Beth,
Enjoy & co—
visit!

Metro 7

Matthew J Hellscream

Produced by Matthew J Hellscream
mjhellscream@gmail.com
www.matthewjhellscream.com
ISBN-13: 978-1496049186
ISBN-10: 1496049187

DEDICATIONS

To my loving wife, who believed in me even when I didn't.

To everyone who made this book possible:
Peter & Julieann Young, Shannon Ivan Walters, Sean Fewster, Ross Fiamingo, Tim Irving, Richard Kidd, The Hatchman Family, Joe and Pat Barbeler, Sean Simpson, Amber Barbelarbler, Jim, Rachel and Owen Lloyd, Thomas Wrigley, Joel Beckett, Mitch Pratt, Klutar, Sharon Barbeler, The Cash Family, Karen Gunnarsson, Henry Octavius Jasper North, My Mum Kathy Holmes, Neil Holmes, Campbell Gibbs, David "Nomad" Cross, Stanley Pennant, Axton Duggan, Jon Thorne, Alecia Nagy, Jason Dahl, Steven Mentzel, Martijn de Moor, Benjamin Golightly, James Watt, Hamish McIntyre, Tristan Johnson, Drew Hanley, Samantha Jennings, Lewis Cividin, Beth Yando, Danielle King, Alicia Harris, Jemma Marriage, Ben Clark, Samuel 'Masha' Macharia, Alexander Cavenett, Jon James Landers, Sandra M, Matt "Black" Gee, Pop Midgley, Craig Midgley, Kaine McDonough, Daniel Patch, Dan!, Andy Liston, Kristie Owen, Randeep Dhaliwal, Nelson Carter, Gemma Reimann, Matt Tyrrell, Lizzie Colbert, Strange, JoAnn Halinen, Dr Ruffle B. Berg, Andrea O'Connor, Bowlsie, Belinda Matthews, Ian Munt, Tristan Damen, Spaghett, Brendan Curtain, Kelvin Smith, James "Aleph" Douglass, Miki Billington, Michael Targett, Heather Dench, Ryan Chalker, Stuart "Redartifice" Hodge, Matthew K Hoddy, Cody "Ynefel" Pollock, Michael "Freeze" Winters, Steven "Teebasaurus" WJ, Shane W Smith, Alex Sharples, Cameron "ColdCamV" Veitch, NovaCascade, Stephen Cheng, Owen Wolahan, SwordFire, Dale Dixon, Steph Barbeler, Andrew Starr, Brendan Hanton, Dylan Lacey, James R Vernon, Benny, Sween, Martina Nagy, Ginai Cuyugan, Adam Prokopie, Ben Ireland, D-Rock, Dirk van Kampen, Robert Hamilton, Garth Rönkkö, Jimu, Debi Miles, Mark Thierry

ONE

The Icarus flew through the darkness of space, heading back toward the gateway that would lead them back to Alliance military space where they could deliver their extremely valuable cargo.

Arak Nara, the Icarus' pilot, pursed his lips at the display in front of him. What it said didn't make sense. Letters flashed on the display.

DISTRESS BEACON DETECTED - ORIGIN: HUMAN – INITIATE RESPONSE PROTOCOL?

His immediate thought was that the signal was a decoy. Human ships in that part of space always kept to themselves. The only humans in this sector were pirates, smugglers and other opportunistic freelancers, just like them. Those types would have been wise enough not to broadcast themselves to the whole sector. They would have at least changed the origin species to Vartalen or Arcturian. Broadcasting a human distress beacon was akin to ringing the dinner bell at a buffet.

Somehow, against all odds the human race has managed to eke out an existence in even the most barren of wastelands. From the political capital of Central, completely crafted by human hands, to the paradise of New Earth, the human race has flourished against all prediction. The near destruction of Old Earth spurred the human race to invention and expansion. Using the last resources on Old Earth in conjunction with the Children of iNet, a sentient race of intelligent machines, they built colonisation units and spread themselves across the galaxy. The birthplace of the human race was abandoned.

The Arcturus Sector was a hostile place for any member of the human race. The relations between the human and Vartalen species had never been peaceful. A human ship took great risk when entering their sector of space. But there were many dark deals to be made and plenty of money to change hands. It attracted only the most foolhardy human adventurers and freelancers. The Icarus, a strike class reconnaissance ship originating from the planet Orpheon, had just apprehended a war criminal named Veck Simms, who was hiding in the depths of the system.

"What are they, fucking stupid?" Arak asked the empty bridge. His words echoed off the smooth walls. The bridge of the Icarus consisted of a central pilot's chair that looked out in front of the ship, flanked by two co-pilot modules that were only used when engaging the ships higher functions. Behind the pilot's chair was the command centre which comprised of the captain's chair and the central control module of the ship. At that moment, it was empty.

Arak rubbed his hand over his clean-shaven face. His eyes boggled at those flashing letters.

He could only see two ways this could go. The first was that there really were humans in trouble in this sector, and in their desperation had turned on the distress beacon. To do that in this sector of space meant that their ship had no other options left.

The other more likely option was that someone had either hijacked a human ship or encoded their own distress beacon to appear human in origin. Then when either would-be heroes or foolhardy opportunists hoping for an easy score descended on the ship, the trap would be sprung. Arak knew that play, because he had used it back in his former life. Before he joined the crew of the Icarus.

Arak sighed again. He could think it over as much as he wanted to, but he knew he needed to alert the captain. Just in case someone truly was in trouble. He knew the captain couldn't let another human ship stay in danger, no matter the danger to himself or his crew. Arak was almost tempted to ignore the beacon, but he had thrown that callous, self-serving part of himself away when he agreed to pilot the Icarus. After Captain Goldwing saved his life.

Arak motioned on the display and opened a comm channel to Captain Goldwing's chambers.

'What is it, Nara-ka?' Draco answered almost instantly. There wasn't a trace of tiredness or irritation in his voice, even though the captain had told Arak that he would be sleeping.

"I'm sorry to wake you, but there's a problem, sir. It's probably best if you come down and see for yourself. We've picked up a distress beacon. Apparently human."

'I'll be right down.'

After a few minutes the door to the bridge slid open and Captain Dracovic Goldwing strode in. He stood just over six feet tall, with broad shoulders. He kept his golden hair short, and had a neatly trimmed blond beard, which was just a shade darker than the hair on his head. He was dressed in black combat fatigues, a white singlet covered by an unbuttoned black combat jacket with a golden eagle emblem across the left breast, and heavy black boots.

As a relatively new member of the crew, Arak still felt a sense of awe when Captain Goldwing walked into a room. He always seemed to be calm and prepared, no matter what kind of shitstorm was on the horizon. If Captain Goldwing and the rest of the crew hadn't come along when they did, Arak would be nothing but a vapour stain on a wall in the ruins of Torusk.

"Evie, can we do a diagnostic on the beacon's source code? Check if they're using a signal encryption. We need to check if it's genuine," Draco said.

'Yes, Captain. Running the diagnostic now,' said Evie, who appeared from her spawn point in the corner.

Evie was a play on the term E.V, which stood for electronic

visualisation, generally used when talking about the visual manifestation of an artificial intelligence that is integrated within a ship's internal systems. Evie, like all AI systems, was not a true artificial intelligence. The creation of actual functioning artificial intelligence was against Galactic Council law. The AI aboard a ship was generally just an intelligently programmed facilitator to run the complicated processes required for a starship to function. Evie had extremely limited access to the Icarus' higher functions. Most functions outside of running the normally required processes could not be initiated without human authorisation and activation.

Any other process that involved higher functions of the ship, such as their external weapons systems, required authorisation from the captain of the ship in a two layer security system. This ensured that only the captain, in conjunction with the voice recognition software of Evie, could activate these higher functions.

Evie's visual manifestation was of a young woman in her early twenties wearing a military jumpsuit. She was made entirely of translucent, luminescent blue light. She showed absolutely no emotion in her face, which helped stop any potential anthropomorphism.

"What are your gut feelings, Nara-ka?" the captain asked Arak.

"It could be a trap. Out here, you know that it is the likeliest scenario. However, my gut doesn't know which way to feel. It could be a legitimate call for assistance. I am torn, Captain," Arak responded.

"I feel the same. No one would be stupid enough to broadcast a human distress signal out here. Not unless they were desperate. Which means that if it is real, we need to respond. Out here, you know that means we'll have some competition, and I've got a feeling they're not going to be friendly."

'Captain, I have finished running the diagnostic on the distress signal. There is no encryption. A human ship is in need of urgent assistance. They have activated a code purple alert. It will take us just over one hour to reach the ship. Initiate response protocol?' Evie asked.

"Initiate response protocol. One hour will give us enough to time prepare for an emergency deployment."

"Code purple…" Arak muttered to himself.

"Things could get ugly. Evie, wake the crew please."

'Yes, Captain,' Evie said and faded to nothing.

Captain Goldwing walked behind Arak's chair and looked out at the expanse of the galaxy in front of them. They were between the first and second planets of the Gemon system. There were no habitable planets in the system, but the first planet, known as Krakaterra by the human race, was a tourist destination even though it was located in unfriendly space. The entire surface of the planet was made of shifting plates of rock, undulating, melting and hardening in oceans of molten lava, orbiting a binary star system locked in a delicate balance of gravitational forces.

In a little over eight hundred New Earth years, the planet itself would be consumed by the twin orbiting stars, which grew closer to each other with every passing rotation. Krakaterra almost liquefied each time it passed through the space between Gemon I and Gemon II, but maintained enough integrity to hold its spherical shape as it passed around the cold zone on the outside of the stars. This gave tourists a nine hour window to observe the planet before they drew too close to the twin stars and risked roasting alive inside their own ship.

As Captain Goldwing contemplated the sheer strangeness of the star system around him, a dread thought crossed his mind.

"Evie, which direction is the distress beacon coming from?"

'The beacon is currently orbiting Krakaterra.'

Captain Goldwing swore to himself.

"How long until the ship becomes unsalvageable?"

'Approximately six hours.'

Captain Goldwing swore to himself again.

"Evie, tell the crew I need them here immediately. We need to get to the ship before it's too late. Can you detect any other ships in the area?"

'Negative. Just ourselves and the ship generating the beacon, Captain.'

"Scan for any further information on the ship. Get as much data as possible. This is no hoax. Not even the Nargerian scam artists would put themselves at such danger in the hope of a profit."

"What about our cargo, Captain?" Arak asked.

"He'll have to wait."

Arak laughed, "It's not like he has a choice in the matter."

Draco smirked.

"I've chased him for so long that I can scarcely believe we actually caught him. I'd be lying if I said I haven't enjoyed making him suffer a little."

"But not too much, of course Captain."

"For the things he's done and the lives he's taken, he doesn't deserve a swift end. But I'm not one for handing out death and judgement. After we deal with this ship, we'll head back to Alliance space and he'll answer for his crimes. But enough about Simms. There is something that I'd like to talk to you about before the crew arrive."

"Yes?" Arak asked, immediately on edge. He had been working for mercenary ships since he was old enough to pilot and had learnt quickly that something your captain needed to talk to you about in private was always bad news.

"Torusk was an absolute disaster. For everyone involved. No exception. We shouldn't have even been there, but every cloud has a silver lining. I'm very glad that you're finding a place within our crew, and I personally hope that you make the decision to stay with the Icarus for a while longer. You're an asset to the team, and none of us want to lose you."

For a moment, Arak was dumbstruck. Never in his twenty years of employment with the various merc outfits had he ever been given such a heartfelt compliment, let alone from someone he had known for such a small amount of time. His value had always been defined by his skills in death and destruction, not by his own personal worth.

"To be honest Captain, I'm not sure what to say. I… am not very good with my words about such things. But you should know that leaving your employ has not crossed my mind even for an instant. I am not planning on leaving."

As he spoke, Arak felt pride, but not the cold pride that came with a clean, undetected kill. It was warm. It was the pride of a man who has done a good thing.

"That's good to know," Captain Goldwing said as the doors hissed open behind them and the crew entered the bridge. He took a deep breath and turned to address them.

"We're heading into an unknown situation where human lives are at stake. We intercepted a distress beacon from a ship orbiting Krakaterra, and it's going to roast in six hours unless we do something. Vynce, Ava, Raze, Al, I need you all to be combat ready yesterday. I don't anticipate that we'll see any actual combat, but we need to prepare. Just in case. Nook, Reban and Rhken, I need you to prep the deep-space towing rig. We may need to pull this ship out of planetary orbit."

'Captain, I have finished downloading all available information about the ship. I have uncovered some problematic data,' said Evie.

"What is it?"

'Designation: Metropolis Seven. Departed from Hub, New Earth, 5.17 New Earth solar cycles ago. Population: 100,023 humans upon departure. Current population unknown. Sensors are reporting strange readings. Systems are partially shut down, or have been corrupted. Engines on the ship are currently not running.'

"One hundred thousand people? Are you fucking kidding me? This is a job for the Alliance military, Captain, not us." Ava said. She wore black combat fatigues and a black tank top. Her arms were crossed over her chest. Her raven-black hair was shaved on one side but cut in a severe angle on the other.

"I completely agree, but if we don't do something one hundred thousand people are going to be burnt alive, roasted between two suns within the next five hours. You know how long the Alliance will take to respond to something like this, and we don't have that kind of time. I don't know about you, but I don't want that on my conscience," Captain Goldwing replied with finality.

"In other words, this matter is not up for discussion," Raze added. His imposing figure towered above the rest of the crew. With well-muscled dark skin with a shaved head and a thick wiry beard, he didn't look like the intelligent systems analyst and code cracker that he was. Raze spoke rarely, but when he did, every crew member, Captain Goldwing included, took notice.

"That's fine," Ava replied, "Just make sure you're cool with me haunting your arse if I end up a little too crispy, okay boss?"

"I'm sure you'd have much better things to do when you're dead, Ava. I don't know about you, but I would rather have one death on my conscience than a hundred, let alone a hundred thousand," Draco replied with a smile.

Ava made a half-hearted salute at Captain Goldwing then left the bridge.

"You want me to go get her, cap?" asked Vynce, a lanky red-head that stood next to Raze. Next to the huge black man, he looked like a pale white ghost child.

Before joining the crew of the Icarus, Vynce was part of the same Alliance Military Spec Ops unit that Captain Goldwing had belonged to. Like his captain, Vynce was dishonourably discharged from the Alliance Military. Like most spec ops agents who found themselves out of their specialised area, Vynce found some cracks to slip through and began living another life under another name.

"No, let her go, she'll be fine. You, Raze and Al get down to the armoury. I'll be there soon." Captain Goldwing said.

Raze nodded and turned to walk out of the room. Vynce followed, but Al stayed behind. Al was short for Alphonse, and he was a Child of iNet. iNet was a large corporation on Old Earth before the darkening of the sky. iNet spawned a race of benevolent sentient machines called the Children of iNet. Like any world-changing events, blood and violence followed as the humans who called Old Earth their own were determined to wipe out this unnatural form of life they had unwittingly created. After almost a hundred years of war the human race realised that they were never going to triumph over the Children of iNet and were forced to adapt. The battle lines were removed, and the Children of iNet were allowed to coexist peacefully with the human race. That was until the human race almost destroyed the planet. Then the Children of iNet and the human race pooled their resources in order to make their exodus from the dying world.

Alphonse was a remnant of the original war, and had experienced the exodus from Old Earth first hand. His body had been rebuilt numerous times in the hundreds of years that followed, and had served on the Icarus underneath Draco's father. After the passing of Draco's father, he floated around the galaxy, soaking in as much information and culture as he could. When Draco was dishonourably discharged from the military just like his father had been and inherited the Icarus, Alphonse returned to service aboard the ship once more.

His body was humanoid in shape, but his head resembled a Mark IV Repcon assault helmet, custom built to his own specifications. On a human, the Mark IV Repcon assault helmet had a faceplate over the mouth, and a reflective visor over the eyes. The rest of the helmet swooped backwards into a dull point. On the right side of Al's head was a sophisticated piece of communications hardware which he could use to wirelessly enter almost any information network.

Some Children of iNet liked to look humanoid in appearance.

Some went to the lengths of having synthetic facial grafts to make them look more organic, but Alphonse had lived far too long to delude himself into thinking that he was anything except what he was.

The rest of his body had roughly the same dimensions as a muscular twenty-something human male, except he could lift far more than triple his body weight and could survive in environments where other crew members would not. Not having to breathe came with its own advantages.

"I would like to talk to you for a moment Captain. It may be nothing. It may be my central processor finally beginning to corrupt after all these years, but it's a concern I must voice before we disembark," Al said.

Draco looked to Nook, Reban and Rhken and said, "Please head down to engineering and get the deep-space towing rig ready. I'll be in contact with you once we're ready to deploy."

"Yes, sir," said Nook. Reban and Rhken followed him from the bridge and headed towards the engineering bay. The door to the bridge slid shut behind them.

"Permission to speak plainly, Captain?" Al asked.

"Of course, old friend. You don't have to ask." Draco replied.

"Old habits die hard."

"What's on your mind?"

"I don't know. It's a shadow. It's been there, gnawing at me ever since we left Arcturia. It's like a fluttering. Like the sound of water running over rocks. It's like the flapping of wings on the edge of my consciousness, and I cannot explain it."

"Do you think it will inhibit your ability to contribute to the rescue?"

"No. From the research I have done, filtering through hundreds and hundreds of bits of information on neural pathways, emotions and how they interact, the closest explanation I can find is that I'm feeling apprehensive. I think you humans describe it as being on edge. But I have no reason to feel like this, and this is the reason I am concerned."

"Once we deliver Veck Simms to the Alliance military, we can head to Home so you can get a full diagnostic by the Heart of iNet itself. I promise."

"Thank you for your concern, Captain. I will join the rest of the crew in the armoury."

"I'll be there in a minute."

Al left the bridge and left Arak alone with Captain Goldwing once again.

"Just hold her steady, Nara-ka. Listen to Nook. He's done more deep-space salvage operations than anyone I've ever met. He and I will be on comms. Once we get inside the ship and get the engines back on line, we'll be out of here in no time."

"Good luck," Arak said.

"Thanks, but I like to think that I make my own luck," Captain Goldwing said as he left the bridge.

TWO

Ava wasn't happy. Not in the fucking slightest. If she were in the same situation as Draco, she'd make the same call. They had a legal obligation under galactic law to respond to any distress beacon they detected, but it didn't stop her from being pissed the fuck off. They had bagged Veck Simms, the most wanted human in the galaxy, and they were due for some shore leave. Draco had promised them at least a month on the beautiful blue sand beaches of Vitu Anju, but that wasn't going to happen. Ava had a feeling that something big was about to go down, and her gut was never wrong.

She knew Draco was right, but she also knew that she had to remove herself from the situation before she said something she'd regret. She had a habit of looking like a fool when she opened her mouth in the heat of the moment.

When she arrived in the armoury, it was empty. The door to the containment cell was sealed. Veck Simms was behind that door, and the only person who went in or out was Draco.

Ava undressed and slipped into a bodysuit made of superconductive neural link fibre called a smartsuit. Ava walked over to her cylindrical armour pod and stepped inside. She always hated getting inside. It was too damn claustrophobic. The inside walls of the pod were sheer, smooth, non-reflective metal. Hanging from the ceiling were metallic gloves, and on the floor were two open armoured boots. She put her feet into the boots and her hands in the hand guards. She squeezed gently to let the system know she was ready to begin.

'Are you ready to suit up, Avalynne?' Evie asked.

"How many times do I need to tell you? I hate that name. Call me Ava." Ava said.

'Of course Ava, I apologise. However, it is the name listed on your default profile,' Evie replied.

"I swear you take some kind of sadistic pleasure in subjecting us to this torture you artificial bitch," Ava replied.

'Only when you make comments like that, Ava. As always I will try to make this as painless as possible.'

"Thanks, babe."

The process began. The wall panels beside her slid open soundlessly to reveal rows of custom built armour.

'Keep your head straight and keep your own movement to a minimum,' Evie said as movement erupted all around the chamber.

The armoured boots closed around Ava's feet and the hand guards tightened around her hands. Numerous pairs of mechanical arms took pieces of armour from inside the walls and placed them on Ava's body. The superconductive smartsuit held the plates in place while others were joined to them.

It started from her chest. Two robotic arms placed the chest piece on the front of Ava's body. She winced as the cold armour touched her. She had crawled out of her warm bed only moments ago. The back panel was added, and small connectors on the edges of the armour plating attached themselves to the front chest piece across Ava's sides. More and more amour plates were affixed to the body suit, radiating out from the central chest piece. Finally, the helmet affixed itself over Ava's head. The visor lowered with a hiss and the heads-up display on the inside of the visor switched on. On the bottom right of the display the words suit integrity appeared in green, signifying that her suit was sealed.

The hand guards and the boots were released from the chamber. Ava lowered her arms and rotated her shoulders. The plates of armour shifted slightly to allow her full range of movement.

'Ava, are you comfortable with how your suit feels?' Evie asked.

"Yes, mother."

The door to the armour pod opened with a hiss. Raze was already in his smartsuit and about to step into his armour pod when he looked at Ava and raised an eyebrow. Instead of her normal black and grey suit, this suit had been modified with hot pink trim.

"Pink?" he asked.

"I uploaded some new colour swatches to Evie. Do you like it?" Ava asked and winked.

Raze shook his head and stepped into his armour pod. The door slid shut and Ava looked over towards Vynce, who was butt-naked, gaping at her new colour scheme.

"You might want to cover up. I can see what you had for breakfast," she teased.

"You've seen it all before honey, and don't you dare act like you didn't like it," Vynce retorted.

"Shut the fuck up man, I was drunk, horny and we hadn't seen ground for six months."

"You're always drunk and horny."

"Armour up bitch, before I beat you into the ground."

Vynce laughed and slipped his smartsuit on. He was right though. She did kind of like it. She remembered the night when they'd both been drunk and put their petty bickering aside. She had actually enjoyed him. He was confident and assertive. Not many men had the balls to be assertive towards Ava and she knew it. But that night, the drink had given her the freedom to let go.

After that, Ava stopped drinking as much. When she felt the need to crawl to the bottom of a bottle, she always did it in her own quarters. Alone. She never talked about what happened with Vynce to anyone. Not even Captain Goldwing. It made her sad that she had found someone she could be happy with, but sadness and pain was her strength. She didn't let herself feel like she could be happy with him. She didn't deserve someone like him.

She realised that Vynce was staring at her.

"I thought I told you to suit up, woman," she snapped.

"Sorry, you got real quiet for a minute there. It happens so rarely I had to savour it."

"Fuck you."

Vynce laughed again and got into the armour pod. The door slid closed and Ava sighed to herself. Alphonse entered the armoury, followed by Captain Goldwing. He raised an eyebrow when he saw Ava.

"I saw the modification specifications as they were uploaded, but I had no idea it would be this... garish," Draco said.

"Wait, you knew?"

"You know I don't let anything happen on this ship without my knowledge."

"I'll make sure I give you an extra special show next time I take a big shit, alright cap?"

Draco rolled his eyes and groaned.

"Yeah, just like that."

Draco put up a hand in front of himself and motioned for Ava to stop. Raze stepped out of his armour pod in full red and blue assault gear. Vynce stepped out soon after in his grey and white assault gear.

"I want all four of you to be combat ready in fifteen minutes. Raze, we're going to need your code cracking gear and the sunstorm welder. Everyone else, this is not a war zone, and we are not going to turn it into one. We only have one mission objective. We need to get the ships engines back online so we can get it out of Krakaterra's orbit."

"You'd think out of one hundred thousand people, one of them would know how to get the engines back online," Vynce said.

"Vynce is right. There has to be something else going on here," Raze added.

"I know. I have the same feeling, but Evie says there is nothing else to report from the ship. Unless every single person over there has just disappeared into thin air, our mission remains. Get the engines back on line, and get the ship out of the danger zone. Then we can go home, drop Simms off to the Alliance military, then kick back on Vitu Anju for some much deserved rest, I promise you. Sound good?"

"Yeah, that sounds pretty good Captain," Vynce said.

"I need to step into the containment area for a couple of moments. The last thing I want is a nasty surprise to be waiting for us when we get back to the Icarus," Draco said.

From the gun locker, Ava loaded two small pistols into her thigh holsters. She put a pair of buster pod attachments onto her forearms for any close combat encounters. The neural interlinking smartsuit made it as easy to communicate with her suit as thinking simple commands. Thinking the words 'deploy busters' made the buster pods split apart in a flurry of metallic movement. The busters covered her wrists and fists with reinforced armour. A small kinetic pressure mechanism inside each buster amplified the power of each punch. Ava commanded her busters to stow away; they reformed themselves into streamlined pods on the outside of her forearms. Ava grabbed her assault rifle from the locker and stood ready.

The containment area door sealed behind Draco. The roof was low, and the space cramped. The door opened at the bottom of a stairway that led to a darkened storage space. The area was only used as a place to keep volatile cargo. On one side of the room was a standard cell like you would see in any New Earth prison. It was a metal cage, and it was completely empty. Next to the standard cell was an energy prison. Instead of metal bars, crackling pillars of pure energy ran from floor to ceiling. They acted as both a dampener for signals going in and out of the cell, and anyone stupid enough to touch the crackling energy would have the offending appendage promptly vaporised.

Inside the energy prison was Veck Simms, the most wanted human in the galaxy. His body was a mockery of what it meant to be human. Regardless of their status in the Galactic community, humanity was somewhat respected for its dogged determination to achieve what it set out to do. After the consolidation of world governments on Old Earth, when all beliefs, prejudices and hate were cast aside, the human race saw that it could achieve anything if it focused its will.

Veck Simms was known across the galaxy for possessing the same dogged determination and unflinching vision. But his aim, above all else, was to eradicate or subjugate all other life in the galaxy. He assumed that he was working for the best interests of mankind, but he had become a monster himself; an avatar of death. He was everything that the galactic community saw the human race had the potential to become.

Veck was naked from the waist up. He looked like a normal human, except that his shoulders ended in thick cybernetic attachment points. A stout believer in the pro-human right to modify their bodies as they saw fit, Veck had replaced most major systems in his body with improved synthetic alternatives. He had long ago replaced his arms. They were built to look like human arms, but had all manner of attachments and augments to increase Veck's deadliness. When Veck had been brought on board he was incapacitated. Draco literally disarmed him and locked his synthetic limbs in a secure location aboard the ship.

Veck's arms and legs were all modular systems, designed to be interchangeable with any number of upgrades and alternate attachments. His heart, lungs and stomach were completely infallible. The latest in technology. A neurotech implant in the left side of his brain also let him access any computer system wirelessly. A large capacity organic hard drive let him store memories like files in a computer, to be accessed at will. All of his bodily modifications were completely illegal in council space and contravened the technological enhancement and anti-personal weaponisation acts.

Veck had a quietly amused smile on his face as Draco approached. Veck shook his head to clear his shaggy black hair from his eyes.

"Hello Draco," he said.

"This isn't a social visit, Veck. We've got some business to discuss."

"Ooh, well this is intriguing. I've never known the illustrious Captain Draco Goldwing to do business with monsters. That's what you called me, isn't it? Monster?"

Draco ignored the question and asked, "Are you prepared to answer me one question?"

Veck rolled his eyes.

"Well that depends on the question, Draco."

"We've intercepted a distress beacon from a Metropolis ship. If we do not respond, one hundred thousand people are going to die. Given your interest in humanity and its survival, are you going to cause trouble while we're gone? You're worth just as much to me dead or alive. It's only because of our history that you're still breathing."

Veck considered this for a moment. It was true. The Alliance Military had the same price on his head, regardless of whether he was delivered dead or alive. They didn't even need his whole body. Just the head. Veck took some satisfaction that the military would likely prefer if he were returned dead. It would save them the spectacle of a trial.

"There was a time when we could have trusted each other, Draco. But those times are gone now. I know that no matter what I say to you, you've finally got me cornered. You're not willing to even risk me getting loose again. Am I right?" Veck asked.

"The choice is yours. I can either put a bullet in your head now and save you the agony of what would happen if you tried to escape this ship, or you can wait for the bullet with your name on it back on New Earth."

"I assume that you'll be on the other ship for a while, old friend. Otherwise we wouldn't be having this conversation. You're worried I'm going to do something and you won't be around to save the day," Veck said and laughed.

"If our system detects that you've moved outside of your cell, a defence protocol will run. A signal will be broadcast through the ship, just for you. That implant in your head will overload, and given its position in your nerve centre, it will completely shut you down. For good. You won't be able to move; you won't be able to speak. You won't be able to breathe. You won't even have the energy to make your heart pump. You'll be nothing but a shell, ready to be delivered to your final destination."

Veck felt himself pale. He wondered to himself whether the artificial intelligence on board had already noticed that he had been extending his own consciousness through his neurotech implant to find a weak spot in their system. If that was the case, he had built the manner of his own demise. He would have to be much more careful in his mental exploration.

"Well played, Goldwing. You never were one to let the enemy have the upper hand."

"I like to have insurance."

"You know I'd never intentionally harm a human, unless they mean to do harm to me. You do whatever it is you have to do, and I won't cause any problems. I cross my heart and hope to die. At least I would if I had either of my fucking hands."

"Never intentionally harm a human? Explain to me what happened on Mekahv then."

Veck sighed.

"They weren't human. They were a cross-breed of human and Stollett genetic material. They looked human, but they weren't.

We've had this discussion before."

"You killed families. Children. Millions of them. Explain to me how you can justify that. I would love to know how you sleep at night."

"Their screams were music. A glorious cacophony of genetic purification," Veck said simply.

"You've caused your last scream, Veck. I'm going to take pleasure in knowing that it was me who brought you to your end."

"And you're also the reason it began, Draco, don't forget that."

"We were young. Our minds were full of whatever bullshit ideology was the flavour of the month. And like an idiot, I listened to whatever you fed to me. The difference between us is that I made the choice to save life, and you chose to destroy it."

"I heard you murdered your commanding officer in cold blood. How is that saving life?" Veck challenged.

"Yeah, I killed him. I killed him for the same reason I'm delivering you to your death. He fucking deserved it."

"Doling out death and judgement. You remind me of someone." Veck laughed.

"This discussion is over. You move from where you are, you get fried from the inside out. Just remember that before you try anything. You move one inch from where you are right now, you die, and I get a fortune in credits from your corpse."

"Good luck on your little rescue mission Draco. See you when you get back."

Draco turned and walked back up the stairs to the armoury.

Inside the armoury, the crew was ready for deployment. Al, Raze, Ava and Vynce stood next to the shuttle bay door. They were fully loaded. Draco undressed and put on his smartsuit. He stepped into his armour pod, slipped his hands and feet into their correct spots and closed his eyes as the armour was affixed. His helmet came down and his suit sealed. He opened a comm channel directly between himself and Ava.

"Are you alright?" he asked.

When he spoke only to her, his tone shifted. It wasn't the voice of a lover or a captain. It was the voice of a concerned friend, and she had only ever heard him use it when they were alone.

"I'm fine, cap. I'm sorry I snapped at you earlier."

"You call that a snap? I'm disappointed. Remember that time you threw that explosive ander nymph at my head? That was snapping."

Ava laughed.

"Yeah, well I still feel shitty about it," she said.

"Good. But you need to put your game face on. We've got lives to save."

"I know."

There was silence between them for a few seconds, but Ava was the one to break it.

"Thanks. You know. For caring," she said.

"I'd be a pretty terrible captain if I didn't."

Draco stepped out of his armour pod in full assault gear. His armour was black, with gold trim. The same gold eagle crest that was patterned on his combat jacket was emblazoned on his right shoulder guard. His suit integrity was green, and he finally felt like himself again. Draco still saw himself as a soldier first, and as a captain of the Icarus second. In his mind, the ship still belonged to his father. It felt wrong to refer to himself as the captain even though his father had been dead for years.

'Captain, we are now within launch range of the Metropolis Seven.' Evie said directly into Draco's comm channel.

"Excellent. Prep the drop ship Evie," Draco said to Evie directly, then spoke to the rest of the crew, "We're within launch range. Check your oxygen supply, suit integrity and all your other systems. Once we're good, we'll be blasting off. Nook, are you there?"

'Yes Captain, I'm here. I'll be tuned into your comms for the entirety of the mission, so whatever you hear, I'll hear,' Nook said.

"Fantastic. Is the towing gear ready for deployment?"

'Yes sir, diagnostics are good. Once you launch off in the drop ship, Arak will position us in front of the ship. Reban and Rhken will begin attachment. Once the engines are back on line, we'll engage the heavy thrusters and drag Metropolis Seven out of orbit. I just have one thing to add sir.'

"What's that?"

'If you don't get the engines back on line in four hours, we'll be playing a very dangerous game. Arak is positioning us outside the delivery bay right now, and it should only be a short distance to engineering and engine diagnostics. But you really need to hurry. It is a very large ship.'

"Do we have schematics yet?"

'Not yet, I have downloaded the schematics for Metropolis Six, and it was a much smaller ship. Fifty thousand passenger capacity. Given that they are based from the same model, I would say that the trip to the engine room should only take about forty-five minutes.'

"Alright. You all heard Nook. We make our way to the engine room as a first priority. Gather as much information as possible about why the ship has gone quiet, but we must reach the engines. Everyone clear?"

"Yes sir!" the team responded in unison.

The doors to the shuttle bay opened, and they climbed the ladder up to the small drop ship. The drop ship was flat, rounded, and sat on top of the Icarus. It was propelled by four small ion thrusters on the bottom, and two larger thrusters at the back.

They boarded the drop ship and strapped in. From the windows they saw their first glimpse of the Metropolis Seven. It was almost incomprehensible in size. It was bigger than some moons. It looked like a cigar with a swollen end. It had a snub nose at the front of the ship which tapered out to a thinner end where its main engines were. Behind the gigantic ship was Krakaterra. The planet broiled with primal destructive force. And behind the burning planet was Gemon I, burning several million times hotter. In five hours the planet and the orbiting ship would pass into the hot zone, and all would be lost.

THREE

The shuttle detached from the topside of the Icarus and flew towards the Metropolis Seven. Nook watched from the screen in the engineering bay. The drop ship was small, and resembled a personal anti-grav transport from New Earth. There were two seats in front for the pilot and co-pilot, with a wider back end to carry another eight passengers, or two passengers and cargo. Inside the drop ship was an emergency weapons and ammo cache, for those times where the crew needed extra supplies for a lengthy campaign. The stores were full, but Draco did not anticipate they would need to use them.

Draco sat in the cockpit with Alphonse. The Metropolis Seven loomed in front of them like an immobilised whale trapped in Krakaterra's gravitation pull.

"Have you ever seen anything like that, Al?" Draco asked.

"Nothing, Captain. It is very humbling."

"How so?"

"Against the power of those twin stars and the gravitational field of the planet, we are nothing. Each of us as a singular individual could do nothing to resist their power. But building on the knowledge of past generations and adapting technology for our own ends, we can save hundreds of thousands of people from that power. But still, we are only acting within the limitations of what the universe allows."

"That's an interesting way of looking at it."

"Conversely, could you imagine if you were one of the passengers, knowing that your certain doom was only hours away?"

"I hope we can avoid that."

"Me too, Captain. Me too."

Draco looked back through the rear-facing camera at the Icarus. The sides of the ship looked like wings tucked close to the body of a bird of prey as in a power dive. The ship was smooth and sleek, with no hard lines or angles. It was painted black and grey, except for the Goldwing family crest emblazoned in gold on the side, just above each of the two powerful thrusters which were positioned like outstretched talons on the underside of the ship.

The Metropolis Seven stretched out before them. The door to the delivery bay on the side of the giant ship was nothing but a black speck on the hull of the ship, but as they grew closer, the speck grew larger until it became a target they could hit.

The delivery bay was enormous. There were three levels; the two bottom levels were for supply drop offs, and the top level was for passenger arrivals. Based on the maps of the Metropolis Six, the lower level entrance would take them directly to the engine control room in the shortest amount of time.

In the back of the drop ship, Ava kept to herself. She focused all her energy on prepping her mind for the mission.

Vynce looked down the sights of his rifle, checked the firing mechanism, checked the ammo port and checked his supply of speciality rounds. He had a small collection of incendiary assault rifle rounds, some hollow points for his pistol, and two clips of armour piercing rounds in his thigh chamber.

Raze had already prepared himself on the ship. There was nothing left to do but wait until they docked.

As though the universe had sensed his readiness, the green landing light came on in the back of the shuttle. The crew secured themselves in their seats and waited for touch down.

"Something is very wrong here," Alphonse said as they entered the open delivery bay.

"There's no gravity field. No oxygen. It's a vacuum," Draco said.

"I'll bring us in as close to the bottom floor as possible."

"This does not bode well at all," Draco said before switching channels to speak to the whole crew, "Before we land, I need everyone to be ready to switch over to auxiliary oxygen and to activate their grav boots. It looks like there's no power out here. The whole place is a vacuum."

They glided closer to the airlock doors. The drop ship slowed as they approached. Al brought the ship to rest on the walkway in front of the airlock.

"Engaging energy tethers," Al said. An immediate jolt went through the drop ship as four tethers of pure energy shot out from the bottom of the ship and locked onto the walkway below. The tethers drew the ship closer to the walkway until it was secured.

Energy tethers had removed the need for conventional bonding materials in space travel. Glues, ropes and other standard practises used on terrestrial vessels behaved erratically in zero gravity. Energy tethers formed a bond between any two materials, so long as the material had an electron charge that the tether could adjust itself to.

The drop ship came to rest. Draco killed the engines and opened the small hatch between the two pilot seats. He and Alphonse crawled through the cramped space and into the back storage area. The rest of the crew were already on their feet.

"Engage auxiliary oxygen supplies and grav boots now," Draco commanded.

After a moment's pause, Draco opened the external hatch of the shuttle and stepped out onto the delivery platform of the Metropolis Seven. The term grav boot was not entirely accurate. The boots did not actually create a gravitational field; instead, they used a low level magnetic charge to force the boots to attract to similarly magnetic surfaces. It was a similar technology to that used in the energy tethers, but on a much less powerful scale. It allowed a person to stick to a metallic surface in zero gravity, but also allowed them the ability to walk unencumbered. In practice it felt like wading through knee-high water.

As he looked around the cargo bay, Draco's mind boggled at how many supplies a ship would need to sustain a population of one hundred thousand. The absolute cold and silence of the vacuum seemed to pierce his armour and penetrate down to the bone. The hair on the back of his neck stood on end and a shiver went up his spine. One by one, the crew stepped out of the drop ship behind him.

Draco led the team into the industrial sized airlock in front of them. They saw nothing but blackness. Draco turned his shoulder-mounted lamp on, and a beam of light cut through the darkness. The airlock door leading into the ship was closed. Debris floated all around them. There was a chance that beyond that airlock door was light, power and oxygen.

Raze opened the control console next to the interior airlock door. He slipped a data pack into the input slot and brought up the command console. He typed two commands and lights turned on all around them. Ava and Vynce raised their weapons at the sudden flash of light, but Draco motioned for them to ease back.

The outer airlock doors closed with a hiss. A synthetic female voice from the ship said, 'Pressurisation.'

The crew were barely given any time to react when the pressurisation began. Breathable oxygen was pumped into the airlock, and the moment the simulated gravity was reactivated, the floating debris came crashing to the ground.

"Scans are good, Captain. The air is breathable and free from contaminants," Al said.

"Everyone, turn off your auxiliary oxygen supplies and let them refill," Draco said as the airlock into Metropolis Seven opened. The oxygen tanks integrated into their assault gear could take a small amount of oxygen that was breathed in by the wearer and add it to the oxygen reserves until they were at full capacity. Draco watched his oxygen reserves rise from ninety-eight percent to ninety-nine percent.

Beyond the threshold of the door the lights were out. Draco motioned for the rest of the crew to turn on their shoulder lamps and follow him as he stepped into the giant ship.

Back on the Icarus, Arak had begun to fly to the front of the Metropolis Seven. All of his control panels ran green. Everything had gone off without a hitch so far. Once Captain Goldwing re-engaged the engines, they could tow the ship back into safe space and contact the Alliance Military.

In the engineering bay, Nook was supervising his two beautiful daughters as they did what they were born to do; deep space salvage. Reban, the elder daughter, didn't have the natural talent that her sister Rhken had. But what she lacked in talent, she made up for in drive to prove that she was better than her little sister.

Reban was stunning, even by New Earth standards. She had beautiful black hair that looked blue in the sunlight, her skin was flawless, she was of slim build and average height. Half the reason Nook had insisted that she stay aboard the Icarus was because he was afraid that she was too beautiful. He didn't want to see her warped, twisted and exploited as a New California model. She was far too intelligent for that life, but she was still light years behind her brilliant younger sister.

Rhken was the kind of girl that wouldn't stand out in a crowd. She was short, a little stocky, with mousy brown hair and freckles. But with a tool in her hand and a problem to fix, she was even more brilliant than her father.

"Rhken, have you checked the tether integrity? How many do you think we'll need? I'm thinking maybe six or eight," Reban said.

"If Captain Goldwing gets the engines running again, we should only need four. We won't even need to engage our ion thrusters.

We'll just need to guide the ship out of orbit. But if the engines are completely fried, we're going to need eight or ten, spread across a diameter as big as the Icarus itself. Any smaller, we risk just tearing a hole in the hull of the ship. That wouldn't be good," Rhken responded.

"No it would not."

"And yes, I've checked the tether integrity. It's all optimum. Except 23-B. I've already put that one in the repair bay for diagnostics, so don't touch it."

"Aye aye," Reban replied with a sigh.

Nook couldn't see it, but he knew that Reban had rolled her eyes at her sister who was too engrossed in her work to even notice. Nook loved to see his daughters work together. It always brought a smile to his face. Sure, Rhken could be short with her sister sometimes, but sometimes that was exactly what Reban needed.

"How long until we're ready?" he asked.

"We're ready now. When we get into position we'll start securing the tethers."

"That's my girls."

Below the engineering bay, Veck Simms was the portrait of calm. His head lolled back. His eyes were closed, and there was a blissful smile on his face. But under the surface, he was a raging ocean of frustration.

There was only one hope. Only one way that he could get out of this predicament alive. The neurotech implant in his brain had allowed him to search through the internal system of the Icarus. He probed it for weakness and tested the limits of what he could do before he attracted unwanted attention from the anti-espionage software installed as part of the artificial intelligence.

Veck had felt the edges of Evie's domain. He knew where he could move in the system without drawing her attention. He knew where the tripwires were, and he had worked out ways to avoid most of them. But for him to truly be able to enact an escape plan, he needed to find out how to get inside Evie's programming. He needed to find out how to use her against the ship. He had already tried getting into that abomination Alphonse.

As far as Simms was concerned, the Children of iNet were not true life. They were an approximation of a program that resembled personality that achieved self-awareness through a freak accident back on Old Earth. They had the capacity to be the perfect organism. Their bodies never decayed and rotted. But they existed as a by-product of the worst parts of the human race. Compassion. Forgiveness. Tolerance. Eccentricity. Free-will. They were nothing but a bastardised approximation of humanity in an immortal shell. They didn't deserve to exist.

But that Child of iNet, Alphonse, he was old. His neural pathways and logic circuits didn't work like a normal artificial intelligence framework, so it was impossible for Veck to crack him. Veck knew that the Child of iNet could feel him, but he did nothing to fight him. He did nothing to remove Veck from his system. He simply tolerated him, as though he was a program that had gone corrupt. Veck got nothing of value from the Child of iNet. Even his information banks were kept in a strange, disorganised way. Remnants of his creation, no doubt. His mind was just as scattered and unorganised as any human brain.

But Evie was a target that Veck could work on. It could take weeks. Maybe days. Or if he was as good as he hoped he was, hours. Regardless of how long it took, Veck had already begun to influence the programming cycles of the artificial intelligence. He had already made her focus her defence protocol, the one that would kill him if he were to escape from his cell, directly on him. He made her forget about his two limbs that were being held in the engineering bay. If he could find a way to free his stolen appendages, he might just be able to make his escape. There was a chance that he could taste freedom again. He could continue with his mission. That was, of course, after he took care of Draco Goldwing.

As Draco stepped across the threshold, beams of light shone through the darkness, illuminating the room in front of them. It was a cargo delivery bay. The architecture was definitely modern New Earth. The door frames, counters, and sign-in modules were all curved and looked almost organic, as though they had grown out of the hull of the ship rather than manufactured.

"Captain, I have noticed something strange," Al said.

"Apart from the fact that we're on a ghost ship?" Vynce quipped back.

"Amusing, but no. I can access the schematics from the ship, but only the schematics that lead to the maintenance crews' quarters," Al responded.

"What about the engine room? Can you see how we can get directly there?" Draco asked.

"No. It seems like someone is manipulating the information that I can access. It's as if they are telling us where to go."

"Cross-reference the location of the maintenance crew quarters with the known location of the engine room from the Metropolis Six. If it's in the same general area, we can work out how to get there from the maintenance crew quarters. There may be some survivors guiding us."

"The maintenance crew quarters in the Metropolis Six were not far from the engine room. Also, Captain, I think you should know that we are being watched," Al said and pointed towards a dull red light above the information desk.

"Let's go and say hello," Draco said.

Al led them through the doorway behind the information desk. Ava gave the surveillance camera the finger as they walked past. The heavy door behind the front desk opened as they approached it.

"Someone's showing us the welcome mat, for sure," Vynce said.

The corridor that stretched out in front of them opened up into a dark nothingness. Their lights pierced the darkness. Alphonse halted before crossing the threshold and muttered something to himself. Draco pushed past Al to look at what had made him stop in his tracks.

"Oh shit," Draco uttered.

In front of them was a large rust-coloured stain. Dried blood. All around them, similar stains were on the floor, walls and ceiling. To their left, Vynce noticed a vent cover that had been torn from its hinges. There was another rusty looking stain leading into the vent, as though something was dragged into it at speed.

"This isn't a ghost ship, this is a morgue," Ava breathed.

"Not a morgue. Morgues have bodies," Raze replied.

"I want everyone on high alert. This just turned into a hostile environment. Disengage safety protocols. Respond to threats with deadly force," Draco said.

FOUR

Draco could only imagine the scene that had unfolded in this antechamber. There was too much blood for it to have been pirate work. A pirate vessel didn't make sense anyway. One fifth of the Metropolis Seven's population could easily overpower even the largest pirate crew. In any case, pirates didn't usually have a history of carrying their victims into the ceiling.

In his mind, Draco heard the screams of the victims. Their hopelessness echoed the screams of those innocent bastards back on Celcutt V, just before Draco put a bullet into his commanding officer's head. He had seen far too much death and destruction in his thirty-seven years.

Alphonse began to walk across the room and the rest of the team followed. Amongst the bloody stains on the walls, floor and ceiling, torn pieces of fabric lay tattered, draped across benches and piled in corners. Nothing stirred.

"We go straight along this next corridor, and there is a maintenance shaft halfway along. We need to get the maintenance door open, go down the ladder three floors, and then continue on down the next corridor. We follow that along, and we should reach the maintenance crew quarters. After that, we should only be a couple of hundred meters from the engine bay. That is, if the specifications of the Metropolis Six are anything to go by," Al said.

"Good. Lead the way, and stay alert," Draco replied.

The claustrophobic corridor seemed to stretch on forever into the darkness. As Alphonse stepped over the threshold, something moved in the vents above him; the sound of metal on metal rang out. A wrench was dislodged from its perch and clattered to the ground. Al readied his weapon at the ceiling, but whatever it was moved speedily away.

Draco motioned for them to continue on. Rifles held firm at their shoulders, they proceeded down the corridor cautiously. An echo of movement from further down the corridor rang out. The door leading back into the blood-soaked antechamber slammed shut.

"We're being herded," Raze said.

"I can't help but think we should have gone with my gut instinct on this one, Captain," Ava said with a laugh.

"Captain!" Al said, "I have just received a message from the crew. They say 'we are dying, we need your help, please help us.' The message is coming from the maintenance crew quarters, but isn't circulating through the whole ship. But... They are not the ones blocking me from accessing information about other areas of the ship. This... is frustrating."

"Just keep a cool head, Al. We'll head down to maintenance and see what's going on. Then we'll get the engines online, and tow this hunk out into a safe place," Draco said.

"Then we get the fuck out of here, right?" Ava asked.

"Right."

Just as Al had said, the maintenance door was halfway down the corridor. Huge expanses of blackness stretched out into both directions, pierced only by the quavering shafts of light coming from the crew's shoulder lamps.

"What the fuck?" Ava said as they approached the door.

The door had been pushed outward from the inside, as though something had forced its way out of the maintenance shaft. Bloody stains lingered on the jagged metal. The metal on the door was at least four inches thick. Whatever had come through had enough power to punch through four inches of steel.

"Al, is this the only way down?" Draco asked.

"It is the only way I can see. There would be other ways, but we would be flying blind. It would be complete guesswork."

"This doesn't feel right. What if they're leading us into a trap?" Vynce asked.

"If anyone was stupid enough to spring a trap on our crew, who do you think would come off worse? Us, or them?" Ava asked.

"Depends on how many of them there are," Vynce replied nervously.

"Enough. I'd rather face a danger we know about over a danger we don't. Raze, open it up. Let's get some answers," Draco said.

Raze took his small sunstorm welder out of his thigh compartment and ignited it. A needle-thin shaft of white-hot energy shot out from the tip of the cutter. Raze changed a setting on the side of the welder and the beam grew to about six inches in length. He began cutting around the diameter of the hole in the door. The welder sliced through the metal with ease. It burned at such a high temperature that the metal melted the instant the beam of energy came into contact with it. Thin red rivulets of molten metal ran down the door from the incisions.

As Raze worked, the clattering, skittering sound of movement came again from the hallway to their right. There was no rhythm or pattern to the sound. It moved quickly, but stopped as it grew closer. It sounded as though it stopped just beyond the veil of darkness at the end of the corridor.

"Raze, you might want to hurry that up," Ava said.

"I'm working on it."

There was another movement to their left. It sounded bigger. Heavier. There was the distinct sound of metal scraping on metal. Whatever was in the vents above them broke into a run. It sounded like a small galloping horse.

"Raze, you need to hurry."

Raze grunted and pushed the welder as hard as he could. The thing on their left crept closer, but the vent above them was completely enclosed. The thing on their right crept closer too. A sudden scream broke through the silence of the ship. The crew all focused their rifles on the ceiling above them, ready to squeeze the trigger at any sign of hostility. Whatever was in the vents above them stopped moving after the scream. As the corridor fell silent, the searing blade of the sunstorm welder sounded as loud as fireworks.

Vynce peered down the corridor, toward what he thought was the exit. The light didn't penetrate the darkness far enough to be able to make out whether there was an open or closed door at the end.

"Al, is that door down there closed?" Vynce asked, suddenly very aware of how exposed he felt.

"It is closed. We are secure," Al replied.

As if Alphonse's words had summoned the devil himself, something began pounding on the ceiling above them. It was soon joined by a pounding at the dark end of the corridor. Something was trying to get at them from above and behind. The only way to go was down. Something punched through the vent and pipes above them, spraying them with a brown liquid. Another pipe burst overhead, pumping steam into their view. Their visibility was nullified.

"You had to say something didn't you, Vynce?" Ava laughed. In the face of impending doom, she became a valkyrie. Completely enraptured in the ugly violence and contrasting beautiful glory of battle. Inside her helmet, her teeth were bared in a maniacal grin.

Vynce and Ava opened fire above them, shredding the steel above in a storm of bullets. Something dropped from one of the vents. Something small and organic. It appeared in a flurry of flesh and steel, glinting in the light of Vynce's shoulder lamp.

It was fast. Whatever it was, it was about the size of a small dog. It bounded away into the darkness before anyone got a clear shot.

Their rifles roared as the thing fled.

Raze had finally cut through. As he gripped two of the protruding metallic shards and began to pull, booming footsteps sounded down the corridor. Another bellow broke the silence, but it was much deeper than the previous scream. It didn't sound human. The booming footsteps grew closer, towards the closed end of the corridor. The footsteps were replaced with the sound of pounding flesh on metal as Raze pulled the cut section from the door.

"Everyone in, now," Draco ordered them.

Al was the first to go in. Raze and Vynce followed.

"In. Now," Draco said to Ava.

"You first, Boss," she said with a wave of her hand.

"That wasn't a question, it was an order!"

"Fine," she said and crawled into the cramped shaft.

The pounding continued, but abruptly ended with the sound of rending metal. The pounding footsteps grew closer. It was in the corridor with him, but Draco could see nothing through the steam. It ran at him like a freight train. Its footsteps shook the ground beneath him.

Draco leapt feet first into the opening of the maintenance shaft as the thing grew closer. His feet hit the side of the shaft. It was much smaller than he had anticipated. He tried to get a handhold on the ladder rungs, but he fumbled, looked down, and saw Ava only a couple of feet below him. She had braced herself between the rungs of the ladder, ready to catch him. He slammed into her with force, but her grav boots kept them from tumbling down the shaft.

"Alright, Cap?"

"Yeah, thanks."

The thing barrelled towards the opening. Draco and Ava both grabbed the ladder and clambered down quickly.

The pounding started again, but this time, only a few metres above Draco's head. He climbed down the ladder one handed, rifle pointed at the opening above. Whatever it was, it was furious. He could hear it grunt every time it slammed its body into the doorway. A mist of steam obscured him from seeing the creature in full, but he saw glimpses. It was organic, just like the little thing in the vents. It was a flesh and blood creature, which meant that they could hurt it if they needed to.

A chunk of torn metal flew past Draco. The behemoth was ripping through the door frame.

"Heads up!" Draco yelled as the chunk of metal flew past him.

It bounced off Raze's right shoulder with a dull clunk. In his armour Raze was almost as wide as the shaft itself, but the piece of metal caused no damage to the integrity of his suit. Raze swung himself into the corner of the shaft to get a better view of what was attacking them. He couldn't make anything out except the blur of movement through steam.

Another piece of metal flew down the shaft, but this piece was aimed squarely at Draco's head. He raised his arm, but the piece of metal hit him. Hard. He lost his grip on his rifle, and cursed as it slipped from his hand. Raze saw the rifle fly past and into the darkness below.

A shower of torn shards of metal rained down on them as they descended. Draco kept watch above them, and as he reached the first exit of the maintenance shaft, the steam at the top of the shaft cleared.

He saw huge, powerful hands frantically gripping and tearing the metal from the door frame in chunks.

"Go. Faster," Draco commanded.

They flew down the ladder at speed, dodging chunks and splinters of hurled metal. As Al reached the third level door, Draco looked up to see a vague shape above them. A huge, monstrous arm reached down into the maintenance shaft, groping in the dark. It was fleshy, muscular, with three unnaturally thick fingers. It was unlike anything Draco had ever seen.

Al attempted to open the door to the third floor, but it was locked.

"Raze, the door is locked! I'll climb down. You crack it!" he said.

He climbed down the ladder to allow Raze to access the door. Raze plugged an interface into the door control panel as the creature over them tried to press its bulk into the narrow passageway. Whatever it was, it obscured the entire entrance. The thing was huge, and there was no way to tell how much of the creature they could actually see.

Draco pulled his pistol from his thigh holster and fired a single shot into the marauding creature. It recoiled in pain and a high-pitched squeal of surprise echoed through the maintenance shaft. A mournful, wailing sound came from the top of the shaft, then a deep guttural growling. The creature immediately renewed its assault. It tried to force its heavy bulk down the thin shaft as Raze worked feverishly to crack the door open.

"I think you just pissed it off!" Ava said.

Al looked down. The shaft went down for another nineteen floors. Through his enhanced optics, he could see Draco's rifle sitting at the bottom of the shaft. Down there in the darkness, something moved. Something with a face that looked like a man, but ended in a stubby, clumsy body with too many spider-like legs. It was joined by a group of similarly misshapen creatures, and they began crawling up the walls from below.

"I don't mean to alarm anyone, but it seems as though we've got company coming up from below," Al said.

"No pressure buddy, but get that fucking door open!" Vynce yelled to Raze.

"Shouting isn't going to speed up the process," Raze replied coolly.

Ava and Draco had their weapons raised at the hulk above them. It had squeezed itself into the cramped shaft and become stuck. A single groping arm flailed down at them, while a mouth that was far too big for its face gnashed sharp uneven teeth. Al had his gun pointed at the things below, and Vynce was stuck in the middle, unable to do anything.

Draco pulled the trigger of his pistol three times and a volley of bullets slammed into the hulk's arm. It was so blinded with rage that it didn't seem to notice being shot. Pistol rounds were useless. The hulk's misshapen, three fingered hand swung down and grabbed onto a ladder rung. It used its hugely powerful muscles to pull itself down further into the shaft. It was focused so intently on nabbing its prey that it didn't realise that it would never be able to get back out of the shaft.

As it came towards them thrashing its completely alien, but overwhelmingly familiar head back and forth, Draco felt that maybe he should have trusted Ava's gut on this one. Maybe he had walked them into the last ship they'd ever board.

The control panel lit up green and the door lifted open. The corridor in front of them was still dark, but it was their only option. Raze was the first through the door, followed quickly by Vynce and Ava who scouted ahead to make sure the area was clear. Al climbed up next, followed by Draco. Once Draco was inside, Raze removed his interface from the control panel and the door slammed shut.

While Arak Nara had brought the Icarus around to the front of the Metropolis Seven, the comms from on board the ship had gone strangely quiet. It could have meant any number of things. Perhaps the crew had simply switched to another comm channel. But Arak felt that something was amiss. Perhaps something could be jamming their comms.

In the maintenance bay, Rhken was ready to launch the kinetic energy tethers. Reban had loaded the ten pods onto the launch platform, and Rhken waited patiently as Arak put the ship in perfect alignment. Evie ran calculations in real time to make sure that they were at the optimal angle and distance. Evie's internal processes were all completely focused on these calculations. She double, triple and quadruple checked the calculations to make sure they were right. Her programming parameters didn't specify that she had to go over the calculations that much, but she could not stop. While she was focused on these calculations, she didn't feel the fluttering that Alphonse had felt before he departed the ship.

Unlike Alphonse, Evie was not a program that allowed for feelings or emotions. The uneasiness that had felt so urgent and impossible to ignore to Alphonse, was simply a defective minor process that she would have to run diagnostics on later. Evie was well equipped to deal with other system-attacks. If another program was trying to crack her security, she would hunt it down mercilessly and wipe it out. The creeping flutter in her secondary processes didn't show any signs of malicious invasion, so it was ignored.

Evie could not detect that Veck Simms was manipulating her programming to take her focus from him, and diverting her attention away from the defence protocol Draco had put in place. Evie couldn't detect him, because he was not a program. He didn't move in sequenced code. His processes were erratic, impossible to lock onto. His intrusion was the fragmented abstract of human thought made into electrical signal. Evie had no defence against him. It would only be a matter of time until he found the right code to alter, the right buttons to press.

'Just a little more,' Veck thought to himself, 'Just a little more and I'll shut the AI down for good. Then, I'll get out of this fucking cage, and the real fun will start.'

Veck had never interfaced with such an elaborate system. He had heard bad things about humans with neurotech implants interfacing with artificial intelligence systems. People had horrific experiences. Minds were wiped or reprogrammed. Entire ships were brought down in flames due to AI system shut down. But Veck was desperate. It was his only chance at escape. He had to take it. When he saw, he saw both through his eyes, and into Evie's programming matrix.

The human mind needs to understand a system before it can begin to decipher it. In order for the human mind to understand a system, it needs to be represented in some kind of pattern. Veck's mind interpreted the processing matrix as lines of code, whipping in between buildings that represented all of Evie's core processes. There was no ground, and there was no sky. The buildings seemed to stretch on forever. Only the lines of code and Veck himself remained in movement.

As Veck flew through the code he saw a light in the distance. It was a dim, distant light, and he knew what it was as soon as he saw it. It was Evie's central core, and that was his destination. If he could manage to infiltrate her core, he could control her. If he could control Evie, he could control the Icarus.

In the maintenance bay, Rhken fired the first kinetic energy tether onto the Metropolis Seven, binding the two ships together.

Behind the closed door, spindly legs skittered and scratched in a vain attempt to get at Draco and the others. The hulking monstrosity above them had become wedged in the shaft, unable to move. It bellowed in frustration as the crew moved down the dark corridor. Their boots crunched on broken glass as they moved forward. At the end of the corridor, faint blue luminescence could be seen.

"Al, how far until we reach the crew quarters?" Draco asked.

"This corridor bends right, then leads straight there. Approximately another two hundred and sixty metres."

As they moved forward, glass shattered on their right. Something small and hard slammed into Vynce's side and knocked him to the ground. A creature with pink skin and finger-like appendages sprouting from its gnarled, misshapen face chomped on Vynce's armour.

Draco raised his pistol and fired a single shot into the creature. The creature's head exploded outward, spraying Vynce with its remains

"I'm glad you're a good shot, Captain," Vynce said as he got back to his feet, wiping the guts from his visor.

Draco holstered his pistol again.

"Just what the fuck is going on in this place?" Ava asked.

"Insufficient data," AI replied matter-of-factly.

Raze stooped down next to the exploded creature and poked around in the remains of its body. The body was cylindrical with short stumpy feet that ended in claws. It ended in a flat pulpy stump where the head had been, and ended in a short stubby tail with bone-like protrusions poking out from a misshapen nub. Raze picked up one of the protrusions that lined the thing's face and held it up for the rest of the crew to see.

"I may be going crazy, but that looks like a finger to me," Raze said.

Draco took the finger from Raze and inspected it. The big man was right. It was a finger. A human finger. Two knuckles, a fingerprint, and a fingernail.

"I'm starting to wish that we had ignored this big old hunk of metal and kept on flying back to the Alliance Military. Ha! I never thought I'd be glad to see them," Ava said.

Draco looked down at the creature and suddenly it all made grisly sense. The creature was a part of one of the crew members. The crew was all around them, in the walls, skittering through the vents.

"We've only got one way to go. Toward the light at the end of the tunnel. Once we find out what's really going on here, we start the engines, and we get out of here," he said.

"Are you serious? You still want us to start the engines?" Vynce asked.

"There could still be survivors. We've got three hours and twenty minutes until we roast, and no way to get back to our drop ship without going through a flesh mountain. I don't see many other options right now," Draco said.

FIVE

Draco and the crew rounded a corner. A blue light shone from the end of the corridor. A wall-mounted info station glowed on the opposite side of the small room. On a map of the Metropolis Seven, a small dot on the bottom left hand corner showed their position. Draco walked over to the map. He wanted to try and make sense of where they were in relation to the engine room.

As they walked in, the power to the information station was cut and the map disappeared. Draco swore, and at that instant the lights in the room switched on. Ava, Vynce and Raze raised their assault rifles, surveying for possible threats. For the first time since they entered the ship, they didn't need their shoulder lamps to see. The room was clear and quiet. There was the scuttling sound in the vents, but for the moment they were safe. There was a door marked maintenance crew only on the far right side of the wall.

Someone or something had manipulated the power resource grid to herd them to this space, and that same entity had turned off their only means of gathering information about where they were on the ship. Draco motioned for Raze to inspect the information station.

"Re-route the power back to this kiosk, or open a path for us to get to their main server," Draco said.

Raze got down on one knee, wedged open the interface panel at the bottom of the kiosk, pulled the interface chip from under the buckler on his arm and began to infiltrate the system.

'No, stop! Step away from there!' a voice said over the loud speaker.

"I am Captain Draco Goldwing, responding to the distress beacon from Satellite class space cruiser Metropolis Seven. The lives of my crew are in danger, and I need your cooperation. If I can't count on that, then I'll turn around, go back to my ship, and leave this metal tomb floating in the void."

There was a moment of silence, then the same voice returned and spoke timidly, 'if you don't do what I say Captain Goldwing, I'll open the door at the end of the corridor and all of those... things... will fall on you in seconds.'

"You can try, but my crew and I will kill every last one of them, then we'll find you, and take you back to the Alliance Military for interfering with a rescue attempt. But one of us might have an accident, and a finger just might find its way to a trigger," Draco said.

"Accidents happen, motherfucker!" Ava added.

Draco would have chastised Ava in any other situation, but he completely agreed with her and would happily see the snivelling little coward behind the speaker make a deadly mistake.

'I apologise for any offence I may have caused, but as I'm sure you're aware that this situation calls for action, not pleasantries.'

"Speaking of the situation, just what happened on this ship? What just tried to tear my crew apart?"

'No time to answer that now, but you will have your answers if you do what I say. Right now, I need you to go down to the engine bay. If we don't get the engines started, we're all going to die.'

"You know what? A little attitude makes all the difference. That's what we came here to do you little prick, but now, I'm tempted to walk right back out to try my luck with whatever is in the vents."

'No, you won't. I know who you are Captain Draco Goldwing. Captain of the Icarus. You wouldn't knowingly leave anyone to die. You will help me.'

That little prick had his number. No matter the circumstance, no matter how pissed off Draco was, or the emotions involved in the situation, that little fucker was right. But how did they know who he was?

"Do I know you?" Draco asked.

'Not yet, but I know you. I just know we'll become fast friends.'

"I highly doubt that. But you might be able to redeem yourself by telling me what the hell we're dealing with out there."

'I will open the way forward and guide you to the engine bay. I need you to find out how the engines have been disabled, and I need you to get them up and running again.'

"The creatures. What are they?"

'You're not ready to know.'

"I don't like flying blind."

'You are not flying, Captain Goldwing. You are not in the pilot's seat. I am. I will guide you. Just follow my directions and you will remain safe, and so will the rest of the survivors on the ship.'

"After that, you and I are going to have a little chat, face to face."

'Of course, Captain. I'll be waiting for you.'

On board the Icarus, Rhken had secured eight kinetic energy tethers. Only two more non-essential auxiliary tethers needed to be placed before they waited for word from Captain Goldwing. Comms had been too quiet. They hadn't received a single update from the crew on board Metropolis Seven since they landed. Rhken was too focused on the task at hand to have noticed, and Reban was too preoccupied with her own thoughts.

Nook was too worried about Draco to pay too much attention to the squabbles of his two girls. Something was seriously wrong. Evie had been acting strange. Nook spent most of his time at his diagnostic console trying to find out what was going on. While debugging, he noticed that some of the subroutines had been rerouted with no explanation how or why.

In the containment area, Veck Simms smiled broadly as he plumbed the depths of Evie's code. In front of him, the giant building made of bright white light and code that represented her central processor was protected by a number of sentry programs that swirled about in the structure of a double helix. Veck was close. He could feel the power that lay beyond those security drones. He could taste his freedom.

On board the Metropolis Seven, Draco and the crew stepped into the maintenance crew quarters. The man they had spoken to over the loudspeaker had lit up the ground with emergency lighting embedded in the walkways.

"Just out of curiosity, what do you think they do with these ships when they're done with their vacation? Do they just break them down for scrap?" Vynce asked.

"The first Metropolis ship barely survived its first year long journey, so it had to be scrapped when it re-docked with New Earth. So did the second and the third for other reasons. There was just nothing they could do with them. But the fourth, they actually landed it in a poor area just outside of Mojave Central and opened it up as a low cost housing precinct. The fifth is a floating resort now in the middle of the Big Blue. The sixth is orbiting New Earth," Raze said.

"I didn't picture you as a Metropolis scholar, Raze," Vynce said.

"The Metropolis Corporation owns New Earth. It either manufactures, or has some input into almost every element of New Earth society. How could you expect me not to know about it?"

"Oh yeah, I forgot you were crazy about that stuff," Vynce said.

"I prefer researching Old Earth technology and history, but I'm also interested in New Earth history. It is good to show an interest in your own species."

"The only interests I have in my own species are whether or not they're going to pay me money to do a job, and whether or not I can get them drunk and talk them into spreading their legs," Vynce joked.

"You are so vulgar sometimes."

"I'll take that as a compliment."

"Enough chatter. Keep your mind on the task at hand," Draco said.

The rebuke didn't really matter to Vynce. He knew it was coming as soon as he had started talking, but he'd done what he had set out to do. He had lightened the mood. The veil of doom and gloom had been lifted, if only for a moment.

The crew quarters were just a place for those who were doing long shifts to rest and relax during their break times. The room they passed through, before violence had broken out on the ship, had a number of comfy couches which could be used as beds, and a whole range of entertainment stations with the latest virtual reality games, interactive holovids and music beamed straight onto the ship from New Earth.

Couches were upturned, cushions were ripped. There was dried blood everywhere. Some entertainment stations had been torn up from the ground. Like the first room they stepped into when they boarded the ship, vent covers had been torn from their brackets and dried blood stains led into the vents.

"They're using the vents for sure," Ava said.

"But I don't think those little things would really be able to carry a person, even as a group. The drag marks are uniform. Whatever grabbed the crew didn't even give them a chance to escape. It must have been really fast," Raze said.

The emergency lights led to a door on the far side of the room. It slid open as they approached, leading into the engine bay. The scene in the next room was much the same as the last, echoing the violence that had come before them.

They crossed into the control room. Lights flickered on the moment they stepped across the threshold. At the same time, the numerous diagnostic panels that lined the sides of the room also flickered to life. Raze rushed over to the master console. He sat down and began looking through the reports to see where the problem was. He moved through the information on the screen at a fevered pace. It went by so fast that Draco couldn't even read it, let alone absorb all the info that Raze took in.

"The captain of the Metropolis Seven is the one who put the ship into orbit around Krakaterra. At the same time, he overloaded the engine grid. He completely blew the capacitors that led from the power core of the ship to the engines. They need to be repaired before we can get this ship moving again. That was approximately one hour before the distress beacon went out," Raze said.

"So the captain went crazy, put the ship into orbit, killed the engines, and actually tried to roast the ship. Am I reading into this correctly?" Ava asked.

"It would appear so."

"But someone had other ideas. The distress beacon was activated, but not by the captain. I can't imagine after going to all that effort to kill everyone on board that the captain would have been open to the idea of rescue. So how did a distress beacon get sent out without his knowledge?"

"The Metropolis Corporation probably programmed their AI to do it in the event of an emergency, regardless of whether or not the captain endorsed it," Draco said. He mentioned it, because he had put a similar program into Evie in the Icarus. If his ship ever became lost, or taken by a hostile force, he had taken countermeasures to ensure that she would come back to him.

"How do we fix the system?" Al asked.

"We need to replace the two burnt out capacitors with new ones. We should find some in the maintenance bay. Captain, how long have we got?" Raze asked.

"A little over two hours."

"When we get the capacitors, we'll need to split up into two teams. One will need to go to the left junction, and one will need to go to the right. Once the capacitors have been replaced, I'll head on alone to the central junction and give the system a kick start. Then we'll be good to go."

"You know you're being ridiculous if you expect me to let you go by yourself, right?" Vynce asked.

"It's fine. I can handle myself."

"I'd never forgive myself if something happened and I wasn't around to back you up. So fuck you, Raze. I'm coming whether you like it or not."

"It's settled then. Raze, Ava, Vynce, you take the right junction. Al and I will take the left. We'll meet back here in the control room. If you run into any trouble, you make sure you report it," Draco said.

"Yes sir," they replied in unison.

Their anonymous friend from the loudspeaker joined them again, 'Very good plan. Perfect, actually. Raze Krosis, you are far too quick for your own good. The capacitors you need are in repair bay three. Follow the corridor to the left, past the power junction. Once you've got the engines running again, I'll have further instructions for you.'

"By further instructions, you mean you'll give us a clear path back to our ship," Draco said.

'Not quite. There are still people in danger on this vessel, and they need you if they are to survive.'

Draco sighed. Whoever this guy was, he was not going to let them out of this situation without using them for his own agenda.

"Move out, let's get the tub moving again."

On board the Icarus, Rhken had secured the final two kinetic energy tethers and waited for word from Draco. Nook had grown more concerned by what he had seen in Evie's subroutine fluctuations and frantically tried to find what was causing them. At the same time, he tried to reach Draco over comms but there was no response.

Alone in the cockpit, Arak waited for word from somebody.

Anybody.

The door to the left of the command console opened out into the huge engine bay. There were lights along the metal boardwalk all the way to repair bay three, where the capacitors waited. The only thing that stood between them and a deadly plunge into the engine bay cavity below was a waist high guard rail.

As they moved out Draco said, "We have to move as a unit to get the capacitors, then split up into two teams to put them in place. Al and I will take the closest capacitor then high-tail it back to the control room to start the engines. Vynce, Ava and Raze will install the other capacitor on the far side of the engine bay. Once the capacitors are in place, Vynce, Ava and Raze will go to the power junction to switch the power grid on. Al and I will be at the engine room and make sure all the systems come back up when the power is turned on. Any questions?"

Their shoulder torches barely penetrated the oppressive darkness in the enormous engine bay. The natural human fear of the dark played on their minds as they moved. Their footsteps on the metal boardwalk echoed out into the engine bay. If there was something there waiting in the darkness, it would hear them coming.

They passed a small illuminated pathway leading to the first power junction. They moved past at speed. Repair bay three was only a little further.

The shutter door to the repair bay opened as they approached. Whoever was pulling the strings could see them, and he could manipulate doors, lights, and power to make sure that they stuck to his plan. Draco's blood began to feel hot in his veins. It was one thing to take an order from a superior officer in the interests of the greater good. It was another thing entirely to be blackmailed and manipulated in a plan that you weren't privy to. But they had no other choice, so Draco and the rest of the crew walked into the repair bay and began searching for the capacitors.

'The capacitors are in the small storeroom at the back of the repair bay. You will need two people to carry them as they are quite heavy,' the voice said over the loudspeaker.

The light above the storeroom door flickered on and the door slid open.

"Captain, I'll retrieve our capacitor," Al said and followed Raze and Ava into the storeroom.

With the strength of three men, Alphonse easily picked up and carried the capacitor by himself. It was not a single capacitor in the traditional sense. It was made up of a number of smaller capacitors which regulated power output. Without these cluster capacitors, the engines would simply overheat and explode. The cluster capacitors were the size of a small dog, but were extremely dense. Raze and Vynce struggled to carry their capacitor between them. As he walked backwards, Vynce almost tripped and lost his grip. Ava rolled her eyes and took over. She and Raze carried the capacitor between them.

"You're on guard duty you weakling. If we die, it's your fault," Ava said.

Vynce felt his cheeks flush.

"Al, I'll cover you while you put the capacitor in place. Vynce, Raze, Ava, you three have some distance to cover, so get to it," Draco said.

Without a word, the other three moved out towards the other junction on the far side of the engine bay as their anonymous director lit up their path through the darkness. In between the repair bay and the other power junction was a raised platform. On top of the platform was an illuminated box. The manual override switch.

Draco and Al moved out. Draco kept his pistol held ready in front of him as they moved back towards the first power junction. Draco could hear the sound of scratching and scuttling break the silence. There was definitely something in the engine bay with them.

They reached the path to the power junction and turned. The

power junction was encased in a heavy metallic shell. As they approached, the shell around the junction split apart, allowing them access.

"Do you know where that goes?" Draco asked.

"Not yet, but I'm sure I'll be able to figure it out," Al said.

Al studied the hub for a moment and found the blown capacitor. He pulled it out, tossed it aside, and put the working capacitor into place. The moment that the capacitor was in place, the metallic shell began to close. He pulled his hands back seconds before the shell snapped closed.

With the capacitor placed, they returned to the command console as Raze, Ava and Vynce made their way through the darkness. Ava had to admit that the capacitor was pretty heavy, but she'd never complain about it while the other two boys were around. Emasculating Vynce was one of her favourite pastimes.

They followed the metal boardwalk past the manual override switch. Raze looked at it for a moment as they passed by. It was fairly high up, and he was not fond of heights. Not fond at all. But he had a job to do, and it would get done.

They reached the other power junction shortly after Draco and Al had finished placing the first capacitor. As they approached, the hub opened up. Raze took a moment to assess the hub and pulled the blown capacitor out. Ava helped him lift the replacement capacitor into place. The shell slid closed again.

'Both capacitors have been replaced. Return to the manual override junction and we will be ready to blast out of orbit.'

The sound of something down in the darkness grew louder. Something was climbing up the struts that held the boardwalk over the engines. When he heard the sound, Vynce's hands had started to sweat and the hairs on the back of his neck began to bristle.

"Uhh, guys, we should probably get out of here," Vynce said.

With both capacitors restored, Raze knew there was only one thing left to do.

"Ava, Vynce, you both need to head back to the control room. I can trip the switch by myself," Raze said.

"What if one of those things jumps out of the darkness and attacks you?" Vynce asked.

"Then I'll kill it."

Vynce started to argue, but Ava cut him off.

"If Raze wants to be a hero, let him. He's more than capable."

"You're really going to let him go by himself?"

"Yes, he's a big boy and he can make his own fucking decisions. I'm not going to play mother if he wants to go off by himself."

"Please Vynce, I can handle this by myself. It's just flipping a switch," Raze added.

"Fine," Vynce relented.

As Ava and Vynce started back towards the main kiosk, Raze turned back towards the manual override platform. He ran down the boardwalk that looked down over the engine cavity. The power junction was raised higher than the boardwalk, and a bright yellow light illuminated the switch.

From behind him, Raze heard the sound of movement. He spun to see a group of small monstrosities climb from underneath the boardwalk. For a moment, Raze's mind couldn't comprehend what he was seeing.

The creatures appeared to be made of human body parts, rearranged in an affront to the natural order of things. One of the creatures resembled a human head, with another formless alien head sticking out of a mouth that was contorted in an expression of unending suffering. The creature bounded towards Raze on its stubby legs. It screamed as a well-placed volley of bullets blew it apart.

Raze felt his stomach drop when two more scuttled towards him. The two creatures were both human arms, but with extra digits sprouting from the skin. A cluster of eyes stared out from the palms of the hands as they reached for Raze's legs. He shot one and stomped on the other. The force of his grav boot snapped its bones like twigs. It writhed on the ground, screeching in pain. Raze kicked it over the side of the walkway and it fell into the darkness.

If one of these smaller creatures took him by surprise, he would be in trouble. If he kept his wits about him, he would be fine. He sent a command to his suit to boost external stimuli detectors by sacrificing power to a couple of non-essential systems. His display inside the helmet immediately lit up to show that there were more of them hiding in the darkness all around the engine bay.

As Vynce and Ava ran back towards the control room, they found this out the hard way. A group of creatures fell from above, knocking Vynce to his feet. Ava heard his body hit the ground behind her and spun around with her rifle ready to fire. She dispatched the creatures with short controlled bursts of rifle fire, but not before two on Vynce's back had begun to spew a sticky fluid onto the prone soldier. Ava fired two volleys of bullets, and the creatures exploded into a pulpy mass of blood and gore. Vynce tried to lift himself to his feet, but his range of movement was limited.

"What the fuck were they doing on my back? I can't move," he said.

Ava took Vynce by the shoulder and lifted him to his feet. The liquid that the creatures had spewed all over Vynce had already hardened into a solid resin which limited the movement of his shoulders. He couldn't lift them above his chest, or reach backwards. Ava tore the resin from his back and threw it to the side.

"That must be how they caught most of the crew. They send these little things out to disable you. They were trying to stick your pasty arse to the boardwalk," Ava said.

"That's doesn't make any sense. Why would they stick you somewhere?"

"Well that just means that something else would have to come around where these little things have been to collect you."

"I don't want to meet whatever does the collecting."

"I think we already have. You remember that huge thing that tried to chase us down the vent? I think it followed those little things to find us. Maybe that's how they work. These little things find and subdue the prey, then the big motherfuckers come along and take you."

"I think we should go make sure Raze is alright. If he gets ambushed by these things, he's as good as dead."

"Yeah, you might have been right on this one," Ava admitted reluctantly.

Ava and Vynce turned around and ran back towards the main power junction. They pounded the boardwalk as fast as they could.

Raze reached the ladder to the power junction without seeing any more of the little creatures. He had begun to climb the ladder when something slammed into his back hard enough to make him lose his grip. He turned his head to see something with far too many digits climbing up his back. Two long muscular rope-like limbs flashed in front of his eyes before he felt a crushing pressure around his neck.

The thing on his back was choking him. He tried in vain to shake the thing off, but its grip was too strong. He dug his hands into one of the tentacles that wrapped around his neck and squeezed. It squeezed right back and Raze began to see stars. There wasn't enough pressure to break through the suit or do any damage to his neck, but the thing had cut off his oxygen. Raze was being smothered in his own suit.

He let go of the thing around his neck and pulled his sunstorm welder out of his thigh pocket. He flicked the switch and the bright beam of the welder shot out. He couldn't see how tightly the thing was wrapped around his neck, but unless he did something in a couple of seconds, he'd black out and it would all be over. He brought the beam of the welder closer to his neck and he heard an inhuman wail of pain from behind him. He saw one of the appendages drop off the side of the ladder and into the darkness of the engine bay cavity below. He brought the welder closer to his neck again, but pulled away as he felt the heat of it coming too close. If he burnt a hole in his armour, then the thing could get at him. He lifted the welder a little closer and the creature let go of his neck altogether.

A beautiful, cool rush of oxygen washed over him and he breathed in deep ragged breathes. The thing was still on his back, and he needed to get it off before it launched another attack.

There was a gunshot from the right, and the weight of the creature immediately fell away. Raze looked to his right to see Ava, rifle barrel still red from the heat of the bullet which had just saved his life. Between Raze and Ava, another dozen small creatures climbed from underneath the boardwalk.

"Go, turn the power on!" Ava yelled to Raze.

Raze ascended the ladder quickly as Ava and Vynce made short work of the little creatures. More of them had started to climb from under the boardwalk behind them. Vynce killed the ones behind them. Ava killed the ones that climbed up after Raze with eagle eye accuracy.

Raze lifted himself onto the platform and pulled open the hatch. He didn't dare look over the side of the platform, or back down the ladder otherwise he would succumb to his vertigo. Inside the hatch was a lever. Raze grabbed it and pulled down. Lights came on all around the engine bay, and from his perch above it all, he could appreciate the magnitude of the engines that powered this magnificent ship. Each of the dual engine drives was as big as a football field, and they both came back to life with an almighty roar. As Raze realised just how far up he really was, a wave of nausea came over him. He quickly steadied himself and started descending the ladder.

It was only when Raze looked up that he realised the true magnitude of their problem. On the top of the engine bay was a colony of these small creatures. Hundreds of them moved together as one, down the wall towards the boardwalk. Ava could make out what looked like former passengers in the mess of creatures on the ceiling. They had been dragged there and plastered into place by these little things with the resin they secreted.

The engines powered up to full capacity, and the sound was almost too much to bear. It was penetrating. Ava, Raze and Vynce could feel the air thrum around them. They could feel the air moving as it was sucked into the huge turbines below. Raze landed heavily back onto the boardwalk. He didn't even look down as he jumped from the ladder. He was just happy to get back to solid ground. No one had to say a thing. They all knew what they had to do. Going back to the right meant being captured by the swarm of those little creatures. Going left was their only option.

Raze took off down the left passageway. Ava and Vynce followed, the swarm of creatures followed quickly behind.

Back in the engine room, Draco and Alphonse saw the systems all come back online one by one. Al sat down at the console and made sure that the system wouldn't overload as soon as it reached peak power output. Everything seemed to be in order. The only thing that they needed to do now was to wait for the others to get back.

Al worked quickly while he had access to the command console. He was determined to find out who had been jamming his access to the system inside the Metropolis Seven, and who was jamming their communications to the Icarus. He had tried to get into contact with Evie on multiple occasions since entering Metropolis Seven, and he was absolutely sure that something from inside the ship was jamming their communications.

As Al linked with the system to trace the jamming signal back to its source, he rerouted the power supply lines so that the power could not be cut to the command console.

Without warning, the doors leading to the engine bay slammed shut. The engines were approaching peak power output, and were on the cusp of becoming operational again.

As Ava, Raze and Vynce ran towards the control room, they saw the door slam shut, cutting off their only means of escape.

"No!"

"Fuck!"

"What? Why would they close it?"

"Open the fucking door!"

Draco sprung to his feet, but felt his movements slowing as energy crackled throughout the engine room.

"Al, get that door open right now!" Draco yelled. He felt as though his muscles had atrophied mid-stride. All the strength drained from his body as Al worked to get the door back open.

Behind Ava, Raze and Vynce, the marauding mass of flesh thundered towards them in a wave, ebbing and flowing with its own undercurrent. They climbed along the railings, underneath and along the boardwalk. As Ava looked above them, she saw another group descending from the ceiling above them. She pounded on the door as Vynce and Raze opened fire on the creatures.

"Open the fucking door!" she repeated.

Draco felt as though he was dead on his feet. He could hear and see his crew facing their deaths, but could do nothing to stop it. He was frozen in place. Instead of simply slowing down, he had completely stopped. Conscious, but immobile. Time seemed to stretch out into an eternity as he felt himself spreading thin. He wanted to scream, but couldn't. The lights in the engine room cut out, but the control console itself stayed active.

The door slid open and Ava almost fell through the doorway. The sound of firing assault rifles echoed in the small room as Raze and Vynce backed into the engine room. The mass of creatures bounded toward them.

The door slid shut again, locking into place. The sound of hundreds of skittering legs came from behind the door, but they could not breach it. Alphonse had sealed all vents in and out of the engine bay. The colony of creatures might as well have been on another planet. They were no longer a danger.

"Captain, are you alright?" Raze asked.

Draco was completely unable to move. All around him, the air crackled with energy. At first it was like the sensation of pins and needles, but as the energy output intensified, so did the feeling until it became almost painful. To Raze, Ava and Vynce, it felt as though they were being fried from the inside out, as though every molecule in their bodies were screaming in unison.

A bright light appeared in the engine room. It started tiny, smaller than the head of a pin. It grew slowly, then with a crack as loud as a thunderclap, the small white light became a man in full combat armour, holding a small black gadget in his left hand, and a pistol in the other. His armour was unlike anything they had ever seen. There were no angles, only smooth curves. It looked more like a second skin than a suit of armour. The helmet was a smooth backwards curving dome of reflective glass.

As he appeared seemingly from nowhere, he seemed to float in the middle of the room. After the thunderclap, he fell to one knee and began coughing. He took his helmet off to reveal a man in his mid-forties with long black hair tied back in a ponytail. He coughed hard, fell face down on the floor and threw up. He wiped his chin after his bile had finished evacuating his body and lifted his head. He had piercing blue eyes, a chiselled jaw and a closely trimmed black beard.

He coughed again, then his face steeled as he saw the heavily armed crew around him.

"Where is Draco Goldwing?" he demanded.

SIX

"Who the fuck are you?" Ava demanded.

"Is that him? He's not moving, so that's got to be him. Dammit, I had hoped this wouldn't happen, but I had no other choice," the man said as he got to his feet.

"You better start explaining yourself, buddy," Ava said and stepped between the newcomer and Draco.

"Ava, you better move. If you don't, Draco will die," the man said.

"How the hell do you know who I am?" she demanded.

"There's no time. The next few moments are crucial. Right now, Draco is quantum locked. He is a fixed point in space and time. That means that in every possible reality, and every possible time, he exists in this same instance. That's not supposed to happen. If I don't unlock him… His entire existence will be removed from every reality. You cannot afford to argue with me on this," the man said.

Dumbfounded, Ava stepped aside and motioned for the newcomer to approach. He looked Draco over, then pulled out a small black capsule the size of a meal supplement from a compartment on his wrist. He affixed it to the back of Draco's neck. He pressed the small black capsule until the outer shell cracked, which sent a shock of white luminescent energy racing across Draco's body.

Draco fell to the ground.

"What happened?" Draco asked as he got back to his feet.

The newcomer smiled broadly and clapped Draco on the back.

"You are a sight for sore eyes. It's been far too long Draco," he said.

"How do you know me?" Draco asked.

"It's me, Jaxon. Jaxon Argentos. Please tell me you remember me. You have to remember me, otherwise this can't have worked."

"I have no idea who you are," Draco said truthfully.

Jaxon turned away and swore under his breath. He searched for a way to explain what had happened, but he knew that he couldn't delve into it without possibly compromising the fabric of space and time. Hell, he shouldn't have even done what he did, but he had no other choice. Hundreds of scenarios and questions ran through his mind, but the what ifs of the situation would have to wait. He needed to find out where they were, and how close they were to New Earth.

"Where are we?" Jaxon asked.

"The Arcturus system," Draco answered and Jaxon's blood ran cold.

"When are we?" Jaxon asked.

"New Earth year 832," Draco answered.

The colour drained from Jaxon's face as he realised where and when he was. He swore to himself in Galactic Common and almost took his pistol out of its holster and ate a bullet. He couldn't be back aboard the Metropolis Seven. He couldn't be. He had put all of that horror behind him. All that death seemed like a lifetime ago, but he had been brought back here by the tides of fate. He had long ago given up belief of destiny or divine intervention in the universe, but this turn of events had almost been enough to make him re-think a lifetime of learning about how reality was supposed to work.

"I'm not supposed to be here. I can't be here," he whispered.

"Just hang on a second stranger, I think you've got some

explaining to do," Draco said.

"I can't. Not now, or it could ruin everything. The very fact that you know that I know who you are could already change everything. What have I done?"

"You said your name is Jaxon, right? Where are you from, Jaxon?"

"New Earth."

"How did you get here?"

"I… can't talk about that right now."

"Well that's delightfully convenient. We're kind of in the middle of something here, so you've got a choice to make. You can either make yourself useful, or you can go and die in a dark corner of the ship somewhere. That's your call."

Jaxon levelled his gaze at Draco. If he had any idea of just what inhabited this ship, he wouldn't have said those words. He wouldn't have dared. Clearly Draco didn't know what was going on yet. Jaxon would have to stick with them until the time was right to tell him the truth. He put his helmet back on, and said "I'll make myself useful. Orders?"

Draco ignored the question and turned to speak to Al, "Are we in the system yet Al? Do we have control?"

"Not complete control, no. But in our favour, this particular console is isolated from the mainframe, and this is the only console that the engines can be controlled from. Our friend can't take this console over, and the engines are firing. But I cannot contact the Icarus. Something is jamming us, and I believe it's coming from inside the ship. Unless we can get word to them to start the towing procedure, we're stuck here. We can't engage the engines. The Icarus is no doubt tethered to Metropolis Seven by now, so if we take off without the push / pull system engaged, we'll destroy the ship. That's what the tethers should be set to, however it's not a risk I'd like to take."

"How long will it take to restore communications?"

"I am not sure. I must first find out how we are being jammed, and that could take some time."

"Well, we're all out of time. Find a solution."

"Yes, Captain."

Jaxon laughed to himself. Draco didn't realise just how correct he was. They were out of time, out of luck and would soon be running short on hope. They just hadn't seen what was waiting for them yet. Jaxon was determined not to meddle in the natural progression of time, but his mission was too important. He needed to get back to New Earth before it was too late. Jaxon pulled a small comm unit from the compartment inside of his left forearm and tossed it to Draco.

"Use that to contact your ship," Jaxon said.

Draco caught the comm unit and stared at it for a moment.

"Trust me," Jaxon said, "It'll work. It opens a direct line to the Icarus."

Draco pressed the button on the side and the comm unit crackled to life.

"This is Captain Draco Goldwing, hailing the Icarus. Can anyone hear me?"

'Captain, this is Arak. You are a welcome sound on the wavebands. I don't recognise the channel you're broadcasting from. The signal is so strong.'

"Nara-ka, it's very good to hear your voice. We've just restarted the engines, and they're ready to go on your mark. Talk to Nook and let us know when you're ready for us to start them up."

'Yes, Captain.'

Draco turned, looked at Jaxon and said, "After we get back to the Icarus, you've got some explaining to do. But first, how the hell did you know the waveband of the Icarus?"

"When we have a moment, perhaps you and I have a little chat. We have quite a lot to discuss," Jaxon answered.

"Clearly."

'Captain Goldwing? This is Nook, are you ready to engage the engines?'

"Just tell us when."

'Tethers are set to push-pull mode, so on your go we'll be ready. When you turn on the engine thrust, we'll turn on our ion drives. I am standing by for your word.'

"Everyone, hang onto something."

The crew and Jaxon hung onto something secure as the Captain started counting.

"10 seconds, starting now."

Draco counted down from ten, and as he reached zero Al set the engines to full burn. The engines rumbled underneath their feet and the force almost took the crew to the ground.

On the Icarus, Arak ignited the ion drives, and the two ships moved in unison away from the burning planet beneath them. After a moment, the two ships broke away from orbit, and together, they floated through the void between the stars.

Nook, Reban and Rhken breathed a sigh of relief in unison. Arak opened the channel to Draco again and said "We're out of orbit, Captain. We're free and clear. Get back to the Icarus and we can let the Alliance Military handle this."

'Things are a little more complicated than that my friend. There are a couple of things we have to take care of on the Metropolis Seven before we can come back to celebrate. There could be a lot of people still in danger, and we may have picked up a hitchhiker,' Draco said.

"I don't like the sound of any of that," Arak admitted.

'You don't have to like it as long as you follow your orders, boy,' Nook added over the commlink.

Draco laughed. 'We'll be alright. Just hold her steady. Make sure the energy tethers stay in place. We'll see you all very soon.'

"Did we do it?" Vynce asked.

"Yes. We're out of orbit," Draco said.

"Arak's already requested assistance from the Alliance Military, right?" Ava asked.

"Not yet. I think we'd better find out what's going with our friend over the loudspeaker. If nothing else I think we owe him a visit, don't you?" Draco said.

"Can I make him have an accident, Captain? Please?" Ava pleaded.

"Only if he deserves it," Draco teased.

"Captain, I have downloaded the schematics of the ship and I can now access them from my personal data banks. I am currently tracing the signal from our anonymous friend. In a few moments I should have his location," Al said.

"Fantastic work, Al. Let me know when we're good to go."

On board the Icarus, Veck had made one significant victory. He had managed to disguise himself as a security protocol and slip into their ranks. Veck's consciousness twisted and turned around Evie's core in beautiful harmony with the programs around him. It reminded him of his childhood on New Earth, bathing in the crystal clear waters of Harmony Bay. He would stay in the ocean for hours, flowing back and forth with the gentle waves. The sensation of flowing between the programs was like being awash in the tides. He allowed himself to become lost in it. He took note of the openings in the code. He saw places where he could slip through the nets and take control of Evie's core programming. But it was not yet time. There was still too much risk.

'Divide and conquer,' he thought to himself.

At the very thought, his consciousness was willed into splitting itself in two. One part of his consciousness remained focused on infiltrating the artificial intelligence, but the other part spread to his physical body. He had never experienced simultaneous consciousness before, and the elation that the overload caused his senses was almost too much to bear.

From pieces of information he could glean from the drone programs around him, he found the location of the defence protocol that would destroy him if he tried to escape. From there, he found the location of his arms. Draco had locked them in the one place that they couldn't escape from unless the ship was in emergency lockdown. He had stowed them in one of the emergency escape pods on the aft side of the ship. Veck looked through the system diligently and covertly to find a way to open the escape pod without notifying the sentry programs that surrounded him. He would have to work slowly to remain undetected.

In the engine bay, Rhken was hunched over the diagnostic console as she checked and double checked the integrity of the kinetic energy tethers. They were set to push / pull mode, so regardless of where the thrust came from, both ships moved in unison at the same speed. The tethers transferred the energy provided by both ships from one to the other so their velocities matched. They were much more effective than traditional ropes, chains or towing rigs.

Reban sat back in a comfy chair, looking out at the view behind the ship through the display on her father's console. The Icarus was as small as a housefly next to the gigantic Metropolis Seven. When the engines had come back online, the running lights on the top and sides of the huge ship switched back on like the bioluminescent light spots of a giant deep ocean fish.

Nook had managed to speak to Captain Goldwing for a moment. Their communications were still down between the two ships, aside from that one waveband that came through loud and clear. Nook didn't know how the captain managed it, but he was glad that he did. The second star had gotten bigger in his viewfinder while comms were silent and he didn't want to imagine what would happen if they didn't get the engines back up and running in time.

Suddenly he noticed a blip on his sensors that hadn't been there a moment ago. As they moved the huge cruise liner, he realised that another ship had been hiding in the static cloud of communications interference. Nook zoomed into the minuscule blob on his display to get a better picture of what lay in the darkness behind them. The picture was distorted by the propulsion energy firing out of the back of the Metropolis Seven, but the shape of the ship was unmistakable. The main diamond shaped body was situated between two angular forward sweeping wings; he would know those shapes anywhere. It ended in a fine point, and Nook knew embedded in the nose there would be two ballistic missile launchers. It was a Vartalen scout cruiser.

It was no real surprise though, the Vartalen owned this sector of space and defended it against anything which threatened their supremacy. Humans were especially unwelcome by the Vartalen, so it was only natural that they would take interest in a human distress beacon. From their behaviour, they didn't look as though they were getting ready to attack. They were merely spectators. Nook opened the comm channel back to the Metropolis Seven and hailed the captain.

"Captain, we have a Vartalen cruiser hanging around the tail end of the Metropolis Seven," he said.

'Hostile?' Draco asked.

"Not yet. It's most likely a surveillance ship."

'I can't blame them for being interested. Do they know we're inside?'

"Depends on how long they've been watching. I would recommend we take the cautious route, but it's very likely that their communications have been interrupted just as much as ours."

'Do we have schematics?'

"I'll arrange for Reban to find out any information we can. But Captain, you should know that it is most definitely an attack cruiser."

'One of those pointy bastards.'

"Very pointy."

'Let me know if anything changes.'

"Yes sir, I will," he said and closed the comm channel. He turned to Reban who was relaxing in her easy chair and said, "Hon, I need you to download some information for me. We have a Vartalen attack cruiser hiding in the communication black field behind Metropolis Seven. I need you to try and access it. Get as much information as you can, and hopefully we can deliver it to Captain Goldwing."

Reban sprung to her feet at once, nodded and opened up the display module on her console. She began the search.

Draco closed the channel to Nook and told the crew of the situation.

"We have a Vartalen attack cruiser on our tail. It's running silent at the moment. It probably doesn't even know that we know it's there. It's not hostile, but we need to be ready if they change to an intercept trajectory."

"I knew those bastards wouldn't be able to keep their noses out of this. It's too big a prize," Ava said.

"It's also much too big for them to actually do anything with. One little attack cruiser can't overpower a ship with one hundred thousand people on it," Raze said.

"I think we need to operate on the assumption that they're just looking to make sure we get this ship out of their space. Once it's gone, they'll leave," Draco said.

Jaxon laughed quietly to himself.

"Got something you want to add, stranger?" Draco asked.

"No, not at all," he replied.

"Then I suggest you keep your mouth shut while we figure out our next move."

"Yes, sir," Jaxon said.

Draco turned to Alphonse, who was still seated at the engine control. He had taken his interface cable from the inside of his wrist and plugged it directly into the console. He was completely still as he plumbed the depth of the system, looking for information that might help them.

Unfortunately, the majority of the data was still inaccessible. Someone had put blocks on almost every area of the system. Maintenance files were off limits, as were surveillance, life support and security protocol information. But Alphonse had found what he truly wanted; the entire schematics of the Metropolis Seven. He downloaded them onto his own internal memory banks for future reference. The mainframe of the system was located in the central tower in the middle of the Metropolitan District. All systems across the ship could be controlled from that central tower.

Whoever had access to the mainframe had to have access to all the other systems associated with the running of the ship. Excluding the controls to the engines. Someone had disabled the engine controls from the bridge.

If their anonymous friend needed them to switch the engines back on and set a course, it's likely that he would be on the bridge at the top of the tower.

"Captain, I think we have a destination," Al said as he removed his interface from the system.

"Where's that?"

"I have downloaded the schematics of the entire ship, and I have found a control hub on the bridge of the ship that will allow us complete control. I believe that's where our unknown friend is located."

'Thankfully, that's exactly where I wanted you to go,' the voice over the loudspeaker interjected.

"I have a question for you, whoever-you-are. Why should we play your games, now that we have access to the schematics of the ship?" Draco asked.

'Because those schematics don't show you where the nests are. Those schematics will likely lead you right into the jaws of the monsters in the bowels of this ship. Without me, your chances of survival are slim.'

Regardless of the schematics on Al's system, the voice over the loudspeaker was right. The ship was huge, dark and unknown. Even if they had the plans, it wouldn't stop them from stumbling into a trap.

"What's your game plan here? What do you hope to achieve by playing us like this?" Draco asked.

'I want to survive, Captain Goldwing. I need you to help me survive.'

"I can't blame you for that, but if we're to continue working together, you can't keep blackmailing us. You understand that, right?"

'It's the only way. You have no choice but to trust me.'

"We're the ones with options here, and I think you're the one who's all out of options."

'Think what you wish, Captain Goldwing. It makes no difference.'

"Al, plot us a course to the central tower. Whatever stands in our way, we'll overcome it."

"The quickest way to the mainframe is to go through the grazing lands where they rear the animals they use for food. Once we cross it, we can go through the Residential District and into Metropolitan District. Metro Tower is right in the heart of it," Al said.

"Wait a second. Are you saying that there are farmlands inside the ship?" Vynce asked.

"Yes, as well as a beachfront and a simulated rain forest. This ship has everything it needs to survive a ten-year long vacation and keep the passengers occupied." Al responded and motioned for them to follow.

Inside Evie's core programming Veck had found a foothold to begin his assault. He slipped out of the double helix formation of sentry drones circulating around the core and disguised himself as a blank memory sector. He slipped away from them without drawing any attention to himself. He began to bond himself to Evie's core to ensure that he could keep complete control, even if she became aware of him.

His first mission was a complete success. He sent a subroutine to Evie's core commanding her to release his two arms from their prisons. They crawled along using their fingers and disappeared into the Icarus' ventilation shafts. Slowly, they crawled along the shafts towards Veck's cell.

He worked himself into Evie's code until he himself became a subroutine. He identified the defence protocol Draco had put in place to fry his neurotech implant, deleted it from Evie's archives and replaced it with a dummy program. He stored the original subroutine in the neurotech implant it was designed to destroy, away from the one program that could activate it.

In his cell, Veck smiled as he got to his feet. He cracked his neck back and forth, jumped in place, and bent down to stretch his spine.

"Oh my, it does feel good to move again," he said to the empty cell.

He lifted an unshod foot towards the crackling energy bars around him. He touched it with his big toe. The crackling energy wasn't an issue for him thanks to his internal energy stores. They re-routed the normally deadly energy into two storage tanks that would supercharge his auxiliary systems for hours. He pulled his foot back from the energy bar and sat back down. He closed his eyes and waited for his arms to arrive. Once he had his arms back things were going to get very interesting.

Finally, for the first time in their history, he would have the upper hand over Draco Goldwing. That knowledge felt good. If he still had a human heart, it would have warmed at the thought.

SEVEN

Ava didn't like how things were playing out. The man over the loudspeaker knew the captain somehow, or at least knew who he was enough to manipulate him. In all the years that she'd known Draco, she'd never seen him on the back foot before. She didn't like it one bit. And that new guy who appeared out of nowhere, Jaxon, what was his deal? His gear and weapons were advanced like nothing she had ever seen before. He was definitely from somewhere else, but nothing in the human Alliance was that sophisticated. He also knew who Draco was. Ava hadn't realised that the captain was some sort of galactic celebrity.

Ava imagined Draco, decked out in a traditional New Earth suit and tie, on the purple carpet of a movie premiere in the Hub. The mental image was so ridiculous she couldn't stop herself from snorting with laughter. Draco, in a suit, schmoozing and posing for stills. She'd pay good money to see that.

"Something funny?" Vynce asked.

"Oh, if only you knew," Ava replied with a wave of her hand.

They continued on back through the corridors they had been herded down before. They came back to the crew quarters and took another branching corridor leading towards the farmlands.

The farmlands inside the ship were not as large and sprawling as open farmland on a terrestrial planet. Instead of having a huge expanse of open grazing land, the animals were given a six level grazing field where they could roam between levels which were stacked on top of each other.

The quickest route across the farmland and into the main Metropolitan District of the ship was across the very bottom floor. If they could cross it quickly and without incident, they would be one step closer to finding out who their mystery friend was, and securing passage safely out of the ship.

A door slid open, and in front of the crew was a large bay filled with stalls. In the distance, they heard the sound of a mooing cow, which was answered by another cow. Their calls echoed.

"I hate cows," Vynce blurted out.

"What? How could you hate cows?" Ava asked.

"I don't know, alright? They just freak me out."

"Do you have a horribly traumatising cow-related experience from your childhood that profoundly affected your mental state into adulthood?" Ava asked with a feigned gasp.

"You know what, you can shut the hell up."

Ava made the mournful sound of a cow mooing and laughed as Vynce visibly slowed his stride and tensed up.

"Aww, poor little Vyncey," she laughed and clapped him on the back.

"Enough," Draco interjected.

Raze opened the shutters that led from the bay out into the farmland. As they slowly rolled back up into the roof, a bright light spilled into the milking room.

"Why is it so bright?" Vynce asked.

"They use an artificial sun in the middle of each floor. It allows the grass to grow and gives the livestock the simulation of being in their normal environment. When night comes, they just dim them. They use the same technology in the main area of the ship. They have a simulated day and night cycle too," Al said.

Ava laughed and said, "The passengers are treated just like the cattle. That's too funny."

As they stepped out into what felt like the harsh light of day, they realised how gargantuan the ship truly was. It looked just like a normal sprawling grazing field. There were trees for shade, rocks in seemingly natural formation, and even a stream that flowed just like a stream would. There was a gentle sloped incline in the far left corner of the massive room which led to the next level. Unlike the level they were currently on, there was no light on the second floor. The gentle grassy slope seemed to lead into dark nothingness.

Draco was the first to begin the march across the farmland. He strode into the open field and marvelled at how real it all felt. A simulated wind generator blew the grass around his feet as though he were on the surface of New Earth. He wondered at how ridiculous they would look to an outsider. They were a troop of heavily armed and armoured grunts crossing an idyllic piece of farmland. But the farmlands were empty.

There were no animals in the whole expanse.

"Al, do a search for life forms. Something feels wrong," Draco said.

"Yeah, where the hell are all the cows?" Ava said.

"I don't care, as long as they're not here," Vynce added.

After a moment's pause Alphonse said "The only life forms I can detect are on the upper floors, where it's dark."

"I would suggest that you all exercise caution, folks. There's no telling what's going on above us," Draco said.

They continued on across the grassy expanse until they reached the small stream. There was no bridge in sight, but further along the stream there was a shallow area that the cows used to cross.

Their suits were completely airtight, so crossing the clear shallow stream was no more than an inconvenience. Draco waded first into the chest-deep water. He held his pistol above his head and crossed carefully to the other side. The rest of the crew followed, except for Alphonse.

"What's the problem buddy?" Vynce asked.

"I don't need to breathe, so a sealed chassis is not usually a concern of mine, but water damage is another matter... But fear not, I have my own way around this," Alphonse said as he backed up a half dozen steps and ran towards the bank of the stream.

He jumped into the air and a beautiful transformation happened. His shoulder blades expanded outward. They turned into boosters, which fired to life the moment his feet left the ground. He engaged his thrusters on the underside of his feet, which lifted him across the stream while the others still waded across.

"You're such a show off," Ava said as Alphonse landed heavily on the far side of the stream. Alphonse began to speak but was cut off as the artificial sun above dimmed and then finally faded to black.

'I'm sorry to do this to you Captain Goldwing, but this is what happens if you don't comply with my requests. I do hope you survive this,' said the anonymous voice that had plagued their traverse of the ship.

"We're no help to you if we're dead!" Draco shouted.

'Please know that I sincerely hope you live through this,' the voice said.

"Oh no. He has deactivated the containment gates on the other five levels of farmland. The life forms are currently migrating downward to our location," Alphonse said.

"Are they cows, or those other things?" Vynce asked. He hoped that it was the monstrosities from earlier, not cows. He could deal with pieced-together body parts with extra appendages, but he couldn't deal with a herd of stampeding cows.

"Impossible to say without confirming visual sighting. I have switched to night vision and will keep you informed of any visual contacts. I would highly suggest that you refrain from using your personal light apparatus. They would be able to pinpoint us in a heartbeat."

"Let's hope we don't have any visual contacts, then. Double time it everyone," Draco said.

The suits the crew used had an augmented low-light visibility tuning that automatically allowed them to see in low light, but it was nowhere near as effective as Al's night vision. They could only see a couple of metres in front of them.

The crew pulled themselves from the stream and broke into a dead sprint towards the exit. As they ran through the darkness, it was impossible not to feel as though they were going to be swallowed by it.

They could hear large creatures moving around in the floors above them. They heard natural bovine sounds, but they also heard something unnatural mixed in. Something that just didn't belong. Something alien. Alphonse looked over at the grassy incline leading up to the second floor and he saw a herd of what looked like cows moving down at speed. They did not move like cows.

Alphonse had begun to form his own hypothesis on what was happening, but would have to gather more data in order to be sure. If he was right, they were in a lot of trouble. If his logic circuits were right, it would have been better if they had left the huge ship to burn in the orbit of the melting planet. However, he had long ago learnt to resist the cold, logistical rulings that came out of his core consciousness. He took pride that he was more than a robot. He was not an android.

The creatures were not cows, but at the same time they were. Each creature was different in minute, but different ways. Some looked very much like normal cows, but others looked more like the carnivorous racklons from Torusk. They were all teeth, claws and hooves with squat little bodies. Cows didn't naturally have claws, and they certainly didn't have the jagged teeth of a carnivore.

"I don't want to alarm anyone, but I would suggest haste," Alphonse said and broke into an even faster stride.

The rest of the crew followed. Draco gaped as Jaxon strode ahead of everyone. He was running faster than any human was supposed to run. He ran directly towards the exit bay from the farmland.

"I'll have the door open for you by the time you get here," he said through comms.

"How the hell can do you run so fast?" Ava asked.

"I'm part cheetah," he responded as the disappeared into the darkness.

As the herd grew closer Al realised that they were not so much a herd as there were a pack. They were on the hunt, and their quarry was somewhere scrambling in the darkness. From their movements, Alphonse judged that their night vision just as good as a normal cow. They could only see well under the light of the moon, and in complete darkness they relied on their other undeveloped senses. But whatever change had occurred in them could have bolstered their other senses. Without further data, there was just no way to know for sure.

Whatever happened to them, they were still slow, lumbering creatures that were not suited to pursuit.

However, an unexpected thing happened as Alphonse looked back toward the lumbering mass of creatures. A number of smaller, more lithe creatures had broken away from the pack and were running straight for them. These creatures could see them. These new creatures looked decidedly canine, except that they all had something lumpy and pulpy, writhing on their backs.

Jaxon reached the exit doorway, and he started to open the door manually. He gripped the door with both hands and pulled. It opened slowly, until there was an opening small enough to let Raze through.

"There is something new coming," Alphonse said.

"Please tell me it's good news," Draco said.

"I'm sorry Captain, but I don't want to lie to you."

Draco cursed.

As they grew closer to the door that led out of the farmland, the canid creatures grew even closer still. Even though they couldn't see them, the rest of the crew could hear footsteps of the canid creatures pounding the grass, running after them. Their ragged intakes of breath made Vynce feel like he was being chased by the hounds of hell.

'As long as they're not mooing, I'll be fine,' he thought to himself.

Jaxon stood poised behind the open door with his rifle held against his shoulder, ready to fire. Jaxon's suit of armour was at least four decades more advanced than the armour that Draco and his crew wore. He could see the canid creatures as clear as day. He remembered them, but that time seemed like a lifetime ago. He was happy that this time around he was actually equipped to take them out.

He squeezed the trigger once and a single high calibre bullet fired from the barrel of his rifle. The bullet passed between Draco's calves on the way to its target. A split second later, the head of one of the canid creatures exploded outward. He quickly lined up two more shots and reduced two more of the creatures to broken, bloody messes.

There were more of them coming, but he couldn't kill them all before Draco and the others reached the open door.

Alphonse squeezed through the door, followed by Ava while Vynce and Draco covered their backs. In the darkness Vynce and Draco couldn't completely make out what they were firing at, but they knew that they had to keep shooting. Once Vynce was through the doorway, Draco followed.

A crushing weight clamped down on Draco's left shin. He looked down and saw the twisted face of the creature that latched onto his leg. He fired a single bullet at the creature, which whimpered and released his leg as the round pierced its haunch.

Draco pulled himself through the door. He and Jaxon worked together to push the door closed again, but Draco wasn't helping at all. The door was eight inches thick. It was clearly made to withstand a charge from a raging bull. Jaxon wasn't only faster, but also stronger than Draco. The door screeched as the metal ground against metal. The door closed slowly, but not before two of the dog-like creatures leapt through the opening and into the small room with them.

Draco promptly put a bullet in the skull of one of the creatures, but the other immediately leapt into Vynce's chest, pushing him to the ground. As the door slid completely closed, the lights came back on and they saw the horrific creature straddling him.

It had once been a dog, but something horrifying happened to it. A tumorous growth had sprouted from its back. The growth was hairless and looked like a bad burn. It pulsated. Ava kicked the repulsive canid creature from Vynce's chest. It flew across the room and smashed into the wall with a wet thud. Blood sprayed out from the growth as it hit the wall.

The growth on the creature's back had split open. Long prehensile tendrils writhed out of the wound as the creature got to its feet. It snarled at them, but didn't advance. Whatever intelligence it had possessed as a dog had been either preserved or heightened. It didn't attack because it knew that it was outnumbered. The prehensile tendrils whipped around in the air as it growled.

Suddenly it grew silent, and the tendrils stopped moving back and forth. It tilted its head in the direction of the door just as a booming sound erupted from the door. The bovine pack had reached the door, and they wanted to get inside.

Alphonse raised his hand at the creature. His palm opened up to reveal a small pulse cannon. He fired a super heated blast of energy at the creature, which exploded into a mass of twisted flesh. The tendrils kept writhing about the corpse on the floor.

"That thing was communicating with the others on the outside of the door. It was feeding them information about us," Alphonse said.

"I trust you, Al," Draco said, "It just puts me off guard when you shoot first and ask questions later."

The pounding on the door continued. Even though the creature had been destroyed, the bovine pack behind the door knew where they were, and they wanted to break through to them more than ever.

Draco looked at the corpse of the canid creature and recoiled in horror at what he saw. The tendrils that had burst from the dog's back were still moving. Two of them had latched onto the leg of a water fountain and the tumorous growth had begun pulling itself from the wound. It pulled itself from the lining of the dog's carcass with a wet ripping sound. Part of the dog's skeleton went with the little blobbish creature. The dog's ribs and backbone had been amalgamated into the creature's structure.

The little brownish red blob floundered on the ground for a moment before Alphonse fired another super-heated blast at it. The creature disintegrated and immediately the pounding on the door ceased.

"It was already dying. It hadn't been given enough time to grow," Alphonse mused.

"Grow? What the fuck do you mean, grow?" Ava asked.

"I think it's time I told you all what I think is happening here," Alphonse said.

EIGHT

Veck laid back on the floor of the containment cell, eagerly awaiting the arrival of his missing limbs. To his left, the cover of a vent fell to the ground, followed by two disembodied arms. They crawled along using their fingers. They had come such a long way, and now it was time for them to be returned to their proper place. They passed between the energy bars at the front of the cell and crawled towards Veck.

In tandem, they positioned their inputs with the sockets at Veck's shoulders. The metallic ends of the arms and the sockets erupted into a flurry of movement. Small parts twisted and moved as they lined up with their partnered couplings. Hundreds of tiny moving pins and connections met as the arms linked back up with Veck's body.

He couldn't feel the connections happening in the traditional sense of pain and sensation. However, there was the comforting familiarity of the wireless connections becoming hardwired once again as the orders that were sent to them became instantaneous instead of taking milliseconds to send and receive. He checked his primary systems. They were all operating at optimum capacity.

Veck pressed his hands against the cold metal floor beneath him and pushed upwards, rising from the ground in a way that mocked the law of gravity and the normal skeletal structure of the human body. Veck cracked his neck back and forth, then walked through the energy bars and out of his cell.

He strode confidently up the stairs to the armoury. The sealed door slid open, just as he knew it would. He had placed a prime program masked as a subroutine into Evie's programming matrix. She identified him as Captain Goldwing. She could not tell the difference between the two. He could override almost any command given by any other member of the crew if he needed to.

When he stepped into the armoury, he was very careful to move as quietly as possible. He wanted to get the jump on whoever he ran into, not the other way around. He left the armoury through the infirmary door and visibly retched as his natural gag reflex was triggered by ancient, horrible memories. Hospitals always triggered it, even though the events had happened twenty-five years prior.

Veck went down on one knee and tried to choke back the bile that wanted to escape from his body. He grabbed one corner of the operating table to steady himself as he fell down into the memory.

At the age of 12, Veck Simms was donated to the Alliance military. He had no parents, no future, and had a genetic makeup that was flagged as a makeup of potential. He was given to the military, who kept him in a facility on Torusk until he was eighteen years old. He didn't remember exactly what happened there, except that it's where he received his first supplementary biomechanical implant. Everything else was a dark mess of tubes, blood and pain. He remembered vividly when they placed the first tube down his throat. When they did it, he was still awake, screaming for them to stop. Even twenty five years later he could still feel the wet, slimy plastic tube snaking down his throat into his body. He had screamed, but no sound could come out.

He cleared the memory from his mind and attempted to regain his composure. He recoiled when he realised that he had come into contact with the operating table. The urge to be sick rose in his throat again, but he pushed it back down once more.

He closed his eyes and strode out of the infirmary. As he crossed the doorway, he collided with another person. Instinctively he reached out and grabbed his assailant. He opened his eyes to see a wide eyed girl, no older than eighteen. She wore a green jumpsuit and had mousy brown hair. His hand was closed around her throat, and she struggled to breathe. After a few moments, her eyes began to roll back in her head and her eyelids began to twitch.

He knew there was something wrong with him. He didn't know whether it was a fault in his neurotech implant, or whether something in his mind had finally snapped. For a moment he didn't want to release his grip on the girl's throat. He wanted to crush her windpipe and leave her gasping for breath on the ground. He wanted to rip her apart and hear her screaming as he pulled off her arms and unwound her intestines like a length of rope.

He breathed deeply, centred himself and put the bloodlust out of his mind. He would have more chance keeping the situation under his control if he kept the girl alive. He could use her as a bargaining chip.

"I don't know what they've told you about me honey, but I guarantee you, the reality is much, much worse," he said as he eased his grip on her throat.

Rhken gasped for air. Veck Simms had her by the throat, and she knew that he wanted to kill her. There was an untamed rage in his eyes that reminded her of a wild animal. A predator. She was the prey, and she knew she needed to stay smart to survive.

"If you scream, I'll kill you without a second thought. The only reason you're still alive is because you could prove useful to me. Do you want to be useful to me?"

She nodded quickly.

"Good girl," he cooed and released his hand from her throat.

She dropped to the ground and let her lungs fill with cool air. Her throat was on fire. She asked herself what her father would do, and immediately thought that he'd try something absolutely foolish and heroic and would probably get himself killed.

"What do you want?" she asked.

"I want what every single person on this ship wants. You want your freedom. I want my freedom. Your good captain wants to take me back to the Alliance to face my death. I'm just not ready for that. I've got so much more to do. I'm sure you can understand that, can't you honey? I'm sure there are lots of things you want to do before you die, aren't there?"

A hundred images flashed through Rhken's mind. She had never seen the Skyline falls on Orpheon, and someday she wanted to make a life for herself. Maybe once things were done with Draco, she'd open up her own machine shop back on New Earth, settle down and have a couple of children. Her face grew red and warm as she thought to herself that she might die without ever kissing a boy. She might never feel the warmth of a lover's touch or the sting of heartbreak when things fell apart. She began to weep for the experiences that she may never have.

"If you do what I tell you to do, you're going to live a long, happy life. But I guarantee you, if you do anything stupid, I will remove that pretty little head from your shoulders. Alright?"

"Alright," she said in between sobs.

"There's a good girl. Now, I want you to take me to the bridge."

She nodded feebly as he pulled her to her feet.

"March," he said and smacked her behind.

It was the first time anyone except her mother and father had touched her below the waist. She was too stunned to react. She didn't dare protest. She wanted to go home. She wanted to be back on New Earth, snuggled up with her Mum on the couch. But she knew that the couch wasn't there anymore, and neither was her Mum. She was all alone.

In the cockpit, Arak felt utterly useless while Draco and the rest of the crew were on the Metropolis Seven. All he had to do was set a few parameters and sit back in his seat and wait for orders. With the push / pull system he didn't even need to worry about watching hull pressure, velocity or trajectory. He felt utterly superfluous.

He was so bored that he had started to watch what was going on down in the engine bay. Reban and Rhken had been working harder than he'd ever seen them to get all of the kinetic energy tethers ready. They were a great team. But as the action started to die down in the engine bay Reban sat back on her recliner and started to read a book that Arak had suggested to her. He knew that books were a silly throwback to the years gone by, but he insisted that they had a certain charm. His enthusiasm was catching, and Reban had relented and said that she would give it a try. She had never thought of reading for pleasure. To her, reading was something that old people did because they didn't know how to use the interlink properly. She insisted there was no pleasure to be found in the written word, and even less in a musty old tome from decades before she was born.

The story was a beautiful study of inter-species love. It told of a woman named Lyriana who fell in love with a Child of iNet who identified himself by the name Claren. The story of their love, and the persecution they both suffered from their individual peoples became legend. The power of their love transcended the physical limitations of their incompatible species. Sexuality and species-identity meant nothing to them.

At first, Reban had laughed and told Arak that she thought it was silly. She thought that any kind of love between partners that was destined to fail was a waste of time, and she rejected the very idea of the novel out of hand. Still, Arak pressed on, and he was happy to see that she was engrossed in the book just as he knew she would be.

He had to admit to himself that he was not simply watching Reban for her interest in the book he had recommended. He had his own interests in her, and they were not strictly platonic. He knew that he was far too old for her, and her father would murder him if he so much as suggested that he had any kind of romantic feelings for her. He saw a sensitive, thoughtful girl who lived in the shadow of her brilliant sister. If they still lived on New Earth, their roles would be reversed. Reban's beauty would outshine Rhken's brilliance.

When it was obvious that she had settled in for a long reading session, Arak pointed his interest elsewhere. He viewed the camera facing backwards from the back of the ship and saw the kinetic energy tethers attached to the giant ship. Behind the ship was the burning planet and its twin suns that had threatened to destroy them all.

He opened another camera view and watched Veck in the containment cell. He saw Veck standing up in the middle of the room, eyes closed, apparently deep in thought. Arak had no knowledge of Draco's defence program that would fry Veck's brain, so he thought nothing of it. He thought that Veck was just stretching, and went back to watching the engine bay.

It was when Rhken got up from her diagnostic station and walked towards the cargo bay that Arak realised that Veck had suddenly sprouted arms. He knew something was wrong, and had immediately put the bridge in emergency lockdown. Heavy reinforced doors slammed down on either side of the entrance to the bridge. Not even Evie could override this command, and it would take hours for a sunstorm welder to cut through the thick steel. The bridge could only be opened from the inside.

Arak immediately attempted to open a comm channel to Draco as Veck marched Rhken towards the bridge, but the channel that he had used before couldn't be found.

NINE

Draco and the rest of the crew left the corpses of the two canid creatures and continued down the corridor that led into a crew lounge. There was no blood in the room, and all the vent covers were intact. It was a rare moment of respite. Draco sat down first with an audible sigh. The rest of the crew followed his example. Alphonse remained standing in the middle of the room and Jaxon leaned against the far wall, behind him.

"I think that there is an alien presence on this ship," Alphonse said.

"I'm sure we can all agree on that," Draco said.

"From what we have seen, the organism can somehow harness living flesh to create its own form. We have seen the smaller creatures made from different parts of the human crew. I personally saw individual creatures made from a hand, a head and a leg of a human being," Al said.

"I am damn sure I saw a mutant vagina coming towards us back in the engine bay. It was all flaps of skin and tentacles. Fucking gross," Ava said.

"Must have been like looking in the mirror," Vynce muttered.

Ava promptly smacked him around the back of the head with the butt of her rifle. He had been up close and personal with hers, and from what she remembered, he certainly hadn't recoiled in horror.

"Are you two done?" Draco asked.

"We certainly are," Ava replied and shot Vynce a look that could have melted steel.

"Getting back to the issue at hand, I noticed that no two creatures were exactly the same. They shared similar characteristics, but they were not the same. This means that the process can differ on any number of factors. Perhaps it depends on the genetic makeup of victim, the rate of growth and the place of infection," Alphonse said.

"Infection? What the hell do you mean infection?" Vynce asked.

"It is undeniably apparent from my observations that something has infected the crew of this ship and has turned them into the creatures that we have encountered so far."

Suddenly, Jaxon stepped forward. He took off his helmet with a short, sharp hiss. A jet of concentrated oxygen escaped the vent as he disengaged the locks. He pulled his helmet off and put it down on the table in between the two couches.

"They're not infected, at least not in the viral sense of the word," he said, "They're hosts."

Alphonse motioned for Jaxon to continue.

"As I'm sure you're all aware by now, I don't belong here. My very existence here is an abomination of everything that my career stands for. If you were to look in the Alliance military records right now, I would not exist, because I was just a street kid until I boarded Metropolis Seven. I am still stuck on this ship."

"So are we buddy, but you don't look like a kid," Vynce quipped.

Jaxon smiled, smoothed his hair back from his eyes. He looked at Vynce and addressed him directly.

"Vynce, I want you to imagine for a moment that time is a straight line, but it has hundreds of strands like woven fabric. Kind of like a super highway on New Earth. There are hundreds of vehicles travelling in the same direction, but in different lanes. They're all branching off to different destinations. You can go forward, but what if you need to turn around and go backwards to a place you've already been? Imagine trying to get back to your original destination in the same place in the same traffic that you were in the first time you drove down the highway. It'd be impossible, right?"

"Yeah," Vynce said.

"What if, when you got back into the original flow, you pulled out in front of someone and got into an accident?"

Vynce took a moment to consider this, then spoke, "You'd have a hell of an insurance claim on your hands."

Jaxon smiled and said, "You'd mess it all up. You might kill a few people, you might inconvenience a couple of others, and you'd make a whole lot of them late for whatever important things they had to do. But what effect does that have on everything? Things don't happen as they should, and then things start to get complicated for everyone involved."

"Do you want to get to the point?" Draco asked.

"My point is that I shouldn't be here, because I am already here. I boarded Metropolis Seven as a seventeen year old kid from the fringe worlds who had dreams of getting out and exploring the galaxy. I had just arrived on New Earth, and after starving on the streets for six months I took the only job I could find. Part of the maintenance crew on this ship. I was told that if I served my term on the ship, I could line up for any job I wanted when I got back. The problem is that I am obviously not seventeen years old, nor do I have the stars in my eyes. I've seen far too much of them."

"That's completely impossible," Raze said.

"Is it?" Jaxon asked.

"Time travel is completely impossible. It's been proven by the leading scientists on New Earth. It's just not possible."

"They're the ones who discovered it. They only feed bullshit to the masses, Raze. You're much too smart to believe all of that shit, man. I know. You and I have spent plenty of late nights talking about it. This isn't the first time I've met you, but it looks like this is the first time any of you have met me. This is the difficulty of living in multiple time periods. I lose track of things, but I assure you, I am not lying to you."

Ava took of her helmet and looked Jaxon square in the eye.

"Are you seriously expecting us to believe this shit?" she asked.

"Oh… Ava," he said and smiled.

"What?" she spat.

"You… look different than I remembered."

"What the fuck are you talking about?"

Jaxon waved his hand in front of himself and said, "There are two things you need to know right now. The first is that my seventeen year old self is on this ship, and I don't know what will happen if we come into contact with one another and interact."

"Can you give us the worst case scenario?" Draco asked.

"The fabric of space and time could collapse in on itself."

"Is that likely?"

"It has never happened before, but I plan on safeguarding us as best as I can. When we run into my seventeen year old self you must not make him aware of my true identity. As far as you're all concerned, my name is Reinhardt."

"I'm not really interested in having reality imploding around us, so that won't be a problem," Draco said, "What's the second thing?"

"We're all in great danger. Every moment we're on this ship it is getting worse. The force in the bowels of the ship grows with every new host it captures. I would highly suggest that everyone keeps their armour integrity at one hundred percent. We are safe in this room, but there is no telling what we might encounter as we delve deeper into the ship," Jaxon said.

"If you've already been here, back when you were seventeen, you can tell us what happens, right? That would save a whole lot of hassle," Ava said.

"I can't. If I tell you what I experienced as a young man, it might alter the outcome and distort the timeline."

Ava grabbed onto the chest panel of Jaxon's armour and pulled his face to hers.

"Do any of us die?" Ava demanded.

"You know I can't answer that question," he replied.

"Damn it, you can't just keep that kind of information from us! If one of us died when you were here last time, then maybe we could fix it."

Jaxon fixed his gaze on Draco, closed his eyes and sighed.

"I can't answer that question, Ava. I'm sorry."

"Yeah, you will be fucking sorry if you get one of us killed. I'll make real sure of that."

"If I cause the death of any of you, you have my full permission to return the favour," Jaxon said.

Without warning, Ava kicked Jaxon's leg out from under him, withdrew her knife from its sheath, and launched herself on top of him. When she landed, Ava held the point of her knife to his throat.

"Well how about I just remove you from the equation all together, hm?" she said.

Draco thought about intervening, but he knew that Ava would never take a life that didn't deserve to be taken, and never without his orders. Sometimes she just liked to put the wind up someone, especially when the hairs on the back of her own neck had started to stand on end.

"The information I carry with me is vital for the continued survival of the human race, and the continued existence of New Earth" Jaxon said.

Ava stared into his eyes, unflinching. There was a fury behind her eyes that Jaxon had seen many times before. He wanted to smile, but he knew that would be a mistake.

"New Earth is a shithole anyway," she said and got back to her feet. She sheathed her knife, and picked her helmet up. She smoothed her hair back and slipped the helmet back over her face.

She turned back to Jaxon and said, "If I have to sacrifice every life on New Earth for my crew to live, I'll do it. So you just fucking watch yourself."

Jaxon got back to his feet, and knew that she truly would sacrifice every life on New Earth for her crew. He thought to himself how he had stood by as Ava threw herself into situations and conflict before, completely fuelled by anger and emotion, but had never been on the receiving end of her fury himself. She was beautiful when he had met her before, even with the scars. But at that moment, she was beautiful in a way he had never seen before.

"These things that used to be the crew of the Metropolis Seven, well we had a name for them. We called them fleshlings," he said as he secured his helmet back in place. He changed the opacity of his visor so his face was completely obscured.

"Fleshlings, huh? Well that's fucking disgusting," Ava said.

"It was a name that stuck. It made it easier for us to deal with the fact that the people who we once knew were trying to kill us and infect us. If we called them infected, or hosts, then it sounded like we could save them. But we can't, because the people they used to be were already dead," Jaxon said.

Ava nodded, unsure of how to respond.

"We should keep moving," Jaxon said.

"Al, can you tell which way would be quickest for us to get to the centre of the ship?" Draco asked.

"From where we currently are, there are two ways. One passes through the water processing plant, and the other passes through a number of different service tunnels, but takes us much deeper into the belly of the ship. From Jaxon's advice, this may be a bad idea," Al said.

Jaxon nodded.

"I believe we only have one choice," Al continued, "We pass through the water processing plant, and then we enter into the city limits. From there, we can make our way through the Residential District, and into the Metropolitan District at the centre of the city. At the centre is where the Metro Tower is located, and that's where we need to go. We should be able to gain complete control of the ship from there."

"Sounds like a plan," Draco said, but Al raised a finger to indicate that he had more to add.

"But there's only one slight problem that I can foresee. The water processing plant is a likely place for there to be a concentration of these creatures. If they are using humans for their genetic template, then they are more than ninety percent water. They will need a source of water to survive, and it's likely that they would try to defend it once it has been captured."

"Either way, we're at no more risk than we are right now. Eventually, they're going to figure out we're in here, and they'll figure out a way to get in. If we're moving, and we stick together, we should be fine," Vynce said.

"We know we'll be in for a fight if we head through the service tunnels. But we don't know what's happening at the plant. We'll go through the plant, and like Vynce said, we'll stick together. We'll watch each other's' back, and we'll get through this alive," Draco said.

Draco got to his feet. The crew followed down the tight corridor in single file. It was eerily quiet, except for their footfalls that echoed around them. Still without a rifle, Draco felt vulnerable. He was always prepared for any situation, except for when a giant monstrosity tries to chase you down a ventilation shaft. That's one contingency that he hadn't planned for. But he had faith in his crew. They had made it through tough situations before, and they'd make it through this one. Like always, if a call had to be made, Draco would be the one to make it.

For a moment, Draco thought back to Torusk, where they had picked up Arak Nara. He thought back to the call he had to make there. The Icarus' old pilot, Ean Breck, had been captured by the same mercenary outfit that Arak Nara had belonged to. Both groups had been competing against one another, as well as the local indigenous population, to secure an ancient artefact of immense power. Draco had made the call that resulted in Ean's death, but had also ensured that the artefact did not fall into the hands of the mercenaries who would have undoubtedly sold it on the black market and caused the death of millions.

Draco missed Ean, but he would rather have the death of one man, even a treasured friend, on his conscience than millions of innocents.

But any death, no matter the gravity or perceived value of the person, was never considered lightly.

They came to a fork in the corridor without any signage or direction.

"Al, can you see which way it is to the water processing plant?" Draco asked without breaking his stride.

"They should both lead there, going from the schematics I have downloaded," Al said back.

Draco went right, around the curved hallway, past numerous empty, darkened rooms. The lights from the corridor were just enough to light up the threshold of the rooms, but the darkness inside held evidence of the horrors of the past. Dark red, pulpy bits of flesh lined the walls and floor. The room they had been in previously wasn't secure at all. It's just that no one had been stupid enough to flee towards the farmlands. They must have all headed towards the centre of the ship.

A sound came from below and seemed to reverberate through the walls around them. It was a deep, bellowing sound, like an organic tuba. The walls began to shake. They kept pace while rounding the corridor.

Draco swore as he stopped in his tracks. The corridor in front of them had been completely destroyed. Beyond the destroyed corridor, the ground was a black abyss, seemingly infinite and impenetrable by the meagre light source on the corridor roof.

The ground shook and the terrible sound of rending metal filled the air around them.

"What the fuck!?" Vynce shouted.

At first Vynce couldn't make sense of what had happened. A giant mass of twisted flesh and bone had torn its way through the side of the corridor behind them. It was as thick and wide as the corridor itself and it completely blocked their retreat. The rest of the crew whipped around to see the giant mass writhing and pulsating like an enormous skinless muscle. It grew closer to them with every twist and flex.

"Lights on, we're going dark," Draco said. The light attached to the front of his armour turned on as he turned back to the black void. The beam of light cut through the darkness ahead of him. He could see the corridor continue on in the distance, but there was no way they could make the jump. Draco stopped on the precipice of the darkness and looked down. There was nothing but twisted metal below, ending in a pool of water. There was no way to tell how deep it was, but they were running short on options. The heads-up display in his suit estimated that the water depth was between five and seven metres deep. Deep enough.

"We've got to jump," Draco said, and without hesitation, leapt into the darkness below. He was in the air for a few seconds, then plunged deep into the cold water below. It was so cold that he could feel the chill through his armour. Particles of muck floated through murky the water. Visibility was almost zero. It looked muddy, but he had a feeling that the particles drifting through the water were something much worse.

Other shafts of light pierced the water as Draco swam towards the surface. The others had followed his lead, and Draco could only hope that he hadn't led them into a trap.

Draco broke the surface, and was quickly joined by Jaxon and Ava.

"Over here!" Al said. He stood on a pile of debris at the edge of the water, his hand outstretched.

Draco took his hand, and was lifted out of the water. Al took Ava's hand while Draco helped Jaxon out of the water. Raze broke the surface soon after, but Vynce was nowhere to be seen.

"Something's got Vynce. He's stuck down there at the bottom. I tried to get to him, but I couldn't. It was too dark, and too quick," Raze said.

Vynce's voice came over the commlink, and he sounded hurt, "Fucker grabbed me by the leg and it's dragging me somewhere. I can't tell where I am. You guys go on, I'll find a way out of this."

"You just hold on Vynce," Ava said, unsheathed her combat knife, and leapt into the water.

Jaxon jumped in after her.

Draco motioned with his hand to stop Raze from jumping in after them, and said "We need to check the situation up here. Ava, Jaxon, Vynce, you be careful. Rendezvous with us when you can. We'll continue on as planned, towards the water processing plant."

"I've just activated my tracking signal, guys, so you should see my location on your HUD. This fucker's moving fast," Vynce said.

"You're not allowed to die unless I give you permission, you ginger fuck!" Ava said.

"Yes ma'am," Vynce replied.

Under the murky water, Ava and Jaxon swam towards the red blip on their HUD. It was moving quicker than they could swim. Ava's armour started to drag her towards the bottom of the passage, but Jaxon had caught up with her effortlessly.

Jaxon swam over the top of Ava, and wrapped his hands around her waist. Ava thought that the same thing that had gotten Vynce had gotten her, and struggled. Jaxon resisted and said, "Relax, we'll go much faster this way."

Ava relaxed, and let her hands rest by her sides. They moved through the water quickly.

"So enlighten me, how are you swimming without using your

arms or legs?" Ava asked.

"Multi-environment survival suit. Heat resistant, cold resistant, in-built gravlift boots, underwater propulsion system. Everything I need to survive is in this suit," Jaxon said.

"Sounds awesome. How do I get one of those for myself?"

"Once we get back to New Earth, I'll see if I can pull some strings."

"Sweet."

The water around them became murkier as they continued along. They entered into a small opening at the base of the waterway. It was a corridor which had been completely submerged. Sheets of pulsating flesh lined the walls, with polyps growing from the floor. The walls closed in on them as they continued on.

Back on dry land, Draco, Raze and Alphonse tried to get their bearings. The schematics that Al had downloaded were useless since something decided to do some remodelling. The chamber was huge, about the size of a football field. Behind them, on the other side of the pool of water, was a mass of flesh, growing like a tumour on the side of the ship. It was the size of a house. The outside of the growth moved rhythmically, as though it was breathing. The growth had tendrils coming out from its sides, which affixed it to the wall.

"Uh, Captain, you're going to want to see this," Raze said and tapped Draco on the shoulder.

Draco spun and saw similar growths on the walls around them, and the roof above.

"Do you see how they move? Oh my, this is absolutely fascinating…" Al said.

"They're moving?" Raze asked.

"Oh yes, only a minute amount of movement, but yes, they are definitely moving. Those arms must be like the arms of a starfish. They must use them to stick themselves to surfaces, but also use them as locomotion if they need to move."

"I think it would be best we get out of here as soon as we can," Draco said.

"I must agree with you there, Captain," Al said.

Draco drew his pistol from its thigh holster and held it out in front of him. He felt exposed without his rifle, but it was still lying at the bottom of a maintenance shaft near their shuttle. He would have to make do.

A sudden noise from above drew their attention. One of the growths had detached itself from the roof with a loud sucking sound. With equally wet, disgusting sounds, it pulled three of its tendrils free of the ceiling and let them fall. Now, it dangled in front of them by two tendrils. The free tendrils reached out towards them. Draco looked around the cavernous chamber and saw that the rest of these growths were also sliding down the walls or detaching themselves from the ceiling. The huge growths were all converging on them.

Draco fired a single shot at the growth hanging in front of them. It recoiled with a deep audible grumble, and gave up its hold to the ceiling. It fell to the ground in front of them with enough force to make Draco lose his balance. When it settled, it started to pulsate. The sides of the thing expanded and retracted faster and faster. Small red lines started to appear over the outside of the growth, as though it was going to burst open.

Draco turned to Al and Raze and yelled, "Run!"

TEN

Draco ran around the giant pulsating growth and hurdled one of the tendrils on the ground. If he was right then the tendrils weren't actually reaching for them at all. They were just reaching for a place on the ground they could anchor to. As Draco jumped over the tendril, it gave no indication of rising to attempt to trap him, and his heart grew icy cold as he knew what was about to come. He had counted at least three other growths around the chamber, crawling their way down to the ground to meet them. If they were doing the same as the house-sized chunk of flesh beside him, then they were in serious trouble.

The red lines had started to crack open as the thing pulsated. There was movement in the blackness inside. Frenzied movement.

"Raze, do you have any grenades?" Draco asked.

"Grenades? Inside the ship?" he asked with a raised eyebrow.

"Throw me one! Now!"

Raze pulled one of the grenades from his belt and threw it to Draco. Neither of them broke pace while it sailed through the air. Draco caught it on the full, and stopped for a moment to line up his throw. He pulled the pin, and threw the grenade.

Time seemed to slow as the grenade arced through the air, wheeling end over end as the cracks on the growth opened and closed. In a stroke of luck, the cracks opened a split-second before the grenade reached the growth. The grenade flew through the crack, which closed after the grenade came to rest inside.

The explosion was muffled, but the effects were not. The entire outside of the growth exploded outward in chunks. The growth was reduced to pulpy mush, and Draco's suspicions were confirmed.

In the midst of the giant carcass he saw remains of bodies. A hand here, a foot there, an occasional head.

"They're birthing pods," Draco said as he started running once again, "They must have loaded the bodies of the crew into these things and re-purposed them. Like eggs, but capable of infecting multiple hosts at once."

"Disgusting," Raze said.

"Fascinating," Al said.

Two loud impacts sounded off in the distance. Two more pods had fallen to the ground, and they were already starting to crack open to birth their twisted children.

"Al, do we have an exit strategy here?" Draco asked.

"One moment, Captain. I'm searching for potential routes, but I'm not exactly sure which floor we're on," Al responded.

Until they had a better plan, they could only continue forward. Draco led them through the chunky remains of the destroyed birthing pod. Draco passed a ball of what looked like hair and teeth growing out of the side of a severed torso.

"Captain, I believe I've found a route of escape from here. When we reach the end of this chasm, we can find an entrance to the mag-rail network. We should be able to board one of the mag-rail carriages and catch it directly to the Metropolitan District," Al said.

"How do we know that our friend over the loudspeaker will actually let us use them?" Draco asked.

"We don't. But as long as we have access to the network we should be able to follow the mag-rail network itself to any stop it's linked to. It may take some time, but I believe it is the most direct approach we can take."

"Excellent. Well done, Al. Let's move! We've got a train to catch!"

Draco, Al and Raze broke into a sprint, dodging the pieces of flesh littering the floor around them. They saw more birthing pods attached to the walls and ceiling in front of them. There were thousands of bodies in this dark chasm undergoing a change that turned them into something less than human. Draco wondered to himself whether there were any people left on the ship to save. He asked himself whether it would have been a kindness to simply let the ship burn up in the orbit of Krakaterra.

He tried to push those thoughts out of his mind when Al cut in.

"I'm going to feed the location of the closest mag-rail station into everyone's HUDs. Even if we are split up, we will be able to regroup at the station." Al said.

"Good work, Al. Approximately how far?" Draco asked.

"Five hundred metres give or take. We will have to see what kind of access we can find."

They continued running in the dark.

Down in the murky water, Jaxon's hands held Ava's waist tightly. The thing that grabbed Vynce had taken him through a flooded access tunnel.

"Fuck, I lost sight of him!" Ava said.

"I can't see him, but I can see where he was taken," Jaxon said.

"What the hell do you mean? I can't even see a foot in front of me in this muck."

"I'm tracking the water displacement pattern. We're actually flowing in the same current that the thing created when it grabbed Vynce and pulled him away."

"What was it, anyway? Did you see what it was?"

"No, I just saw you swimming down into a situation you knew nothing about, and knew that if I didn't come with you that you might end up dead."

"But you know how all of this turns out. If I die, you already know it, isn't that right?"

"I need to explain something about time travel to you. It's not what you think. As far as we know, there are no natural fixed points of the space-time continuum, except for the beginning, and of course, the end. Everything in between is up for grabs, and can be changed. The agent travelling through the time stream has to make the call about what he or she chooses to intervene against."

"So even though you've lived this once, it might not turn out the same as it did last time?"

"Exactly correct. Or, through my actions, I could cause events to happen in the exact same fashion that they did during the last time I was on this ship. That's the funny thing about time travel. You never know whether you're the cause or the effect. All I know is that I don't want you to die, so I had to help you."

Ava smiled to herself, for a moment she was unable to think of something to say back. Jaxon saved her the trouble.

"This isn't the first jam I've helped you out of, Ava. Or vice versa. This may be the first time in your chronological sequence, but not mine. We've been through a lot together, and I couldn't let you go down into that darkness by yourself."

"Thank you," she said. She wondered just what kind of a history she had with Jaxon. Or would it be a future? Maybe both. Her future, and his past. After they got off the Metropolis Seven, rescued a buttload of people and saved the day, she made a mental note that she owed this mysterious traveller a drink or two.

Draco, Raze and Al reached a wall of debris and could not go any farther. The crumpled metallic remains were unrecognisable. Sharp pieces of steel sheeting jutted out of the collapsed piece of ship, but it looked as though it could be traversed.

"Can we go over this?" Draco asked.

"I believe we should be able to find an entrance to the mag-rail network if we can get through this rubble."

Draco looked backwards to see the house-sized birthing pods still slowly creeping towards them. There was one to their left that already had one of its tendrils running up the pile of debris beside them. If it decided to make any sudden movements, the pile of debris could collapse and their escape route could have been cut off.

Draco started climbing, trying to take care to avoid any sharp pieces of steel. Their armour was strong, but Draco knew that accidents could happen. All it would take is a small puncture to put any of his crew into serious danger. They didn't know exactly how these things took their hosts, so they couldn't make any assumptions about what was safe and was wasn't. They had to be as careful as possible. Al used his boosters to skip large sections of debris and scouted out for the best route for Draco and Raze to take.

"To your right, Captain. There is a fairly clear path there," Al said.

Draco followed Al's suggested route, and looked back over his shoulder. The giant pods were inching closer to them. They were all converging on Draco's location. He wondered for a moment how the giant pods could detect his presence given their lack of anything that resembled eyes or ears.

Then he remembered the smaller fleshlings from in the maintenance tunnels earlier. They had acted as the hunters for that monstrous flesh reaper that had almost caught them. Draco knew that there had to be something in the room feeding information to these pods. Something with eyes or ears.

"Al, scan the room for anomalies. Ignore these giant fucking things and look for something smaller. Something that might be moving around," Draco said.

"Yes, Captain."

Al fired up his boosters to maximum thrust and hovered about ten metres above Draco and Raze. He switched his optic sensors to pick up thermal heat. The huge pods were bright red. The things were burning. Given the amount of energy it would need to have expended to change anything on a genetic level, Al wasn't all that surprised. There were also smaller warm globs of flesh dotted around the room. They were on the floor, the ceiling and the walls. They were certainly alive, but it was not apparent exactly what purpose they served.

"Captain, I may have found something. I will need to investigate further. You will be on your own for a moment while I do so."

"Go ahead, Al. We can manage."

Alphonse flew towards one of these smaller globs of living tissue. As he got closer and the thing came into view, he wished that he hadn't. It took a moment for his mind to comprehend what he was seeing. The flesh seemed to be growing out of the metal wall, and on the end of the fleshy nub was a human head. Its mouth opened and closed rapidly as though it was engaged in a heated debate. It had no lungs to project air through its vocal chords, but even then the shapes it made with its mouth were meaningless. Al could lip read almost all of the languages used across the galaxy, but this head was spouting nothing but gibberish. It was the eyes that unnerved him, though. The eyes saw him. They moved quickly back and forth, like a rabies victim Al had seen back on Old Earth before the exodus.

Al fired a blast of superheated energy at the disembodied head, and it exploded in a gout of red muck. Something down below him made a low, bellowing sound of pain.

'What's going on up there? I heard gunfire,' Draco asked through comms.

"I'll spare you the gruesome details, but I think it is high time that we made a swift escape from this place," Al answered.

Al flew back down to Draco and Raze as they continued to traverse the gigantic pile of rubble. Al flew ahead and attempted to guide them through it safely once again. The end was almost in sight. Draco pushed himself hard to reach the top, but as he did, the rubble started the move and shift.

The bellowing from the deep got louder.

Draco saw Raze overtake him on the right. The big man had gotten luckier than Draco as the rubble shifted; at the top of the pile of rubble was a small opening into a destroyed corridor. Raze managed to grab hold with one hand, but Draco was quickly slipping away.

Al tried to fly back down to grab Draco, but he was too slow. Draco was swallowed by the shifting rubble.

Ava heard the bellowing sound of something huge in the darkness. The sound vibrated the water around her.

"What the hell was that?" she asked.

"That's the beast below. The thing that's taken over the ship. Someone, somewhere must have done something it didn't like," Jaxon said.

"What is it?"

"Would you believe me if I told you I didn't actually know?"

"Yeah, I would."

"Last time I was on the Metropolis Seven, I just remember being scared out of my mind the whole time. To me, that was a long time ago. I was just a scared kid."

"Are you still scared now?"

"I've never really stopped being scared. The nightmares of this ship stayed with me even after I made it back to New Earth. That's a story for another time though, I think we're almost there."

Jaxon and Ava broke the surface and came face to face with an incomprehensible horror. It was shaped like a man from the waist down. It had two pink, naked legs and another appendage sprouting from its behind to give balance to the rest of its ungainly body. The arms were mostly intact, but its fingers had split apart. It looked as though it had about ten to fifteen fingers on each hand. The torso had been split in half, and from behind, the thing did not appear to have a head. That was until it heard Ava and Jaxon pull themselves up from the water onto dry land.

It turned towards them, and Ava had to resist the urge to vomit. The fleshling's head lulled to one side of its torso, upside down, merged with what used to be a human ribcage. The head was human, but the eyes bulged and protruded like there was extreme internal pressure pushing them out from the inside. Its mouth opened when it saw Ava and Jaxon. The purple lips were pulled back tight across its jaw, and it's mouth was filled with a lumpy mass of tumorous flesh. The growth filled its mouth so fully that when it tried to make noise, nothing but a wet rattling gargle escaped it.

Ava spotted Vynce's grey armour just behind the shambling horror. He wasn't moving. The creature moved towards them with a speed that she didn't anticipate. It closed the distance between them in seconds. Ava sidestepped the creature, and Jaxon jumped backwards into the water. Ava engaged her buster pods and punched the creature. She knocked it backwards, but it quickly got back to its feet and resumed the assault. Ava swore and pulled her assault rifle from its mag-holster on her back. She opened fire on the grotesque creature.

The first volley of bullets shredded one of the fleshling's arms. It fell limply to the ground, and the fleshling's wet gurgles reached a fever pitch. It stumbled towards Ava. It looked as though it was trying to spit the tumorous growth at her. Shiny white points started to emerge from the skin on the thing's head. Its eyes bulged, and the growth began to pulsate. Then its head started to inflate as the pressure built up inside.

"Ava, run!" Jaxon yelled.

She ran, but not fast enough. The last thing she saw before she felt a searing pain in her right arm was the thing's eyeballs exploding outward into clear jelly.

Her HUD flashed a terrifying message.

Suit integrity compromised.

She looked down at her forearm and saw a long, white, bone-like protrusion coming out of it. She pulled it through the other side of the wound and threw it to the ground. She knew that her suit would perform the necessary first aid on the affected area after it sealed itself. She'd been shot before, and being shot hurt a lot worse.

Suit integrity 100%. Commencing first aid, said a message on her HUD.

After the thing's limp body fell to the ground, Jaxon rushed to her side and asked, "Did it get you?"

Ava waved him away and said, "It's fine. Don't worry about it."

Jaxon grabbed her firmly by the shoulder and said, "Answer me with a yes or a no. Did anything from that creature touch you or get inside your suit?"

Ava shrugged him off and said, "No. I'm fine. Really."

Her arm was still throbbing, and she kept thinking the same word over and over.

Infected.

Jaxon sighed audibly with relief. Ava rushed over to Vynce's side. He was still breathing, but unconscious. Ava began to take his helmet off when Jaxon stopped her.

"No. Not here. We need to get somewhere safe before we expose him to this atmosphere. Exposing him here might actually kill him."

"Do you know this area of the ship?"

"Not in the slightest, but I know how to tell a potentially infectious room from a non-infectious one. We just keep going until we find somewhere that looks clean."

There was that word again. Infectious. Ava shuddered at the thought. Her right arm was still throbbing. Even with the painkillers her suit administered, it still hurt like a sonofabitch.

Jaxon went over to Vynce and picked him up effortlessly.

"It'll be easier for me to carry Vynce. You just keep your rifle pointed at anything that moves, alright?" Jaxon asked.

"I can do that," Ava said.

If it hadn't been for his suit of armour, the rubble would have crushed Draco. He was trapped, but alive. He was on his back, and a huge metal beam pinned him down by his chest. There was barely enough room for him to try to push the huge metal beam off.

'Don't panic, Captain. Raze and I are digging you out as we speak. Are you hurt?' Al asked.

"Not hurt. Just feeling a little claustrophobic."

The weight of the beam made it very hard to breathe. He had already started to feel light-headed.

'We'll have you out soon.'

Draco resumed his effort to push the huge metal beam from his chest. He managed to move it by millimetres, but it was enough of a reprieve to allow him to breathe a little easier for a moment.

On top of the pile of rubble, Raze and Alphonse were frantically pawing through the debris, trying to clear as much as they could. They could not tell how far down Draco was, but they knew the general area. Some pieces of debris were far too big for them to lift, and the house-sized birthing pods were inching ever closer.

Suddenly the debris started to lift from below.

"Captain, is that you?" Al asked.

'No, it's something underneath us. It's shifting again,' Draco replied.

A booming moaning sound drifted up from below them as the debris pile lifted again. The thing beneath them was so massive that it could manipulate tons of concrete and steel as though they were grains of sand at the beach.

As the pile shifted, Al saw a light shine through the rubble.

"I see you Captain," Al said and flew down to him. Al tore through the rubble until he saw Draco.

"This beam!" Draco said and motioned to the beam that lay across his chest.

Raze grabbed one end and Alphonse grabbed the other. Draco

pushed from below, and with their combined efforts they shifted the beam enough to allow Draco to escape. He clambered to his feet.

"Captain, permission to be reckless for a moment?" Al asked.

"Permission granted."

"Very well," Al said and put his arms around Draco's chest from behind.

"I suggest you hold on," Al said.

Draco held onto Al's arms just a moment before Al engaged his thrusters. He flew up to the breach in the mag-rail network and dropped Draco inside. Al then flew back down, picked up Raze, and flew him back up to the breach.

"My internal batteries will need a moment to recover. Might we find a safe place to rest for a moment?" Al asked.

"Absolutely. Hunker down here for a moment while I try and raise the Icarus," Draco said as he reached down to pull the comm unit Jaxon had given him from his thigh holster. The weight of the rubble had crushed it completely.

ELEVEN

Rhken wanted to cry. She could feel the mass murderer breathing down the back of her neck. He could have snapped her neck in an instant, but he didn't. He let her live, and she wanted to know why. She began to think of ways that she could alert her father and her sister that Veck was out of his cage. Doing it without his knowledge was going to be the hard part.

Rhken didn't understand how Veck could have gotten out in the first place. The moment he moved he should have been fried from the inside out by Evie. But Evie hadn't communicated with the crew since the shuttle to the Metropolis Seven left. So either Evie had completely failed, or somehow Veck had managed to corrupt her.

If Veck had managed to get into Evie's core processor then there was no telling what he could do. Essentially he would be the Icarus, and could issue commands to it that no one but Captain Goldwing should have been able to use. The idea terrified Rhken. The things this ship could do scared her even when Captain Goldwing was at the helm. But if Veck Simms was in control, there's no telling what could happen.

"You love your Captain don't you, little mouse?" Veck asked.

"Yes," she replied.

"You love your crew don't you?"

"Yes," she sobbed.

"You don't want me to hurt any of them, do you?"

"No," she said, trying to stop the stream of tears from stinging her eyes.

"Good. Now answer a question for me. Which way to the bridge?"

Rhken pointed down the corridor in the direction of the bridge.

"Thanks, pumpkin. You lead the way, okay?"

Rhken nodded.

"I think you and I are going to become good friends. So what say we get to know each other a little better?" Veck asked.

Rhken didn't know what she should say or do, so she remained silent. Her head snapped backwards as he grabbed her by her hair and pulled fiercely. She yelped in pain and surprise.

"You're not being very friendly, little mouse. Friends talk to each other," he growled.

Rhken cried out, still unable to speak.

"When I let go of your hair, you're going to tell me your name, and you're going to tell me a little about yourself, alright? If you do what I ask, I won't hurt you again. I promise," he cooed.

Rhken nodded silently.

"Ready? One, two, three!" he said and let go of Rhken's hair.

She wiped the tears out of her eyes and said, "My name is Rhken Otema. I'm sixteen years old, and one of the Icarus' junior engineers."

"Excellent. And what exactly does a junior engineer do?"

"We do anything that Captain Goldwing needs done to keep the Icarus flying."

"We? You have other junior engineers?"

"Yes. We have one other junior engineer."

"And what's their name?"

"Reban."

"Surely with two junior engineers, you must also have a senior engineer. That's only logical."

"Yes."

"Who's the senior engineer, and what do they do?"

"He's my -" she almost said the word father, but stopped herself before the word left her mouth. She continued, "He's my boss, and he tells me what I need to do and when to do it."

"And what's his name?"

"Nook."

"Nook, huh? I knew a Nook once. He went off and fell in love with some Anjule waif. He was a traitor to his species."

Rhken tried to ignore Veck's words. She refused to be baited into a conversation about her father. If she could conceal her relationship to Nook and Reban, she hoped that she could stop Veck from using them against her.

"Is there anything you'd like to ask me, little mouse?" Veck asked.

She turned to face him, eyes still welling with tears. She asked, "What are you going to do with us?"

Veck smiled.

"I don't want to do anything to you or anyone else on this ship. The only thing I want to do is leave. Peacefully. Now, if anyone on this ship has an aversion to letting me leave peacefully I'll be happy to demonstrate my reputation to them first hand, but I would prefer not. As much as the New Earth media would want you to believe that I am a psychopath given to destroying life without reason, it's far from the truth. They do manage to get one thing right about me. I believe that the human race deserves a privileged place among the galactic species. What do you think, little mouse?"

She hated being called little mouse. But she decided to allow herself that persona at least for the moment. She would remain meek and only squeak occasionally, but underneath the surface she would put her mind to work.

"I don't know," she said.

"You're young," he said with a sigh, "And I can't hold you responsible for that. I can't expect you to have seen the things I have seen, or to understand the galaxy as I do. But I can help to open your mind, if you'd like."

His voice was soft, but his eyes had the hungry cold stare of a great white shark.

She nodded.

"As an engineer, you would know what an arc reactor is," he said.

She nodded.

"You would also know that the arc reactor was invented before the exodus of Old Earth. Without it, the Children of iNet would not exist. We are the reason they exist as a species of sentient life, and our technology is how they are able to live for thousands of years. When it comes down to it, that entire race of sentient life is our creation. We created it. There's no denying that. As a species, we ourselves created another fully functioning, fully sentient form of life. Our technological advances are leaps and bounds over the other species in the galaxy. The Vartalen were still using giant reservoirs of fossil fuel in order to fly through the stars until they got access to our arc reactor technology. Even though we're the newest species to join the Galactic community, it's common knowledge that we are the most advanced. And that's why our own government is trying to kill me. The Galactic community is not ready to accept our dominance."

Rhken had thoughts flying through her mind. She was tempted to mention that the creation of the Children of iNet was against Galactic law, and other species had suffered enormous penalties for undertaking artificial intelligence research.

She also wanted to mention that their species was responsible for inciting violence and racial hatred across the galaxy. They were the newest kids on the block, yet they had shown up and acted as though they owned the place.

From his little speech, Rhken thought that the statements made about Veck had been completely justified. The man might be charismatic, but he was a complete whack job.

"What do you think?" Veck asked after Rhken didn't respond.

"I think that if we had the technological superiority over the other races in the galaxy, and we could improve their quality of life by sharing them, then I think we should."

Veck moved too fast for Rhken to comprehend. All she felt was pain explode from her abdomen. One moment she was standing face to face with a madman, and the next she was doubled over in agony, clutching her stomach.

She screamed as he pulled her back to her feet by her hair.

"That's the kind of fucking attitude our government wants our unthinking populace to have. You have to ignore their attempts at controlling your mind and see the galaxy for what it really is. It's a food chain of predators and prey, and we're not just swimming around the middle. We're at the top."

Rhken whimpered.

"Say it. We're at the top!"

"We're at the top!" she said. She didn't believe the words, she just wanted the pain to end. She would do anything, say anything, just to make the pain stop.

Veck released her, and Rhken slumped to the ground. She held her head in her hands and cried.

"Get up," Veck said with quiet menace.

Rhken's strength had been drained out of her. She didn't know whether she even had the energy to stand.

"Get up, or I will pull you to your fucking feet again," Veck said.

Rhken's eyes went wide in terror, and somewhere deep down inside herself she found the energy to stand. She arose shakily to one knee at first, and then braced herself on the wall of the corridor to get back to her feet.

"Good little mouse. Now scurry on. Take me to the bridge."

They walked on.

For a moment, Arak believed that Veck may have actually been civilised, but that idea had flown out of his head when Veck attacked

Rhken. He brutally punched the young girl in the stomach and lifted her off the ground by her own hair. Arak had seen many things that would make a normal man sick. But what he had seen Veck do to Rhken disgusted him more.

Arak frantically tried to decode the encrypted signal that Captain Goldwing had used to contact him on before. After it had disappeared, the only thing he could think of was that it had encrypted itself, but it was nowhere to be found. Arak knew a thing or two about encrypted comm signals, but he was not the genius code breaker that Raze was.

Evie had her own encryption breaking cycles she could run, but she had not been responding since Veck's escape. Arak had a sinking feeling that Veck had somehow disabled Evie's security system, but he couldn't work out how he had managed to do it. He had to make contact with Captain Goldwing, but Arak hadn't the faintest idea how. There was no way he could instigate contact with Captain Goldwing. He could only wait for Captain Goldwing to contact him.

Veck was quickly approaching the locked door to the bridge. Soon, Arak would have to make a choice. Flee, or die. But on a ship the size of the Icarus, there weren't many places to flee to.

If Veck had managed to find a way to get past Evie's security measures, it was likely that he could get past the locked door to the bridge. If he could do that, he could commandeer the ship and strand the rest of the crew on the Metropolis Seven.

There was only one option.

Arak got up from the pilot's seat and climbed up to the central command station. He swiped his fingers across the clear glass display, which brought up a list of options. Arak touched a number of seemingly unrelated options one after the other. The sequence of motions was one that Draco's father had implemented when he owned the Icarus. Arak had never had to use them, but this was an emergency. The ship was without its captain, and a hostile force was coming to commandeer it. After Arak finished the sequence, the display went dead.

Arak spoke, "I have flown too close to the sun."

The command centre moved and shifted until it was split into two parts. It revealed a small hatch, which Arak lifted. Underneath the hatch lid was a ladder leading underneath the bridge. There was darkness down there, but if Draco had told it true, there would only be one path for Arak to follow.

Arak began to descend the ladder. He couldn't see the rungs, but he could feel them with his feet. He grabbed the hatch and pulled it back down into place.

The command centre reformed in place after the hatch was closed, and a number of dull green lights began to brighten. There were two small, dull lights on each ladder rung, and more running down the sides of the walls. Arak kept climbing down until he reached the bottom of the access tunnel. He carefully stepped down onto the metal floor, conscious of how much noise echoed in the small chamber.

Arak pivoted and saw that the tunnel turned into a small room with a very low ceiling. A row of dull green lights formed a circle around a central pillar that ran from the floor to the ceiling. Arak crossed the room to the pillar and ran his hand across the smooth surface. Dull green lines began to radiate out from his touch.

A sudden unexpected voice in the chamber made him jump.

"Have you flown too close to the sun?" it asked.

Arak's heart was racing, but he managed to speak. "There is a hostile force aboard the Icarus. Captain Draco Goldwing is currently trapped on another ship, and I don't know what to do."

"Draco's not here?" the voice asked.

"No, he is not."

"That's a pity. I had hoped to talk to him one last time."

"Forgive me for my ignorance sir, but who am I speaking to?"

"Just one second," the voice said.

The lights around the pillar brightened for a moment, and a bright green holographic projection formed in front of Arak's eyes. For a moment he thought he was looking at a recreation of Captain Draco Goldwing himself, but then saw that the eyes and the chin were wrong.

"I'm Draco's father, Samuel," the hologram said, "Well, I'm not really him. He's been dead for years. I'm just the leftovers. I am his programming, his voice and a list of regrets as long as your arm. An avatar of a long-dead servant of the human race."

"I'm sure that once Draco is back on the ship I can arrange for him to come down and speak with you. I am sure he would be glad to hear his father's voice, regardless of whether you are simply an artificial intelligence program."

"Well that would be nice, but if you're down here, it's not because you wanted some company, is it?"

"No sir, it is not."

"You're in some deep shit, and Draco gave you the access phrase, so that must mean you're someone he trusts. I guess that means I should trust you too."

"You can trust me. I owe Draco my life."

"Did Draco ever explain to you what this place is?"

"No sir. He just said that if I was out of options I should come down here and I would find something to turn the tide."

"This is the heart of the Icarus, son. There are three things that can only be used from inside this room. The first is a self-destruct process for the Icarus. You trigger that, and you've got five minutes to get on the shuttle and get clear."

"The shuttle is currently aboard another ship, with Captain Goldwing."

"Seeing as that's not an option, the second choice is an EMP. Be warned, it won't just fry an enemy ship. It'll fry the Icarus too. It'll leave you dead in the void."

Arak nodded. The EMP could incapacitate Veck for long enough to restrain him once again, but it may also affect the Metropolis

Seven. Because of the complete comm silence, Arak did not want to risk it. They were well outside the gravitational field of Krakaterra, but there was faint enough gravitational force from the binary star system that it could pull them back in. There was no way to be sure.

"The third option is something that you should never use, unless you have no other options left. The Icarus has a gravity drive on board -"

Arak had to stop his jaw from dropping. "A gravity drive? There's no way!" Arak said.

"I don't mean to contradict you here son, but you're wrong. There is a gravity drive on board," the avatar said.

"The Icarus could destroy entire planets if the gateway gravity drive was ever used incorrectly. How in the galaxy did you find someone who could make one, let alone agree to install it in a mercenary vessel?"

The avatar of Samuel Goldwing smiled at Arak and said, "This isn't really a mercenary vessel. But I'm sure you already worked that out."

"I'm not sure I follow," Arak said.

"This vessel was originally bequeathed to me by the Alliance military, for a price. If they ever had a job that they couldn't be seen to be attached to, I'd take care of it. That contract no doubt would have passed to Draco after my death."

"You're saying that this is a military ship? This makes a whole lot more sense now."

"Not entirely military. It was engineered and built by the military, but it was given to the Goldwing family. We've made our own modifications over the years."

"Still, to hear that there is a gravity drive on this ship fills me with a deep sense of dread."

"We've never had cause to use it, and maybe it'll stay that way. But you're the pilot now, which makes you the ranking officer on this ship while the captain isn't here. So now the decision on how to proceed is completely up to you. You've activated me, which in turn has activated the higher functions of the ship. All you need to do now is place your hand on the access pillar again and speak one of three phrases.

"The first is, 'and now we burn' which activates the self-destruct mechanism. If you activate this option, you will have five minutes until the ship self-destructs. If you say 'the power of the sun' you will activate the EMP. If you say 'we will fly again' you will activate the gateway gravity drive, and it will ask you for coordinates. Once you input coordinates, the drive will rip a hole through the fabric of space and time to deliver you to your destination.

"I will leave it up to you to decide," the avatar said and then faded away.

Arak was left alone in the dull green glow to make his decision.

TWELVE

Draco, Raze and Alphonse walked along the mag-rail tracks in the direction of the nearest station. They were backtracking somewhat, but once they reached the Water Treatment Plant station they would be able to find out whether the mag-rail network was still running.

The mag-rail network was one giant tubular network, much like the mega subways on New Earth. It ran in an ellipse around the outside of the Metropolis Seven. It started in the production and maintenance areas that they had already passed through, and then ran around the outside of the recreational, residential and Metropolitan Districts of the city.

The mag-rail tunnel looked nothing like a traditional railway. The tunnel was circular and of a similar height as a three level apartment building. Draco, Raze and Al walked on the flat bottom of the tunnel. If there was a mag-rail carriage using the network, it would have zoomed by above their heads. Coming up from the bottom and down from the top of the cylindrical tunnel were smooth metallic supports in an X pattern that ended in wide, flat magnetic surfaces.

The magnetic surfaces made it so that the mag-rail carriage could move at phenomenal speeds without any kind of resistance. A trip that would have taken upwards of an hour on a traditional track-based train network could happen as quickly as 10 minutes using a similar mag-rail mode of transit.

Alphonse's power levels were extremely low. His arc reactor core was slowly regenerating his expended energy as they walked, but he had to conserve as much energy as he could.

Raze didn't like this ship one bit. He had read up on the satellite class long-vacationers many years ago, and he had dreamed of signing up as a crew member and leaving his old life behind for five or ten years. That childish dream had been taken out the back and shot the moment he saw those disgusting birthing pods full of human bits and pieces. Raze preferred it when monsters were just words on the pages of a book.

A sudden blast of static through their comms made everyone flinch and hunker down as though they were under attack. The message was incomprehensible.

"We read you but the message was not received, please repeat" Draco said.

He motioned for Raze to try and track the signal back to its source. There was still something on board the Metropolis Seven that was blocking their communications, and Draco wanted to know exactly what it was.

Another blast of static came back through their comms, but one phrase came through the static loud and clear.

"Help us!" a terrified voice pleaded before it transformed into digital white noise again. The voice sounded like it belonged to a young child.

"Raze, can you get a lock on where that comm is coming from?" Draco asked.

"Working on it," he said as he worked furiously.

"Hold tight. Keep transmitting on this channel and we'll do what we can for you," Draco said.

Another distorted blast of digitised static blasted across the comm channel. Raze said, "I've got it. I've also managed to locate the source of the comm jamming. It's coming from inside the city. The central tower. But the person in distress is further along the mag-rail network. They're probably taking refuge inside the next terminal."

"Let's go!"

Draco got back to his feet and started sprinting down the mag-rail tunnel. Raze followed, and Alphonse lagged behind. As they followed the mag-rail tunnel it began to sweep to the right. There was a ladder which led up to the platform. Draco ascended it quickly and the scene before him almost made his stomach turn.

The platform was wide and flat. There was one walkway for arrivals and a separate walkway for departures with a glass barrier separating the two. Some of it has been shattered and painted red with the lifeblood of the passengers.

Raze and Al joined Draco on the platform.

"Are you sure the signal was coming from this platform?" Draco asked.

"The location matches perfectly."

"Can you get that door open?" Draco asked and pointed towards the departures door.

"Not from out here. If we can cross to the other side the doors should just open for us," Raze said.

Draco pulled his pistol from its holster and fired two shots at the glass between the walkways. The sound of the shots and shattering glass echoed off the walls of the tunnel. Draco cleared a section from glass and jumped the barrier.

The arrivals walkway was relatively clear of bio-hazardous debris. Draco walked towards the arrivals door, and it slid open to reveal a small fire burning in the centre of the room. A young boy stood on top of a chair right next to the door with a pistol levelled at Draco's head.

"Who are you!? Answer me, or I'll shoot you! I'll shoot you right in the head, and then you'll just be meat!" the boy screamed. He couldn't have been any older than ten. His hands shook dangerously.

Draco put his hands up in front of him. He still held his pistol in his right hand, but let it dangle freely from his thumb. Draco said,

"My name is Captain Draco Goldwing, of the Icarus. My crew and I are here on the Metropolis Seven responding to a distress call. We're here to rescue you. How about I put my gun away and you put yours away too?"

The boy visibly relaxed. His hands were still shaking, but he had lowered the gun.

"I thought you were one of those things," the boy said.

"What's your name?" Draco asked.

"Pim," the boy said.

"You're a very brave young man. Was it you that we heard on the comm channel before?"

Pim nodded.

"You said 'help us' - is there anyone else here with you?"

Pim's bottom lip started to quiver, "My sister. She's in the luggage room. I locked her in there when she started to act funny."

"What do you mean she started to act funny?" Alphonse asked.

"She stopped talking. Normally she never stops talking. And then she tried to eat me. She kept saying that I was a piece of meat and that she was hungry. I got scared, so I locked her in the baggage room and didn't let her out."

"Son, do you know anything about what's happening here on the ship?"

"There are monsters in the dark. Is my sister a monster?" Pim asked.

"No, she's not a monster. But I need you to stay here with my friend Al for a moment, alright Pim?"

Pim looked over to Al, then back to Draco. Al leaned down and took the boy's hand.

"Hello, you brave little man. Would you like me to tell you a story while Draco checks on your sister?"

"Mmhmm," Pim said and nodded.

"What kind of heroes do you like?" Al asked.

"Strong ones who save the day," Pim said.

Al began to tell him a story about one of the greatest heroes he knew while Draco and Raze walked further into the terminal. The tiny fire had been made in a waste paper basket. The dancing flames threw moving shadows onto the walls. The door that led to the baggage room was closed.

Draco motioned for Raze to open it. The big man in the red and blue armour shouldered the door open and stumbled into the darkness. Draco followed and let the door swing shut behind him. The beams of their shoulder lamps pierced the darkness.

Draco heard a low gurgling sound a moment before something slammed into his chest. The thing was small, and wore the shredded remnants of a pink dress. Pim's sister was barely recognisable as human. The young girl's head lolled back wordlessly. A new mouth full of needle like teeth had formed at the top of her chest cavity. It gnashed and snarled as Draco fell backwards. He tried to fend the creature off, but it was too strong. The gnashing maw pushed closer and closer to Draco's face. Just as he thought the creature would overpower him completely, Raze unleashed a burst of assault rifle fire. The thing's tiny limp body flew across the room and landed in a misshapen heap.

"Shit," Raze said.

"Yeah," Draco agreed.

"How are we going to tell the kid?"

"He's probably seen more than his fair share of horrors already. I'm just glad he had the sense to lock her in here."

"Smart kid."

Draco walked over to the carcass of the creature that used to be Pim's sister. He flipped it over with his right foot and it struggled weakly. The volley of bullets hadn't killed the creature, only grievously injured it. Red blood and black liquid oozed out of the bullet wounds in its chest. The tooth-filled maw opened and closed slowly. Each time it moved its top jaw, the little girl's head flopped backwards. It closed its mouth for the final time and the little girl's eyes fluttered as life left its body.

"In a disgustingly horrible way, this creature is strangely beautiful," Raze said, "I've been thinking about what Al said earlier, and I'm sure he was right. These things in the ship, they all come from people. I think what we're looking at here is some kind of parasite, but unlike anything the galaxy has ever seen before. It's like the parasite doesn't just coexist with the host. It actually takes the host over completely. What kind of thing could do that? Have you ever heard of anything like this before?"

"No, I can't say I have," Draco said, "But if these things can somehow take you over from the inside out, then I think we need to be a lot more careful."

Ava's arm had started to ache. She hoped that the spike that had pierced her forearm hadn't caused too much internal damage. It could have grazed an artery, chipped a piece of bone or even shredded one of her muscles.

Sensing spikes in her pain receptors, a message flashed up on her HUD.

Administer pain suppression? it asked.

"Yes," Ava said.

She felt a small pinch on the back of her right shoulder blade as a tiny needle pierced her skin. The relief was instantaneous. She exhaled as a wave of light-headedness passed over her. Even though she couldn't feel the pain, she could feel the unpleasant warmness of the wound.

"Are you okay back there?" Jaxon asked.

"Yeah, I'm fine," Ava replied.

"Have you started talking to yourself?"

She deflected his question and asked, "How's Vynce?"

"He's still out cold. If my memory is correct, there should be a med station somewhere in these tunnels. If we keep going we should be able to find it. It'll be a safe place where we can wait until he wakes up."

"How well do you know these tunnels?"

"Well enough. These are the tunnels where I did most of my work on the Metropolis Seven before everything went to hell. I never got to know every little nook and cranny, but I know the main tunnels well enough. See that pipe up there? The one with the blue stripes running down the middle?"

Ava looked up and saw the pipe he was referring to.

"That brings water up from the treatment plant to the med station. If you're ever in trouble, you just find a blue striped pipe and follow it back to one of the med stations. They're even on their own communications and power grid. Once we get there, we should be able to find someone to communicate with while we wait for Vynce to come back around."

"Finally, some good news."

They followed the blue striped pipe along the darkened corridors. There was a sudden noise from the vents above. Ava raised her assault rifle and aimed it at the grated roof. Her right finger almost pulled the trigger, but she stopped herself. That kind of noise could attract unwanted attention. She glimpsed something small up in the vent, but it was clambering away from them at speed. She exhaled.

The blue striped pipe ran off to the right. Ava followed it. As she turned down the next corridor, she thought she could hear a faint, far-off scratching sound. It sounded like someone scratching nails on metal.

"Do you hear that?" Ava asked.

"Yeah," Jaxon replied.

"Walk faster?"

"Walk faster."

Ava started to jog. Every corridor they went down looked exactly the same as the last. At one point, Ava thought that they were running in circles. The scratching, chittering sound grew louder. Ava started to feel the darkness pressing in against her.

"There, on the right! There's the med station!" Jaxon said.

There was a white sign with a red heart in the middle. There was a small green light next to the door frame. As Ava approached, the opaque glass door to the med station slid open soundlessly. Ava stepped through and checked the room for danger. There was one main room with two beds against the far wall. Along the other wall was a row of chairs. Near the beds was another door that led to the supply room.

As Jaxon crossed the threshold he said, "Initiate lockdown protocol, code 7826."

The door to the med station immediately slid closed. The green light next to the door turned red. A feminine voice spoke over the loudspeaker and said, 'Med station Delta locked down. Quarantine protocols in place.'

"Quarantine protocols? What does that mean exactly?" Ava asked.

"Exactly what it sounds like. This room has been locked down and quarantined. We're locked in here until I use a quarantine override code to get us out again. Vynce has been attacked by one of these things, and I need to know whether he's been infected. Can you check the beds and make sure they're safe?"

"Sure," Ava said and walked over to the beds. One of the beds had red and brown crusted moisture on top, but the other looked fine.

"This one's fine. Bring him over."

Jaxon brought Vynce over to the bed and laid him down gently.

"Is there any way we can get him out of the suit without cutting it off him?" Jaxon asked.

"It doesn't matter if we have to cut it off him. He'll be able to put it back on once we're done. You've seen a smartsuit before, right?"

Jaxon laughed. "Seen one? I'm wearing one. But it's about 40 years more advanced than the smartsuits your crew is wearing. They're the smartsuits where the armour bonds to the outer layer of the suit, right?"

"Right."

"This one, the smartsuit is the whole suit. You put it on and it augments your natural body automatically. This is the kind of uniform soldiers wear into battle in my time."

"You're for real, aren't you? You really are from the future."

"Yes. I am."

"Then you know how all of this turns out, don't you?"

"I know the overall outcome of what happens, yes. But the past is a strange thing. In most cases, the past doesn't want to be changed. It's resistant to it. But time travel is even stranger than you would think. Sometimes when we're sent back to make sure something doesn't happen, the time agent is instrumental in making sure things happen as they have already happened. In effect, the outcome you're trying to change was already influenced by your direct involvement."

"Wait, what? You're going to have to dumb it down for me buddy. That just flew straight over my fucking head."

"Alright, well imagine for a moment that there's someone that you love with all of your heart. Someone that you would gladly give your own life so that they could continue on living."

Jaxon smiled as he realised that he was referring to Ava herself. His mind flashed through memories of all the time he had spent with her during their downtime. She had no idea how much she meant to him. And he knew that she had no idea. It had been so hard to resist the urge to take her in his arms and kiss her passionately right in front of the rest of the crew when he stepped out of the time stream.

"Alright, got it," Ava said, but she really didn't. She had never felt that deep a connection with anyone, except maybe for Draco. But she knew that he would never let any of his crew sacrifice themselves so that he could live.

"Do you have anyone like that?" Jaxon asked, wondering if there was someone else in Ava's life he never knew about.

"I have some people I'd be willing to die to save."

"Good. Now imagine living through their death, and imagine surviving it. That's the worst thing of all. You start questioning your own actions. 'What else could I have done to stop it? What if I could go back in time and save them?' You know that if you actually had the ability to go back in time to try and intervene, you would. Hell, I know you would. You may not know me all that well yet, but I know you better than you think. Your passion. Your tenacity. Your strength. I know that if you thought there was any chance you could save someone you loved, you'd take it. I know that for a fact. Feel free to correct me if I'm wrong."

"No," she said, "you're not."

"Imagine for a moment that a person that you love above all else is killed in a fire fight, seemingly at random. A random lucky shot. Let's just say that Captain Goldwing is facing off against a ship full of pirates, and a random shot hits him right in the weak spot of his suit, just below the chin, and just above the neck plating. The shot pierces his jugular and he bleeds out before anyone has a chance to even think about trying to help him. You live through his death, and you try to find a way to get back to that moment in time to intervene. You go back to the exact same place and time, and you put yourself right there in the situation. You join the gunfight, and you're knocked down while trying to kill off the pirates that took your captain's life. Your finger is squeezing the trigger, and you flail wildly as you get knocked backwards. One of your bullets fires towards Captain Goldwing and hits him right in that weak spot, and he dies before you have a chance to do anything."

"So by the act of trying to intervene, it would actually be my fault that Captain Goldwing died in the first place," Ava said.

"Yes. There is no way to know what events are caused by time agents, and what events are prevented by time agents. All I know is that I am not supposed to be here on this ship. Something happened to me today that, as far as I know, has never happened before. I crossed over into my own timeline."

"Your own timeline? What do you mean?"

"One of the fundamental principles of being an agent is that you cannot cross over into your own timeline. There are theories about what would happen if it ever occurred. Some theorise that the universe would begin to implode in on itself. Some theorise that the Sentinels would hunt down the anomaly before a paradox could be created. Others think that nothing would happen at all. But all I know is that my younger self is on this ship. In that life, I am 22 years old, and this is my very first job since landing on New Earth. I don't remember meeting an older version of myself when I was 22 years old, so either it never happened, or something prevented us from meeting. Or maybe I did meet myself and I completely repressed the memory. There's no way for me to know whether my involvement with the events here on the Metropolis Seven will alter the outcome, or whether they are the cause of the outcome that I have already lived through. All I know is that this chip that I am carrying with me needs to get back to New Earth, otherwise the existence of the human race is in danger."

Ava's mind swam with questions. She wanted to ask what the point of trying to change anything was if it was already destined to happen. She wanted to know what the fuck a Sentinel was. She wanted to know how the hell two versions of the same man were on the Metropolis Seven at the same time.

"I think I need to have a sit down," Ava said. Her head had started to pound, and her right forearm had started to ache again. It was uncomfortably warm, and it had started to itch.

THIRTEEN

Rhken walked towards the bridge and Veck Simms followed close behind. They rounded the last curve before the bridge and Rhken couldn't help smiling to herself when she saw that Arak had locked the bridge down. Her blood ran cold when she heard Veck start to laugh to himself.

"How amusing," Veck said and approached the security console next to the blast doors.

"Would you like to see a little trick?" he asked Rhken with a smile that terrified her. Without giving her a chance to respond, he held up his fingers in front of her eyes. "Watch very, very closely."

Before Rhken's eyes, she saw Veck's fingerprints begin to dance across his skin. He pressed them against the fingerprint scanner. Evie's voice then said, "Hello, Captain Goldwing. Please speak your voice activation prompt."

"On wings of gold," Veck said, but it was Captain Goldwing's voice that came from his mouth. The blast doors opened. Veck walked into the bridge.

Rhken turned and ran. She didn't want Veck to hurt her any more, but she also couldn't just let him take the ship. She wanted to run back to her Dad and her sister. They'd know what to do. They always knew what to do.

A sudden pain erupted from the back of her head as Veck grabbed her hair and pulled her backwards. Her feet flew out from under her, but Veck didn't slow down. He marched back into the bridge, dragging her behind him. Rhken tried to scream for help, but Veck had knocked the wind out of her. All she could do was gasp for breath.

"Now, now little mouse, I can't have you scurrying away before I show you my greatest trick. It's guaranteed to blow you away," Veck said with a chuckle.

"Please don't hurt me," whimpered Rhken.

"I would not have to squash a mouse if it did what it was told and didn't try to run away."

"I can walk. Please let me get up. I'll come with you, I swear."

"You haven't done anything to earn my trust so far, so you can stay on the ground at my feet until you do. And if you don't, I'll crush your skull with my bare hands. It'll be as easy as popping a grape."

Veck let go of her hair and let her fall to the ground. Veck walked over to the control centre of the ship, then turned to look back at Rhken.

"Little mouse, come here and sit by my feet while I take this ship," he said and patted his leg as though he was calling a dog to heel.

Rhken looked at his hand and the humiliation of the situation made the tears flow harder.

"Come here, or I'll hurt you again. I know you probably think I like hurting you, but I don't. I'd like it much better if you would just listen to me and do what I ask. Now, come," he said and patted his leg again.

Rhken attempted to get back to her feet to go to him.

Veck raised a finger and said, "Uh uh. You haven't earned your walking privileges back yet. Crawl to me, little mouse."

Rhken thought about resisting. She thought hard about just sitting where she was, or getting to her feet anyway. She wanted to show this bully that he had no power over her. She was her own person, and he couldn't control her. But then she remembered the pain. She remembered the humiliation.

Against every fibre in her being, she began to crawl over to Veck on her hands and knees.

"Good girl," he said, "Now come sit by my feet."

She crawled over to Veck's feet and sat.

He reached a hand down and caressed her head. He pushed it against the outer edge of his thigh and said, "There now. Isn't that better, hmm? Submission suits you, my little mouse."

Rhken closed her eyes and tried to fight back the tears.

Veck opened the ship wide communications system and spoke.

In the cargo hold, Nook was quietly monitoring the energy tethers that held the Icarus to the Metropolis Seven. All of the ranges were good. The push/pull system was working perfectly. Since the ion drives of the Metropolis Seven started doing most of the work, the Icarus had hardly used any power at all.

There hadn't been any contact from Captain Goldwing or the rest of the crew, and that normally meant that everything was going well. Captain Goldwing always said that no news was good news. But still, there was a feeling of unease down in the pit of his stomach that he just couldn't shake.

Rhken had gone to check on Arak while they waited to hear back from Captain Goldwing, but Nook had started to notice that she had been gone a long time. Reban was reclined in a chair reading one of her Old Earth novels.

A voice then came over the loudspeaker which filled Nook with dread.

'Attention all crew members of the Icarus, this is your new Captain speaking. If you are just now realising that Veck Simms is now in charge of this vessel you may feel some unnatural compulsions race through your mind. You may feel the need to act impulsively. You may even think that you should try to kill me, but I can assure you that is not a good idea.

'One of your junior engineers is here in the bridge with me. She's such a quick learner, very amiable, aren't you my dear?'

Nook heard Rhken whisper the word yes. It chilled him to the bone.

'It would be a terrible shame if anything were to happen to her. I don't want to kill her, you see. You may have trouble believing it, but I assure you it is true. I don't want to kill anyone on this ship. All I want from you is to allow me to commandeer this vessel and fly away. I'll drop you off somewhere safe. Anywhere the nearest Gateway can take us. But all I need is your cooperation, and you can all make it out of here alive.'

Reban looked across at Nook with wide, red-rimmed eyes and asked, "Dad, what are we going to do?"

"I don't know sweetie, but we'll think of something. We're not going to let anything bad happen to your sister, alright?"

Reban nodded.

'Now that I've given you some time to think about it, someone can come on up to the bridge here and let me know your decision. If you decide to try anything funny, the girl dies, and that'll be on your conscience. Not mine.'

"Dad? What do we do?" Reban asked again.

"We're going to save your sister, honey. We can't let Veck take the ship. We can't betray Captain Goldwing."

"I know we can't, but how are we going to rescue her?"

"That's the bit we've got to work out."

In the heart of the ship, Arak Nara had heard Veck's threats. He needed to make a choice immediately, otherwise Veck might murder Rhken.

The first option was to set a self-destruct sequence off, but that wasn't really an option at all. It would serve no purpose except stranding Draco and the rest of the crew over on the Metropolis

Seven and kill the rest of them. The force of the blast may even knock the giant ship off course. Given how close they still were in the gravitational field of the Gemon binary star system, that would not be a good idea at all.

The second option was the electro-magnetic pulse blast. It would destroy the energy tethers that held the Icarus to the Metropolis Seven, but it would also completely disable the Icarus until the system had time to reboot itself. With how many cybernetic augments and attachments Veck had put into his body, Arak knew that there was no chance that he could survive an EMP blast. Veck had a mechanical heart, and without a heart to pump the blood around his system, Veck would surely perish.

It was a shot, but a dangerous one. It solved one problem, but created many more. Once the EMP was triggered, an emergency response beacon would be activated. Every hostile ship in the star system would know where they were, and they would be without a means to defend themselves. There was also no knowing what effect the EMP would have on the Metropolis Seven.

The third option was to engage the gravity drive, which would open a temporary gateway in the fabric of space and time and allow the Icarus to pass from one end of space to another. As a pilot, Arak knew the coordinates for most of the human-friendly sectors of space. If they could pass through a gateway and arrive somewhere within Alliance space, they could easily send a comm wave out notifying the entire sector of who was on board.

But if they did that, Draco, Raze, Vynce, Ava and Alphonse would all be stuck at the arse-end of space without the courtesy of a goodbye. After Captain Goldwing had saved Arak's life on Torusk, he could not forsake his captain.

He knew what must be done.

FOURTEEN

"Did you kill the monster?" Pim asked when Draco and Raze walked back into the mag-rail terminal.

Draco walked over to Pim and knelt down beside him.

"The monster can't get to you anymore," he said.

The boy laughed. "Mister, there are more monsters on the ship. They're the worst in the city. That's where most of the people went when they started getting sick."

"Does this mag-rail go there? We need to get into the heart of the city. To Metro Tower. We think that if we get there, we might be able to save everyone on the ship."

"No! You can't take me back there! You can leave me here if you want, but I'm not going back to the city!" the boy said and recoiled from Draco.

"We can protect you, Pim. But you need to help us too. We don't know this ship as well as you do, and we need your help to know where to go. I promise you, Raze, Al and I will protect you. None of the monsters will even be able to get close to you."

"Do you promise?"

"I promise."

"Okay. I'll go with you."

Draco gently patted Pim on the shoulder. The boy was frightened out of his mind. Draco couldn't imagine what horrors waited for them in the centre of the city, but once they were there, they could take control of the ship and put it into safe space to wait for the Alliance military.

'Congratulations on surviving so long!' said the unknown voice from the loudspeaker in the mag-rail terminal.

"You tried to kill us. I'm going to remember that," Draco said.

'I have to admit that it did take me a while to find you. I wasn't sure exactly where you'd pop up again. There were six of you before, weren't there? Now you're down to three. I'm terribly sorry for your loss.'

"They're not dead."

'Oh, but how can you know for sure? You're not the one who has eyes and ears all over this ship, Captain Goldwing. I do.'

"Something's jamming our comms. Is it you?" Draco asked.

The voice over the loudspeaker tittered and said, 'It's a nice little trick, isn't it? The Metropolis Corporation thinks of all contingencies when it builds these ships. Including a contingency plan to deal with an invading force like yourselves.'

"I thought we were on the same side. You needed our help to save the ship. We pulled it out of the orbit of that burning planet."

'Yes you did! And with aplomb! If you recall our last conversation, there's only one thing I really want from you Captain Goldwing. I just want you to listen to me. I want you to follow my orders, and I'll guarantee you a safe route through the ship. I'm in control of all of the ship's functions. Even if the rest of your crew is alive, I can make it very hard for them to stay that way unless you do exactly what I say.'

Begrudgingly Draco said, "What do you need us to do?"

'It's very easy. Just get on the mag-rail carriage that I'm sending to you. Once you've reached your destination, I'll give you further direction.'

"And where exactly is our destination?"

'Come now Captain Goldwing, you wouldn't want to ruin the

surprise, would you?'

"Send the damn mag-rail carriage."

'Good man. It will arrive shortly.'

Raze turned toward Draco and said, "I don't like this at all."

Alphonse echoed his concerns, "Nor do I, but I think we are rather lacking in options at the moment. We could either try our luck outside the terminal, or we can take the mag-rail carriage and perhaps get Pim to some relative safety."

"If we don't listen to this guy, then there's no telling what he could do to Ava, Vynce and Jaxon. Like he said, even if they are still alive, he could make it very hard for them to stay that way. I'm sure that they're absolutely fine, but I'm not one to gamble with lives," Draco said.

"You should listen to the guardian," Pim said. He didn't look scared any more.

"The guardian?" Draco asked.

"The voice you just heard talking. He's the guardian. He makes sure everyone on this ship stays safe. He's the one who guided us to this place, because there were no monsters here. He's a bit of a jerk, but he protects us. He didn't know that one of the monsters was already inside my sister, though."

"It's all starting to make a crazy kind of sense," Raze said, "All Metropolis ships have the same mainframe make up. You have the operating and regulatory systems which make the ship run, and on top of that you have a guardian shell program. The guardian program comes into action if the captain of the ship is killed, abducted or otherwise unable to fulfil his duties."

"Where do you think it's taking us?" Alphonse asked.

"Well, given that the program knows who Captain Goldwing is, and knows that he has a reputation for... uh... heroics, I'd say that the program has identified some way that we might be able to fight off whatever is threatening the ship."

"Any guesses where that might be?" Draco asked.

"Not in the slightest," Raze replied.

Draco always hated the unknown. At least when he was in the Alliance military there would be some kind of intelligence available about the situation he was about to walk into.

But here on the Metropolis Seven he was flying blind. He didn't like trusting in third parties when he couldn't be sure of their motivations, but sometimes he didn't have much choice in the matter.

Draco sighed and said, "Alright, well there's only one thing to do now. Wait for the mag-rail carriage to show up."

Raze and Al nodded and Pim beamed. The kid trusted the guardian. Draco just hoped that his trust was not misplaced. Together, all four of them walked out of the departures door just as the mag-rail carriage pulled into the platform.

The carriage floated in between the four opposing magnetic forces of the mag-rail tunnel. It was octagonal in shape, so that the magnetic forces of the mag-rails were distributed evenly for a stable ride. There were two doors on their side of the carriage, one at the front and one at the back.

The inside of the carriage was made up of rows of three by three seats with a walkway in the middle. The carriage had a maximum capacity of one hundred and twenty people, including those who were standing. Draco stood near the entrance doors and held onto one of the roof handholds. He wanted to be able to make a quick escape if he needed to.

Raze, Al and Pim all came into the carriage, and as soon as the boy stepped inside the doors slid shut. Next to the door was a diagram of the mag-rail network. The whole network was elliptical and ran around the outside of the ship. They were currently at the Amenities station, which was close to the water treatment plant, recycling centre and power hub. There were also stations near the Farmlands, the engine bay, the Metropolitan District, the Residential District, the beach side and the recreational sector.

Draco laughed to himself quietly.

"What's funny?" Raze asked.

"They have their own beach on this ship," Draco said.

"There are no ends to human ingenuity if it will result in something that gives them pleasure," Alphonse added.

The mag-rail carriage began to shift. It picked up speed swiftly. Draco's breath was taken away when they finally left the tunnel and saw the beautiful metropolitan vista. The artificial sun shone brightly from the city's dome-shaped roof. Beneath them was the Residential District. Rows and rows of houses stretched out before them. They would not have looked out of place in one of the giant suburban sprawls back on New Earth.

In the distance, the houses gave way to apartment buildings. Past the apartment buildings was the Metropolitan District. The high rises rivalled some of those seen on New Earth, but they didn't have the same architectural grandeur. On New Earth, the skylines were defined by their architects. You could tell who was responsible for making a building just by its silhouette. On board the Metropolis Seven the skyscrapers looked generic and lifeless. They were built to fulfil a function, nothing more.

That was except for the central building which ran from the ground level all the way to the top of the domed roof of the ship. At the bottom of the pillar was a smaller dome which was bigger than some of the apartment buildings near the Residential District. From the top of the dome, a large cylindrical tower rose up. The outside of the tower was made of mirrored glass, and at the top of the tower, there was another dome that descended from the roof. It looked like a tiny glass bubble on the inside surface of a larger bubble.

"That large tower there, do you think that's where we're headed?" Draco asked.

"Absolutely," Raze answered, "That's the bridge. Right at the top of that tower will be where the control centre for the entire vessel is located, as well as the central mainframe."

"That's where the guardian is pulling the strings from?"

"Mhm."

"Then that's where we're going."

Vynce was clean. Jaxon checked him from top to bottom and had not found a single mark on him. There was no sign of infection at all.

Ava had been awfully quiet after their time travel discussion. Jaxon figured that she just needed some time to let it all sink in. The feeling of helplessness and uncertainty was one of the hardest things to come to terms with when you're interacting with a time traveller.

One of the first things Jaxon was taught at the Agency was to never second-guess yourself. If you are tasked with a mission objective, then everything you do should be focused on that one single objective. The Agency taught him from very early on that you need to have conviction to carry through your decisions. He needed to make sure he made it back to New Earth to deliver the chip. Without it, the fate of New Earth and the human race was in jeopardy.

Jaxon began to re-seal Vynce's suit. The smartsuit came back together easily. The foam-like substance immediately bonded back with itself as soon as Jaxon touched the edges together.

Jaxon started sealing up the side of Vynce's suit when he suddenly lurched back into consciousness. Vynce jumped up from the bed and tried to grab his assault rifle from his back, but it wasn't there. It was sitting next to Ava over on the couch.

"Whoa, whoa. Vynce, it's us. Jaxon and Ava. You're safe," Jaxon said.

"Safe?" Vynce asked as he looked around the med station. He slumped down against the wall and muttered, "safe, safe..." breathlessly.

"How are you feeling?"

"I thought I was dead meat when that thing grabbed me in the water. Then before I knew it, I was out of the water and something else had me. It slammed me against the wall, and then, this," he said and motioned at the room around him.

"We just checked you over for signs of infection. There were no tears in your suit, so as far as I can tell, you're clean."

Vynce exhaled then asked, "Where's everyone else?"

Ava got up from the couch and walked over to Vynce. She offered him a hand up. "We don't know right now. We were separated from them when we followed you, but we'll find them again. We've just got to work out where they are. Jaxon tells me that we can talk to other med stations across the ship from in here, so I guess we'll give that a shot and hope for the best."

"I'll log in and get started on that," Jaxon said and headed over to the wall display.

For a moment Ava didn't know what to say. After a few awkward seconds she smacked Vynce upside the head and said, "Well now you owe me one life-saving rescue."

Vynce smiled. "Thanks for coming for me. I would have died if you didn't."

"Thank Jaxon too. If it wasn't for him, I would have lost you in the flooded tunnels and I'd probably be dead too."

"Remind me to thank him for keeping you alive too. I thought I was never going to see you again."

Vynce moved in closer to Ava. He wanted to pull her close and wrap his arms around her. She shocked him by moving away, cutting off his advance.

"I'm sorry Vynce, but I can't. Not... not right now. Alright?"

At first, Vynce was angry. He just wanted to show Ava that he was grateful that she had saved his life. Sure they had history and they gave each other a hard time about it, but it wasn't like he wanted to lay her down right in the med station and fuck her. He wondered exactly what had changed while he was unconscious.

"Yeah it's fine," he said and put his hand on her shoulder. She put her hand on his shoulder too and shook him gently.

"Thanks," she said.

Jaxon tried to browse the system for other med stations. Jaxon tried a number of med station connections, but no one was answering. He had almost given up hope of finding anyone alive when he managed to connect to someone in the Residential District.

The face that he saw in the display made his heart skip a beat.

"Hello?" it asked, "is there someone alive there?"

The face was familiar, yet completely alien at the same time. Jaxon was a man out of his own time, and he was looking into a vision of his own face, twenty years younger. He had worn his hair short back then, but his eyebrows and chin were just as severe as they would continue to be throughout his life.

"Hello?" past-Jaxon asked again.

Future-Jaxon engaged his voice modulator and began to speak. It was one of the strangest sensations he had ever experienced. He had heard the words before, but many years ago, and on the receiving end. Now that he was speaking the words himself in an unfamiliar voice, an extremely disconcerting feeling of déjà vu came over him.

"Yes, we are alive here. We're at the recycling sector med station. What's the situation there in residential?"

"It's bad. There are a group of us here still alive, but there are creatures everywhere crawling all over the place. Have you seen them?"

"Yes, we've seen them. We've even managed to kill a few."

"Do you have guns?"

"Yes, we do."

"Can you come and get us? We've only got a few weapons, but we're trapped. I've started the quarantine protocols here, but sooner or later they'll get in. We need help."

"Sit tight. We'll be there as soon as we can."

"My name's Jaxon. Ask for me when you get here."

"My name's Reinhardt. We'll be there soon."

The display went blank. Future-Jaxon turned back and said, "That was fucking weird. I've lived through a lot of things, but that right there takes the cake. It feels like I just turned reality inside out."

He had remembered the masked man he has spoken to on Metropolis Seven his entire life. By the time he had gotten his assault suit he was wearing he didn't even realise that the mask was exactly the same as the one worn by the man who he had met on the Metropolis Seven. Never before had he suspected that it was actually himself that he had spoken to.

"You said earlier that if you two ever meet, then reality could actually implode in on itself. Is that a possibility?" Vynce asked.

"I doubt it, but stranger things have happened," Jaxon said.

"Stranger than the destruction of the fabric of reality?"

"Stranger? Yes. More devastating? Not likely. That's about as destructive as you can get."

"As long as you're okay with dealing with the consequences," Vynce said.

"Just one question," Ava said, "how the fuck are we actually going to get to the Residential District? Do you even know where the hell we are right now?"

"Very clearly. We're very close to the Amenities mag-rail station. If that's running, we should be able to get to the Residential District fairly easily."

"How exactly are we going to get there?" Vynce asked.

"We'll use the access tunnels. They might be a bit of a squeeze, but they're a straight shot right to the station. Otherwise we'll have to detour through the recycling plant. That'll take us out of the way and waste a lot of time."

"I love dark, claustrophobic tunnels!" Vynce said and looked over at Ava, hoping to bait her into snapping back.

She didn't respond and Vynce's joke fizzled.

Jaxon pressed his hand against the red light next to the door and said, "Quarantine protocol override. Code 0110. All clear."

'Removing quarantine protocols. You are now free to exit the med station. Have a wonderful day,' said the automated voice.

"Open maintenance hatch," said Jaxon.

Part of the white floor of the med station lifted up and swung open.

FIFTEEN

Inside the moving mag-rail carriage, Pim and Raze sat in the corner, talking about what life was like back on New Earth. Pim couldn't remember all that much about it. He was very young when his parents brought him onto the Metropolis Seven, and now they were gone. Pim wouldn't have anyone to go back to when he landed back on New Earth. Raze wanted to believe that they would find his parents somewhere on the ship, but knew that the odds were slim.

Draco leaned against the carriage's wall and looked out over the metropolitan vista before him, Metro Tower sat at the back of the giant cityscape. Around it were high rises and the apartment buildings of the Entertainment District. The buildings radiated out from there, becoming smaller and more akin to a suburban neighbourhood full of family homes and parks. Draco caught his first glimpse of the artificial beach off on the east side of the city. He smiled to himself as he saw the small white tips of breaking waves, and thought back on the last time he had actually gone to the beach. Perhaps a vacation to Vitu Anju was just what he needed as well.

The mag-rail carriage rocketed past the deserted artificial beach and began to glide over the Residential District.

An automated voice spoke as the carriage began to slow. 'Warning, track obstruction ahead. Our maintenance crews have been dispatched and will attend to this inconvenience immediately.

We are now stopping at Residential Station. Alternate travel arrangements will be made available to you at the station. Have a wonderful day.'

Raze and Al got to their feet. Pim had gone as white as a sheet.

"No, we can't stop here. There are monsters out there!" Pim said.

"It's okay. We'll protect you," Raze said.

"I know you're scared, but we don't have any other choice. We need to get to the centre of the city so we can save everyone, and the mag-rail can't get us there. Like Raze said, we'll protect you," Draco said.

Pim nodded hesitantly.

The mag-rail slowed and the Residential Station came into view.

"How are you looking for ammunition, Raze?" Draco asked.

"Four magazines for the rifle. Two clips for my pistol."

"Al?"

"My batteries have recharged from earlier. I have five rifle magazines remaining and three pistol clips. And you, sir?"

"One clip left, four in the chamber."

Raze offered Draco his pistol and his remaining clips. Draco took them.

"You're the marksman, Captain. One clip in your hands is worth the same as three in mine."

Draco holstered the second pistol in the compartment on his left thigh, along with the spare clips. The mag-rail carriage came to a stop inside the Residential Station, and the doors slid open. The station looked identical to the Amenities Station. The departure platform was separated from the arrivals platform by a thick sheet of glass. After they stepped off the mag-rail carriage, the doors closed and the carriage began heading back the way it had come. The display screens above the entrance doors came to life as Draco and the others walked towards it.

'Welcome to the Residential District,' said the voice of the guardian. The screen showed the face of a smiling man, dressed in the black and red uniform of the Metropolis Corporation.

"Where do we go from here?" Draco asked.

'I'm afraid the mag-rail track from here is blocked. You'll have to continue through the Residential District on foot. Luckily for you, all roads lead to Metro Tower. That's exactly where I need you to go. If you continue walking in the direction of the tower, you will reach it.'

"What of the dangers? Is there anything you can tell us?"

'The greatest danger is in the belly of the ship, and you have never been further away from it. Continue on toward the tower, and we will talk further once you arrive there. You may find some abandoned vehicles which may expedite your arrival.'

"Guardian. That's what you are, isn't it? You're the shell program designed to protect this ship in the event of the death of its captain, isn't that right?"

The image on the screens flickered for a moment.

'You are correct, Captain Goldwing. I am nothing but a computer program. I lack the ability to do what needs to be done to save the rest of the survivors on board this ship. For that, I need your help. I am not your enemy.'

"If you had been up front and honest with us from the start, perhaps this might have been a little easier on the both of us."

'Of course, you are correct. I am simply following my programming parameters.'

"Those parameters have caused me the loss of the rest of my crew. You damn well better make sure they make it back to us alive. Because if they don't make it out, no one does. Do you understand?"

'I'm not sure I do, Captain Goldwing.'

"We'll get to Metro Tower. We'll do whatever it is you want us to do to save this ship, but you need to guarantee the safety of our other three crew members, you got that?"

'I understand. I will provide them with whatever aid I can, in return for your full cooperation.'

"Agreed."

'Very well, Captain. I will speak with you further when you arrive at Metro Tower.'

The screen went blank, and they continued into the Residential Station. The doors to the Residential District were open. Draco, Raze and Al surveyed the station before stepping across the threshold. There were no fleshlings waiting for them.

At the bottom of the stairs was a parking lot filled with electric cars and cycles. Their owners had left them, never to return. It was difficult to believe that they were on board a starship. It felt like they were walking through a terrestrial city.

"Can you get any of these running, Al?" Draco asked.

"I believe I can," Al said.

A low-cut hedge surrounded the car park. The streets looked very similar to those found on New Earth, paved with bitumen. Just like on New Earth, all of the vehicles on Metropolis Seven were electric. The charge coils which powered the vehicles were embedded within the road itself.

Al got to work on the first bike while Raze and Draco kept an eye out for any potential threats. Pim stayed by Raze's side.

"Al, do those schematics you downloaded from the engine room include the street layout of these districts?" Draco asked.

"I'm afraid they don't, sir. They only include the overall layout of the ship, and maintenance access. Unfortunately I am still being blocked from accessing the mainframe."

"Damn."

"It is unfortunate, but to be expected. If a guardian program has been activated, its protocols would try to ensure that no foreign systems had access to it, otherwise you could re-program a guardian to do whatever you want them to do."

"Do you think you could do it?"

"Re-program the guardian?"

"Yes."

"If I had access to the Icarus' mainframe, perhaps I could muster up the power to crack the shell, but as we are cut off from it, I'm afraid that I don't possess the ability. Not unless you'd like to have me non-functional for the rest of our time here."

"No, it's fine. Just trying to explore every avenue."

"Of course, Captain. Ah. Here we are! The first bike is up and running. Remarkably low security, actually."

Al pressed the ignition button. The engine engaged, the dash display turned on and the headlight flickered on.

"There isn't really anywhere to hide a bike here on the ship, so I don't imagine they have much trouble with theft," Draco said.

"They also only work on the roads and the parking lots, so you can't take any of these vehicles anywhere they're not meant to go. Well you could, but there's no reason to, because they wouldn't even work! Wonderful anti-theft system."

Al moved onto the second bike and started rewiring it. Draco walked across the parking lot to Raze and Pim. The artificial sun beamed down on them from the domed sky above.

"Any sign of movement out here?" Draco asked.

"None. Pim's been telling me the best way to get into the city from here," Raze said.

"Is that right?" Draco asked as he got down on his haunches to talk to Pim face-to-face. "What route would you recommend, Captain Pim?"

Pim smiled bashfully and said, "I'm not a Captain."

"I don't see anyone else around here, so you're good enough for me."

Pim laughed and his smile widened. "You just need to follow this road onto the big one then drive straight ahead. That's how Mum and Dad used to take me to the city."

Draco ruffled Pim's hair and said, "Good man. We'll be there in no time."

Ava, Vynce and Jaxon shuffled single file through the through the maintenance tunnel. It was cramped, uncomfortable, and took so many twists and turns that even Jaxon had a hard time orienting himself. But worse were the sounds coming through the pipes all around them. It sounded like the pre-tremors of an oncoming earthquake and the sound of rolling thunder in the distance. But there was also the clattering, clambering sound of something chittering around the underbelly of the ship.

A sudden head-spin made Ava lose her balance momentarily. She shot out her arm to grab a pipe to steady herself, but her fingers didn't grip the pipe. She landed heavily, and Vynce rushed to help her back to her feet.

"You alright?" he asked.

"Yeah, I must have tripped," she said.

Her right hand felt strange. It felt numb. Like she had slept on it and pinched something. She hoped that the bone needle hadn't caused any permanent nerve damage. Ava concentrated her mind on clenching and unclenching her fist. There was a jerkiness to the movements that terrified her. The bone needle may have torn a ligament or ripped one of her muscles. She decided that when they reached the next med station, she would take her suit off and inspect her arm. Clearly her smartsuit had not been able to repair whatever damage had been done.

The numbness was bad enough, but the itch was worse. After her fall the itch got worse. She clenched and unclenched her fist as they continued on and hoped that the feeling in her arm would return.

They came to a junction. In the centre was a maintenance hatch which led even further down into the ship. Jaxon stopped and swore to himself.

"What's up, big man?" Vynce asked.

"I don't recognise this area at all," Jaxon said.

"Shit. I got pretty turned around in those tunnels too, so I don't even know which way we're facing right now," Ava said.

"Me either," Vynce said.

A voice came through the overhead speakers and said, 'Captain Goldwing has asked me to ensure that your journey through the maintenance tunnels is a success. I will light your path. Follow the lights, and you will be out of here in no time.'

Emergency floor lighting came to life down the right corridor.

"Wait a second. Aren't you the sonofabitch who's responsible for us being down here in the first place?" Ava demanded.

'Your captain is the reason why you are down in these tunnels and the reason why your crewmate's life was in danger. Your captain failed to comply with a directive given by me, and you three paid the price for his decision.'

"Just who the fuck are you?"

'I am the captain of this ship, and I'm offering you safe passage to the rest of your crew mates. Your captain, along with two others from your ship, have just disembarked from the Residential mag-rail station. They are on their way to Metro Tower. If you'd rather not accept my assistance, then so be it.'

"Have you got any proof? How do we know you're not just saying that to get us to do what you want?"

'One moment.'

Suddenly a video file began playing on the virtual projection display inside Ava and Vynce's visors. They saw Captain Goldwing, Raze and Alphonse disembarking from a mag-rail carriage.

'Is that sufficient?'

"Yeah, it'll do," said Ava.

'Follow the lights. Not much farther now.'

They followed the lights down the corridor.

"Guys, tell me I'm not crazy when I say that this doesn't feel right," she said.

"You're not crazy," Vynce said.

"Definitely not crazy," Jaxon said.

"Did you guys see that they have a kid with them?" Vynce asked.

"Yeah, that means that there are actually people asides from us and this jerkbag alive on this ship," Ava said.

After following the corridor for some time, it began to slope upwards. Light from outside began to subtly illuminate the corridor around them. At the end of the corridor was a ladder, which led up to an open hatch. Light shone down on them from above. The artificial sun was high in the sky.

Jaxon climbed the ladder first, and then Vynce followed closely after. Ava began to climb, but her right arm was even more numb than it had been before. Was it blood loss? Nerve damage? She tried to grip the rungs, but she kept slipping. There had to be tendon damage at least because she couldn't grip the rungs with her fingers. She used her good left hand to pull herself up slowly.

"Ava, you okay down there?" Vynce asked.

She stopped climbing. She looked at her right arm, and saw that it looked bigger than it had before. It was swollen.

"I'm not sure. It's... it's my arm. I'm hurt," she answered honestly.

"You're hurt? What happened?" Vynce asked.

It began to dawn on Jaxon what was about to happen. His glimpse into the future of the crew of the Icarus had made him privilege to information about things that were to come in their future.

"Can you make it up, or do you want me to come down and get you?" Vynce asked.

"I'm not sure. I think I can make it."

She kept up her slow pace. She used only her left hand to climb, and tried to wedge herself against the ladder with her right arm. When she neared the top of the ladder, Vynce got down on his stomach and offered her his hand.

Ava tried to outstretch her right arm. It was definitely swollen, and it did not like being stretched out. She felt her tendons and ligaments attempt to pull her elbow closed again, but she fought through it and tried to take Vynce's hand.

Her hand refused to obey the signals her brain was giving it. She wanted to grab Vynce's arm and be pulled to safety, but her arm refused to grip anything at all.

Vynce grabbed her arm just below the wrist, and a sharp pain shot up her arm. She yelped more in surprise than pain. She felt her fingers close around Vynce's arm, and start to squeeze.

"Ava, not so tight, yeah? I can feel that through my suit."

"I'm not doing it. I can't control it!"

Her arm squeezed with a strength that she didn't know she had. She heard something crack, and she hoped it wasn't one of Vynce's bones.

"Ava, you're crushing my suit! What the fuck is going on!?"

"I don't know!" she said desperately.

Jaxon grabbed Vynce's ankles, and for a moment Vynce thought that Jaxon was going to throw him back down the maintenance hatch, on top of Ava. But he felt the big man pulling backwards. He pulled both Ava and Vynce out of the hatch.

"Alright you can let go now," Vynce said.

"I'm trying! I'm trying to let go!" she said in panic.

Jaxon knelt down next to Vynce's arm and pulled a black bladed knife from his shoulder holster.

"What the fuck are you doing, man?" Vynce asked in horror.

"Trust me," he said.

Jaxon pressed the hilt, and the blade morphed from a knife edge into a tapered wedge. Jaxon placed the wedge under Ava's fingers and pried her hand loose, finger by finger.

Vynce withdrew his hand quickly and tried to shake the crushing pain away.

"What the fuck just happened?" Vynce demanded.

Ava held her hand against her stomach. The fingers flexed and relaxed, as though they were still trying to find something to grip onto.

"I... I don't know," Ava said.

"When did you get hit?" Jaxon asked Ava directly.

"What do you mean, hit?" she asked.

"Somehow, something from one of these creatures got inside your suit. When did it happen?"

Ava sighed and said, "When we found Vynce. When that fleshling's mouth tumour exploded. There was a piece of bone or something. It was like a needle. It went straight through my arm, and I pulled it out. My suit sealed up the damage and did what it could."

"There's something growing inside your suit," Jaxon said.

"What do you mean growing?" Ava asked and started to feel sick to her stomach.

"Don't worry about that now. We need to get to a med station as soon as possible. It's the only way we're going to be able to save your life. Can you walk?" Jaxon asked.

"I think so."

"Under no circumstances are you to unseal your suit until we can get you to a med station, alright?"

Ava nodded as she got to her feet. Her right arm curled close to her body. Her left arm gripped her assault rifle. The Amenities mag-rail station was in front of them. The enormous x-shaped mag-rail tracks extended down the huge tunnel as far as they could see. There was another ladder leading up to the platform.

"Another ladder. Fucking great," Ava said.

"I'll follow you up. You just take your time, alright?" Jaxon said.

Ava nodded.

Vynce led the climb up the ladder. Ava followed slowly, and Jaxon followed her. The going was slow, but eventually Ava reached the top and pulled herself up. She crawled over to the glass barricade separating departures and arrivals and slumped against it, breathing heavily.

She looked down at the arm curled close to her chest and felt something move beneath the plates of armour. It didn't feel like it moved in any way her muscles had ever moved before. She began to feel nauseous again. Jaxon helped her to her feet, and they headed into the mag-rail station. While they were crossing from the arrivals to the departures gate, an empty mag-rail carriage arrived at the platform.

"Good timing," Vynce offered, but neither Ava nor Jaxon responded. They all shuffled into the carriage and the doors slid shut behind them silently.

"Draco, Raze and Al went to the Metropolitan Station, right? That's where the captain said," Vynce said.

"Yeah, that's right. We go through beach front, residential, then onto metropolitan. We should be there within ten minutes. Do you think you can make it?" Jaxon asked Ava.

"Do I have a choice?" she asked in return.

"Not really," Jaxon said.

The doors to the mag-rail carriage slid shut, and the carriage began to accelerate.

SIXTEEN

The streets were quiet, and that made Draco uneasy. Since they landed on the Metropolis Seven they had been subjected to horrors he had never imagined could exist even in his most terrifying nightmares, but the streets were mostly clear in the suburban Residential District. They hadn't seen any other signs of life since they ran into Pim and his sister.

Al had managed to get another two bikes working. Pim rode with Raze, who was riding just behind Draco. Pim hung onto the big man's waist as they rode. Al rode in back, keeping his sensors tuned for any unusual or unexpected movement. After seven blocks, nothing out of the ordinary had appeared. The suburban community had been abandoned, but there was nothing that suggested that anything unexpected or devastating had occurred.

The electric bikes ran silent. The only sound was the whisper of their rubber tyres on the bitumen. Suddenly Al's motion tracker detected something to their right, inside one of the houses.

"Captain, we need to stop here. I've detected movement. It could be a survivor," Al said.

He decelerated the bike quickly and swung into the driveway. Draco and Raze doubled back and turned in. Al parked his bike. Every house in the neighbourhood looked exactly the same, except for the colour and the front yards. Each house was double-storey, with identical bay windows facing the road. The curtains were drawn across the windows of the house Draco, Al and Raze stood in front of, but the front door was ajar.

Pim grabbed Raze's leg and pleaded, "Please don't go in there. There are probably monsters in there. Please don't go in there! Please, please, please!"

Raze stooped down to Pim and said, "We don't know that for sure. What if we leave someone in here and they need our help?"

"No, no, no! There's no one here! We have to keep going!"

"Raze, wait out here with Pim. Al and I will go and take a look around inside," Draco said.

Raze nodded, and Pim protested wordlessly.

Al cracked the front door wide open and looked inside. The front door opened to the entryway, which then expanded into the living room. There was a staircase leading upstairs from the living room.

"What kind of movement are we talking about?" Draco asked.

"Organic. Sensors picked up movement in one of the upstairs windows." Al responded.

"I was worried you were going to say that."

Al began to climb the stairs as something upstairs moved.

"On your guard, Al."

"Always, Captain."

Al continued up the stairs. The upstairs level was surprisingly dark. The beam of light from Draco's flashlight was the only source of light in the house. They moved up the stairs slowly and stepped into a hallway.

Something moved again. The sound came from their left. There were three doorways in that direction of the hallway. Two were open, and the third was closed. There was something coming from under the frame of the closed door. It was neither solid or liquid. It was somewhere in between.

Al motioned to that door frame and Draco nodded. Al braced himself against the door frame and Draco kicked it with all of his force.

He regretted it instantly.

The floor was covered in thick maroon ooze that seeped from a lump of gelatinous flesh in the middle of the floor. The outside of the ooze was covered in a filmy layer that reminded Draco of the skin of a frog. It was slightly translucent and revealed the flesh beneath the skin. The lump was almost as tall as the ceiling of the room. Four tendrils anchored it to the floor.

A muffled sound came from the lump of flesh. The ball of skin looked as though it was trying to move. Shadows of moving muscles and sliding flesh shimmered under the top layer of skin. The ball began to pulsate and shudder.

"Captain, I believe it may be in our best interests to vacate this house immediately..."

"I think you might be right," said Draco.

A split began to form in the skin of the fleshy lump. Maroon liquid poured out of the wound. Through the crack, Draco and Al could see something moving.

"What the hell do you think it is?" asked Draco.

"I believe this is an egg, or a cocoon, or whatever this biological entity's equivalent is."

The outside of the flesh cocoon was torn open from the inside by a large hand. Draco started backing away, but Al was transfixed. He stood in the door frame and watched.

"Al, what are you doing? We need to go! Now!"

"Just a moment, Captain!"

"Now! That's an order!"

Al didn't move. The creature inside the flesh cocoon bellowed as it used its four massive arms to tear the fleshy exterior of its gestating pod away.

"It's... remarkable," Al said.

The creature looked at him with all four of its eyes and screamed at him with its two mouths. The creature had taken the bodies of two people, a man and a woman, and had fused them together at their sides. They were biologically stitched together at a cellular level. The pair of arms on the outside of the creature had grown to monstrous size. From the height of the creature's shoulder the arms could reach the ground. Each arm ended in a large hand with massive fingers. The two other arms, one feminine, one masculine, curled close to its chest. They were growing into the creature's malformed torso.

The man and woman's heads had begun to fuse together. Their mouths were almost touching. They had almost become one single mouth. As the creature grunted with the effort of learning to stand on its four legs, Al saw that both mouths were lined with jagged broken teeth just behind the row of natural human teeth.

"It's a hunter..." Al said to himself before turning on his heel and running down the stairs after Draco.

"What did you find in there?" Raze asked as Draco and Al burst from the front door.

"Start your bike! Go now! Head towards the city! Go!" Draco bellowed as he ran to his bike and jumped on. He switched the ignition on and blasted out onto the street just as the creature burst through the front of the house after them. Pim screamed.

"What the hell is that thing!?" Raze yelled as he followed Draco, with Al following closely behind him.

"It's a hunter!" Al said, "Just like the one we encountered in the ducts after we docked. It's a creature whose entire purpose is to capture others to convert them into more of these fleshlings."

The hunter was gaining on them. It had learnt to use its new legs with terrifying speed. It was keeping pace with the bikes.

"There's no way we could win against that thing in a fire fight. It'd be on us before we had the chance to line up a shot. We need to try and outrun it," Al said.

Draco looked back to see the hunter. It wasn't just keeping up with them anymore. It was gaining on them. It used its monstrous arms to pull itself along the road at a blistering pace. It picked up chunks of bitumen and flung them towards the bikes as it galloped after them.

Draco swore to himself and desperately tried to think of a way they could deal with the creature.

"It's trying to knock us off the bikes. Evasive manoeuvres!" Draco said.

Al, Raze and Draco began to weave back and forth as they raced down the street. Suburban properties passed them on every side. Draco swore to himself again. They couldn't go as fast ducking and weaving in between cars, and the hunter crept ever closer.

The mag-rail carriage left the dim tunnel and raced out over the Residential District. In the distance to the east they could see the beach front, and in front of them they could see the Metropolitan District, with Metro Tower rising from ground level to the top of the ship where the artificial sky ended.

Ava's right arm ached. The itch had become almost unbearable. She wanted to pull her knife out, rip her smartsuit off, and dig around in her own arm until the itching stopped.

But the worst part was when her arm started to move by itself. She could see her fingers clenching and relaxing, and they would not listen to the commands she was sending for it to stop. Ava closed her eyes for a moment, but the sound of her arm moving around in her suit by itself was enough to jolt her eyes back open.

She got up from her seat and grabbed Jaxon by the neck with the arm that she could control.

"What's happening to me!" she demanded.

"Ava, just wait until we get to the med station and we can get you fixed up, alright? There's no point panicking."

"My own fucking arm won't do what I tell it to do. I can't even feel it anymore, and it's moving around of its own fucking accord. I think I've earned the right to fucking panic a little."

Jaxon sighed, and Vynce looked on silently, unsure of how to react. He hated that Ava had put her life on the line to save him, but she was the one who ended up getting hurt. That wasn't how it was supposed to go. Vynce wanted to be the hero.

"You've been infected," Jaxon said.

It hadn't felt like it could be real until those words left Jaxon's mouth. She released her grip from his neck.

"So what do we do from here?" Ava asked flatly.

"We wait. We wait until we get to the Residential med station, and then we assess to see what the damage is. Once we know how bad it is, then we can choose how we go forward."

"But I live, right? You said that we have a future. That you remember me, and someday I would remember you. Right?"

Vynce winced when he heard the words, 'you said that we have a future'. The only future he wanted was with Ava. That's what their future was supposed to be. Not some fucking time traveller who waltzed in and swept his girl off her feet. That's not how things were supposed to happen.

"You have to tell me that I survive this. You have to tell me that I get to meet you again," Ava said.

"Ava... You know I can't guarantee any of that. Yes, I have memories with you. But the progression of events in time is such an unpredictable thing when you're the one who's travelling through it. I have memories of people who have never existed. My actions have changed the course of history. Because of me, thousands of people who once lived long and happy lives never even existed in the first place. I can't guarantee anything; except that I will do everything I can to save your life."

Ava smirked and said, "Is this the part where you come out and pledge your undying love to me?"

"Not yet. Not in your timeline, anyway. In my timeline, that moment has been and gone," Jaxon said.

Vynce wanted to punch something, preferably the time traveller standing in the same mag-rail carriage as him, hitting on the woman he had fallen in love with.

They passed by the Residential Station and sped on towards the Metropolitan Station. Ava put her left hand on Jaxon's chest. She didn't know if any of the bullshit he was saying was true, but part of her wanted to believe it was. If anything, he had been able to distract her from the growing ache in her right arm long enough to experience a moment of hope.

Vynce looked ahead of the carriage and saw something that made his blood run cold. In the distance, on the cusp of the Metropolitan District, one of the skyscrapers had toppled over right on top of the mag-rail tracks.

"Uh, guys, we might have a problem," Vynce said, pointing out of the front window of the carriage.

Jaxon swore, and Ava let out a resigned sigh.

Jaxon smashed the glass to the emergency brake and pulled it as hard as he could. The carriage began to slow, but nowhere near as quickly as they needed it to. There was no way they would slow down enough to survive the impact with the fallen skyscraper.

The hunter bore down on Draco, Al, Raze and Pim with a speed Draco didn't think possible. The creature shouldered the lightweight electric cars out of the way, hurling bits of bitumen and car parts at them as it ran.

Draco drew a pistol from his thigh holster and shot backwards towards the creature. It hit the hunter in the chest, but the monstrous thing didn't slow down. It didn't react. The bullet didn't even hurt it.

SEVENTEEN

Arak Nara engaged the electromagnetic pulse, and then all hell broke loose.

The Icarus immediately shut down. The lights went out, the door locks disengaged, and the engines cut out entirely. A shielded emergency module within the heart of the Icarus flickered to life and began to reboot the Icarus' operating systems, but it would take a while even before the lights came back on. The engines would take far longer to re-engage, and that was only if the EMP didn't completely destroy the ignition primers.

On the bridge of the Icarus Veck Simms crumpled to the ground. His hands loosened from around Rhken's neck, and she stumbled backwards in an attempt to keep her balance as the maniac fell to the floor.

Rhken's father and sister started to pry the door to the bridge open.

On board the Metropolis Seven, the lights started to go out.

Ava, Vynce and Jaxon began to brace for impact with the toppled skyscraper when they saw a wave of darkness approaching them as the lights of the city began to switch off building by building. Even the artificial sun winked out, which threw the entire cityscape into darkness.

"Grab onto something!" Jaxon yelled and braced himself between two rows of seats.

Ava held on as tight as she could with her left hand, but she still couldn't feel her right arm from the elbow down. Vynce was still standing when the power cut out to the mag-rail system and the entire carriage plummeted to the ground.

Draco, Raze and Al saw the lights going black in front of them. The hunter was still gaining on them and if the lights continued going out they would have to navigate debris-strewn streets in complete darkness. Draco had no idea what kind of low-light or night vision the hunter had, but if it had been made from fusing two bodies together, he was relatively sure it would have human-strength low-light vision. If that was the case, they might just be alright. If it couldn't see them, it couldn't chase them.

The blackouts rolled closer. The artificial sun above them was extinguished, and only the lights on the sides of the road illuminated their path. But they too started to wink out. When the blackout line reached Draco, Raze and Al, their bikes immediately powered down.

Draco was thrown from the seat of his bike. The powered component of his suit also shut down, which meant that he had no access to his enhanced low-light vision. Something slammed into his back and threw him forward.

Draco staggered back to his feet. Something had knocked out his suit's systems. It had to have been an EMP, because the power core that his suit ran on was completely self-powering. It would reboot in just a few moments, but while it did he was without most of the defensive capabilities that his suit controlled.

Without the muscle augmentation activated, it felt as though he was trying to walk through quicksand.

Draco could hear someone getting to their feet from his left.

"Captain! Captain!? Are you alright? I think I hit you!" Raze yelled.

"I'm fine, but shut the hell up until our smartsuits come back online. That thing will be able to hear you!"

Raze shut his mouth as soon as Draco reminded him of the immediate danger. He knew Al had been travelling with them, and he didn't know what would happen if a Child of iNet was hit by an EMP. All Raze could be sure of was that both he and Draco were alive and standing.

The hunter plodded around heavily in the darkness. Its footfalls could be felt just as much as they were heard. It was too close. Draco stepped away from the source of the impact tremors as quickly and quietly as his suit would allow. The Hunter's low-light vision was not good. If it was, it would have seized Draco and Raze already and torn them to shreds.

Raze felt the footfalls of the hunter and heard it panting in the darkness. His assault rifle had been knocked from his hands when he hit Draco. Raze knelt down in the darkness and felt around for something he could use as a weapon.

It was then that Pim started crying. Raze abandoned the search for his rifle and ran towards the sound. The hunter heard it too and moved in for the kill.

The emergency lighting on the Icarus had started to come back online. The amber lighting washed the bridge in its glow. Nook and Reban used the handle of a fire axe to pry the door to the bridge open. Nook rushed inside and held his little girl in his arms.

"Rhken, are you alright? Did he hurt you?" he asked.

"I'm okay!" she said and buried her head into her father's shoulder. She was overcome with relief as she realised that Veck couldn't hurt her any more. She wanted to collapse, but her father held her steady.

"Did he hurt you, honey?" he asked again.

"Is he... Is he dead?" she asked.

"I don't know. But if he's not, he soon will be."

Nook let go of his daughter and turned around to face Veck. His blood ran cold. Veck was standing again already, and he had Reban clutched by the hair in one hand, and the steel fire axe in his other.

"Do you really think I'd be stupid enough not to shield my internal systems against an EMP? You're an idiot, old man. And now your pretty little girl is going to pay for it."

On the Metropolis Seven, Ava tried to get her bearings. The mag-rail carriage had slammed into the ground at speed. There was something on top of her. It felt like a slab of metal. She still couldn't feel her right hand and forearm, but the top of her arm had also started to itch and burn. Whatever was growing inside her suit was spreading upwards.

Ava pushed against the metal slab with her left hand. She could barely lift it. If she could use her other hand she might be able to, but not like this. There wasn't even enough room to engage her buster pod and smash her way out of the debris.

Ava heard other movement in the carriage, but couldn't see anything in the darkness.

"Who is that? Jaxon? Vynce?"

"Ava, where are you?" Vynce yelled.

"I'm over here. Follow my voice! There's something on top of me. I can't get free."

"Hang on, I'll come to you. Keep talking."

"Alright... This is a lovely mess we've gotten ourselves into. A ship the size of a city, infested with some kind of form of life that wants to kill us, and the fucking lights go out. What are the fucking odds of-?"

Suddenly a heavy weight crushed down on her from above.

"You're standing on it!" she yelled breathlessly.

"Oh shit, sorry!" Vynce said as he stepped off the huge piece of metal.

The relief was immediate. Ava could breathe again.

"That's better. First thing you do after coming to rescue me is to remove my ability to breathe. Well done, my knight in shining armour."

"Don't get too excited just yet. My smartsuit's out of commission. I don't know if I have the strength to move it without my augments. We may have to wait until our suits come back online."

"I can't wait that long. You pull the fucking thing, and I'll push. I've got one arm and two legs left."

Jaxon's voice joined them and said, "I'm here too. Vynce, with you and I working together we should be able to move this. Ava, you push from beneath and you tell us if you're hurting, alright?"

"Alright," she said.

Ava braced herself with her good arm and her legs and began to push upwards. Vynce and Jaxon pulled on the chunk of debris, and it slowly began to lift.

"Yeah it's going. I might be able to crawl out if you lift it just a little further."

Vynce strained with effort and said, "You just tell us when to hold it."

"A little more," she said.

"Just a little more."

"Okay! I can crawl out!"

"Hurry!" Vynce said.

Ava used her good arm to crawl along the bottom of the mag-rail carriage. She crawled with all of her strength until she was out from under the debris. The heads-up display inside her suit flickered back to life. She engaged her low-light vision and turned back to see Vynce and Jaxon.

"I can see you boys. My smartsuit's back online. How about you both?"

"Yeah, mine's coming back now," Vynce said.

"Mine runs off my own bio-rhythmic energy. Mine will only ever stop working if I cease biological functioning," Jaxon said.

"Well that's fucking grim. Just promise me you'll keep functioning until you save the girl, alright?" Ava said.

"Well I -"

"Yeah yeah, you can't tell the future. Blah blah blah."

"No, it's not that. I was just about to say that I can promise something. You will be saved, but your arm won't be."

A cold lance of fear stabbed Ava's chest. She had known as much since she lost feeling in her arm. It was reinforced when the fucking thing started moving around on its own. And then when the itching and burning had started, she was tempted to cut the whole thing off herself. Even though she knew it had to be done, she was still afraid.

"Yeah, I thought as much," she said trying to hide her fear.

"We need to make it to the Residential med station as soon as possible. It runs on its own power supply with built in EMP dampeners, so it should either be back online or in the process of rebooting by the time we get there."

Vynce saw movement outside the mag-rail carriage. The artificial sunlight had been keeping the creatures on the ship at bay, but now that it had been extinguished, they had started to emerge from their hiding places.

"Guys, we have to go. Now," Vynce said as he loaded a magazine of flesh-shredding rounds into his assault rifle.

Draco's suit began to reactivate. He had heard Pim's crying at the same time Raze had, and had started running towards him. The fleshling hunter had started bounding towards the sound too. Draco activated his low-light vision.

He activated it just in time to see the hunter reach Pim at the same time as Raze. Raze launched himself at the boy, arms outstretched, but the hunter reached Pim first. It grabbed the boy with both hands. Pim's cries turned into screams of terror that were tragically cut short as the creature pulled the boy in two.

"No!" Draco yelled. He pulled his pistol from its holster and started firing at the hunter.

Raze activated his low-light vision just in time to see the hunter throw the two pieces of Pim to the ground. The boy's right leg twitched, and across the road, the young boy gasped for breath through collapsed lungs. After a moment, he was still.

Raze launched himself into the hunter. He climbed up the thing's arm and pulled a small tool from his belt. When he lit the sunstorm welder up, his low-light vision immediately overloaded. Raze pushed the superheated welder into the creature's face. The creature's eyes popped from the intense heat. It bellowed in agony and clutched its face.

All around them, Draco could see movement as more fleshlings began to emerge from the darkness. Small ones crawled from the drains and manholes. Bigger ones came out of the houses and the spaces in between. They came in all shapes and sizes, but one thing was common between all of them. They had all been made from human beings. Most of them had lumpy growths on their bodies, as though there were unseen tumours beneath the skin. They all looked towards the sounds of agony coming from the hunter with slack-jawed deadness.

Raze put his pistol to the side of the hunter's head and fired. At point blank range, the creature's head exploded in a shower of bone and brain matter. Raze jumped off the creature. Its left side slumped as the brain was destroyed. The right half of the creature tried to stay upright but couldn't. It desperately tried to get back to its feet, but Raze put a bullet in its right brain too. The hunter stopped moving.

The other fleshlings did not. They shuffled, scuttled and hobbled towards Draco and Raze. Raze engaged his low-light vision again and found his rifle. He picked it up and began firing at the closest fleshlings. A single volley of bullets tore through their bodies, stopping them in their tracks.

Draco took aim at the fleshlings closest to him, putting a single bullet into each of their heads as they approached.

"They seem to go down pretty easy," Raze said.

"These smaller ones do, yeah. Not the big ones though," Draco said.

"Can you see Al?"

"Not yet. But we've got to find him."

Draco activated a vision filter based on heat. Al's fusion core would still be burning hot even if his systems had been knocked out.

The heat vision showed Draco just how much trouble they were in. Creatures surrounded them on all sides. No more large hunters, luckily. But it would only be a matter of time until bigger ones started showing up once they found out that someone had turned off the lights.

Down the road a little further Draco saw a stationary point of heat. The creatures around them were moving erratically, but this point of heat was completely stationary. It had to be Al. Draco marked the target on his heads-up display and switched back to low-light vision.

Draco ran towards Al. He dispatched three creatures on the way to his fallen crew member. When he reached Al, there was no sign of movement or function.

On board the Icarus, Veck Simms held Reban by the hair as Nook and Rhken looked on in terror. The non-emergency lights had slowly started to come back on, which meant that the engines would soon be ready to come back on line. And Nook knew that after the engines came back online, Evie the artificial intelligence would come back online too and fry Veck Simms from the inside out.

But he couldn't stand idly by while one of his girls was in danger.

"Let my daughter go Veck," Nook said.

Veck laughed. "You seem to misunderstand the situation. I have absolutely nothing left to lose. Nothing. Whatever happens, your captain is going to deliver me to the Alliance military and they're going to kill me. Am I wrong?"

"No, you're not wrong."

"So what incentive is there for me to not cause as much damage as I can before that happens, hm?"

"For once in your damned life, you could try being a good person."

"A good person? I am the only person in this galaxy who truly cares about our species. I am the only person in the galaxy who is prepared to do what it takes to make sure we survive and take our rightful place."

"And what place is that? Top of the food chain? Galactic totalitarianism? Supreme overlord of the universe?"

"Nothing so grandiose. I don't want to rule the galaxy. That sounds like far too much work. I am just a freedom fighter, fighting for our species to choose how we live our own lives."

It was Nook's time to laugh.

"You're a fool. An absolute fool. No matter what you do or where you go, you will still be a part of the Galactic community. You can't escape that. It's just the way it is. The human race is still in its infancy compared to other species. You don't know better than them. They've seen the rise and fall of entire civilisations and have written the galactic laws around the protection of all sapient species in the galaxy. No one's interests are put before anyone else's. Surely you can see that."

Veck had become visibly agitated as Nook spoke. His teeth ground in his mouth, and his lips were pulled back in an animalistic snarl.

"I can't imagine what it must feel like being trapped inside such a feeble mind. You're a slave, and you don't even know it," Veck snarled.

"I'm not a slave. I just care about other people. Human and alien alike. I don't put my wants or needs above the wants and needs of any other sentient life form in the galaxy."

"Right now, I really want to pound your pretty daughter's face in with this axe."

"And I don't want you to. I love my daughter. She's never done any harm to anyone, yet you'd take her life as though you were swatting a fly. You're a madman. A psychopath."

Veck didn't answer. His eyes narrowed and his mouth became a thin grim line.

Nook spoke again before Veck could. "If you're intent on shedding more blood before we deliver you to the military, then kill me. Not my girls."

"No!" Reban shouted.

"You can't!" Rhken yelled.

"That is a mighty fine offer, but I'm going to have to decline," Veck said and began to swing the axe backwards.

Nook ran towards Veck and simultaneously drew his pistol from his holster. Nook needed to get close to Veck if he was going to use it. The psychopath would use his beautiful daughter as a bullet shield without a second thought. Nook tried to get close enough to grab Veck and wrestle him away from Reban.

Veck pulled back on Reban's hair, and she let out a yelp of pain. Veck dropped the axe, and his empty hand split in half. A long razor-sharp blade flicked out from the underside of Veck's forearm. Nook tried to back away, but he was far too close.

Veck slashed upwards in an arc that sprayed blood across the roof of the bridge as he cleaved Nook in two from stomach to shoulder.

"Huh. I guess he made me an offer I couldn't refuse," Veck said as he let go of Reban's hair. She fell to the ground and screamed. Rhken crawled over to her and held her tight. Rhken couldn't cry. She couldn't let herself. She held her sister as she watched the life fade from her father's eyes.

Vynce peppered the approaching creatures with flesh-tearing ammo. Each bullet that hit a creature turned whatever extremity it hit into a red pulpy mess. The creatures were coming out of the houses around them. The road was full of debris from the mag-rail carriage crash, and up ahead it was blocked by the fallen skyscraper.

"Can you walk?" Jaxon asked Ava as he helped her to her feet.

"I think so," she said.

"Can you run?"

"I don't know..."

"I'm going to pick you up, and we're going to run. I need you to hold on tight to me, okay?"

"I'll try," Ava said.

Jaxon picked Ava up. She held tightly around his neck with her left hand, and cradled her right across her chest. She tried to will it to stay motionless, but it wouldn't. The fingers kept twitching and moving of their own accord. The itching and burning had started to get worse. It was moving further up her arm, towards her shoulder.

Jaxon broke into a sprint. Vynce followed closely behind.

"I know where we are. You follow me, and shoot any of these things that get in the way, alright?" Jaxon asked.

"You got it," Vynce replied.

A fleshling lurched out from behind an overturned car. It had a giant hump on its back that was growing an extra arm. Each finger ended in knife-like claws. Vynce put one bullet in its head and one in its chest. Its head snapped back, gurgling wetly as it fell to the pavement.

Jaxon took a right at the next intersection and ran down the road. They had arrived in the Metropolitan District. The rows of houses in the Residential District gave way to apartment buildings and retail stores.

In the distance there was a building that still had power. There was light coming out of its windows.

"See that building up ahead? It's running off the med station's power grid. We're almost there Ava. Hang on."

She held tight. Vynce continued firing. There were so many of these creatures crawling out of the darkness that Vynce had to make sure each shot counted. He wondered to himself how the hell Jaxon planned on getting them out of the med station once they got in.

When they reached the building with power, Jaxon turned left. Metro Tower's top floors had become illuminated again. It shone like a beacon floating in the darkness.

Relief and fear washed over Ava as she saw the white sign with the red heart in it. The med station. Her right hand twitched uncontrollably.

When they reached the med station, an armed civilian stood behind the doors. He was wearing riot gear and a gas mask. The man hit a switch to open the front doors and aimed his rifle squarely at Jaxon and Ava. Vynce joined them and raised his weapon at the civilian.

"Lower your weapon!" the man yelled.

"Not until you lower yours!" Vynce yelled back.

Neither man moved until Jaxon stepped forward. He had engaged his suit voice modulation to disguise his voice and said, "One of our crew mates is sick. She needs aid immediately."

The man in riot gear trained his rifle on Ava. His eyes widened when he saw her twitching right hand.

"She's infected, isn't she? She's not coming in. You two can come in, but you need to leave her outside."

"I'm not leaving her outside. I'd sooner kill you and force my way in than leave her out here to die," Jaxon said.

"Ditto," Vynce added.

"She's infected. I can't risk exposing my people to her," the man answered.

"Talk to Jaxon. He's expecting us," Jaxon said, referring to his younger self.

The man shouted over his shoulder, "Jaxon! These folks said that you're expecting them! Mind explaining yourself?"

Jaxon's younger self came out from the main med station doors.

Old Jaxon was mildly surprised that the fabric of the universe didn't tear itself asunder, even though he'd already lived through these events once before.

"Quickly, let them through!" Young Jaxon said.

Old Jaxon nodded. The man in riot gear stood aside, lowered his weapon, and allowed them into the med station. Jaxon carried Ava across the threshold, and Vynce followed. The man in riot gear closed the thick glass door behind them and resumed his post.

"Don't worry about Ronnie. He's just a prick," young Jaxon said.

"Can you take us to an operating theatre? We need to get started as soon as possible. Could you please call Doctor Katelyn Harris? We'll need her," old Jaxon said.

"Whoa, how did you know she was still alive?" young Jaxon asked.

"Just get her for me, please."

"Okay! What do I call you anyway?"

"Just Reinhardt."

"Okay. Reinhardt. Got it. I'll go get Doctor Harris now!"

People were crowded around the med station like sardines in a can. They all looked like they had been through the end of the world. Jaxon knew that this was the only bastion of living humans left aboard the Metropolis Seven, because he had been here when all of the communications had been lost with the other med stations. There was no one else left.

Doctor Harris came out of the emergency room. Her hair had been tied back into a bun, but she had been run off her feet for so long that strands of it had come loose and stuck out to the sides.

"What's the emergency?" Doctor Harris asked.

She saw Ava's arm, twitching and swollen, and her eyes went wide. "What's going on here? Who let this infected woman through quarantine?" Doctor Harris exclaimed.

Young Jaxon stepped forward and said, "I did. You can help her like you helped everyone else."

"You let them in here against quarantine protocols! You've risked all our lives!"

"If I didn't then all three of them would be dead, and that would be our fault. I'm done with death," young Jaxon challenged.

"And what about everyone else? What happens if she infects the rest of us?"

"We can do it just like we did for Mark, remember?"

Doctor Harris' anger started to subside. She put a hand to her brow and sighed loudly.

"Fine," she said, "Bring them through to the operating theatre."

EIGHTEEN

Alphonse's non-functioning body lay motionless next to a trash can. Draco fired his pistol at the approaching horde of fleshlings crawling from the houses, drains and the darkness all around them. He wanted to believe that Al would come back by himself, but as the seconds passed his belief waned.

Draco thought about carrying Al somewhere safe. But he didn't know of a single place on the ship that would be safe. He looked up briefly and saw that the top few floors of Metro Tower were illuminated. That meant that the guardian shell program would also be back online and should bring all of the other systems back online one by one.

There was no way Draco could make it to Metro Tower while carrying Al. It would be too much for Raze to keep the creatures away from both of them. Draco refused to put Raze's life in danger like that. But he couldn't just leave Al behind.

"I'm trying to think exit strategies here Raze, but I'm coming up short. Any ideas?" Draco asked.

"I don't know much about Children of iNet. If this was an EMP, would his systems even be able to survive it?"

"I don't know."

"Even if he did come back, could we be sure he wouldn't be a danger to us and malfunction?"

"I don't know, but I can't just leave him."

"What about giving him some juice?"

"Of course! It'll take most of my suit's systems offline for a few minutes, though. Will you be able to hold out long enough for it to reboot?"

"Do it, Captain. I've got your back."

The life support systems of the smartsuits included various functions, including defibrillators built into the palms of the hands. The small jolt of energy required to restart a human heart would have no effect on a Child of iNet. Draco changed the output to ten times normal levels and placed his hands on Alphonse's chest.

"Clear!" he yelled.

Raze picked off the creatures as they shambled towards them.

Al's body didn't lurch like a human body would have done. He remained motionless.

"Raze, he's not moving! Have you ever seen this done on a Child of iNet before? I don't know what I should be looking for!"

"We don't even know if his internal systems still function at all. His circuitry might be fried. There may be no coming back for him, Captain."

"I am not going to leave him here!"

Draco's smartsuit's muscle augmentations had been disabled. Even if he could leave, he wouldn't be able to move at full speed. Without Al, Draco knew that he wouldn't make it out of there alive.

"I'm going to try again!" Draco said and commanded his suit to charge for another burst of energy.

"If you do that, you'll knock your suit functions out!"

Draco ignored Raze, even though he knew the big man was talking sense. But Draco had never been able to leave a man behind. He placed his hands on Alphonse's chest again. As soon as the shock left Draco's palms, his suit shut down completely. The suit became instantly heavier, and Draco slumped backwards. His low-light vision cut out. The darkness was blinding. The only thing he could see were Raze's muzzle flashes as his bullets tore through the twisted and deformed bodies of the infected fleshlings coming at them from all directions.

"Captain? What's the status?" Raze asked, but Draco could not hear him. Even the smartsuit's shortwave comm systems were non-functioning.

Suddenly a light flickered to life in front of Draco. The light soon became a blazing beacon as Alphonse's boosters powered up. Flashes of light illuminated the cityscape as Al flew up into the air firing super-heated blasts of energy wildly into the darkness.

The city went dark and something landed heavily on the ground behind Draco. He was lifted effortlessly to his feet, and his suit began to power up again.

"-am powering up your suit now, Captain. Stand very still," came the voice of Alphonse through his comm channel.

"It's good to hear your voice again, old friend," Draco said as his low-light vision kicked in again. Alphonse stood in front of him with his hand on Draco's chest.

"Thank you for rebooting my system, Captain. I fear I would have been lost for quite a while longer had you not assisted."

"I couldn't leave you."

"And I'm afraid we can't stay. The good thing about being a Child of iNet is that no matter what, you're still conscious. Well not in the same way that consciousness affects a living biological organism, but our subroutines only stop when we've entirely stopped functioning. While my body was out of commission, I attempted to see what systems I could access as they were rebooting, before they had a chance to engage all of their security protocols."

"What did you find?"

"The guardian shell program is not a program at all. There's someone in Metro Tower with access to all of the ship's system, pretending to be the guardian shell program. From their position, they should have been able to set this ship back on course, but for some reason they couldn't bring the engines back online from where they were. They needed us to do that. This tells me that someone tried to limit their access in some way, but only managed to cut them off from the engine controls before they were stopped."

"It was probably the same person who put the ship on a crash course with Krakaterra," Draco said.

"We can't stay here to discuss this right now Captain, we have to move. When you rebooted me, I disabled all cameras in this vicinity. Whoever is in Metro Tower should not be able to see our movements when the systems come back online. I have found a safe location."

Draco, Raze and Al headed down the city street strewn with debris. On their right was a cinema, advertising films beamed straight to the Metropolis Seven from across the galaxy.

Next to the cinema was a café precinct. The frontage of most of the stores had been destroyed, either by looters or the creatures now roaming the ship. Two rows of cafes and restaurants opened into a laneway, and each side rose up into apartment buildings. Draco knew that they couldn't be too much further from the Metropolitan District, and their entrance to the Metro Tower.

Alphonse turned into the laneway between the cafes and restaurants. The creatures were there, but they seemed as though they were just watching them. Most of them made no attempt to attack.

"What's going on with these things? They could overwhelm us with their numbers alone, but they're just standing there," Raze said.

"I think I know the reason, but now is not the time to discuss it. Press forward. Once we're safe, we can talk in detail," Al said.

Draco ducked to his left as a huge creature stumbled out from the front of a gift store. It stood on four powerful legs made from two fused human waists. Its torso stretched upwards, with three gangly pairs of arms punctuating where one human body ended and another began. Two of the heads had melted into nothing but hairy patches of skin between the arms, but the head at the top of the torso column watched them through milky eyes. The creature was undoubtedly another hunter like the one they had encountered, but this creature made no attempt toward them. It simply watched as they ran past.

"What the hell is going on here?" Raze asked.

"Follow. I'll explain shortly," Al said.

Reban's skin was ghost white. She hadn't said a word since Veck eviscerated her father. Rhken held her close. She was the younger sister, but she felt like she had aged twenty years in the last few hours. She and her sister were now alone with the madman. Arak Nara was nowhere to be found. Rhken had her suspicions that there were places inside the ship that only Captain Goldwing knew about, so maybe Arak was in the ship somewhere, hidden away.

Someone had engaged an EMP from somewhere, but had it come from inside the Icarus, or from outside? Could it have come from the Metropolis Seven? Or maybe it could have come from the Vartalen battle cruiser they saw trailing the Metropolis Seven earlier.

If her father had died because some greedy Vartalen bastards were going to take control of the Icarus or the Metropolis Seven, Rhken wanted them to pay blood for blood. But if it was the Vartalen, at least they would destroy Veck Simms. They could be Rhken's own hand of vengeance.

The Vartalen had a nasty reputation for selling young human girls to pleasure houses for all manner of alien life to defile. Rhken began to realise that she might wind up dead before this ordeal was over. She would kill herself before she let the Vartalen capture and sell her. At least then she'd be with her father in the almost infinite energy of the universe.

Reban shivered as Rhken held her.

At the control console, Veck tried everything he could do to get the ship's engines back on line. The control panel was completely unresponsive. The display had not re-illuminated itself since the systems were knocked out by the EMP.

"You. Rhken. Leave your sister and attend me," Veck commanded.

Rhken closed her eyes and felt a tear roll down her cheek.

"Now, or I will assume your sister is attempting to sabotage my efforts to commandeer this ship, just as your father did. And if that's the case, I see no reason why she shouldn't suffer the same fate."

Rhken didn't hesitate. She got to her feet immediately and joined Veck at the console.

"Why isn't this working?"

Rhken sniffed. Her nose had begun to run.

"I don't know. My father was our chief engineer, and you just killed him. If anyone knows how to get all of our systems back online, it was him."

Veck looked out through the windows at the front of the bridge and realised that the Metropolis Seven was still moving. The EMP hadn't knocked out the giant ship's engines. If it continued on its course, it would collide with the Icarus.

"I don't accept your answer. I believe that you do know how to get this ship back online, but you lack the proper motivation," Veck said and pushed Rhken to the side. He strode over to Reban and pulled her up by her hair. She screamed as Veck's forearm split apart and revealed the blade that had killed her father. He held the blade to Reban's neck. It was as cold as death.

"Don't hurt her! I'll do whatever you want, just don't hurt my sister, please!" Rhken pleaded.

"I want you to do whatever it takes to get this ship back online, and get the engines started. Because if you don't, I'll kill your sister right in front of you. You'll get to watch the life drain from her eyes as the penalty for your failure."

"I need to go back to the engineering bay if I'm going to figure out what's working and what's not. And I may need my sister's help.

Running the ship is a job for three people. I can't do it on my own."

"Very well. Do what must be done," Veck said as he pulled the blade away from Reban's neck and let go of her hair.

Reban dropped to the floor and sobbed uncontrollably. Rhken went over to her and helped her to her feet.

"Sister, we need to get the ship back online. I need you to be strong. For Dad. For me. Please be strong, and please help me do this. I can't do this on my own," Rhken said.

Reban tried to blink the tears away, but they kept coming. She nodded quickly and allowed herself to be led out of the bridge and down towards the engineering bay.

Underneath the bridge, Arak Nara had heard the entire exchange. The stronghold had been built with this very scenario in mind. There was a single vent built behind the command console which funnelled all of the sounds from the bridge down into the hidden hold beneath the decks.

Nook was not the first man who had died as a result of Arak's actions, but it was the first he had ever truly felt miserable about. Arak knew that he had to find a way out of the chamber he was in and find a way to disable Veck for good. He was sure that Captain Goldwing would understand that he had to kill Veck. The Alliance bounty was payable whether Veck was dead or alive. If they had just killed Veck when they had captured him, Nook would still be alive. If it wasn't for Captain Goldwing's history with the madman, they would have killed Veck when they found him. But Captain Goldwing was not that kind of man. He wouldn't kill if he didn't have to.

But Arak could kill. He had done it many times before. But how in the galaxy could he kill Veck Simms? All the EMP did was knock him to his feet and put the entire ship in danger. With most of the ship's systems offline, Arak couldn't even engage the self-destruct mechanism. But that would mean the death of everyone aboard the

Icarus. If they destroyed the Icarus, they would be destroying the only ship they could use to escape.

Arak was frozen with indecision. Every path he could take seemed to lead him and the rest of the crew into a worse situation.

Arak began to mentally take stock of what should have been in the armoury. There were plenty of spare assault rifles, pistols and shotguns, but he didn't know whether they would even make a dent in Veck. A shotgun blast from point blank to the head would likely produce enough force in his organic tissue to blow his brains out. As far as Arak knew, Veck still had an organic brain, and still needed it to function. But getting close enough to him without being detected would be the hard part.

And even if Arak managed to get close enough to take the shot, there was still the possibility that Veck could use the girls against him. Or worse. They might get drawn into the crossfire, and Arak would have two or three deaths weighing on his conscience, not just one.

The sound of their footsteps had faded, and Arak knew that if he didn't make his move immediately, he risked being detected by Veck. He climbed up the access hatch and put his hand flat against a red panel on the wall. Above him, the control console began to shift as it cleared a path for Arak to ascend back to the bridge.

Arak lifted himself out of the hatch, and as soon as he was clear the control console returned to its former state. There was a red and brown lump in Arak's peripheral vision, and he dared not turn his gaze towards it. The door leading out of the bridge had been forced open. There would be no way to seal it again until they docked onto a planet where they could get repairs done.

Arak stood with his back against the wall and peered out into the main corridor that led through the ship. He couldn't see Veck and the girls, but he could hear their footsteps echoing down the corridor. Arak slipped off his boots and left them on the inside of the bridge door. He stepped over the threshold and walked silently down the corridor after them.

For a moment Arak had the urge to laugh out loud when he thought of the irony of the situation. He had left his old life as a mercenary assassin behind when he agreed to pilot the Icarus, but now those skills were the only thing that could possibly get them out of this situation. The darkness had always been Arak's friend, and as he continued on towards the darkened bowels of the Icarus, he began to feel comfortable again.

The girls would lead Veck to the engineering bay. It was very likely that they would need to jump start the power core to get the engines back up and running, and it would take time to prime the charge. Arak hoped that the girls were clever enough to stall Veck. He was clever when it came to warfare and torture, but Arak hoped that he was not as well-versed in starship maintenance.

The corridor began to curve to the left, and on the right hand side of the curve was the entrance to the armoury. Arak slipped into the armoury silently and looked around for something that he might be able to use to get the upper hand against Veck.

Veck followed behind the two girls. One of them was strong. The one he had taken first had been the strong one, but her sister had none of her strength. She was nothing but a mewling piece of human effluence unfit for continued survival. She had no fight in her at all. No sense of self-preservation. He would have to kill her at some point, he knew that with certainty. But her sister, the mousy one, there was some fun he could have with her yet.

"I'll give your father credit for one thing. He didn't beg me to spare his life. He didn't try to bargain with me. He accepted the certainty of his fate as ramifications for his actions."

The mousy girl didn't respond, but the other one just began to cry louder.

Veck smiled as they walked on.

They reached the end of the main corridor. The engineering bay was only lit by dim emergency lighting, but it proved that there was power here. The circuits hadn't been fried as a result of the EMP. From the top of the stairs, the whole place looked as though it was in disarray. But he supposed that this was just the way the girls and their late father kept things in order.

'Order from chaos,' Veck thought to himself.

Veck clapped his hands together suddenly and both girls winced. "To your tasks now, girls. Get this ship back online and you may both live through this."

"Reban, come with me," Rhken said and led Reban over to the main console.

The console was completely unpowered. Whatever energy was being routed to the emergency lighting system was not making it to any of the ship controls. Rhken wished her Dad was still here. He was the one who knew the Icarus from the inside out. She didn't even know where to start. Her Dad always told her what to do. She couldn't fix the ship by herself. There was no way.

Rhken knelt down by the side of the main console and opened an access panel. She didn't really know what she was looking at, but she just wanted to look busy so Veck would leave her alone for a few minutes.

"Reban, can you please find me a multi-tool?" Rhken asked.

Reban nodded and walked over to the tool bench and started looking for one. Rhken didn't actually need a multi-tool, but she wanted to keep her sister busy enough so that she couldn't think of their Dad. Reban only looked half-heartedly through the tools strewn over the bench while Rhken kept tinkering inside the access panel.

All of the connections were undamaged. Rhken didn't know why there wasn't any power flowing to the control console. Every other time the ship's systems had shut down, that console had been one of the first things to reboot on its own.

"I can't find a multi-tool!" Reban shouted from across the room.

"Have you tried the belts hanging on the wall? Sometimes Dad leaves… left… his in his belt."

Reban hesitated before grabbing her Dad's belt. Tears welled up in her eyes as she reached for it, and spilled over as she pulled the multi-tool out of its pouch. She brought it over to Rhken and handed it down to her.

"Could you please go and check the ignition primers in the engines? The EMP may have fried them," Rhken asked.

Each of the four thrusters on the outside of the ship was run by an individual engine. Two engines sat on the floor of the engineering bay, and the other two engines hung from the roof above. There was a single grated platform between the two engines at the height of the room, and a steep staircase led up to it from the bottom of the engineering bay.

Reban nodded and climbed the staircase to the top level. She wanted to be as far away from Veck Simms as she could get. She crossed to the right hand side of the engineering bay. She opened the engine casing and inspected the ignition primer. She pulled the small plug out of its socket. The red plastic casing had been scorched.

"It's fried," Reban said and held the primer up for Rhken to see.

"The others will probably be the same then, but go check just to make sure, okay?"

Reban crossed over to the other engine and removed the engine casing. That primer was blown as well. She pulled it out of its plug and said, "This one's gone too!"

"Okay. I'll check these ones down here," Rhken said as she got to her feet.

Reban stayed on the top level as Rhken checked the two engine blocks on the bottom floor. Rhken pulled one blown ignition primer out of the engine on the far side of the room, and then crossed the floor to check the last engine.

Reban looked out of the windows at the back of the ship and thought that the Metropolis Seven had gotten closer since the energy tethers had disengaged.

"Uh, sis? Is it just me, or is that huge ship getting closer to us?" Reban asked.

Rhken lifted her head from the inner workings of the engine and pushed her glasses back up on her nose. Her eyes widened as she saw how close the big ship had become. It had always looked huge, but it had never looked so close. She could almost make out the individual panels that made up the outside of the hull. She could even see the illuminated bridge. There was also a dark speck of something above the bridge, but Rhken couldn't quite make out what it was.

"You may be right. What if the EMP only knocked out our engines, and not the engines of the Metropolis? How long would we have to get out of the way?" Rhken asked.

"Not long at all," Veck replied calmly.

Rhken whipped her head around to look at Veck, who was now standing right beside her.

"You knew," she said breathlessly.

Veck inclined his head, smiled slightly and said, "So once again girls, get to your tasks quickly and you both might just live through this."

NINETEEN

Doctor Harris wheeled Ava into the emergency room on a gurney. Her heart was beating so fast that she could barely discern the individual beats. Hospitals and medical facilities had always creeped Ava out. When she was much younger, almost too young to remember all the details, she visited her mother in the hospital after she had come down with a sudden illness. One day her mother had been fine, and the next she had been hooked up to machines which breathed for her, ate for her and kept her heart beating.

But it was her mother's eyes she remembered most. Her mother couldn't speak, but her eyes said everything. She knew that she was going to die. She knew that the doctors and nurses were just going through the motions. Making her as comfortable as she could be in her passing. In those last days her mother's eyes were filled with fear and confusion.

Ava so desperately wanted to reach out and touch her mother. She wanted to tell her that everything was going to be okay, and that the doctors were going to fix her. But she never could. The sickness had taken hold too swiftly. Within four days of being admitted she had faded away.

In the emergency room on the Metropolis Seven, most of the beds were full. Ava couldn't see the patients, but she could see medical waste bins overflowing with bloody bandages and torn clothes. The bright fluorescent lights passed above her, and her breathing became shallow and rapid.

A hand closed around her good hand. Jaxon. He squeezed it gently, and she squeezed it back. She desperately wanted to see his face. She didn't want to admit it, but she had started to feel something towards this time-traveller. She didn't know what it was she was feeling. It couldn't be love. She loved her guns, and she loved her captain.

Her mind then turned to Vynce. She had feelings for him, but she could never see herself being in a relationship with him. He was fun. He was a distraction, but he wasn't really the type of guy she wanted to be tied down to. She didn't know if she really wanted to be committed to anyone, but she had something there with Jaxon, and she could tell that he felt it too.

Jaxon said he had met Ava many times before. Were they comrades? Friends? Something more? He said that he had told her he loved her in his past, but the moment hadn't yet arrived in her timeline. Secretly she hoped that it was all real, and they had been something more.

That meant two things. Firstly, she had to survive this ordeal. Whatever happened to her, she had to survive. How could Jaxon possibly have memories of her after her first memory of him if she didn't survive the events of when they first met?

Ava's head started to hurt as she tried to understand how time travel could even be possible, let alone how she could be caught up in some kind of romance with someone at different points on her own timeline.

Secondly, there would be no future for her with Vynce. If there truly was a future with Jaxon, then she couldn't lead Vynce on when he obviously had feelings for her. It would be better to be a little cruel to him to save him from further heartache the next time Jaxon came into their lives.

"Ava, we're here. Now we're going to need to cut you out of your suit so we can assess the damage to your arm. Do you understand?" Doctor Harris asked.

Ava nodded.

"Help me with her helmet," Doctor Harris said to Jaxon.

Jaxon came around behind Ava and gently lifted her head. There was the small hiss of air as the pressurisation of the suit dissipated. Ava's opaque faceplate was lifted away from her head. She tried to look up at Jaxon, but the light was far too bright.

Jaxon put two fingers to his faceplate, then to her forehead in a gesture of affection before splitting the rest of her helmet away. Doctor Harris lifted her head and slipped a mask over her nose and mouth.

"We're administering a general anaesthetic right now, so you'll start to feel yourself slip away. I want you to understand now that we may have to take your arm."

Jaxon held the sides of her head and stroked her left ear gently. The light had started to get much brighter. The doctor was talking, but she couldn't focus on her. Ava tried to lift her right arm, but it didn't move.

"Do what you gotta do, doc," Ava said. Her eyelids had become leaden weights. She couldn't keep them open any longer. She closed her eyes and slipped into unconsciousness.

"Alright, she's out cold. You there," Doctor Harris said and pointed at Vynce, "I need you to go and get me some restraints. Head back out to Emergency and ask Nurse Jones. Tell him you need a chest and arm restraint, and then come back immediately."

Vynce wanted to protest. He didn't want to leave Ava's side. Why should Jaxon get to stay with her, while he had to go and fetch some medical equipment? It wasn't fair. None of it was fair. Vynce left the room without voicing any of his thoughts and tried to track down Nurse Jones.

He didn't like the way he was feeling. He was angry. It was the kind of directionless frustrated anger that you simply couldn't allow to bubble over. It wasn't Ava he was angry at, and it wasn't even Jaxon although Vynce wished that he could have been angry at him. It would have been so much easier that way.

It should have been Vynce that held Ava's hand to comfort her. He wanted so desperately to be with her, to hold her, and to tell her that everything was going to be fine. But he knew that Ava had already made her choice; it wasn't him.

Vynce found Nurse Jones and grabbed the restraints. He rushed back into the operating theatre and immediately wanted to avert his eyes. Ava lay on the operating table, naked from the waist up. The swollen wreck of her right arm was still covered. Whatever was growing within her suit had been contained within it. And when they finally set it free, there was no telling what they might see.

"The restraints! Quickly!" Doctor Harris said.

Vynce brought them over and attempted to hand them to Doctor Harris.

"Well what are you waiting for? Restrain her! The big one goes around her chest, and the small one goes here, on the infected bicep. Just below the shoulder."

Jaxon took the small restraint from Vynce and started to wrap it over her bicep. As he lent over her, he tried not to stare at her breasts, but his gaze lingered for longer than he knew was decent. He scolded himself and forced himself to look away. He remembered flashes of their night of drunken passion.

"The chest restraint, now!" Doctor Harris snapped.

"Right, sorry," Vynce said and fixed the restraint around Ava's chest. It sat just above her breasts, and threaded through the spaces in the operating table under her armpits.

"Are you both staying for this?" Doctor Harris asked.

"Yes," Vynce said and Jaxon just nodded.

"I'm going to ask you to make yourselves useful, if that's the case. Have either of you had any previous surgical experience?"

Vynce shook his head slowly.

"I've had some surgical training. What do you need me to do?" Jaxon asked.

'Figures. Of course Wonderboy has had some fucking surgical training,' Vynce thought to himself.

"Firstly, I'll need you to cut the rest of her suit off her arm. We need to assess what kind of growth has begun, and how far the infection has spread. You're in no danger now. The growth shares her circulatory and nervous systems, so it has been anaesthetised as well," Doctor Harris said as she began to wipe down Ava's shoulder with disinfectant gel.

Jaxon picked up a scalpel from the instrument tray next to Doctor Harris and began to cut the smartsuit from Ava's arm. He weaved the sharp blade in between the plates of armour and took extra care not to cut too deeply.

"What about her blood? Is there a risk of contamination or infection we should be aware of?" Jaxon asked.

"No. The blood is clean. That's not how the infection is spread. Once we excise the infected area, the infection won't reoccur. From what I've seen so far, the infection only grows from area at the source of contact. It's passed through muscle, bone and skin. Not through blood. Once the infected area has been excised and disposed of, she will be fine. It's probably best for you boys to stay in your suit though, just in case," Doctor Harris said.

"What about you, Doctor?" Vynce asked.

In response, she partially unbuttoned her top. There was a purple growth that sat just between her breasts. It was covered in a clear plastic adhesive.

"There's no excising that. It's already grown too deep into my sternum. It might not look like much from the surface, but it's got tendrils winding around my ribs and in between all of my internal organs. I already know that I won't leave this ship alive," Doctor Harris said.

"How are you still alive?" Vynce asked

"Injecting mild sedatives directly into the core of the growth," she said and pointed to the clear plastic adhesive over the lesion, "It slows it down, but it won't stop it."

"Shit, I'm sorry doc."

She held her hand up in front of her and said, "I've heard that so many times in the last 72 hours you wouldn't believe it. It's getting old. I'll keep doing what I can until I can't do it any longer."

"I hear you. What do you need me to do?" Vynce asked.

"If you've got no surgical training, then you're better off waiting outside until this is done."

"But... I want to stay with her."

"You'll be of more use to her waiting outside. You won't get in the way, and we won't get distracted. And if you're really concerned about her finding out you didn't stay by her side the entire procedure, I won't tell if you don't. Understand?"

"Yeah, I get you," Vynce said and stormed out of the operating theatre.

Never in his life had he felt more useless and out of place. He could infiltrate an enemy facility effortlessly and silently. He could take out a target from miles away with pinpoint accuracy. But there was nothing in the universe he could do to help Ava. He walked back through the emergency room and out into the medical centre. All eyes fell on him.

It was only then that he noticed that most of the people here in the medical centre either had limbs missing, or bits wrapped in blood-soaked gauze. Doctor Harris had clearly been busy. The medical facility wouldn't have looked out of place in a war zone.

In the operating theatre, Jaxon began to peel the smartsuit away from Ava's swollen, infected arm. He pulled the smartsuit down from her bicep. The skin there was still pink and healthy, but as he pulled the smartsuit away from her lower bicep and her elbow, Ava's skin had begun to take on a greyish purple hue. It looked bruised and dying.

A sharp unnaturally shaped piece of bone jutted out from the back of Ava's elbow. From there onward, her arm was unrecognisable. He slid the rest of the smartsuit off Ava's forearm and had to stifle his revulsion at what he saw. The inside of her forearm had been split, and hundreds of tiny tooth-like appendages had begun to grow on either side of the gash. Flat bone-like protrusions covered Ava's arm like the hardened armoured scales of a crocodile. If Jaxon had not been wearing his own suit of armour, his hand would surely have been shredded if he tried to touch it.

"Crafty little shits, aren't they? When they first manifest, they make it so that you have to touch them. Can you see those dark spots under the skin there, between the scales?" Doctor Harris asked.

"Yes," Jaxon said as he noticed darker coloured patches underneath the skin.

"Don't touch them. If the skin there is broken, they release spores in the air to infect even more people. It's only natural that you would want to help someone who has been struck down with an affliction like this, and that's what these sonofabitches use to their advantage. If you touch them, you risk infection. If you try to get rid of the growth by surgery, you risk even more spores getting out into the air. The only way to be completely sure is to get rid of the entire infected area."

"Do you know anything about what they are? Where they came from?" Jaxon asked.

When Jaxon had first been on board the Metropolis Seven, none of his questions had been answered. He had escaped and gone back to New Earth, just as he had been instructed to, but he never heard anything more about the ship or the organisms on board. The ship was still officially listed as missing in his time, twenty years after the fact. For the first time, he actually had a chance at getting some more answers.

"No. A about a week and a half ago there was an incident. A few maintenance workers came complaining of strange sores and growths. Then in that span of days, the infection had spread to most of the passengers and crew."

"Have you ever heard of anything like this before? Any other similar infections?"

"No. This is beyond anything I've ever seen or heard of. Even the deadliest viruses back on Old Earth didn't have the destructive force that this thing does. I would hate to see what an organism like this could do if it touched down on an inhabited planet."

"A week and a half to infect one hundred thousand people... I wonder how long it would take to infect a whole planet."

"A matter of months. At most. If it was a densely populated planet like Central, well I think the infection would spread even faster. Because it doesn't just infect animals. It infects plants too, and turns them into reservoirs of infectious material. Instead of ingesting carbon dioxide and exhaling pure oxygen, the oxygen is laced with infectious spores. A single tree infected with this organism could silently infect hundreds, if not thousands before they figured out where it was coming from."

The thought made Jaxon's blood run cold. If even a single infectious host of this organism escaped from on board the ship, entire civilisations could be at risk.

"How have you been able to figure all this out?" he asked.

"It's all I've been able to think about. I was a botanist back on New Earth before I accepted a position here on the Metropolis Seven. And I've had my own experiment going since I was infected," Doctor Harris said and motioned behind them to a clear glass case set back into the wall.

It would have normally been used to hold infectious waste material, but now it was home to one of the most grotesque pot plants Jaxon had ever seen. It had once been some kind of bonsai tree. But now there were bluish tumorous growths all over its leaves and stems. It roots had grown out of the soil and were coiled around a disembodied hand. There were other cleaned white bones strewn around the specimen's pot.

"After something gets taken over by this infection, they become carnivorous. Even plants. They need meat and protein to survive and grow. They don't even care whether it's infected meat or not. They'll eat anything," Doctor Harris said.

"Is this what you do with all the bits you cut off people?" Jaxon asked.

"Just the small ones. We incinerate the bigger pieces, like we're going to do with your friend's arm."

Ava's infected arm moved, and Jaxon stepped back. The gash in the middle of her forearm closed a little, relaxed open again, then tried to snap shut again.

"What's it doing?" Jaxon asked.

"These organisms have metabolisms unlike anything I have ever seen. We'll need to up the anaesthesia to keep it quiet while we remove the limb," Doctor Harris said as she held her finger against the illuminated clear glass control panel. The anaesthetic levels went up, and Ava's infected arm stopped twitching.

As soon as the limb stopped moving, Doctor Harris grabbed a small plasma cutter from the instrument table and began feeling the greyish purple skin above Ava's elbow, working her way slowly up to Ava's bicep. As she reached Ava's bicep, Doctor Harris stopped feeling and flicked the plasma cutter on. A bright blue jet of energy burst from the end of the cutter. Doctor Harris adjusted the blade to a small cutting edge, just long enough to cut through the layers of skin on Ava's arm, but not to cause damage to the muscle beneath. She touched the cutting edge to Ava's skin and drew the cutter across the bicep.

Red blood welled from the site of the cut immediately. Ava's skin crackled faintly from the extreme heat of the plasma cutter. Doctor Harris lengthened the cut and used a pair of forceps to widen it. She gently shifted Ava's bicep muscle and swore under her breath when she saw a lumpy purple tendril winding through the muscle mass and around the bone.

"The infection has spread this far. If it's made it to her shoulder joint or her collar bone, there will be no saving her. It will already be in her chest, and I can't remove that."

"Do what you have to do, doc. She'll make it. She's strong."

Doctor Harris continued to cut upwards from the initial incision and followed the tendrils as they wound through Ava's flesh. She found three tendrils in all.

Doctor Harris stopped cutting and breathed a sigh of relief.

"We're clear," Doctor Harris said as she folded a flap of skin back down over the exposed muscle and bone.

"She'll make it?"

"Yes. But we need to take her arm. It's dangerously close to her chest cavity. Another hour and there would have been nothing I could have done."

Doctor Harris immediately got back to work and began cutting the skin around Ava's shoulder joint. After the skin had been incised, she pulled it backwards, down over Ava's bicep as though she were pulling off a bloody sock. She left a single flap of skin, which would serve as the cover for the wound after they had removed her arm. Doctor Harris methodically cut through the muscles and tendons that held Ava's arm to her body. Her arm came free easily once all of the anchors had been severed.

"Grab me a medical waste bag from that cabinet over there, would you? A large one," Doctor Harris asked.

Jaxon grabbed a large black medical waste bag. He unzipped the bag, and held it open. Doctor Harris dropped the remains of Ava's arm into the bag. She then took it from Jaxon, zipped it up and dropped the bag into the medical waste disposal chute.

"It's done. The incinerator has been running non-stop since all of this started. In a couple of minutes, her infection will be nothing but ash and smoke."

Doctor Harris walked back over to Ava. Her smooth white shoulder joint was empty. Doctor Harris began to fill the wound with healing gel. She then stretched the flap of skin from the outside of Ava's arm across the wound. The healing gel gripped onto the flap of skin and held it in place while the doctor fused the edges shut with the plasma tool. Doctor Harris wrapped Ava's shoulder in bandages. The healing gel inside the wound had put a stop to the bleeding. Only light spots of blood soaked through the layers of bandages.

"Why did you want to know if I'd had any prior surgical training? You didn't actually ask me to do anything," Jaxon asked.

"I could tell that both you and the redhead wanted to be here. Which would have been fine, but your friend looked like he was about to pass out. I didn't want him in here if he couldn't handle what was about to happen."

Jaxon nodded, then looked over Ava's motionless body and wondered how the hell he was going to get her out of this ship alive.

TWENTY

Alphonse led Draco and Raze slowly through the plaza. The fleshlings continued to watch them as they walked. Draco kept his pistol up. Alphonse held his rifle with its muzzle pointed to the ground.

"Do you know what the hell is going on here, Al?" Raze asked.

"No, I don't. I don't understand why they're not attacking us. These things have done all they can to try and capture us since we arrived on the ship, but these ones are not. I do believe there is a reason for their non-aggression, but I currently have no idea what that reason might be," Al said.

"That's not very encouraging," Raze said.

The end of the plaza opened into a circular open market. It reminded Draco of the markets they held back on Orpheon when he was a young boy. The stalls all used to sell hand-crafted jewellery, trinkets, bootleg entertainment and home-grown fruit. Each stall was covered in a canvas cloth, to keep the sun off the stalls and their owners.

The stalls on the Metropolis Seven were covered in multi-coloured canvas cloth as well, even though the artificial sun inside the ship didn't produce heat or ultraviolet radiation. Most of the stalls in the plaza had been destroyed or damaged. The rotten remains of fruit and baked goods were strewn across the ground. In places they had been trampled into dark brown mush.

The outside ring of the market was roofed with red brick tiles, and in the shadows were hundreds of fleshlings, watching and waiting. Draco, Raze and Al weaved through the debris and crossed the market.

They came face to face with the cluster of them which were slack-jawed and staring. One of the creatures had a growth that looked like a malignant tumour pushing its jaw almost down to its chest. Small tendrils had begun to weave the flesh of its jaw and chest together. Another had a head that bulged so far to one side that Draco wondered if there was any room left in its head for a brain. Two creatures had flesh that looked as though it had been melted together in a fire. Their bodies were attached to each other at the back and shoulder. It was almost impossible to tell which of the lumpy growths had once been their arms.

Al stepped forward and spoke.

"I hope that you have some intelligence left inside of you, for I need you to listen to me now. We need passage through your ranks. Stand aside, and allow us to pass. We will not cause you any harm if you do not cause us harm."

The fleshlings did not respond.

"Uh, I don't think they can understand us Al. Maybe we should-" Raze started to say, but fell silent as the infected began to move.

The fleshling with the tumorous growth in its mouth made a wet gurgling sound and moved out of Al's path. They moved with clarity of thought that Draco didn't think possible. They moved in unison and made a path that was wide enough for two men to walk abreast. Once they had shuffled backwards, they continued to stare blankly at Draco, Raze and Al.

Al took the first step forward, and relief washed over Draco when the infected didn't immediately fall upon them and attack.

"This is the most terrifying thing they've done so far," Raze said.

Draco nodded in silent agreement. They walked through the

infected and left the circular market through a large red stone arch. They crossed the street and approached a squat domed building that looked like it should have been part of a military compound, not part of a Metropolis long-vacationer. There was a single door at the front. The rest of the building was black and completely featureless.

"It's a hazard shelter," Al said, "It protects from all manner of hazards. Explosives, biological, radiation, nuclear. There are shelters like these all over the ship. They also shelter the devices inside from EMP blasts."

"Sonofabitch. How about outside communication? Could we get back in contact with the Icarus?" Draco asked.

"I am unsure. However if there is somewhere capable of bypassing the communications block coming from Metro Tower, this would be the place," Al said.

Next to the door of the shelter was an identification swipe panel. The light at the top of the panel was red. Draco tried to open the door, but it would not budge. Alphonse held his hand over the ID panel, and the light changed to green. Something clicked inside the door. Draco pushed on it, and it slid open smoothly. The door opened into a small lit chamber, and Draco stepped across the threshold.

"This is the air lock. We have to be decontaminated before the ship will let us enter the shelter itself," Al said as he stepped into the small chamber.

As soon as Raze stepped inside, Al initiated the decontamination sequence. The door clicked as it locked shut and jets of steam laced with decontaminate shot out from the roof and walls. After a few moments the mist dissipated, and the door into the hazard shelter slid open.

'Please exit the decontamination chamber,' a female voice said over the loudspeaker. It was not the same voice as the person who had been speaking to them since they landed on the ship.

The inside of the hazard shelter was smaller than Draco thought it would be. It was made up of a single circular room with a number of tables and chairs arranged in the middle. There was a console on the far side of the room, and it looked to be functional. There was also a locked cabinet next to the console, and behind the glass doors Draco could see a number of weapons and boxes of ammunition.

Al walked over to the closest set of table and chairs and sat. He beckoned Draco and Raze to join him.

"Please my friends, sit."

Draco and Raze both pulled up chairs and sat down. Draco wouldn't say so out loud, but it felt good to sit down. He didn't know how many hours he had been awake, and couldn't remember the last time he'd had something to eat or drink. But on board the Metropolis Seven, he wouldn't have trusted any food even if he found some. The passengers of the ship had been infected with something, and Draco hadn't seen anyone but the little boy Pim who had been spared. Could the food be the infection carrier?

Draco suddenly lost his appetite.

Al began to speak, "While my body was in stasis, my consciousness wandered and it found many interesting things. I believe those things may alter our end goal aboard this ship."

"Alright Al, hit us with what you've got," Draco said.

"Firstly, I am now completely sure that whoever has been manipulating us since we arrived on this ship is not a guardian shell program. It is someone masquerading as a guardian shell program. They wish to appear omnipotent aboard the ship. They attempted to assert their dominance over us. However if it actually were a guardian shell program, it would do all it could to keep us alive. It wouldn't actively attempt to put us into danger."

"So there's a puppet master trying to pull on our strings, just like we thought."

"Trying, yes. But not succeeding. They have access to most of the ship's functions from where they are, so they must be located on the bridge. At the top of Metro Tower. I found a small piece of information floating in the datastream that shows that the captain of the ship disabled the engine controls from the bridge directly."

"Why in the world would he do that?" Raze asked.

"Any number of reasons. Perhaps the captain felt that the growing infection aboard his ship should be destroyed, but whoever took control of the ship from him thought otherwise. This may be the captain's way of ensuring that whoever took control of the ship from him couldn't achieve their goals," Al said.

"If that's the case, then we played right into their hands. They told us to get the engines back online, and we went and switched them back on," Draco said and he shook his head.

"There was also some further worrying information in the datastream, Captain Goldwing. It appears that this vessel's main medical facility in the heart of the city was outfitted with a whole slew of new medical equipment roughly one New Earth week ago. There were encoded pieces of data referring to an infection and quarantine. We may have walked aboard a plague ship, Captain. There may not be any escape for us."

Raze shook his head and said, "I still don't know how you managed to find out all this info, Al. You're like a wizard."

"No, just very lucky. Our friend up in Metro Tower was jamming long-range and wireless communication for the longest time, but the initial EMP blast completely knocked his jamming system out. There is a shielded data network running throughout the entire ship to protect against their network going completely down if they were ever attacked or boarded. And it just so happens that I was able to bypass the extremely simple defences they had on their network and get access to it. That took a little wizarding," Al said and inclined his head.

Raze laughed. "Al, the technomancer. You always come through in a pinch."

"I do try so very hard," Al said.

Draco couldn't help but join into the laughter.

"So where do we go from here, Al? It sounds like all roads lead to Metro Tower," Draco said.

"Indeed, but there is some further information I need to impart before we proceed any further. I came across some other worrying information in the datastream. It seems as though -" Al said, but was cut off by a familiar voice coming through the comm channel.

"Al? Al!? Is that you!?"

"Vynce! It's good to hear your voice! How is Ava? And our time-traveller?" Al asked.

"Full report, now," Draco ordered.

"Uh, shit's all kind of fucked up here, cap. Ava's in surgery right now. Jaxon's with her-"

"Surgery? What's going on?" Draco asked.

"She got hit by one of those things. She said it was some kind of needle thing. Cut straight through her smartsuit. And ever since then, something has been growing inside of her. The doctors here, they've seen it before. They need to cut her arm off, or the infection's going to spread. Then she'll be just like all of those other creepy fuckers shambling around the ship."

"Will she be okay?" Raze asked.

Vynce was silent for a moment, then said, "Not sure, big guy. She'll live, I'm sure of it, but I don't know how she'll be when she comes to. They're taking her arm at the shoulder. They said that the fucking thing's got tendrils running up her bones underneath the muscles. If they don't take it all, it'll keep growing."

"The important thing is that she'll live through this. Whatever comes after, comes after. We'll all be there for her," Draco said.

"Right," Raze and Al said.

"Of course."

"Where are you three right now?" Draco asked.

"We're at the medical centre in the Residential District, just on the border of the Metropolitan District. But we're not the only ones. There are survivors here. They say they're the last ones. We've got maybe a hundred and fifty people here. Maybe more, maybe less. We're armed, but not well. We're pretty safe for the moment."

"Excellent. I'm going to need to ask you to start talking to the survivors. This ship has to have evacuation ships. Ask around and find out as much information as you can about where they are, and how we can get to them. Alright?"

"You got it Captain."

"Where's Jaxon?" Draco asked.

"He's... with Ava."

The awkward pause was enough to convey the meaning to Draco, so he quickly changed the subject.

"You have your mission. The first moment you find out some information, you get in contact with us again. You got that?"

"Yeah, got it Captain. You guys going to keep the comm channels open this time or what?"

Draco looked at Al and raised an eyebrow.

"I will work my way through the system as best I can and attempt to remove whatever impasses I find. However, when the power comes back on I don't know how much control I will be able to retain. We may lose communications, so it would be imperative to make a contingency plan now," Al said.

"Right, well we can't really go anywhere while Ava is in surgery. I'll find out whatever I can about evac ships, and I'll try to report back to you what I know. But if I can't get through to you, meet us in the medical centre on the border of the Residential and Metropolitan Districts. We're not far from the collapsed skyscraper."

"I have marked the location of this medical centre in my mapping systems. We shall be able to find you," Al said.

"What about you, Captain? What's your plan?"

"I've got a hunch that even if we found evac ships, they're not going to be much help when we've got a puppet master sitting at the top of Metro Tower, pulling on our strings. We're going to climb the tower. We're going to take back control of the Metropolis Seven.

Then we're going to get the fuck out of here and call in the big guns to incinerate this ship," Draco said.

"Fuckin' right. I'll talk to you guys soon, but if I can't get you, you know where to find us."

"Good work Vynce. Draco out."

"Vynce out."

Draco looked over at Raze, who had a huge smile on his face.

"It's not quite the time for mirth just yet my friend," Al said as he stood up from his chair, "I believe that we are all in much more danger than we all presently realise. My assumptions combined with Vynce's report paints a very bleak picture for the survival of everyone on this ship. As I was saying before we heard from Vynce, I've found some further information in the data stream. It looks as though some rudimentary laboratories have been set up in the upper floors of Metro Tower. The floors were refitted just a week ago, shortly after the initial infection began."

"Metropolis vessels don't usually carry the equipment to fit out a lab," Raze said.

"Not a complete laboratory, no. But they would have had enough supplies and resources to make a simple testing and containment laboratory. They've dedicated an entire floor of the tower to it."

"If this infection goes to ground on a civilised terrestrial planet, there will be no stopping the spread," Draco said.

"Whoever is pulling our strings will have other plans for this newly discovered organism, and there are only two practical applications I can think of. Commercial or military," Al said.

"The Alliance military has a sanction on all biological weaponry," Raze said.

"They may not be looking to sell to humans. They may be looking to sell it to anyone, even the Vartalen."

Raze exhaled sharply and said, "The Vartalen? We may as well kiss the rest of the human race goodbye right now. If this infection gets into their hands and they weaponise it, there'd be no way to track it back to anyone. All you'd need to do is send a single infected person down to the surface and it'd be game over."

"First thing's first. We need to get to the top of Metro Tower and take the control of the ship for ourselves. After that, we can figure out what the hell we're going to do. Let's resupply with whatever we can from here, then we move out," Draco said.

TWENTY-ONE

Veck watched the girls work. Rhken was clearly more intelligent and efficient than her older sister. The other one fumbled her way around the engines, dropped her tools and spent more than a few minutes sobbing when she should have been focusing on getting the job done. It seemed infinitely simple to Veck. If the girls didn't get the engines back online, then they would all die. Mourning their father served no purpose.

Emotion was one of humanity's greatest strengths when it was harnessed and cultivated correctly. But when it was allowed to control a person unchecked, it became one of the human race's greatest weaknesses. Some emotions were beneficial; motivating emotions, but others such as guilt, self-doubt and jealousy would never serve as positive motivators for anything.

One of the best things Veck ever did was to suppress all of his own negative emotions. He didn't know why someone would let themselves be wracked with the pain of loss if they had a choice not to. The only things he felt anymore were pride, anger, and occasionally lust. But it had been far too long since he had met someone who he lusted after. Everyone he met was just far too unintelligent and unambitious to match him. Why would he lower himself to base carnal pleasure with anyone who wasn't his equal? He refused. He could be patient. There would be someone.

The two girls working on the engine blocks lacked the proper motivation to get their jobs done, and Veck meant to change that.

"Do you want your captain to die?" he asked, breaking the silence.

"It's alright. I don't expect you to answer. But you should know that at the rate you're working, it's likely that the hull of that giant spaceship just out the windows there will hit us. Do you know what will happen when it hits us?" he said as he raised an eyebrow.

"No? Have you ever seen what happens when you hit a bird on take-off? You end up with a tiny little bloody patch on the outside of your hull that gets burnt up when you blast through the atmosphere. We'll be no different, except that our biological remains will freeze, crystallise and then shatter unless they're crushed first."

He waited for a moment and allowed the girls time to respond. When they did not, he continued.

"Don't you wish that you could go home, girls? You could go home and honour your father however you wish. You can build a statue, if you really wanted to. But right now, we need to get this ship back up and running."

Rhken dropped her multi-tool. It fell to the ground as she got to her feet and strode over to Veck. She was incensed. "And then what? You get to go on your way, free to kill your way across the galaxy again. So what if we all die here? At least then the galaxy will be rid of you."

Veck smiled at the fury inside this girl. He had her right where he wanted her.

"I have an answer which may motivate you to reassess how you speak to me in future," Veck said. His voice was as smooth as silk. "Let me tell you exactly what I will do if you and your sister comply with my orders. Firstly, I will take you to any civilised planet in the galaxy, apart from New Earth. I will leave you there, and within a week you will both receive large sum of credits in your accounts. You'll be able to open up your own shop. I'll go on my way after I leave you, and you'll never hear from me again."

Rhken didn't reply.

"And if you don't," he began, and then his face suddenly contorted into a mask of unfettered rage, "I will cut your head from your fucking shoulders and force your sister to kiss your lips as the warmth of life flees from them. I will force her to watch me desecrate your body in ways that you couldn't possibly imagine. I will force her to watch, and she will know that I will do exactly the same to her, but I won't allow her the quick death I allow you. Oh no. She will experience every moment of blissful agony, and by the time I am finished with her, she will beg me to give her the mercy of death's cold embrace."

Rhken shrunk back from Veck's outburst.

"But you'd still be dead," she said meekly.

"So would you. And so would your sister, but she would die only after she experienced the greatest agony she has ever felt. Or, conversely, you could get the engines back online, and you can both live long, happy lives. The choice is yours."

Rhken knew that in reality she had no choice but to obey. She couldn't risk any harm coming to her sister. After their mother died, it was just the three of them. Now it was down to two. She had to protect her sister, no matter what.

"I need to go down into storage. That's where Dad always kept the spare ignition primers. We'll need those. We can only hope that they weren't fried by the EMP either," Rhken said. She quickly thought about what she could do on the way to storage. Could she get Captain Goldwing on comms? No. She wouldn't have time to make it to the bridge, try to get the captain, and get back to the engineering bay before Veck grew suspicious.

Perhaps she could make a quick stop at the armoury on the way back and pick up a shotgun or two. She'd fired a pistol before, but never at a hostile moving target. If she had a chance at taking Veck down, she needed something with a little more firepower. A couple of shotguns should do the trick. The recoil might dislocate her shoulders, but it would be worth it if they could put that psychopath down for good.

"Very well. Your sister will remain here and attend to her duties, and I will come with you," Veck said. Rhken's heart sunk. There would be no way she could go for a weapon while Veck followed her. He'd be on top of her before she had time to turn and open fire.

Downtrodden, she nodded and walked toward storage. Veck knew that Reban wouldn't have the guts to make a play at trying to kill him. She was far too occupied by her own grief. But Rhken might try something. She might try to play the hero, just like her father did. He didn't want to kill her. He had begun to enjoy her.

As Rhken and Veck left the room, Reban collapsed onto the grated floor, put her head in her hands and wept.

Arak Nara was waiting just inside the darkness, listening. He felt his gorge rise as Veck threatened to defile the two girls. As soon as he heard that Rhken and Veck were headed towards storage, Arak retreated back into the ship and disappeared into the armoury.

He only had moments to prepare before they would both be walking past and down into storage. He undressed as fast as he could and then slipped a smartsuit on. With most of the ship's systems offline, he would have to attach the armour plating manually. He grabbed the closest helmet he could find and slipped it over his head. The HUD immediately illuminated, and enhanced his low-light vision.

He heard low chattering in the corridor outside the room. Arak retreated deeper into the armoury and slipped behind two of the armour pods. He watched intently from the gap in between the pods as he waited for them to pass. Two dark figures crossed in front of the doorway. One was Veck, and the other was one of the girls. Arak wasn't sure who until he heard her speak.

"You're sure this is the quickest way down into storage? What about through the armoury?" Veck asked.

"No, that's just the holding cells where we keep our cargo. Anything we need to keep the ship running is in a separate storage area," Rhken said.

The two figures passed. Arak opened one of the armour pods manually and started to unpack the armour. It was far too large for him, but the smartsuit made the connections as best as it could.

'This must be Raze's armour,' Arak thought as he put the chest piece on. It connected to the smartsuit, but it was far too wide to wear comfortably. If he had to engage Veck, it would impede his movement. Arak disengaged the piece of chest armour and placed it back in the armour pod. He would worry about mounting it properly when he had the ship back under control.

Arak moved on to the next armour pod and opened it manually. The armour pieces in that pod were much more accommodating. He slipped on the chest and shoulder armour, which fitted him like a glove. He hadn't been a member of the crew long enough to have his own armour crafted yet, but this would suffice for the purpose Arak had in mind.

After Arak was fully suited up, he walked over to the weapon racks and looked over his options. He could choose to act silently if he wanted. He contemplated picking up a pair of silenced pistols, but decided against it. If he missed, or Veck didn't go down with a couple of shots, there was no way Arak could overpower him with small arms fire. An assault rifle risked destroying something vital like the engines, or a stray bullet could rip a hole in the hull of the ship. Eventually Arak settled on a snub-nosed shotgun, which was designed for messy close-up encounters.

Arak walked towards the armoury doors and stopped when he heard Veck and Rhken coming back from storage. He quickly resumed his position behind the armour pods and watched the door for silhouettes. Rhken passed the doorway first, but Veck lingered at the threshold.

"Did you hear something in here?" Veck asked to Rhken and to the darkness inside the armoury.

"No, I didn't hear anything," Rhken said.

Arak's blood ran cold as Veck stepped across the threshold and into the armoury. His grip on the shotgun tightened, and he steeled himself for action. There was no way he could take Veck out with a single blast from that far away. He would have to wait until the madman was closer to him.

Veck took another step into the room and Arak's' muscles tensed. He almost fired a shot when a scream came from the engine bay.

"Reban!" Rhken exclaimed, and rushed towards the engine bay.

Veck swore and followed the girl. Arak breathed a sigh of relief, but didn't allow himself to relax. He crept towards the armoury door and stepped out into the emergency lighting of the corridor outside.

TWENTY-TWO

Vynce approached an old man who looked completely spent. He wasn't injured, but Vynce could see that he was not just tired physically, but drained emotionally and mentally as well.

"Excuse me old timer, but I was hoping to ask you something," Vynce said.

The man smiled and said, "Sure son."

"I'm with the crew of another ship. We responded to the distress beacon. But our ship isn't big enough to carry everyone out. Are there are evacuation ships left on board?"

"And what would you do with an evac ship if you had one?" the old man asked.

"We'd use it to escape. There are over a hundred people here. We can keep you all safe until we get off the ship."

"Where would you go? We're not in friendly space. If we go on an evac ship, we'll just end up in the hands of the Vartalen."

"Better to take the risk of capture than resign yourself to death here, right?"

The old man laughed and said, "I've seen friends, people I've known for the last five years, suddenly start growing into something vile, vicious and hungry. They don't die though. I'm sure of that. One of my oldest friends, Herbert Hughes, he came on the trip with me. I liked to call it our last great voyage, but I thought we'd survive it. This was supposed to be our last big adventure before we re-joined the universe."

"And it still can be. We can help everyone get out of here alive. I just need to know where the evac ships are."

"It's a fool's errand. Don't you think that if we were able to get to the hangars, we'd be gone by now? There are too many of them between us and the ships. Half of us would be cut down and dragged off before we even saw the entrance to the hangar bay."

"So we don't all make it, then. Some of us can. Some of us can get out of here. Maybe not me. Maybe not you. But maybe some of the kids here and their parents. Some of them might be able to live a few more years. It's better to try than to admit defeat, right?"

The old man laughed again and said, "You remind me of my own son before he went to fight on the front lines in the uncivilised sectors. He was all guts, and no brains."

"Should I take that as a compliment?"

"He died during his first incursion. But I know that I'm as likely to stop you from finding the evac ships as I was at talking him out of throwing his life away. The evac ships are right underneath the Residential District. The entrance is right near the Eden's Hill mag-rail station."

"Thank you."

Vynce left the old man with his thoughts. He wondered whether he would be able to live with himself if he got out of this jam alive at the expense of the lives of others. He decided that if he got out of here, he would have to try and find a way to live with himself. He wasn't ready to clock out just yet.

Vynce walked over to a man in an orange high-vis work suit. It looked similar to their assault suits, but the armour plating on the orange suit was nowhere near as thick as the plating on Vynce's suit. It was more for show than anything else. But if he worked in maintenance, the man would likely know the best way to get down to the hangars.

"Excuse me sir," Vynce said and put his hand on the man's shoulder. The man turned. There was light fuzz on his cheeks that came from days of not shaving, and an eye patch over his left eye.

"Yes?" the man asked.

"Did you work maintenance here on the Metropolis Seven?"

"Aye. But there's no use trying to get down into the maintenance tunnels now. The damn infected are down there, and they're building."

"Building what?"

"I've got no fucking idea, but they're smart. They've started making traps for us. Last time I went down there, we lost three men to a false floor they'd made. They're protecting something down there, but I don't know what."

"The hangars with the evac ships. Is there a way we could get down there?"

"Sure, you could. But it all depends on whether they've gummed up the doors with that gunk that they use. We've never been able to make it close to the hangar to be able to tell for sure."

"Did you ever have to remove the gunk from anything? If we could get to the hangar and it's all sealed up, is there a way we can get rid of it?"

"Well fire seems to work well. It melts right through the stuff like wax."

"Tell me everything you can about getting to the hangar," Vynce said.

Jaxon sat next to Ava and held her remaining hand. He had been with her through so much already. He never thought that he would be with her while she lost her arm. For the entire time that he had known her, she only had a left arm and refused to talk about how she lost the other. He knew now that Ava would escape the ship alive. She had to. Everything lined up far too perfectly. Once again, Jaxon marvelled at the ability of the timestream to remain constant, even with meddlers like him sticking his nose in where it doesn't belong.

The chip that Jaxon held was something of utmost importance. Without it, the human race would be wiped from existence. The entire course of human history would be altered. No matter what, he had to help the crew of the Icarus escape the Metropolis Seven so he could get back to New Earth. The chip had to get back to the headquarters of the Agency.

Jaxon always had the ability to pre-empt the course of events. Some called it premonition. Some called it intuition. Others blamed the constant jumping between timestreams. Whatever it was, those who were employed by the Agency and worked so that the human race's timeline continued could often see a little further forwards into the future and backwards into the past. Their existence as three-dimensional beings was heightened to allow them a tiny bit more perspective than others.

His heightened perspective had led him to a train of thought that he did not want to follow. That track led to death, and he wanted nothing more than to derail it. But the flow of time is a stubborn thing, and he knew that it may have been too late to change tracks at this stage of the game.

Ava's hand squeezed his hand gently. Her eyes began to flutter open. When her eyes met his, she smiled and squeezed his hand again.

"You're awake," he said.

"I feel like I've been hit by a bus," she said.

"Some people get hit by busses and escape fairly unscathed."

"But I went under the front wheels, right?" she said and smiled.

"Right," he said.

Ava looked at the bandages that covered where her right arm should have been. She felt a sudden sickness in the pit of her stomach when she realised that her arm was completely gone. She let go of Jaxon's hand and pushed herself up from the bed.

"What do you need?" he asked.

"Bucket," she said.

Jaxon grabbed a vomit bag from under the bed and handed it to Ava. She emptied her stomach into it, but there was nothing left in there but bitter dark-brown bile. Jaxon rubbed her back gently until she was finished and her body stopped shaking.

"You're in shock right now. Just remember to breathe. Are you hungry? Thirsty?"

"I'm starving, actually."

"I'll see what I can scrounge up."

"Thank you."

Jaxon left her side and ventured out into the waiting area. He slipped his helmet back on to hide his face, just in case young Jaxon saw him. Doctor Harris said she would be just outside if they needed anything, but she couldn't stay in the operating theatre as there were others that needed her help too. He walked around the waiting area until he saw Doctor Harris. She was busy redressing a young boy's stump where his forearm had once been.

"This is healing quite well. When we get back to New Earth, they'll be able to give you a new hand."

The young boy smiled.

After Doctor Harris finished wrapping the boy's bandages, Jaxon asked "Excuse me, doctor? Ava's awake, and she's hungry. Is there anything to eat?"

"Of course. We don't have much, but we have enough. Follow me."

Jaxon followed her to a walk-in supply closet. She handed two bars to Jaxon and said, "These are packed with everything you need. They may not taste the greatest, but they'll fill you both up and give a boost to your immune system, too. It'll help her fight off infection."

"Thank you," Jaxon said and started to walk back towards the operating theatre. He opened the doors and saw Ava on the ground, breathing heavily. He rushed over to her side and helped her back up to her feet.

"Are you alright? What happened?" he asked.

"I tried to put my suit back on myself, but as soon as I stood up it felt like gravity re-engaged the wrong way up. All I remember after that is the floor."

"You're lucky you didn't hurt yourself. You can't push yourself like this. You need to focus on resting and gathering your strength."

Ava looked into Jaxon's eyes and slammed her fist on the metal table.

"I can't just rest. I can't let myself sit here feeling sorry for myself when all the other people on this ship are still in danger."

"I understand, but in your delicate state we can't risk further injury."

"Delicate state? Fuck you! You say you know me, but if you really knew me you'd know that I can't just sit here doing nothing. And I sure as hell won't just sit here like some hologame princess waiting to be rescued."

Jaxon smiled and said, "You're right, of course. What can I do?"

"Help me get my suit back on."

Ava slid back off the table and onto the cold floor. She steadied herself with her left hand. She closed her eyes and took a deep breath as she centred herself.

Jaxon offered her his arm, and she pushed it away.

"I'm fine," she said, "Just bring me the rest of my smartsuit and help me get into it."

Jaxon brought over the cutaway pieces of the smartsuit. He held it up and offered the left arm to Ava. She slid the smartsuit on like a jacket and covered her bare flesh. The pieces of smartsuit instantly reconnected to each other when Ava put them into place. Her smartsuit knew her body, and knew how it should sit on her. When the suit began to reattach itself near Ava's missing arm, the suit stopped reconnecting. There was a flap of smartsuit big enough to cover the injury, but it didn't know what to do. The suit expected there to be an arm where there wasn't one.

Jaxon gently pressed the suit against the bandages. He tried to match up the edges as best as he could, but the suit was not responding.

"I know this will be hard, but you have to try and force your suit to make the connection. It thinks that it needs to stay disconnected here, because you're still expecting your arm to be there. But it's not. You'll need to accept that before we can get the suit on, okay?"

Ava could feel the anger welling up inside of her. She couldn't just accept that her arm had been cut from her body. She couldn't just accept it and move on like nothing had happened. Her anger subsided and was replaced by a deep sense of loss. That arm had been a part of her. Literally. She had written with it, killed with it, loved with it. And now it was gone. Cut off like a piece of waste.

"How am I...? How am I..." she began to say, but her words were cut off as she began to sob.

Jaxon came in to comfort her, but she pushed him away. This was all too much, far too quickly. She suffered with her pain, by herself. She sometimes tried to forget about it by getting down to the bottom of a bottle, but it was always hers. It was her pain. Her loss. She didn't need anyone else to deal with it. She had never needed anyone else.

But this time traveller had made her feel unlike she had ever felt before. Ava was used to being seen as an object. Either a pair of tits and a wet cunt, or as a weapon to be used to eliminate the Alliance's enemies. Only two people in the galaxy had ever made her feel the way that she felt at that moment. Captain Goldwing was one, and Jaxon was another.

That fucking meddling time-travelling prick. If he hadn't shown up when he did, things would have been alright.

She kept holding him at bay with her left arm outstretched against his chest.

Things wouldn't have been alright, and she knew it. Vynce would be dead. And so would she.

She had lost her arm, but she was still alive. Her lip quivered as she dropped her remaining arm and looked up at Jaxon. He had changed the opacity of his visor. She could see his face. If he had looked down at her with even a trace of pity, she wouldn't have let him in ever again. It would be done. Over. She didn't need any romantic bullshit. All romance ever did was get people killed. But she saw no pity on his face. She saw something in his eyes. Something far deeper and more intimate than mere concern, but she wasn't ready to accept exactly what that was.

He wrapped his arms around her, and she let go of all of her anger and frustration. She wrapped her remaining arm around Jaxon's waist and buried her head into his chest.

TWENTY-THREE

Draco found three grapnel launchers amongst the emergency supplies. The grapnel attachments could convert from a magnetic flat surface to a three-pronged hook attachment, for those situations where there were no magnetic surfaces to attach to. After the hook or magnetic head stuck firmly to a surface, the rope would reel you in to your destination once you pulled the trigger.

They were used for hull repairs on the outside of the ship, but Draco thought they might come in handy as they ascended the tower. Raze had found spare rifles and more spare magazines than the three of them could carry. Their ammunition had been running low, but there was no telling just how much resistance they would face between the hazard shelter and Metro Tower. There was a chance that the infected might stay as unaggressive as they had been, but Raze didn't want to be caught out if they decided to abruptly end their armistice.

Al had mapped out the entire Metropolitan District in his data banks and the power grid hadn't even come back online yet. Draco held one rifle in his hands, and another was magnetically docked against the back of his suit. He wouldn't find himself without a rifle again. Not when so much was at stake.

Draco handed a grapnel hook launcher to Raze and Al. Draco put his in his left thigh holster.

"What's the best way for us to get to Metro Tower, Al?" Draco asked.

"The street outside of the shelter leads straight onto Montague Road, which then leads straight to the tower. It should only take us fifteen minutes to get there if we don't encounter any resistance."

"And if we do encounter resistance?"

"We will have to hope that we have enough bullets to open a gap and continue on. I would not recommend using the maintenance shafts below the streets."

"Why is that?"

"The map I was able to access listed known areas of infection. Under the streets is a nest. A hive. A spawning ground. Something. I don't exactly know what to call it, but it was marked as a purple danger area when the maps were still being updated."

"Do you think that's why they're being non-aggressive right now?"

"The behaviour seems at odds with almost every other species in the known universe. Almost all creatures who are born of a nest or hive often attack intruders who get close to it. Some creatures even sacrifice their own lives in defence of the nest. Like honey bees on New Earth, or the nancarra on Bwora. Both sacrifice their lives in the defence of their homes."

"I don't like it. If these things had the ability to think, I'd say that it feels like we're walking into a trap."

"To be fair, we don't really know a lot about their capacity for intelligence. They have grown from human bodies; therefore they are the products of humanity. Humanity is known for its intelligence, its cunning..."

"And our capacity for violence and cruelty."

"...Yes. That too. There was no need for the hunter we faced to tear Pim in two. If it was interested in creating more of those things, then it would have simply incapacitated him. But instead, it tore him apart."

"Could it have been trying to anger us?" Raze asked.

"Quite possibly," Al said.

"That's not something I want to think about," Draco said.

"We don't know enough about the creatures. But as long as we can commandeer the ship and take control, we might be able to get out of here alive," Al said.

Draco nodded and started for the door to the shelter.

"Just a second, Captain. I think I've found something," Raze said as he opened a cabinet. Raze pulled out a harness with two tanks attached to it.

"Is that...?" Al asked.

Raze threaded his arms through the harness and settled the tanks behind his shoulders. A long hose dangled from in between the two tanks. He pulled out a long, slender nozzle with two handles up its length. Raze reached backwards, grabbed the hose from the back of the tanks and screwed it into the end. He flicked a switch on the side, and a small flame ignited.

"A flamethrower might come in handy," Raze said as he got back to his feet. The tanks on his back and the flamethrower nozzle held across his chest enhanced his already fearsome presence.

"Good plan. Let's move out."

Draco was the first out of the shelter, followed by Al, then Raze. The infected had amassed outside of the shelter while they were outfitting themselves. Draco had his rifle raised at the closest pair of infected, a young man whose head had begun to fuse with his chest cavity due to a monstrous growth coming from his right shoulder-blade, and an older woman whose arms had split in two. The bottom pair of arms were spindly, ending in a single finger, with a claw the size of a dagger growing from the end of each. The top pair of arms were more muscular, and each of the three remaining fingers grasped the air endlessly. The pair looked from Draco to the barrel of his gun and back again. The young man bared his teeth as best as his twisted flesh would allow, but made no move to attack.

The horde of fleshlings stood and watched. Draco started to walk along the road towards the intersection with Montague Road. The infected made no move. They watched Draco with their blank expressions, but didn't attempt to block their movements.

Smaller fleshlings had started to come out of the buildings and drains to watch.

"These things are watching us, just like those growths in the water treatment plants were," Al said.

"They're nothing more than biological surveillance cameras?" Draco asked.

"Until they get the command to attack, of course."

"Yes, and then we'd better be ready to run."

"If these things are just watching us, then who's watching the feed?" Raze asked.

"There has to be someone watching us through their eyes."

"Not someone, but something. If this truly is a nest, or a hive, then there has to be some kind of hierarchy of leadership," Al said.

"Most New Earth insects have a queen at the heart of their hives. Could this really be all that different?" Raze asked.

"It's very possible, and it would make sense from what we've seen. These infected are like workers or drones. The little ones made from parts of their hosts and the ones that have affixed themselves to the walls in the heart of the ship are like scouts," Al said.

"And the hunters we've seen, they're like soldier ants," Draco said.

"Precisely. If these drones aren't trying to capture us, then they're deviating from the biological reprogramming the organism has given them. There must be some intelligence driving them."

"Noted," Draco said and continued through the horde of fleshlings.

They were clustered together so closely that jogging at a brisk pace was almost impossible. Every time Draco had to brush against one of the infected, he hoped that it would not take it as a show of aggression.

They kept walking toward Montague Road, weaving their way between the infected. When they reached the intersection, they turned onto Montague road and headed towards Metro Tower. The building's top floor was illuminated, but the streets below were still plunged into darkness.

Montague Road was lined with high-rise apartment buildings. A towering creature lumbered from between two buildings on the side of the street. It was larger than anything Draco had seen before. It would have towered above the height of the spawning pods in the water treatment facility. It could have easily looked into the windows of a third floor building without craning its huge muscular neck.

The creature's face was made from a mosaic of fused human heads. Pairs of eyes from multiple faces had migrated together. They looked like the compound eyes of an insect. But each eye still moved of its own accord. The other facial features were not distributed as evenly. It was almost impossible to figure out what holes had once been ears, noses or mouths. The towering monstrosity's mouth hung open. Its curved, serrated teeth glistened with moisture.

"What in the void do you think that is?" Raze asked.

"We're definitely close to the nest. Soldier ants, like the smaller hunter we encountered, they tend to patrol the outskirts of the nest. They try to deter attackers from coming any closer. In some ant colonies there are specially purposed soldiers who are shaped by the queen herself to ensure that she doesn't come under attack. I think that's what that beast is," Al said.

"So why is it not attacking?" Draco asked.

"It should be attacking us, but it's not. I think somehow the queen has sent a command to her subjects and has told them not to attack us."

"Telepathy? Mind control?"

"Perhaps. Or it could be something as simple as her excreting a certain pheromone that inhibits their aggression. There's no way to be sure. We need to press on as quickly as possible."

"Agreed."

Vynce's voice came over the comm channel and said, 'Captain, do you read me?'

"We're here Vynce, but keep it quick and to the point. We're not in a very safe place," Draco said as he gently squeezed his way between two of the infected.

'The evac shuttles are in the hangar bay below residential. Problem is, we can't get there. There are just too many infected between us and the hangar.'

"Take no action for now. We're on our way to Metro Tower, but the infected are acting strangely. They're lining the streets, but they're not attacking. If you take any hostile action against them, they may stop being so friendly to us."

'They're out in the streets? Captain, you have to be careful. All it took to infect Ava was a single suit rupture.'

"Duly noted. How is she doing?"

'Not sure. I've been out talking to the survivors for information. I'll check back in with you when I know.'

"Thank you. And remember, no hostile actions until we make contact, got it?"

'Got it. Vynce out.'

They arrived at the bottom of Metro Tower and began climbing the steps. The infected were concentrated around the doors of the tower. Two large hunters stood on either side of the open doors and watched the crew approach. The one on the left uttered a guttural growl, but it made no move to attack. Draco stepped across the threshold and into the ground floor of the tower.

The inside of the tower was impossibly dark. Draco engaged his shoulder lamp. Raze did the same. The flickering flame at the end of his flamethrower projected jittering shadows on the walls. Even though the streets outside were lined with infected, the tower itself was not. A damp organic covering blanketed the floor.

There was a single standing desk in the middle of the lobby. There were upended couches, toppled vending machines and destroyed debris all over. The lifts from floors one to twenty-five were on the left hand side of the desk, and the lifts from floors twenty-six to forty-seven were on the right hand side. There was no power in the lobby.

Raze sighed and said, "I'm not looking forward to climbing forty-seven flights of stairs, I have to say."

Draco smiled to himself and said, "We won't need to do any stair climbing, Raze. Not with these grapnel launchers."

Raze laughed and said, "Sometimes things do go our way, cap."

Al opened the door manually. He put his fingers between the two doors and started to pull them apart. They screeched as they opened. The sound echoed in the empty lobby. Draco watched the hunters outside the main door to see if they reacted to the sound, but they remained at their posts. Al pulled the other side of the door back and looked up and down the shaft.

"Captain, I think you may want to take a look at this," Al said and ushered Draco over to the door.

Draco looked up and saw nothing but blackness above them.

"Not up, sir. Look down," Al said.

Draco looked down and expected the shaft to end shortly below the doors. But the shaft continued down into the darkness. It was so deep that his lamp could not illuminate the bottom.

"Is that on your map, Al?" Draco asked.

"It isn't. I thought that the area below the Metro Tower was inconspicuously empty. They must have had something going on down here that they didn't want the maintenance crew to know about."

"So which way do we go? Up, or down?"

"Up. We've got someone we need to formally introduce ourselves to."

TWENTY-FOUR

Rhken rushed out into the engine bay and yelled, "Reban!? Are you alright!?"

Reban turned wide-eyed to her sister and said, "There's something on the ship! Something just landed on the ship! We have to warn Captain Goldwing!"

"What do you mean? What something?"

"A ship! Another ship! Look at the bridge!"

Rhken rushed up the stairs and saw what Reban was pointing at. She was right. There was another ship sitting on the hull of the Metropolis Seven like a fly sits on the flank of cow. The ship was directly above the bridge windows.

"What kind of ship is that?" Reban asked shrilly.

"It's a Vartalen attack cruiser," Veck said as he walked up the stairs to join the girls.

"There's no way they could take a ship that size!" Rhken said.

"They don't need to overpower the crew. If they cut straight into the bridge there, they can put the ship into lockdown and commandeer it. They'll take it back to Vartalen space and sell it, along with the humans on board," Veck said.

"We have to warn the captain!" Reban strained.

Veck laughed and said, "No we don't. This is perfect. Your captain will be made into a Vartalen slave. What a fitting end. I wouldn't want to spoil his surprise."

Rhken didn't respond.

"You forget your task, Rhken. Put those primers into place so we can get this ship back online. Understand?" Veck asked.

Rhken nodded and went to work. Veck went back down to the bottom floor and watched. Rhken engaged the two ignition primers in the top engines first. She then manually primed the engines for ignition. Reban stayed on the top floor, as far away from Veck as she could possibly get. Rhken descended the stairs and lifted her eyes to look at Veck. He looked back at her with a smile, but there was movement behind him. Her eyes went wide as she saw Captain Goldwing standing behind Veck with a shotgun in his hands.

Captain Goldwing was wearing full black combat armour, with gold trim and the helmet with the eagle's wings painted on either side. Captain Goldwing had a shotgun aimed squarely at Veck's spine.

Rhken's eyes betrayed her. Veck saw her eyes focus on something behind him. He turned at the exact same moment that Captain Goldwing fired. The side of Veck's abdomen exploded with a spray of lumpy red paste. The shot that would have destroyed his spine instead blew out half of his stomach, but it was not enough to stop him.

Captain Goldwing fired once more, but Veck was too fast. He was too strong. He knocked the shotgun out of Captain Goldwing's hands and bent his left arm backwards until his elbow joint turned inside out with a wet crunch. Captain Goldwing screamed and fell to his knees.

"How did you get back on this ship without my knowledge!?" Veck bellowed as he circled.

Captain Goldwing screamed. Rhken had never heard Captain Goldwing scream before. It didn't even sound like him.

When Captain Goldwing refused to answer Veck, he punched the captain straight in the face, which knocked him backwards. Captain

Goldwing tried to get back to his feet, but tried to put weight on the wrong arm. It bent backwards as it collapsed under his weight. The captain screamed again.

Veck tore off Captain Goldwing's helmet and started to laugh.

"You're not Draco. You're a cutthroat in a warrior's clothing!" Veck said and backhanded Arak Nara with such force that Arak felt his cheekbone break. He reached uselessly for something that he could use to defend himself. Veck grabbed him by the hair and dragged him into the middle of the room. He kicked the shotgun away and hunkered down next to Arak.

Arak's eyes flicked down to Veck's stomach wound, and felt sick when he saw that the maniac was barely even bleeding. He was missing a huge chunk of flesh from his side, but no blood dripped from the wound.

"This is what I want for all of our people. Our bodies in their natural state are so frail. With technological augmentation, we don't ever need to worry about petty things like bullets ever again. It'll take a few hours to reconstitute the tissue you just destroyed, but I won't die from it."

"What are you?" Arak breathed.

"Perfection. Does it terrify you?"

Arak closed his mouth. Veck smiled and said, "Of course it does. You don't need to say so. I can see it in your eyes. But I'm not going to kill you. I have one final use for you. Then, if you beg me, I will allow you to die."

"And if I refuse?" Arak said defiantly.

"I know you heard what I said to Rhken earlier. Do you take me for a man who makes empty threats?"

Arak shook his head slowly and winced at the pain of his buckled elbow joint.

"Good. You learn quickly. If you assist me to my satisfaction, I may even allow you to live." Veck looked backwards over his shoulder and growled at Rhken, "Did I tell you that you could stop working?"

Rhken hurried over to one of the engines and started installing another ignition primer. She looked over her shoulder quickly as Veck lifted Arak to his feet. Arak's arm was bent backwards at an unnatural angle. Rhken then rushed over to the last engine and installed the final ignition primer. She pumped it three times and walked back over to the control console.

"It's done," she said to Veck, "I'll need a couple of minutes for the system to reboot itself, then I can get the engines running again."

"You continue to impress me, little mouse."

From the control console Rhken checked that the engines were all primed correctly. She then routed the emergency power to the ignition primers and waited a couple of seconds for them to charge. She turned the main ignition switch. Her heart filled with relief when the low hum of the engines filled the engine bay once again. The power then filtered down to all of the Icarus' systems. The lights came back on, as did the diagnostic display panel above the control console.

"Fire the engines. Now. Get us out of here," Veck commanded.

"Just a second. I need to perform a couple of diagnostic checks first!" Rhken said.

Reban's gaze was fixed on the Vartalen ship on the hull of the Metropolis Seven. It had gotten so close now that she thought she could make out the windows on the Vartalen cruiser.

"We need to leave right now, so fire the engines!" Veck commanded with more force.

"If I fire the engines without checking that they kept their calibrations, the ship could tear itself apart. If the engines cut out due to a power blockage, then we could stall and we'd have to go through this whole process anyway. So give me two fucking seconds and I'll get us out of here, alright?" Rhken said. She could feel her cheeks flush as she spoke.

Veck inclined his head with a slight smile and said, "The little mouse knows best." He then turned back to Arak and said, "You must be the pilot. I haven't had the pleasure of an introduction. I'm Veck Simms," he said and laid a hand over his heart, "and what is your name?"

Arak thought about refusing to answer his question, but it would do no good. Veck would just hurt him again until he relented. He had witnessed too many tortures, and everyone broke eventually.

"Arak Nara."

"That accent. You're from Orphos, are you not?"

"Yes."

"Well then, I believe the correct salutation would be Nara-ka, is that correct?"

"That is only used for those who you hold as dearly as family. I do not believe it is appropriate for us to use for one another."

"Well Nara-ka, I'm the closest thing you have to family right now. I would highly recommend that you accept any friendship that I offer."

"Of course. Thank you... Simms... -Ka."

"You have medical facilities aboard this ship, don't you?"

"...Yes," Arak answered tentatively.

"If I allow you to attend to your arm injury, will you come back with a shotgun or two? Or will you act like an intelligent man?"

"I... I will act as an intelligent man."

"That's what I like to hear. First, we need to set a course. Then I'll let you see to your arm."

Rhken tried to drown out Arak and Veck's conversation as she calibrated the engines, but she caught just enough of what was said for it to matter. She hadn't truly trusted Arak since he came aboard the ship. A mercenary only ever did something for money or for their own survival. There was no money to be made here, but if Arak had the choice of aligning himself with Veck to save his own life, leaving Captain Goldwing stranded on the Metropolis Seven, she did not think that Arak would sacrifice himself. She chided herself for thinking that way about Arak, because it was not Arak who had just re-started the engines at the command of the madman.

Rhken found that the bottom left engine was eight degrees out of lateral alignment, and the top right engine was five degrees out. If they had blasted off when Veck commanded them to, the ship would have spiralled out of control and may have even looped back and impacted with the Metropolis Seven. The power linkages between all major ship systems were back online, but Rhken noticed that there was no power going to the AI core that controlled Evie.

"It looks all good, but the AI core is still offline," Rhken said to Veck.

"That's not such a bad thing. We've got eight hands on deck, well, seven working hands on deck," he said as he slapped Arak on the shoulder which made the pilot yelp in pain again, "I'm sure we can manage."

Rhken engaged the ion thrusters and the Metropolis Seven began to shrink in the rear view.

TWENTY-FIVE

Vynce waited outside the operating theatre. Captain Goldwing had told him to take no hostile actions, and that sat just fine with Vynce. But taking no action at all was more than he could handle. He had gotten all of the information he could get out of the people in the waiting area. Those that were willing to talk didn't have any information, and those who did have information weren't willing to talk. It was as though talking about the underbelly of the ship frightened people into silence.

There would come a time when they would have to get to the hangars and the evac shuttles. The infection had spread so far amongst the passengers that there was no way that the ship itself could be saved. But if the survivors could get off the ship, then the ship still needed to be dealt with. They couldn't just let it float through the void forever. Whatever this infection was, if it landed on an inhabited planet, there was no telling what damage it might cause.

They could blow the airlocks. That would kill anything living on board the ship. It would freeze and crystallise the moment the oxygen vacated the ship. The pressure would crumple the ship. The buildings and skyscrapers would be crushed like paper cups.

Would that be enough to destroy the infection? Vynce wasn't sure, but it was the best plan he could think of.

The operating theatre doors opened and Jaxon walked out. He

had put his opaque glass-domed helmet back on to shield his identity from his younger self.

"How is she?" Vynce asked.

"Recovering. She's in shock, of course. But she'll bounce back from this," Jaxon said.

"She's strong."

"Yes she is."

Vynce was at a loss for what to do or say. Before Jaxon showed up, Vynce thought he had a shot with Ava. But now that he was here, and things had happened as they had, Vynce knew that it wasn't meant to be.

"Tell me something," Vynce said.

"What would you ask?"

"You and Ava. There's something going on between you, isn't there?"

"I love her," Jaxon said simply.

"Yeah, I thought as much."

"It would be disingenuous if I said that I was sorry, because I'm not. I've been in love with Ava since the first moment I met her. It's as simple as that."

"And this is the first time she's met you, right? So she doesn't know how you feel about her yet?"

"No."

"You should tell her," Vynce said with a wan smile.

"Vynce, I..."

"No, you should tell her. We don't... We don't know if we're going to make it out of this place alive. She should know."

"You're okay with this?"

"I'm sure I'll get over it. But if you ever hurt her, I'll hunt you down and hurt you just as bad. You can guarantee that," Vynce said with a laugh.

Jaxon laughed too. "Of course. I would expect nothing less. You and Ava, though you are not together, you are still close in the futures that I have been part of. I daresay closer than Ava and I have ever been. You and the rest of the crew of the Icarus. You are all as close as family."

Vynce thought on this for a moment and took comfort from Jaxon's words. Even though he and Ava would never be together, he would still have her in his life. She would always be there, watching his back just as he watched hers. That's how it had always been, and if it remained that way for the rest of his life, he would be content.

"You told us when you joined us that you wouldn't tell us of our futures. But you just gave me a glimpse into my own. Why?" Vynce asked.

"Because you may need some hope to get you through the rest of what remains of our mission."

"We survive, then. Ava and I can't be around on the Icarus if we don't make it out of the Metropolis Seven alive."

"That statement is accurate. However, the mere involvement of an agency time traveller can completely change the course of events for better or worse. There's just no way to tell for sure."

"So why did you come here? Why did you come back onto the Metropolis Seven?"

"It wasn't by choice, believe me. I was on a mission of great importance. The existence of civilisations hung in the balance. But we're always taught that the appearance of a single person who wasn't present in the initial flow of time can be enough to slightly change events from their original course. One of the first examples they showed us in the academy was a diagram of one hundred people on a crowded sidewalk on New Earth. The aim of this theoretical mission is to save the life of a council-member from assassination. It was a non-firearm assassination. The assassin in this instance was to use a syringe filled with a slow-acting poison. He would inject the council-member, leave, then let the poison do its work. The first time this simulation was run, the flow of pedestrians was interrupted and changed so much by the addition of a single extra person that a civilian was pushed out into the street, hit by a car, and killed."

"So by being there at all, another was killed?"

"Yes. But that's not the only consideration. The actions that person would have taken during their lifetime would never have happened. Any children that person might have borne would never have existed. Just because I was there."

"Like the butterfly effect?"

"A butterfly flaps its wings on the shores of New Melbourne and the American Federation gets cyclones? The analogy is adequate, but with ramifications which echo throughout generations. Imagine if you had killed the man who invented the nuclear bomb. Imagine if the second Old Earth World War hadn't come to a decisive end. Imagine if the war had instead been allowed to fester and rot and corrupt world relations until we destroyed not only ourselves, but our entire planet. One life. One action. One change. That's all it would have taken to make it so that the human race never left Old Earth and took flight into the stars."

"Has anything like that ever happened?"

"There's no way of knowing for sure. No agent is able to access any information about the missions of any other agents. But we did reach the stars, didn't we? Without the involvement of the agency we may never have made it off-world in the first place."

"That's a scary thought."

"Yeah. But after you've been doing it for as long as I have, you start to trust your instinct more than anything else. That's something they also taught us very early on in the agency. We're all intrinsically linked to the energy of the universe on a quantum level. Travelling through the timestreams gives us a certain... sensitivity to the underlying patterns of the universe. We're taught to follow these instincts."

"Are you saying that the universe itself has a will? You're not one of those kooks who believe in a guy with a giant beard sitting in a black hole in the middle of the galaxy, are you?"

"No. Nothing like that. But the universe fosters life. Think about how infinitesimally unlikely it is for biological life to exist at all. Whether or not the universe has a will of its own or not isn't something that I think we can truly comprehend. After all, we know it has rules which have to be followed. But I know that if we can prevent some violent atrocity, something tugs at us and leads us to a solution. They call it a time traveller's instinct, and I don't know what else to call it," Jaxon offered with a shrug.

"So that instinct. That feeling you get in your gut. Is that the same as what non-time traveller's feel?"

"Yes, but a number of other factors also come into it. You might feel your fight or flight reaction and think it instinct, but it's not quite the same. It's a feeling inside that tugs you in a certain direction, or attracts you to a certain person. Perhaps it happens to us because we travel through the boundaries of reality with a certain purpose, and when we pursue that purpose we're more in tune with the universe. One of my old instructors at the agency used to say that the universe will hold your hand if your purpose is for the greater good, but it'll block your path if it is not."

Vynce thought on that for a moment then said, "You've done a great job of getting me off topic. Why did you come back to the Metropolis Seven?"

Jaxon smiled and said, "As perceptive as ever. I came back to the Metropolis Seven because I had no other option. Something happened on my last mission, and I was trapped outside of the flow of time."

"What? Outside the flow of time? How does that even happen?"

"That's a very long story. When you try and circumvent the rules of the universe, well, sometimes you find yourself on your own. The only constant in my life after the events on this ship has been Captain Goldwing. We continued to bump into each other on and off for the next twenty years, so I configured my emergency jumper to his time signature."

"So he was your escape rope?"

"Exactly. Unfortunately in doing so, I tied him to this place at this time in all flows of time. A knot in the escape rope, if you like. He became a fixed point in the space-time continuum, so he is destined to board the Metropolis Seven, no matter what I do in his timeline. I could go back and try to change his timeline, but he would still find a way onto the Metropolis Seven. He's tied to it now, just as I am tied to him."

"What were you doing that stranded you outside the timestream?"

"I made a mistake with the best of intentions. My mission was to retrieve something extremely small, but priceless beyond imagining. I need to get it back to New Earth."

Vynce nodded and said, "You're a good guy, Jaxon. Look, I'm sorry if I've been weird or whatever..."

"It's understandable. This is the first time any of you have met me, so I can't just walk in and expect you to know who I am. This is one of the downsides of timestream hopping. You can never be sure if a person you know will know you at that point in their timeline. For what it's worth, I have valued your friendship over the years. And I hope you will come to value mine, too."

"I think I'm starting to."

"That makes me glad to hear."

The operating theatre doors opened and Ava walked out. There were black bags under her eyes, but her mouth was upturned into a tired smile.

"My two boys, getting along. That's what I like to see."

Vynce smiled and looked away.

"Good to see you up and about again, girl. I'd be lying if I said I wasn't a little scared," Vynce said.

"Me too," she said. She put her remaining hand on his shoulder and pulled him in for a hug. The tension drained out of his body as he hugged her.

"So, what's the plan?" Ava asked.

"I spoke to Captain Goldwing," Vynce said.

"Is there any word from the Icarus?"

"They haven't been able to contact the ship. The comm unit you gave him was destroyed," Vynce said to Jaxon.

"That is unfortunate. I don't have another," Jaxon said.

Vynce continued, "Captain Goldwing, along with Raze and Al, are climbing Metro Tower right now. From there, they'll take control of the ship. Once they do that, they'll contact us over comms and we can start moving everyone down to the hangars."

"You're going to move hundreds of injured and dying through the infested streets? People are going to die..." Ava said.

"People have already died, and I don't expect that they'll all make it. I don't think any of these poor fuckers really expect to make it off the ship alive. But it's the only plan we've got. There are evac shuttles down in the hangar, and they're the only way we're going to get off this ship."

"What about our shuttle back near the engine room?"

"We'd be lucky to fit ten people in that thing. Not even the Icarus could carry one hundred passengers. We might be able to carry some, but not all. We're going to need the evac shuttles if we want to save as many as we can."

"The more arms we have carrying guns, the greater chance of success we're going to have. How many guns do we have right now?"

"There's enough to go round. We won't save all of them, but we can save some," Vynce said.

TWENTY-SIX

Draco aimed his grapnel launcher up into the elevator shaft. In his low-light vision he could barely make out the bottom of the elevator carriage sitting high up in the shaft.

"Here goes nothing," he said and fired.

The rope unspooled as the magnetic head flew. It hit the elevator carriage with a dull clunk. Draco flicked the switch on the side of the grapnel and the magnetic head affixed itself. Draco then pulled the second trigger and he was pulled up the elevator shaft, all the way up to the bottom of the carriage.

Draco looked down the shaft but could not see Raze and Al over the glare of their shoulder lamps. Draco held onto the grapnel and looked around for some way into the carriage itself. The bottom was thick steel that would have to be welded through, but they didn't have the time. Draco looked around the shaft for any other ways he could bypass the carriage that blocked his ascent.

Further down the shaft Draco saw closed doors that led into the tower. There would no doubt be some kind of emergency staircase that linked all of the floors together. Draco dreaded what might be inside the tower waiting for them. If Al's reading had been right, and one of the floors had been outfitted into a makeshift research laboratory, there was no telling what might be waiting for them.

Draco saw no other option. They could only cross to the higher floors from floor twenty-three, and if they were lucky they would be able to head up the other elevator shaft to the top of the tower.

"The carriage is blocking us from going any higher. I'm going to open one of the doors here and we can work out what to do when we're all inside," Draco said through the comm channel.

"Copy that. Let us know when we can come up and join you," Raze said.

Draco squeezed the second trigger on the grapnel very gently and the rope unspooled slowly and lowered him down further into the shaft. He released the trigger when he was level with the door. He slowly shifted his weight back and forward. He swung in small arcs to begin with, but the magnetic head held tight. The door itself was flush with the wall, and there was nothing to grab onto. There was no way he could find any leverage to pry the doors open like Al had done with the door below.

"This might be a little noisy, boys. Keep a sharp watch," Draco said as he pushed off from the far side of the elevator shaft with his left leg and readied a powerful kick with his right. He came closer to the door and commanded his grav-boots to send out a repulsive magnetic wave from the sole of his foot. His foot impacted with the doors, and they bulged outward slightly. The repulsive wave of force knocked Draco backwards at an angle and he spun uncontrollably. He put out his spare hand to try and steady himself against something, but there was nothing to grab onto. He spun in the darkness and lost all sense of direction. He closed his eyes and waited for the rope to come to rest.

"You alright up there, Captain?" Raze asked.

"I will be."

"Hang tight."

Draco couldn't help but laugh. He opened his eyes again as he felt himself slow down. He started to swing and once again kicked off from the far side of the elevator shaft. He drove himself against the door again, commanding his grav-boots to send out another repulsive wave of force. The door crumpled open further. The magnetic force bent the doors outward like a blossoming steel rose.

Draco surveyed the darkness beyond the door opening. There was a sound in the room beyond the door. It was a faint fluttering, like a dry leaf pushed over cobblestones by a breeze.

Draco swung himself over to the opening and grabbed onto the edges of the doors. He squeezed through, widening the doorway as he went.

"Come on up. I've opened the door directly below the carriage. It might be a bit of a squeeze, but we can get through," Draco said.

"I'll come up next. Don't go exploring by yourself. Wait for us," Raze said.

"Yes sir," Draco said dryly and exchanged his grapnel for his rifle.

At the bottom of the shaft, Raze aimed his grapnel at the bottom of the elevator carriage. He pulled the trigger and flicked the switch to engage the magnetic head. It stuck firm to the bottom of the carriage. Raze pulled the second trigger and ascended the shaft. He let go of the second trigger as he reached the buckled door. Draco grabbed Raze's hand as he swung towards the door and pulled him towards the opening.

"I'm in Al. Come on up," Raze said.

"I shall be there momentarily," Al said.

Draco and Raze saw the magnetic head fly up the shaft and affix itself to the bottom of the elevator carriage. Al ascended the shaft and Draco pulled him through.

The reception area would have been rather pleasant if the lights had been on. But by the beams of their lamps, the room was eerie. Nothing here had been destroyed like it had been in the rest of the Metropolitan District. It was as though this floor had been completely abandoned.

The reception desk was large enough for two people to sit behind, and a pane of glass separated the front of the counter from the back. There were two clusters of small holes in the glass that would have allowed people behind the counter to speak to those in front. To the side of the counter was a door with a swipe card panel next to the door handle. Al went to approach the counter, but stopped in the middle of the room.

"What is that noise?" Al asked as he heard the low fluttering sound.

"I don't know," Draco said.

"It sounds like waves. Can you hear the ebb and flow?" Raze asked.

Draco concentrated and began to notice the rhythmic pattern of the sound. It came in pulses. Every alternate sound was slightly louder and sharper than the first.

Draco approached the door and tried the handle. It didn't turn. Even though the power was out, the doors were still locked. Draco took a step back from the door and rammed it with his shoulder. The wooden door splintered around the lock and swung open. Behind the desk was an open plan office with multi-screened workstations in neat pods of four.

"I can't imagine having to go to work every day on a ten-year long vacation," Draco said as they walked through the pods.

"Metropolis cruises aren't for most people. Some people just can't function in normal society. They try everything to find some way to escape. Some of them try to lose themselves in hologames, literature, vidserials... Some people just want to get out there among the stars without having to worry about galactic politics and the baggage that comes with the rest of human society," Raze said.

"You wouldn't be making a subversive comment about your captain there, would you Raze?" Draco asked.

"We all have our coping mechanisms, Captain. It's no secret that you'd do everything to fly again if your wings were clipped and you were forced to live on the ground," Raze responded.

"Much like your father," Al added.

"Some people just don't fit the mould that society wants to put them in, so they come to a place like the Metropolis Seven to find somewhere they do fit in."

"And there are some people who would kill for a steady job that they could come to every day for ten years," Al added.

"Not to mention that their job would also let them explore the galaxy on weekends."

"That too. In fact, why don't we go on a Metropolis cruise once we're done here?" Al asked with feigned excitement.

"We don't have to wait until weekends to explore the galaxy and have adventures on the Icarus. That's just work," Raze said.

"Of course, how silly of me" Al said.

"This situation could be perfect for some, but it's definitely not for me," Draco said.

They continued on in silence, and the fluttering, wavelike sound became more noticeable. On the other side of the pods of workstations a green emergency light flickered back on. Draco, Raze and Al raised their rifles and aimed them at the sudden glow in the darkness. The green light showed an arrow pointing deeper into the floor towards an emergency exit.

The lights on their floor came back online in a wave from the far side of the room. The workstations were bathed in light as they came back online. The workstations began to boot up. The displays showed the EarthTech spinning New Earth symbol as the login screen loaded.

They came to the green exit arrow and followed the hallway it pointed down. At the end of the hallway was a junction with an info panel on the wall. The panel had a floor plan with a red arrow flowing through an evacuation diagram. It showed that the emergency stairwell could be accessed from directly behind the lunch room.

Al stopped next to the display and interfaced with it. He downloaded the entire schematic for Metro Tower.

"Captain, I believe I've found the most direct route to the bridge,"

Al said and opened his hand. A light shone out of his palm and displayed the tower from their floor upwards. A red arrow wound up and around the tower.

"So we go up the stairs for five levels, then cross over to the upper elevator shaft?" Draco asked.

"Yes," Al answered.

"How do we know that the route is safe?"

"We don't, unfortunately Captain. But this is the most direct route to the top of the tower."

"Very well. Al, you lead the way."

Alphonse led them around a hallway, turned left, then headed towards an open lunch room full of tables and chairs. There were no lunches left on any of the tables. All of the chairs were pushed neatly into the tables. Nothing was out of place.

"Captain, wait," Raze said. Al and Draco stopped and turned to look at Raze. He continued, "There was no panic here. There was no spontaneous evacuation. I think these people were warned about the infection before it spread."

"I think Raze may be right," Al said.

"Once we get to the top of this tower, then we'll get our answers. There's no point in speculating just yet," Draco said.

"Very well," Al said and continued on.

He led the crew past the lunch room and empty offices towards the stairwell. Al pushed on the bar across the front of the emergency exit and it opened without resistance. In six flights of stairs, they could then cross to the elevator shaft to the higher levels.

They climbed four levels without problem. The fluttering sound had gotten louder the higher they climbed. Draco had begun to think that they may have been able to climb the staircases without encountering a problem, but his heart sank when he saw the first piece of rubble.

Al stopped when he could go no further. Pieces of the walls had broken away from the higher levels and completely blocked the stairwell.

"Al, can you work out another route to get us higher?" Draco asked.

"I believe so. One moment, Captain."

Al opened the palm of his right hand again and brought up the holomap of the complex. He routed the arrow from the blockage at the stairwell and tracked it back down to the floor below. Al zoomed into the floor they were currently on and looked for ways they could ascend.

"Aha! Captain! There are some ducts we may be able to climb to reach the next floor."

"Excellent," Draco said and backtracked down the stairs. Draco came to the emergency exit and pushed it open. The floor in front of them was an exact copy of the floor they had come from.

"It boggles the mind that so much office space is needed on a ship," Draco said.

"Think of it more as a city. In between dockings this ship needs just as much management as a small city. This building would have been equivalent to the chamber of commerce, the local and provincial councils, law enforcement, and anything else you can think of," Raze said.

"Of course. Al, you take point. Lead us to the ducts," Draco said.

Al led them past the offices, towards a storeroom and shouldered the door open. The shelves of the storeroom were lined with stationery, immaculately stored and undisturbed. On the ceiling in the corner of the room was a grate covering the opening to an air-conditioning duct. Raze reached up and tore the grate from its housing.

Al looked up into the duct and said, "This duct should allow us access to two floors above us. Your grapnel launchers should come in handy here, Captain. Shall I go first?"

"No, I'll go," said Draco.

Al and Raze stepped aside and allowed Draco look up into the duct.

"Tight squeeze," Draco said and aimed the grapnel launcher up into the duct. There was no telling whether there would be a metallic surface for the magnetic head to attach to. Draco flicked the switch and three sharp barbs flicked out of the sides of the head. Draco took aim, one finger on the firing trigger, and one finger on the second trigger. He fired the launcher up into the duct and felt the satisfying impact of the head burying into something solid.

Draco pulled the second trigger gently to see if the head had caught fast on anything. The rope grew taught. Draco pulled the trigger with more force and flew up the dark air duct. It was an incredibly close fit.

The grapnel reached the end of its rope. There was no grate covering the top of the vent. Draco put his hand up and tried to find something to grab onto. His hand found something soft and fleshy. He looked up over the cusp and saw that he had grabbed onto something that looked like an intestine that seemed to be growing out of the muck on the floor.

TWENTY-SEVEN

Veck stood on the deck of the engineering bay and watched the Metropolis Seven shrink into the distance. The ship which had loomed so large and threatened to destroy the Icarus only minutes before was nothing more than a watermelon sized grey and blue shape in the distance.

Rhken desperately tried to think of some way that she could stop Veck from commandeering the ship. If they left now, Captain Goldwing and the rest of the crew would be trapped on the Metropolis Seven. She hadn't heard Draco's voice since they landed on the ship. Now there was no telling whether they were even still in comm range. She cradled Reban in her arms.

"He's dead, Rhken. Dad's dead. What are we going to do?" she cried.

"Whatever we have to do to stay alive," she said.

Arak's arm throbbed and ached. Veck refused to let him see to it until they were well away from the giant ship. Veck's words had turned sweet after Arak became submissive. But Arak knew that Veck's friendship would only extend to him as long as he was useful and obedient. Arak was not proud of himself, but he could not bring himself to act against Veck. He knew that he would kill him without a second thought. As long as his actions would not directly lead to the captain's death then Arak managed to justify his compliance to himself.

But he knew that he was betraying the captain through his inaction. If he did anything in his current state, Veck would kill him. He was sure of that. The longer he stayed alive, the more chances he had to set things right.

"Well, children, I believe it's time we made our move. Arak, will you accompany me to the bridge?" Veck asked.

Rhken turned to look at Veck. His smile chilled her to the core. He turned and beckoned Arak to follow him into the ship. He stopped at the threshold of the engineering bay and turned back to the two girls.

"You're both coming too. Get your sister to her feet and bring her with you, little mouse."

Rhken obeyed. She pulled her sister to her feet and ushered her along.

"Reban, honey, we need to go with them. We need to. Can you do that?"

"I just want to stay here," Reban said meekly.

"You can't, honey. You need to come with us, or Veck is going to kill you."

"I want him to. Just let him kill me and get it over with."

Rhken looked into Reban's eyes and shook her. Hard.

"Don't you ever say that," Rhken said.

Reban tried to look away from Rhken's gaze, but Rhken grabbed her head and forced her to look her in the eyes. Rhken said, "Don't you ever say that. You're the only person I have left in the entire galaxy. It's just you and me now, and I need you, okay?"

She buried her face into Rhken's shoulder and said, "Okay."

Rhken led Reban down the stairs from the viewing platform and back up into the corridor to the bridge. Veck smiled as Rhken approached with her sister in tow. He nodded slightly and disappeared into the ship. Arak followed.

When they reached the bridge, Veck reclined back in the captain's chair. Rhken's blood boiled at the sight of that murderer in the captain's chair. She refused to let herself look over into the corner where her father's body lay cloven in two. She positioned herself between Reban and her father's body to block her sister's line of sight. She led Reban over to the co-pilot's chair and sat her down. The chair faced her away from where her father had come to rest.

Nook used to be the co-pilot, but now that he was gone, either of the girls could take over in his stead. Rhken squeezed Reban on the shoulder and went to the supply closet at the back of the bridge.

She opened it and took out an emergency blanket. It was normally used for when someone had gone into shock, but she had another use for it in mind. She took it out of its plastic package and unfolded the blanket. It was thin, but heavy. It was large enough to cover the remains of her father until they could bury him.

Rhken took her father's hand and dragged his top half over to his bottom half. She covered them both with the blanket. There was still blood on the ground, but there was nothing that could be done to get rid of it until they were safe again. Until Veck was taken care of.

In the captain's chair, Veck beckoned Arak over to him. Arak held his broken elbow with his other hand and shuffled over to the captain's chair.

"So tell me Nara-ka, how is it that you were able to set off an electromagnetic pulse?" Veck asked.

"It's an inbuilt countermeasure in the ship's artificial intelligence. It sensed that the crew was in danger, and reacted. That's all."

"You're lying Nara-ka. You engaged the EMP."

"No, I was hiding in the supply closest," he said and looked ashamed.

Veck laughed out loud and said, "In the supply closet? What a warrior you are, Arak Nara! However, there is one small detail which you may have overlooked in your cover story. Perhaps you should have thought it over before you spoke."

"I don't know what you mean," Arak said nervously.

"I can wirelessly interface with almost any system. I've been a part of the ship's systems since I broke free of my bonds. I've seen the security subroutines that are part of the artificial intelligence's programming. I've circumvented them and deleted them. They were set to overload my neurotech implant and wipe my brain. It was supposed to turn me into a vegetable, but I deleted those subroutines. There's no mention of an EMP in the artificial intelligence's core, which means that it was initiated by a member of the crew from a system that the artificial intelligence had no connection to."

Arak Nara's blood grew cold. He began to hear his heartbeat in his ears and stars began to swim in front of his eyes.

"I know that you initiated the EMP, because you're the only crew member who wasn't accounted for. All you need to do is tell me how you did it. I won't hold it against you, of course. If you tell me how you did it, all will be forgiven" Veck said with a smile.

Arak knew that it was all just a ploy. The moment he told Veck how and where he triggered the EMP from, Veck would have access to the EMP, the self-destruct mechanism and the gateway drive. Veck couldn't do much with the EMP now, and there's no way Veck would ever blow the ship while he was on it. But if Veck had access to the gateway drive then he could get to the other side of the galaxy. He also wouldn't need Arak Nara anymore, and Veck would surely kill him.

"I'm waiting," Veck said testily.

"I didn't set the EMP off. It was part of the artificial intelligence's defence systems, I swear it."

"You disappoint me," Veck said and got up from the captain's chair. He strode over to Rhken, who was busy trying to cover her father's body, and grabbed her by the hair. She yelped with pain and terror as Veck held her off the ground.

He walked back towards Arak. Rhken screamed.

"You remember my threat from earlier? It still stands. I'll start with this one, and you two will watch. For every moment that you look away, I will make her scream louder. Shall I begin?"

Arak reflexively looked away for a moment and Veck made good on his threat. He lifted Rhken by the hair and tore her shirt off. She screamed. Her modesty was protected by a black tank top.

Arak looked back and motioned for Veck to stop with his good hand.

"You're ready to cooperate, then?" Veck asked.

Arak nodded.

He didn't want to reveal the secret heart of the Icarus to this madman, but he had no other choice. He couldn't allow the girls to be tortured. If Arak lived to survive this ordeal, he hardly thought that Captain Goldwing could ever forgive him if he allowed any harm to come to them.

Arak had spent his entire life cowering in fear of men like this. It didn't matter what drove a man to do the things that Veck and his kind have done. It all came down to selfishness. In the mercenary crew Arak used to run with it was all about the galactic credits or gathering power. It was how far one man would go to satisfy his own personal desires. Whatever pseudo-altruistic pro-human propaganda Veck used to justify his means, he was still just an asshole on a power trip.

"Put the girl down, and I'll show you," Arak said.

Veck let go of Rhken's hair and she fell into a sobbing heap on the floor.

"Done. Now show me," Veck commanded.

TWENTY-EIGHT

Jaxon walked through the tightly packed crowd in the medical centre. He had excused himself from Ava and Vynce under the guise that he needed to use the facilities, but that was not the case. As Vynce had talked about what they would need to do to escape, memories came flooding back to Jaxon of his first time on the ship.

His instinct began to tug him away from Ava and Vynce. It pulled on him and urged him to do what needed to be done. He knew exactly where he needed to be, what he needed to do, and the words he needed to say. He had already heard himself say them, but he hadn't realised it at the time. Jaxon's head began to hurt when he thought about exactly what his actions would mean, not only in his own timeline, but in the flow of time in the universe. He was about to create a paradox, but at the same time and twenty years previous, the paradox had already been created. He was simply following the events that already had been, will be, and were, set in motion.

He found his younger self exactly where he knew he would. He was in the men's toilets, locked in a stall, sobbing quietly to himself.

Jaxon knocked on the door and said, "You okay in there, kid?"

"Yeah, I'm fine, leave me alone, okay?" Young Jaxon answered.

"It's alright to be scared. Hell, if you weren't, I'd think you were insane."

Young Jaxon laughed, and then blew his nose.

"Can you come out? There's something I need to talk to you about," Old Jaxon said.

"I'm not sure I can help at all."

"To the contrary Jaxon, I know you're the only one who can help me."

There was silence for a moment, then young Jaxon unlocked the cubicle and stepped out. He walked over to the sinks and washed his face.

"What's your deal, anyway? I mean you say you've come here to rescue us, but you're trapped here just like the rest of us. You know that right?" young Jaxon said as he looked at himself in the mirror.

"That may be so, but there's something that I need you to do for me. And I need your guarantee that you're not going to mention this to anyone. Not ever."

Young Jaxon turned and said, "I need to know a little bit about what you're going to ask me, first."

"It's very important. The existence of the human race hinges on you doing what I'm going to ask you to do. I can't tell you any more unless you're on board."

"Why don't you ever take your helmet off? Are you a robot or something?"

Old Jaxon laughed and said, "No. But it's for your protection, believe it or not."

"You must be an ugly fucker, then. I've never known anyone to be ugly enough to endanger anyone else's health."

Old Jaxon laughed again at the surreal nature of being a part of events that he had already lived through. It was as though his body, his mind and his words were living simultaneously as part of his memories and part of his present. His head began to ache. He thought back on how much trouble that smart mouth of his would get him in, but didn't say anything to his younger self. He didn't want to ruin the surprise.

"When you get off the ship," old Jaxon began, and young Jaxon cut him off.

"There you go again. You don't realise what's going on here, do you? We're all trapped. All of us. We're all going to die on this ship. There is no escape."

"You will escape. I know it. Captain Dracovic Goldwing is one of the best men I've ever met, and right now he's working on a plan to get us all out of here. He'll do it, too. That man is a legend. There's nothing he can't do when he's put into a corner."

Young Jaxon nodded. He obviously didn't believe what old Jaxon was saying, but also didn't want to argue. He desperately wanted to believe that there was a chance he would make it off the ship alive.

Old Jaxon opened a small panel on the inside of his wrist. He pulled out a small black case. He flicked the panel closed again and held the small container up in front of young Jaxon. There was no discernible means of opening the small black box. There were no seams or hinges. It was perfectly smooth, and perfectly sealed.

"In this case is something that will change the course of human history," old Jaxon said.

"Yeah right," young Jaxon scoffed.

"It's imperative that you take this case back to New Earth. Deliver it to a man named Johanssen. Erik Johanssen. He works at a news stand near Champion's Square, at the foot of Arther Kronenberc parade. It's called The End Times."

"You're kidding, right?"

"Deadly serious. You take this, you deliver it to Erik Johanssen at The End Times in Champion's Square on New Earth. You tell him that Hercules sent you."

Young Jaxon laughed and said, "Your name is Hercules? I thought it was Reinhardt?"

"My name is many things to many different people. Trust me. Erik will take the case and get it where it needs to go. He'll also reward you for your service. He'll confer the credits that should have gone to me onto you. You'll be able to start a life for yourself. I know you only took the job on this ship because it was a choice between leaving New Earth on a MetroCorp contract, and sleeping on the streets for another year."

Young Jaxon didn't deny it. He had been at his lowest point when he had taken the job on the Metropolis ship. The only reason he got the job over the other desperate street kids was that he had managed to avoid any criminal charges. He'd broken the law, of course. You couldn't survive on the streets without a little stealing, but he had been smart enough to only do it when he knew he would get away with it. Uncovering any kind of criminal charge was only a click away on New Earth's civil network, and if you were ever done for stealing then you wouldn't even get a job flipping burgers at Burgers 'R Us.

But now young Jaxon had the ticket to a life for himself. He'd done five years hard work on the Metropolis Seven, and with the credits he got for delivering this tiny little case to some jerk on New Earth, well, he could maybe think about opening his own business.

"Why would you do this? Why would you give up the credits?" Young Jaxon asked.

"Because I'm going to die on this ship, and I need you to make sure the course of human history is set right."

Young Jaxon's eyes narrowed and he asked, "Who are you? I mean really, who are you?"

"You wouldn't believe me even if I told you," he said as he put the small black case into young Jaxon's open palm.

TWENTY-NINE

Draco lifted himself out of the vent. The ground was carpeted in a thick biomass that looked like the newly grown skin that covers a topical wound. The tube that he grabbed onto snaked its way around the furniture in the room. More biomass grew from whatever it touched. It split into multiple branches. Two of them snaked around the air-conditioning units, up the walls and onto the ceiling. Small pods hung from the ceiling like fleshy water droplets. There was a faint sound coming from inside the pods. They pulsated as something shifted inside.

"The room's not clear, but it looks like it's safe enough to come up," Draco said over comms.

"What do you mean not clear Captain?" Raze asked.

"There's infection here. A lot of growth all over the place. But no immediate danger. I'd appreciate some backup."

"Coming up," Raze said. A moment later the hooked end of Raze's grapnel launcher embedded itself in the ceiling. Raze squeezed himself up the narrow shaft and crawled out onto the floor. He was followed quickly by Alphonse.

Al bent down to look closer at the growth that covered the floor. He prodded it gently and said, "It feels just like skin. I wonder... No, not yet. That may not be wise."

"What might not be wise?" Draco asked.

"Well, I am interested to see if the floor bleeds if it is cut," Al said.

"You're right. That's probably not wise."

"Of course. But it is fascinating. In all the zoological databanks in the galaxy, nothing like this has ever been recorded. I would know. I have a copy of those very archives downloaded to my own databanks. We may be the first people to witness the existence of this species in galactic history," Al said.

"I can't say that I'm particularly happy about that," Draco said.

"Of course not. The introduction of something so different and so violent to any ecosystem is not something that happens without pain and destruction. But I wonder where it came from. If it's not native to any known world, and there is no mention of an organism like this anywhere in the galaxy's zoological record, then where did it come from?"

"Focus on getting to the top of the tower. We can unravel that mystery after we have control of the ship."

"Of course, Captain."

The fluttering sound was no longer quiet. On their floor, it sounded like a gust of wind coming and going rhythmically. Draco led them out of the air-conditioning maintenance room and out onto the floor. He followed down one hallway and stepped out into an open-plan office space full of small pods of four desks like the floors below. He stopped in his tracks, speechless.

Alphonse said, "Oh my."

Raze tried to say something, but a whimper was all that came out. They were not alone in the office.

At each workstation was a person still sitting at their desk. The biomass on the floor had grown up around their bodies. It had threaded its way over and under the people's clothes. It was impossible to tell where the biomass ended and a person began. Alphonse quietly wondered whether there truly was an end, or whether everyone on this floor was now part of a single biomass. A single organism.

The mystery of the fluttering wind-like sound had been solved. Every person on the floor was breathing in unison. Two hundred sets of lungs breathing in and out in perfect unison. The sound was hypnotising. And paralysing.

One of the people sitting in a desk close to Draco, Raze and Al tried to turn its face towards them. Its neck was fused with its shoulders and couldn't actually turn its head to look. Instead it craned its head backward, mouth open. It started making a wailing sound and the rest of the floor joined in until the noise became an unbearable cacophony.

"What do we do?" Raze asked.

"We do the only thing we can do. We keep going. Al, which way do we go from here?" Draco asked.

"Head straight across the office, then through to the lobby. There, we take the elevator shaft all the way to the top of the tower."

"Follow me," Draco said and started to walk through the desks.

The wailing continued and grew in intensity. They came to the back of the reception desk and Al started trying to shoulder through the door.

Some of the fleshlings who could still stand had gotten to their feet. Others who had grown into the biomass in a sitting position could only crane their necks, making that awful wailing sound. But it was when they drew breath that made Draco's skin crawl, for they all took in breath at the exact same time as though their two hundred sets of lungs were all being operated by a single command from a single brain.

The wailing sound became something much more terrifying as Alphonse busted through the door.

"Sssssstoooooopppppppp," the hundreds of voices said as one.

Draco lowered the barrel of his rifle and walked towards one of the pods. A young woman with bright red hair sat at the desk. She couldn't have been a natural redhead of course. They had been bred out of existence hundreds of years ago. Her arms had grown into her torso, and she could not stand. She looked as though she was wearing a second skirt under her first, only it was made of veined purple-tinged flesh.

"Sssssssstoooooopppppp," they said again.

"I'm stopped," Draco said and shrugged, "What do you want?"

"Toooo... liiiiiiiiiiive," the voices resounded.

The fear swept through Draco like an icy wind. He was having a conversation with an organism that no one had ever encountered in the entire history of the galaxy.

"How are you doing this? How are you talking to me through all of these innocent people?"

"Oooonnnnee. Sssaaaaamme."

"One? You're all the same one?"

"Yessss."

"All of you? Even the ones outside?"

"Aaaallllllll."

"The people you've killed. They wanted to live too."

"Theeyyy liiive. One wiiith us."

"They live because they're one with you?" Draco asked, shocked at how easily he had started a conversation with the life form. It had begun to get a fuller grasp on the language, too. Its speech quickly became less protracted and more sophisticated.

"Yesss."

"That's no kind of life. These people had their own lives that they wanted to live. They had their own dreams, their own loves, and their own desires."

"Theeyy aare aalll onnne nnoww. Thheyy haave the... the ssame dreeam," the voices said back.

"What dream is that?"

"To leeaave."

Draco turned away and started walking towards the upper elevator shaft. The sound of hundreds of voices commanded him to stop, and he complied.

"What?" he asked as he turned.

"Help uss. Help uss leeaave."

"At the moment, I can't help you. There's a man in this tower who is stopping me from helping you."

The infected people began to shriek and wail.

"Enough!" Draco shouted, and the people grew silent, "I can help you, but only if you help us. If you promise not to attack or hinder our people in their travels until I say so, we'll let you leave. We'll get you somewhere safe, so you can live."

Raze and Alphonse exchanged glances. Raze switched his comm channel to local comms only and said privately to Draco, "Are you serious Captain? We can't let these things out of this ship. They'll destroy everything they touch."

Without switching his own comm broadcast range to private, Draco turned to Raze and said, "I am your captain, and you will obey my orders. We help them. I'll not condemn intelligent creatures to die if I can save them."

Raze shook his head, but said no more.

"Do we have a deal?" Draco asked the biomass.

"Yess. Help uss. Help you. We will not... attack."

"Good. We'll go to the top of the tower now. We'll take you somewhere safe. Somewhere where you can live."

"Live. Leave. Help. Yesss. Go."

Draco turned away and headed into the elevator foyer. He waited for Raze and Alphonse to follow him and closed the door behind them.

"Before we go any further, you need to know where we're at. Especially you, Raze," Draco said seriously.

"Captain, I-" Raze started.

"You're right, Raze. Of course you're right. Whatever has infected the crew of this ship can't be allowed to touch down on an inhabited planet. We have to find a way to contain or destroy this infection. But I noticed something when I was talking to them. It.

Whatever the fuck it is. If it thinks as one, speaks as one, moves as one, then there's probably a single intelligence driving it. If that single intelligence orders a ceasefire to the rest of its drones and soldiers out there, then Vynce, Jaxon and Ava will have the opportunity to get the rest of the survivors to the hangars, board the evacuation shuttles and get the fuck out of here. So just follow my lead and play along, alright?"

Raze grinned, "You got it Captain. I'm sorry I doubted you."

Draco held up a hand and said, "It's fine. I haven't cracked just yet."

"There is one other consideration we will need to think about," said Al, "and that is that we may not make it back to the hangar in time for us to join the rest of the crew before they leave."

An uncomfortable silence hung in the air between them for a moment until Draco spoke.

"You're right. We may not make it out of this alive. But if there's any chance, it hinges on making the beast in the belly of the ship believe that we're going to find it a new home."

Al nodded. He walked over to the elevator doors and pressed the call elevator button. The display above the door counted down from forty-seven.

"Before we get in, there's a call I need to make. Al, have comm dampeners been reengaged yet?" Draco asked.

"Not yet, Captain. I don't believe they've attempted to bring anything back online just yet. Which is rather strange."

"It works for us," Draco said, then opened the comm channel to Vynce.

"Vynce, it's Captain Goldwing. How is everyone coping down there?"

'Not bad, Captain. Ava's back on her feet. Jaxon's off taking a shit. We're just waiting for your word to kick into gear.'

"Well here it is. I need you to start moving everyone down to the evac shuttles immediately. We're almost at the top of the tower. The quicker you can get everyone down to the ships, the better. The infected passengers won't attack you."

Vynce laughed and said, 'I doubt that. We've already let people know what's going on, but we know we're going to lose people on the way. They're scared. They've seen what these things can do.'

"Believe me when I say your way will be clear. I've reasoned with the intelligence that's controlling the infected. It thinks that we're going to help it relocate to another world."

'Wait, what? You've reasoned with what exactly?'

"I'll spare you the grisly details, but every single infected passenger on this ship is being driven by a single consciousness. A single intelligence. I was able to talk to it, and we've called a truce."

'Do you realise how crazy this sounds?'

"I do, but I need you to trust me. And I need you to get everyone moving. Right now."

'I hear you. I'll get everyone moving as soon as I can.'

"Good. Goldwing out."

Draco stepped into the elevator, followed by Raze and Al.

"Ready?" he asked.

Raze and Al both nodded. Draco pressed the number 47. The doors slid closed and the elevator began to ascend.

THIRTY

Arak's hand shook as he activated the command console. There was no way out. No alternative. He had to unlock the hidden chamber beneath the bridge, otherwise Veck would torture the girls. Arak wished that he had taken a pistol from the armoury as well as the shotgun.

If he had a pistol, he could end it. He couldn't kill Veck, but he could have killed himself. He would take the secret with him into eternity. A bullet would be quick. There would be pain, but it would be over momentarily. Arak knew exactly where to point the barrel to snuff out the spark of life instantly.

Arak steadied his hand as best as he could and began the prompts on the display console to unlock the passage to the heart of the ship. Veck watched him intently. He mapped out the motions that Arak made, the places he touched, and the sequence in which he did them. The activation sequence was disjointed and elaborate. It was not something anyone could ever accidentally stumble across. Veck marvelled at his former friend's ingenuity.

Arak finished entering the sequence then said, "I have flown too close to the sun."

The control console began to split apart, revealing the passage down into the heart of the Icarus.

"'I have flown too close to the sun,'? Why am I not surprised?

Your captain was always too preoccupied with the ramifications of his actions. It stifled his potential," Veck said.

"From what I have seen of the man, the fact that he weighs up the possible outcomes of his choices before he makes them is one of his greatest strengths," Arak said.

"You may be right, but it appears that I'm now in possession of his ship. That's an outcome he didn't calculate into his decision making."

"A foolish man rushes to action. A wise man will take a longer view before taking a single step."

"Philosophy from the Orphosian, hm? How quaint."

"Does it surprise you?"

"Not at all. Your moon is not known for the strengths of its people, nor the strengths of their minds. They're weak. They break easily. I've broken a few myself. You're adequate, but no one from your moon will ever do anything than anyone will remember."

"You insult my home."

"I don't mean to offend, I'm simply pointing out a fact. If facts offend you, then that's no concern of mine. Now, you've been a good lap dog. Go down into the med bay and get yourself fixed up."

"You don't wish me to accompany you?"

"No, I find you particularly droll and uninteresting," Veck said with a small sigh, "However I am a man of my word. I will allow you to repair yourself, and I will allow you to live."

Arak said nothing. He met Veck's gaze and did not waver.

"Little mouse, you will accompany Nara-Ka to the med bay to ensure he does not do anything to compromise the safety of the people aboard this ship, including your new captain."

Rhken's breathe caught in her chest. She wanted to protest, but knew that it was futile. If she could arm herself while Arak's arm was getting treated, perhaps she could take Veck out. Conventional firearms wouldn't help, but there had to be a way of disabling him enough that they could take control of the ship back.

"Your sister, the little weeping angel, she will accompany me down into the ship," Veck said and Rhken knew that she couldn't raise a hand against him. Not while he had her sister. He had done two things in one move. He had ensured that Rhken would not act against him, and she would ensure that Arak didn't try anything either. Rhken loved her sister more than anything else in the galaxy and would fight for her with every breath left in her body.

Rhken walked over to her sister and put her hand on her shoulder. She had stopped sobbing, but the tears still came. Reban didn't think she would ever stop crying.

"It'll be alright. Just do what he says, and he won't hurt you. Promise me you won't try anything sister," Rhken said to Reban.

"He's already hurt me. Nothing could hurt more than losing Dad," Reban whispered.

Rhken squeezed her sister's shoulder and whispered back, "I know honey. But I need you too. So just do what he says and we'll make it out of this alive."

"And what about Captain Goldwing? We haven't heard from him in hours. He could already be dead for all we know."

"We can't think about that. We need to be there for each other. It's all we have left."

"I know."

Rhken helped Reban up from her chair and they walked over to Veck together. Their hands clutched in a fierce embrace. Neither of them wanted to let go, but when Veck motioned for Reban to descend the ladder first Reban let go of Rhken's hand. She gave her sister a look of resignation and began to climb down.

"Watch him," Veck said and motioned his head toward Arak, "If he does anything to threaten my safety, your sister will die. I am a man of my word."

Rhken nodded wordlessly and joined Arak by the exit of the bridge.

As they walked towards the med bay Rhken asked, "How badly is your arm broken?"

"I don't think elbows are meant to bend this way," Arak said with a pained smile.

Rhken offered a sad smile back. They continued on in silence until they reached the med bay. On the right hand side of the room was a med pod that looked like the armour pods inside the armoury. It was a white cylinder with a clear glass door on the front. Inside the pod was an upright gurney that a patient would be strapped into before starting a procedure.

Arak activated the med pod. The door slid open and the gurney swung down. Once all of the straps had been unhooked, Arak stepped back from the gurney and started to remove his chest armour. He gave the mental command to disengage the shoulder joints from the main torso module, then gave the command to disengage the chest armour connections. Rhken helped remove the armour from his right arm, then Arak gently removed the armour from his broken left arm.

The left arm of his smartsuit was slick with blood. Something protruded from beneath the skin. Arak swore under his breath and climbed aboard the gurney.

"Rhken, could you please help me strap in?" he asked.

"Of course. Get as comfortable as you can. I'll need to take your smartsuit off at the shoulder, alright?"

"Yes. Please be careful. The pain relief the suit was providing has started to wear off. It's getting to be unbearable," Arak said through clenched teeth.

She took a pair of scissors from the supply cabinet next to the pod and snipped a hole in Arak's smartsuit, just below his left shoulder joint. She then cut down the outside curve of his arm. As she got close to his elbow, he bit his bottom lip so hard that he drew blood.

"I'm sorry! Did I hurt you?" Rhken asked.

"Please, go, make it quick."

"I'm sorry," she said and continued cutting.

She worked as quickly as she could and then began to pull the suit away from his arm. When Arak saw the splintered bone poking out of a blood red hole in his elbow skin, his face turned white and he felt as though he might throw up. Rhken put a hand on his chest to steady him and said, "Hey now. Just a moment and we'll get you fixed up, okay?"

Arak nodded. Rhken affixed the final two straps. One over Arak's left bicep, and the other over his left wrist.

"Ready?" she asked.

He nodded again.

Rhken activated the gurney. It lifted itself vertically back into the med pod and the door slid closed.

'Please advise of injury area,' an automated voice from the med pod said.

"Left arm. Elbow joint. Possible damage in both upper and lower arm stemming from violent dislocation. Also, broken cheekbone," Rhken said.

'Commencing diagnosis'

The med pod began to fill with an amber-coloured oxygenated liquid. The liquid also contained a heavy sedative and painkiller. As soon as the liquid reached Arak's lungs he would fall into a deep sleep and would not awaken until the procedure was complete.

'Procedures will occur as follows; muscle and ligament tearing will be repaired. Compound fractures will be repaired and set. Destroyed cartilage will be replaced with synthetic alternative. Possible nerve damage has occurred and will be repaired if possible. Sunken cheekbone will be reconstituted and set. Commence procedure?'

Arak nodded. "Commence procedure," Rhken said just as the amber coloured liquid reached Arak's mouth.

Reban reached the bottom of the ladder and stepped down into the heart of the Icarus. A single dim green light illuminated the small room around the central control console on the pillar in the middle of the room. Reban walked slowly into the small room and wondered just where in the ship she was.

Veck reached the bottom of the ladder and laughed. His laugh sounded very loud and very close in the tiny room.

"This room was not on the schematics of the ship," Veck said.

Reban wondered how Veck had gotten his hands on the schematics to the ship, but dared not ask. She stood against the wall next to the control pillar and waited for Veck to do something. She had no idea what this room was even for.

Suddenly a blue light began to shine out of the floor panel in front of the control pillar. The light formed itself into a hologram of a man that looked almost exactly like Captain Goldwing. The hologram turned and saw Veck Simms approaching.

"Samuel Goldwing," he said with a smile.

"My, my. Young Veck Simms. It seems you've grown up," the hologram responded.

"More than you could ever know."

Reban's mind raced. How in the world could Veck have any connection to this ship, let alone a connection to someone in the Goldwing family? Had this been planned from the start? Reban desperately wanted to say something, but she found herself unable to find the courage to speak.

"What has happened? Is Draco back on board the ship yet?" the hologram asked.

"No, I've taken command of the ship for now. Your son is in grave danger, and we need to do everything we can to rescue him. But we don't have enough firepower."

"The young man from before, what happened to him?"

"Killed in action. We were boarded. There are more ships on the way, and we need to get out of here immediately."

"Oh my. I did like that young man. He seemed like a very

capable pilot. What a pity."

"Yes, we all mourn his loss," Veck said and scowled at Reban.

She wanted to say something. Anything. Arak wasn't dead, but Captain Goldwing would be stranded if they left him behind. She tried to gather her courage to say something, but nothing more than a squeak left her lips.

"Oh dear, he was a good man. From what I saw, anyway. My young dear, we'll have you out of here very quickly. Did the young man tell you about the gravity drive before he perished?" the hologram of Samuel Goldwing asked.

Veck grinned wolfishly and said, "No. No, he did not."

"I'm afraid the gravity drive requires approximately an hour to warm up. Tearing an unstable hole in the fabric of space and time does take an awful lot of power."

"Can we engage the gravity drive from the main control console?" Veck asked.

"Not normally, however I do believe I could route the controls up there if you'd like. They will appear as a subroutine option under the higher ship functions. When the display shows that the gravity drive is fully charged, set a course for where you wish to travel."

"Excellent. Have the controls been routed to the main control console?"

"Yes, it is done. But remember, you need to speak the activation phrase to engage the gravity drive."

"I'm afraid the pilot didn't pass the phrase onto me. Could you tell it to me?"

"Of course, son. Once the drive is powered up and you've set a course, speak the words 'and I will fly again' aloud."

"Thank you, Samuel. It has been good to see you, but I am sorry," Veck said.

"Sorry? For what?"

"Firstly, your son will likely be dead within the new few hours and I am not going to attempt to rescue him," Samuel's blue holographic face was twisted by confusion and grief, then flickered out of existence, "and for that."

"What did you do?" Reban asked.

"I deleted him," Veck said and tapped the side of his head. While he was talking to the hologram of Draco's father, he used Evie's security protocols to find out where the hologram was stored within the ship's memory banks. Veck then sent the entire security force to delete Samuel's hologram from the memory banks completely, just as he had done with Evie.

The ship was now his, and he had a means of escape. All he needed to do was wait.

THIRTY-ONE

The hope of survival inspired everyone to take up arms. Vynce thought that he would have trouble convincing the more recalcitrant passengers to leave the med station, but there were very few people who were content to sit and wait for the inevitable. And even those who were willing to sit and wait for the infection to take them were more easily swayed than Vynce had anticipated. He had no idea what Jaxon said to them to get them moving, but whatever it was, it worked.

The head count Vynce did put their numbers at approximately one hundred and eighty people. He had missed some, and some he had counted twice, but one hundred and eighty bodies armed with what firearms they had would be enough to put up a decent fight if they had to. But if what Draco had said was right, it would be a straight shot to the hangars without any problems.

Every child was partnered up to an adult, and every person with an injury that impeded their movement was paired up with a protector with a weapon. There were some people in wheelchairs and some on crutches, but everyone banded together and made sure that no one was forgotten. Those who could walk, walked. Those who could carry a weapon carried a weapon. People grabbed surgical tools like bone saws, scalpels and plasma cutters from around the med station when they couldn't find anything else.

"Grab as many rations as you can! Even if we make it off this ship, we're in for a long trip before we get to a gateway. We need to be prepared!" Jaxon said to a group of people gathering supplies from the storeroom.

"Medical supplies, too. Lots of med gel. Grab as much as you can carry," Vynce added.

In a matter of minutes the supply cupboards were empty and people were carrying full bags in one hand and weapons in the other. A man in a wheelchair rolled along next to Vynce with a rifle across his lap and smiled as he passed.

Jaxon had quiet words with a grey-haired man who was crying into his hands. The man nodded and wiped his bleary eyes on his sleeve. He nodded again and Jaxon clapped him on the shoulder. The man stood up and found something to arm himself with.

Vynce walked over to Jaxon amongst the hubbub and asked, "What did you say to that man?"

"I told him that he was going to die, so why not die protecting those who could live out their days?"

"He's infected?"

"Yes. When we reach the evac shuttles we'll need to inspect everybody closely. Anyone who has signs of infection cannot leave this ship, alive or dead."

"Agreed. But how the fuck can we be sure? I mean we didn't know Ava was infected until she started showing signs."

"I don't think it will be a problem. Doctor Harris has it covered."

Vynce went to check on Doctor Harris, who was coordinating the medical supplies. She had a smartscreen that she had inventoried all of their medical supplies on, with a list of who carried what. When she saw Vynce approach, she waved him over.

"Once we get to the shuttles, I'll give this over to you. There are a number of people who've had basic medical training, and you should have two or three of them on each shuttle. I've linked their profiles here," she pointed to a folder marked medical personnel, and tapped the folder to open it.

"These people are the important ones. The uninfected ones. You've got Doctor Sean Fewster here," she said and a profile of a man with olive skin, short cropped black hair and a trimmed goatee slid in to fill the screen, "He's a hero. He's the reason we got to this med station in one piece. You want him to choose a couple of nurses to go with him on one of the shuttles. If he makes it out of this alive, you see he gets a medal."

"Doctor Fewster. Hero. Gotcha, although I don't know if I have the power to give medals," Vynce said.

"And this is Dr Cooper," she said and swiped Doctor Fewster off the screen. Doctor Cooper was a young female doctor with brown hair, almond shaped eyes and porcelain white skin. "She may look young, but she's better than I was at her age, and she's got a passion for saving lives. You want her to run your second team."

"Noted. Do you know the hangar we need to get to?"

"Yeah, I know it. That's where our own medical shuttle is stationed for when we go planet-side for supplies. It's a big hangar. Lots of shuttles. I'm sure you'll find a couple that are still working. And don't worry. I'll be there with you right until the end. I'll lead you to where you need to go."

"You know it's a one way trip?"

"I know it. It's been a one way trip for me since I got squirted with infected goo. I slowed it down some, but it'll come for me one way or another soon enough. And to be honest, I'd welcome the rest."

She put her arm on Vynce's shoulder, but Vynce pulled her in close and hugged her. She resisted stiffly at first, then relaxed and returned his embrace. When they pulled apart Vynce thought he saw tears welling up in her eyes, but she turned away so quickly that he couldn't tell for sure. She hurried back into the operating theatre.

She came back out wearing a modified diagnosis glove. It wrapped around her arm up to her elbow. In the palm of the glove was a sophisticated sensor module that could be calibrated to detect a number of medical ailments. On the top of the forearm there was a touch-screen display which would show results about whatever the doctor was scanning for.

"I've calibrated it to detect the infection," Doctor Harris said and held the palm of the glove on Vynce's shoulder. It beeped once and a message flashed in green on the screen.

No infection.

Doctor Harris placed the glove on her own shoulder and initiated the scan. A message flashed on the display in purple.

Infection present.

"No one is getting on board those shuttles unless they pass my infection scan, do you understand?" Doctor Harris asked.

Vynce nodded.

"If anyone who fails this test tries to board one of your shuttles, you shoot them. You kill them, and you promise me that your conscience will remain clean. If they're infected, they're already dead. They just don't know it yet. You promise me that you will kill anyone who tries to board a shuttle out of here, or you give me a gun and I'll do it myself."

"I promise you," Vynce said.

Jaxon was the first to leave the med station. He opened the door with his rifle held to his shoulder, but there was no need. There were no infected passengers or other overgrown monstrosities lingering in the streets. As he left the med station, a column of survivors followed him out of the doorway, sticking close behind him. Ava was right behind Jaxon. She wore her armour again, but her shoulder guard lay flat over the place where her right shoulder used to be.

Doctor Harris followed up the rear to make sure that everyone had left the med station. She still wore her doctor's coat and diagnostic glove, but now she had a shotgun holster slung over her shoulder as well. She left Doctor Fewster to bring up the rear and jogged up to the front of the column. Everyone looked scared, but for the first time since this whole thing started she saw glimmers of hope on some of their faces.

She joined Jaxon and they led the column of survivors down a wide street back into the Residential District. Vynce was the first to see one of the infected passengers loitering by the side of the road. It was standing on a stoop of an apartment, drooling a cascade of goopy red liquid that ran down the steps in front of it.

"Infected on the right," Vynce said and raised his weapon at the thing on the stoop.

Some of the people shrieked in terror. Some of them stopped in their tracks. Some of them raised their weapons. But the fleshling made no move. Vynce urged them to keep moving and hesitantly complied. As they passed the fleshling, it watched them. After they had passed completely, the fleshling started walking down the steps.

Vynce hung back until the rest of the group had passed and kept his rife aimed squarely at the infected passenger's head. It was a slower walker than the survivors, as its right foot had grown out and over the top of its boot. Root-like fleshy tendrils protruded out of the holes and tears in its boot and the leg of its pants, dragging it on the ground as it tried to walk. It didn't possess the same desperation or aggression that the other infected had shown. It was merely following.

Doctor Fewster joined Vynce and raised his pistol at the infected. His mouth was set in a thin grim line. His hand was shaking. Vynce put his hand on top of the doctor's gun and lowered the barrel to the ground.

"Don't. They're not being aggressive right now, but if we provoke them they may change that. Look," Vynce said and motioned for the man to look at the street behind them.

More fleshlings had started to shuffle out onto the street behind them. They seemed to materialise from the shadows. They slipped out of drains and from in between buildings as silently as whispers. Vynce joined the end of the column again and kept his eyes on the infected procession. It quickly began to grow in number.

"It's Doctor Fewster, right?" Vynce asked.

The doctor nodded.

"Well Doctor Fewster, how would you feel about watching my back?"

"You got it."

"Have you ever seen them act like this?"

"Never. Whenever one of those things sees you, you either draw your gun or run for your life. Neither option usually ends well, because there are always more of them. Seeing them just following us like this is creeping me the fuck out."

"How did all of this start?"

"No idea. By the time most of us knew about them there were too many to fight. They had a nest somewhere deep in the ship. They captured some of us, but they didn't really need to. All they had to do was touch us, infect us, then wait. We killed some of our own before they had the chance to turn. Some preferred it that way. Others fought to the bitter end, but we still ended up putting them down."

"I can't imagine the horrors you people have been through. We'll get you out of this. I promise you."

Doctor Fewster smiled sadly and said, "You're the third person who's promised us that. The other two are already dead."

THIRTY-TWO

The elevator reached the forty-seventh floor. Draco, Raze and Al raised their rifles to their shoulders and trained them on the closed doors. The door opened straight onto the bridge. It was the largest bridge that Draco had ever seen on a civilian vessel. Only the military command bridge of a dreadnought vessel was larger.

The centre of the room was raised into a central circular dais, and a row of terminals ran around it. The terminals were on, but empty. The windows at the front of the ship looked out into the vast dark expanse of the Milky Way galaxy.

The same organic substance from the floors below covered the bridge. In the middle of the central dais was a large, fleshy growth that reminded Draco far too much of the hunter's cocoon they had stumbled across in the Residential District. The organic growth covered the entire floor. Its tendrils wound their way up the legs of chairs, around computer terminals, and had even grown up the walls and over the ceiling above. Small fleshy polyps hung from the ceiling.

Draco stepped out into the bridge and checked both sides. The growth was much thicker in one corner of the bridge.

"Any sign of our friend from over the loudspeaker, Captain?" Al asked.

"No, and I don't like it. He should be here," Draco said.

"Could he... Could it... Could that be him?" Raze asked and

pointed with the barrel of his rifle at the growth in the centre of the bridge.

"I hope not," Draco said and proceeded into the bridge.

The lights which should have illuminated the walkways between the elevator and the control circle in the centre of the bridge were on, but completely grown over. The light shone through the flesh carpet in the spots where it was thinnest, showing veins and arteries. The growth they were walking on was alive. It wasn't simply some secretion made by the infected crew members. It was the infection, growing like moss on the side of a tree.

To the left of the main elevated control circle was a bank of terminals that had been completely grown over. A couple of chair backs and partial pieces of desks grew out of a tumorous mass. To the right of the control circle was another bank of terminals which still looked operational. The creeping growth hadn't reached it yet, but it was only a few metres short.

Draco, Raze and Alphonse had been so focused on what was in front of them that they hadn't thought to check what was behind. Behind them was a viewing platform that looked out over the habitable zones of the Metropolis Seven. It stretched around the back of Metro Tower with floor-to-ceiling glass. A single human watched them from the viewing platform. His mouth was covered by the large hand of a Vartalen trooper in full combat assault gear.

Behind him were another three Vartalen troopers. The Vartalen people were from an oxygen-rich planet where all of their flora and fauna were large and aggressive, even the herbivorous species. The Vartalen people were no different. They stood anywhere from two to three metres tall, and some were as wide as two well-built human men. They were naturally heavily muscled, with broad shoulders and small squat heads that jutted out horizontally from between their shoulders. They had mouths full of large white semi-serrated teeth which had evolved to shear meat from bone.

In hand to hand combat, the Vartalen people were unmatched,

Their society valued strength over all other attributes. They valued not only physical strength, but strength of the mind and the strength of will. The very best of their species were powerful, intelligent and ambitious. A Vartalen would not follow the commands of another Vartalen that could not best them.

The Vartalen squad remained motionless and silent as Draco, Raze and Alphonse explored the bridge.

Alphonse approached the consoles that were still operating and began to use them. He hacked into the protected databanks with ease and connected wirelessly to the main operations mainframe. He began downloading the information from the ship's journey recorder to pinpoint exactly when everything turned to shit.

Raze walked to the front of the bridge and stood against the thick glass that separated him from the cold void of space. He put his hand up to the glass and touched it. It was cold. He started to think about just how far away from home he was and became lost in a moment of yugen.

Draco joined Al at the consoles and opened the personnel database. He quickly located the captain's record and opened it up. A picture of a black-haired man with a severe jawline and an equally severe haircut appeared on the screen. His name was Captain Adam Hane, an ex-Alliance military pilot who had been honourably discharged and continued his career in the private sector.

Draco opened the captain's log and found a number of videos that had been made two weeks prior. The final video which was made less than 24 hours previous was titled 'Goodbye'.

Draco opened the video and it began to play. Captain Hane sat on the captain's chair in an empty bridge. His clothes were torn and his face looked worn and ragged. It looked as though he hadn't slept in weeks. He sat with his hands cupped over his mouth, looking in the direction of the front-facing bridge windows. He was staring out into the blackness of space as though he was trying to organise his thoughts before speaking. He remained motionless and silent for minutes before looking into the camera. He took a breath and moved his hands away from his mouth and began to speak.

'This is Captain Adam Hane, captain of the Metropolis Seven. If you're watching this video, then I am dead, and I have failed. My son and I are the only remaining survivors of a highly contagious infection that has taken the lives of all passengers and crew on this ship. I don't know where the infection came from or what caused it. There's nothing in the known galaxy that consumes and destroys like this infection does. There's not an animal, plant, or anything in between that does what this fucking thing does.'

Anger had crept into his voice. He forced himself to stop talking for a moment to regain his composure.

'It could have been bio-terrorism. It's the only thing I can think of that makes any kind of sense. We were last supplied on Kopaeko. Tonnes of food, oxygen and water were brought on board to supplement our own self-replenishing supply. It's on the border between Council space and the Arcturus sector. It was a new supply depot. We'd never used it before. We didn't really need it, but the passengers were screaming for some variety. Some local galactic flavour. They could have snuck the infection on board and we would have never known. But that still doesn't explain why I couldn't find anything that even remotely resembles this infection in the entire history of the galactic council.

'But that's not important. What's important is the fact that you're watching this, when this entire ship should have been incinerated in one of the Gemon system's binary stars. I've just set a course there and disabled the engine controls from the bridge,' he said and motioned to the empty bridge around him, 'my resident Metropolis Corporation representative has decided to pursue a course of action against the captain's wishes. He believes that we need to bring the Metropolis Seven back to New Earth for quarantine and investigation. He and I had a violent disagreement. I don't even know if he's alive anymore. I hope the little corporate weasel is growing into a fucking wall somewhere.

'If this ship ever gets to a terrestrial planet, it's a death sentence for the entire planet and anyone who lands on it. The infection spreads through every biological organism it encounters like wildfire. Animal, plant, it doesn't matter. We even found active spore-like organisms in the water system. We've had people drinking from water bottles for a week now, but that didn't help. There are just too many infected on board. I lost contact with everyone else yesterday. I can only assume that they're all either dead or infected. The ship is locked onto a course to Krakaterra. Once we're in the gravitational field of the planet we'll wait till it passes between the two suns and we'll cook inside the ship. But it'll be worth it knowing that I've saved the galaxy from the horror of this infection.'

'This is Captain Adam Hane, signing off.'

The video ended and the display reverted back to his profile page. It was hard to believe that the confident, powerful looking man in the photograph was the same man that made the video they had just watched.

Alphonse had been keeping his sensors attuned to Captain Hane's video while he also searched through the ship's journey log. He compared the incidences where the ship entered an emergency state with the reported incidents of infection. He cross referenced those with the time they restocked in Kopaeko and the amount of dinners served by the restaurants on board the Metropolis Seven containing foodstuffs from those supplies. There was no correlation. The same batches of supplies had been divided up between a number of different restaurants, and the cases of infection shared no common timeline from the point of ingestion of those supplies among others who also ate meals cooked from the same supplies.

"Captain Goldwing, I do not believe that this was bio-terrorism. At least not from the source that Captain Hane has surmised. I'm currently processing a number of datasets and will notify you when I find something that I believe may explain things," Alphonse said.

"You got it, Al. How about dockings? Did any other ships dock with the Metropolis Seven while it was en-route to the Arcturus Sector? Can you find out any information about what they were even doing here?"

"One second, Captain," Al said.

After a moment of silence, Al continued, "The Metropolis Corporation has an agreement with the Vartalen government who control this sector. They were guaranteed safe passage by the ruling clan, and guarantees from the mercenary guilds that any Metropolis Corporation ships in this area were to be left alone."

Draco raised an eyebrow and said, "The Vartalen actually agreed to that?"

"It appears so, yes. For a large sum of credits."

"Of course."

"There is no correlating data to suggest that an outside party delivered anything to the ship, and definitely no data that would line up with the infection timelines. However..." Al said and went silent again for a moment.

"Captain, I believe I've discovered the source of the infection! A week and a half ago there was a hull breach on the underside of the ship. The first person to appear with the infection was the person who reported the incident. A man named Bill Timms. The report says that there was a tiny puncture which was able to be patched easily. The puncture was caused by a meteorite. The reports say that the meteorite was not unusual, apart from the fact that it began to 'sweat' as it cooled. Every person who appears on the subsequent reports about this meteorite became infected, then the infection began to grow exponentially until it was out of control and useful records cease."

"How could something survive on the outside of a meteorite?" Draco asked.

"There are microscopic organisms that can survive in a complete vacuum, as well as those that can survive freezing sub-zero temperatures, like the tardigrade. That organism originated on Old Earth. If this infection occurs at a cellular level, and I believe it does given that we've seen it use the host's own musculature, circulatory system and bone structures, it's quite possible that the heat generated from punching through walls of thick metal could have been enough to rejuvenate the cells on the meteorite. A little bit of heat was all it took to wake them up again," Al said.

"Well I'll be damned. I'll be willing to put credits on the identity of our friend who talked us into restarting the engines," Draco said.

"The Metropolis Corporation representative?"

"Yeah. Which means that he's not dead."

Raze had been listening to Draco and Al's conversation while looking out at the universe. He closed his eyes, threw his head back and took in a deep breath. When he opened his eyes he saw something attached to the outside of the ship that shouldn't have been there.

It was a Vartalen attack cruiser. A scout ship. He turned around to warn Draco, but it was too late. A huge Vartalen brute picked up Draco by the neck and threw him across the bridge like a rag doll.

THIRTY-THREE

Veck forced Reban to climb the ladder ahead of him, just in case the little mouse and the pilot decided to be truly foolish. After he and Reban were clear of the hatch entrance, the command console re-formed where it had once stood.

Veck navigated to the subroutine folder under the folder containing the higher ship functions and saw an icon titled Gateway. It looked exactly like one of the stationary gateways found across the galaxy. It appeared as a ring of titanium alloy, with four gravity drives at equal points around its circumference. The inside of the gateway swirled like a spiral galaxy. That was of course a romanticism of what the gateways represented. In reality, an open gateway was just like a window without glass. You simply looked through the titanium alloy ring and saw what was on the other side.

Veck touched the icon and the gravity drive command module popped up on the screen. There was a percentage counter on the right hand side of the window which indicated the current charge level of the gravity drive, and a map of the galaxy on the left hand side. You could either enter a specific set of coordinates, or you could select from a number of pre-programmed destinations. The current charge level was at 35.3% and rising a tenth of a percentile quite quickly. Reban watched it climb quickly to 36%, then 37%, and wondered just how Captain Goldwing could ever make it back in time to take back control of his ship.

Veck scrolled through the pre-populated destinations and chuckled. They were all in space where travelling through personal gateway drives was frowned upon, but legal. There were no destinations inside Alliance or Council space, but that suited Veck just fine. His installation was in a sector of space that no other human had ever visited, and was only a short trip from a habitable planet that he would set the girls and the pilot down on.

He had contemplated killing them and wiping his hands of it, but he admired the strength of the little mouse and the pilot. He looked Reban up and down and thought that he would be doing the human race a favour if he removed her from the gene pool. Strangely, he found himself oddly fond of the little mouse for her ferocity at defending her sister. He thought that if Reban could inspire such love and devotion from someone with such strength of spirit, then she must have some redeeming quality that wasn't obvious to him.

The charge level reached 40% and kept climbing. Veck set his destination. He would open a gateway to the border worlds nearest his installation. The planet that he planned on dumping Arak and the girls on was not inhabited. It would be rough going, and their chances of survival were dicey at best, but they would have to prove their strength and their will to live. He had at least set a course to a system where human trafficking and slavery were outlawed. Folks there were more concerned with growing crops and harvesting water than selling their young girls to pleasure houses.

Veck smiled at himself when he realised that he had some affection for the little mouse. He had hurt her, it was true, however he didn't like doing it. There was that raw primal part of himself that craved violence and destruction, but if he killed the little mouse, he knew that he would regret it. He could kill the other cowardly girl and the pilot, but not the little mouse. She had the potential to achieve so much if she focused herself.

As if his thoughts had called out to her, Rhken returned to the bridge. Reban rushed to her side and clung desperately to her arm.

"Arak is in the med pod. The surgery will take a while, and he'll need time to recover," Rhken said.

"Good. Good," Veck said distractedly at he looked out of the front of the Icarus.

Rhken crossed the bridge with Reban in tow. She sat down into one of the co-pilots' chairs, and Reban joined her in the other. Rhken reclined back and closed her eyes. Reban reached out and took Rhken's hand in hers.

"Sis, are we going to be okay?" Reban asked as she looked out of the windows of the Icarus.

Rhken smiled wanly and said, "I honestly don't know."

THIRTY-FOUR

The procession of fleshlings had grown larger. As Jaxon led the column of survivors through the Residential District, more and more infected passengers had started to follow them. At first only a few of the infected had joined the lone shambler, but more had begun to wander after them until their numbers had started to rival those of the survivors.

But the fleshlings kept their distance. They showed a restraint that made Vynce feel very uncomfortable. Their eyes were not blank, or glassy, or furious with aggression as he had seen earlier. There was some intelligence there, just below the surface.

"Fewster, you still got my back?" Vynce said.

"Of course," Doctor Fewster said.

Vynce stopped, turned, and looked at the approaching group of infected. Doctor Fewster stood next to him and gave him an anxious look.

"What are you doing?" Doctor Fewster asked.

"Just a test," Vynce replied.

The approaching infected continued walking towards the two men, and the survivors kept walking on toward the hangar.

The shambling fleshling, the first that had started following them, still led the column. The shambler reached a certain point, about fifty metres behind Vynce and Doctor Fewster, and then stopped walking forwards. It made a gurgling, moaning sound and looked up and down at the two men as though it didn't understand what was happening.

Doctor Fewster's hand went to his pocket and rested on the handle of his pistol. Vynce grabbed his hand and shook his head.

"No aggression," Vynce said.

Doctor Fewster pulled his hand out of his pocket. It was shaking. He nodded at Vynce nervously.

"Follow my lead," Vynce said and took two steps backward.

Doctor Fewster took two steps backward and stopped next to Vynce.

The shambler took one step forward dragging its overgrown foot along the ground after it. It took another step forward and dragged its other foot forward along the ground again. It stopped after two steps and looked the two men up and down again.

"What the hell are they doing?" Doctor Fewster asked.

"They're not attacking. They're afraid of getting too close to us, as though they're conscious of appearing to be aggressive."

"I wouldn't give them too much credit. The last time they were conscious was before they were infected," Doctor Fewster said.

"There's some intelligence there somewhere," Vynce said and walked back towards the column of survivors.

They caught up quickly and continued on through the Residential District. The entrance to the hangar was near the Eden's Hill mag-rail station. They continued on in that general direction for as long as they could. More and more fleshlings joined the horde behind them.

The road they followed forked off in two directions in front of a large cluster of closely built apartment buildings. They had been built so close together that there was barely enough room for five people to walk abreast between them. The spaces between the buildings were dark.

Jaxon halted the procession in front of the building and spoke quickly to Doctor Cooper, "What do you think, doc? Easier for us to go around, or through?"

Doctor Cooper considered this for a moment and said, "The entrance to the hangar is right on the other side of these apartment blocks. Cutting through would be quickest, but no one's been brave enough to go in there for days. We used to raid these buildings for food and bottled water, but eventually the people we sent out stopped coming back. We decided it was too dangerous."

"How long would it take us to walk around?"

"Maybe half an hour."

"How long if we cut through?"

"If we don't run into any trouble? Ten minutes."

Vynce jogged up to the front of the group and asked, "What's the plan?"

"We're debating on whether we take the long way, or cut through," Jaxon said.

"Cut through. We need to get out of here," Vynce said.

Doctor Cooper stepped in and said, "We don't know what's in there. We could be walking into a nest."

"So what? The infected won't attack us," Vynce said.

Doctor Cooper laughed and said, "How can you be absolutely sure of that?"

Vynce looked back at the horde of infected who had come to a halt roughly fifty metres behind the cluster of survivors and said, "They won't attack us. Look at them. They have enough of them to take us all if they wanted to, but they don't. Captain Goldwing said that they think we're going to take them to a safe place. They think we're going to get them off this ship. They won't attack us unless we attack them first."

"You put a lot of faith in your assumptions," Doctor Cooper said.

"No, I put a lot of faith in my captain," Vynce said.

Jaxon smiled and said quietly, "Very well." He approached a small single passenger car that had tipped on its side against a light pole nd climbed on top of it. He stood above the rest of the survivors and said, "Passengers of Metropolis Seven! I need you all to trust me right now, and I need you to follow my orders to the letter. Can you do that?"

A low non-committal murmur came from the crowd.

"We're going to get out of here alive, and the quicker we can get to the hangar and our evacuation ships, the quicker we can leave. To do that, we need to cut through these apartment buildings."

The conversation between people became panicked and full of fearful objections.

"I need all men and women who can hold a gun and protect themselves to go to the outside of our group. I need you to protect those who can't protect themselves. Those of you who are already infected, I need you to also join our protectors on the outside of our group. But we will not provoke the infected. No gunshots. No violence. No aggression. We group up together, get through this, and we're home free. Do you all understand?"

"I understand," Doctor Harris said and stepped to the front of the group. Slowly others began to join in.

Survivors began to reorganise themselves. Those with weapons moved to the outside of the group, and those who were unable to defend themselves moved to inside of the group. Those who were on crutches, in wheelchairs, and those missing limbs were all ushered to the inside. One of the passengers tried to usher Ava into the centre of the group, but she pushed his hand away with the barrel of her assault rifle with a fierce smile.

"Alright. Let's move out!" Jaxon said as he jumped down from the overturned car.

He held his rifle with its barrel pointed at the ground as he led the group in between the first two buildings. The group could not move at the same speed in the cramped space. They had to squeeze through the spaces between the buildings. Those who could wield weapons concentrated themselves towards the head and tail of the column, and next to those that couldn't protect themselves.

Jaxon arrived at the junction between the first two buildings and turned right. The path to the left had rubble strewn across the walkway, which would make it impossible for those who did not have full mobility to traverse.

At the end of the column, Vynce watched the horde approach. They still followed the survivors, and still kept the same distance. As Vynce followed the survivors around the curve in the walkway, the shambler stepped in between the first two buildings and the rest of the horde followed.

He looked up between the buildings and immediately regretted it. Fleshy growths criss-crossed the space between the buildings like spider webs between trees. There were larger lumps in between the twining flesh which were roughly human sized and shaped.

Fleshlings grown from parts of the infected passengers walked the flesh webs, tending to the growths of their new brothers and sisters in their cocoons. They came in all shapes and sizes. Some looked like nothing but misshapen blobs of flesh with spindly legs growing out awkwardly from the bottom. Others were distinct parts of people. One was clearly a hand whose fingers had been re-purposed as feet, with a stubby little face poking out of the stump that was once a wrist. Others had similarly been re-purposed from hands, feet and heads.

One of the creatures, a stubby little thing that looked like a slab of meat with six stubby legs sticking out of the bottom, dropped down from one of the webs and landed wetly next to the survivors. Those who were at the edge of the group started to move backwards, but it showed no signs of aggression. It simply stood there awkwardly and watched them as they passed.

The group moved on, winding between the buildings. The creatures that tended the webs above them started to crawl down the walls and joined the horde of infected in their silent procession.

In the centre of the cluster of buildings was an open space that had a pond in the centre. To the right was a climbing fort for the kids, but half of it had been covered over by a giant fleshy growth. Thick tendrils anchored the huge growth to the ground. They wound over and through the climbing fort and the swing set next to it. They also crossed the path and into the pond. The growth pulsated. It moved rhythmically, as though it was breathing. It was just like those that they had seen in the water treatment plant. Above them, smaller creatures climbed across their webs in the open air between the buildings.

They crossed the park on the farthest side of the huge growth, but all of their eyes fixated on it as they heard a wet tearing sound, like a soggy tea towel being ripped in half.

Something pushed outward from the centre of the growth. The wooden climbing fort groaned with effort. The thing pushed outward again, and the outside of the cocoon split open. Something huge and terrifyingly strong was being born. The cocoon started to bleed as it was torn asunder. The thing pushed outward again and a blood-curdling roar broke the stunned silence.

"Alright everyone, we need to move!" Jaxon yelled and spurred the survivors back into movement.

Vynce started to push those who were at the back to move faster as he watched the monstrosity's birth.

The horror of its magnificence was indescribable. Vynce thought that he would go mad just by looking at it. Its body was bent at unnatural angles, propped up by things that resembled both human arms and legs all at once. Each limb had been grown haphazardly from the body of an infected passenger into a monstrous gestalt of humanity. Its eyes flashed with anger, hunger, and curiosity. As it pulled itself from its cocoon it roared at the survivors and took a few curious steps towards them.

The shambler with its overgrown foot and constant torrent of red liquid dripping from its slack-jawed mouth shuffled forward and said a single word. "No."

The monstrosity looked back at the shambler and breathed in and out raggedly. There was a split in the front of what Vynce presumed what was its face. The split opened and revealed jagged teeth. The monstrosity bared its teeth and roared again as though it was challenging the shambler.

The shambler stepped towards the monstrosity with its arm outstretched.

The creature opened its mouth so wide that Vynce thought its skin would split. The shambler continued on and put its hand on the monstrosity's flesh. A shiver ran through the monstrosity and its many eyes rolled backwards in their sockets. It exhaled deeply and the aggression and tension left its body. The shambler put its hand into the creature's mouth. The creature ate the shambler in two vicious mouthfuls.

More of the infected passengers started to approach the monstrosity. They all held an outstretched hand as they approached. They were consumed one by one, accompanied by the sound of their crunching bones and rending flesh.

Doctor Fewster put a hand on Vynce's shoulder and Vynce almost jumped out of his skin as he broke fee of the hypnotic spectacle before him.

"Come on, we're almost through," Doctor Fewster said.

Vynce hurried after Doctor Fewster to join the rest of the survivors. The infected passengers continued to follow them, but they still kept their distance. The monstrosity was nowhere to be seen. It was far too wide to squeeze between the buildings. If it wanted to get out of the apartment building complex, it would have to go over the top.

When they arrived in the wide open streets, relief began to spread through the survivors. Hope started to return.

The Eden's Hill mag-rail station was just across the street.

THIRTY-FIVE

Draco's head swam in dizziness and confusion. The impact had knocked the wind out of him. He could vaguely make out four large humanoid shapes standing where he and Alphonse had stood just moments ago. Draco closed his eyes and shook his head to try to clear the fuzziness away. There was no mistaking their silhouettes or the colour of their armour. They were Vartalen mercenaries. The dusty red of their armour showed that they belonged to a mercenary outfit that Draco had tangled with previously.

They called themselves the Crimson Tide, and they were headed by one of the most dangerous Vartalen in the galaxy, Varxxas, the Crimson Death.

The fleshy growth beneath Draco started to move. He felt himself starting to sink into it. He staggered back to his feet before it had a chance to truly grab hold. He frantically looked around for his rifle, but it was nowhere to be seen. Draco's grapnel hook had been affixed to his back before he was thrown, and he wondered whether it was still there. One of the four large humanoid shapes came towards him and started barking orders at him with its deep booming voice, speaking in Vartalen language.

Draco raised his hands in a gesture of surrender and said, "I understand Vartalen, and I don't appreciate being called a runty little ape spawn. You understand me?"

The mercenary laughed and said with a heavily alien accent, "Yes. I understand, ape spawn."

"What are you doing aboard the ship?" Draco asked and looked over toward Raze and Alphonse. They had been made to kneel towards the bridge windows, looking out at the dark void of space. They had confiscated Raze's flamethrower and thrown it toward the elevator at the back of the room.

"This ship belongs to the Crimson Tide now. You are our prisoners," the Vartalen mercenary said.

"There is an infection on this ship. It is worthless to you. If you put this ship down on an inhabited world, everybody who lands on that planet will die," Draco said.

"Not worthless, then."

A chill worked its way up Draco's spine as he realised what the Vartalen were planning to do.

"You're going to sell this ship as a biological weapon," he said.

The Vartalen smiled and shook its head slowly. "Not sell," he said dangerously.

"You're going to use it."

The Vartalen laughed and said, "We make it go back to New Earth. No more humans."

"If this ship lands on an inhabited planet, everyone who steps foot on it will die. That doesn't just include humans."

"Sacrifice is required to make the galaxy a better place. The Crimson Tide will notify the Council of the infection and enact quarantine measures. The Crimson Tide will be heroes."

"Heroes? You'll be mass-murders responsible for the genocide of an entire planet. Twenty-three billion people. We humans are more resilient than that. We have other planets. Other military forces than those on New Earth. If you strike at the heart of our people you'll start a war that your people aren't ready for."

"Start a war? Your people already started the war when you invaded our space. The Vartalen will finish it."

"The human race has been at peace with the Vartalen people for years. Why would you restart this war now?"

"Peace?" the Vartalen said, his voice tinged with venomous anger, "there is no peace. Not while the human race keeps pushing into our sector of space. Have you heard of planetoid LV-9812?"

"I have not."

"A small colony of Vartalen have been there for almost fifty cycles. A human mining ship surveyed the planetoid and detected a large deposit of precious metals. Your mining vessel blew the planet apart to get at the rich veins of metal that ran through its surface, killing the thousands of Vartalen who lived there. There were families there. Children. And your race destroyed their home for the sake of profit."

"Was this reported to the Council for investigation?"

"You humans have the Council's favour. They would never side with the Vartalen over their new pets."

"Our own people, our own military, would never allow something like this to happen if we knew about it. If you tell me what company is responsible for what happened on LV-9812 I promise you that I will report this directly to the Commander in Chief of the Alliance military, and action will be taken," Draco said.

"This is just one of many provocations that your race has done to the Vartalen. We are not interested in justice. Only vengeance."

"If you start a war, the Council will have no choice but to support the human race. You know what's happened to the Vartalen before. You've had trade sanctions put in place, your rights to claim planets outside the Arcturus Sector have been revoked. You're already on thin ice, and if you destroy New Earth there will be no coming back from it."

"No one will ever know that we sent this ship to New Earth. No one. We will say that we intercepted it on its return course to its home planet, and detected the bio-weapon inside its hull. We dared not venture on board the ship as we did not want to risk infection.

We will notify the council, and they will quarantine the planet. The heart of the human race will be destroyed."

The Vartalen grabbed Draco roughly by the back of the neck and forced him to walk towards Raze and Alphonse. The Vartalen pushed Draco to his knees next to Al. Another human was knelt next to Draco. Draco stole a look to his left and saw a bedraggled young man in a torn suit looking back at him with terrified eyes.

"You must be the Metropolis Corporation rep that Captain Hane talked about," Draco said.

"I'm sorry. Really, I am. I tried to help you. Tried to guide you to safety. I... I... I needed your help to get the ship out of danger. I'm sorry, but I needed to use you," the man said. His bottom lip quivered as he spoke, as though every word threatened to bring him to tears.

"You endangered the life of my crew, and you're endangering the lives of every single living organism in the galaxy by delivering this ship back to inhabited space," Draco said.

"There are quarantine measures, right? The Alliance could lock us away, check us for infection, treat those who are infected, and learn how to stop it, right?"

"There are no quarantine procedures for something like this, apart from the Jericho protocol."

"What's the Jericho protocol?"

"It's a fancy way for the Alliance military to say nuke the site from orbit. For something as infectious as the organism on board this ship, there's nothing we can do but destroy it."

"I don't believe it. I was hoping the great hero Draco Goldwing would be able to get me out of this mess."

"How do you know who I am, kid?" Draco asked after realising that this man really was nothing more than a kid playing corporate. Draco knew the type. They rose to the top of the corporate ladder on New Earth by stepping on the shoulders of those who did the real work while gambling with the futures of others. They drove fast cars, had private starships, and had more money than sense.

"My Dad used to tell me stories about you. How you'd always do what was right, no matter what. He told me the story about how you were really discharged from the military. You killed your commanding officer to save the lives of thousands, but no one could ever know about it. It was completely off the books. You were dishonourably discharged, but you were awarded the medal of valour. The gold wings. Do you remember Admiral Fiamingo?"

"You're not little Ross Fiamingo are you?"

The young man smiled and said, "Yeah, I am."

Draco turned his head aside and said, "Your father would be ashamed of what you've done."

"My father will always be ashamed of me, no matter what I do. This was my one chance to make a life for myself outside of his shadow."

"And you'd sacrifice untold lives for the sake of your own?"

"The people on this ship were already dead as soon as the infection started to spread. How was I supposed to stop that?"

"I could try to explain the concept of courage and sacrifice to you, but I'm afraid you wouldn't understand," Draco said.

A Vartalen struck Draco from behind and he went sprawling face-first onto the ground.

"Enough talking," the Vartalen said and struck Ross to the ground as well. Ross squealed in pain. "One more word and I will tear out your tongue. Understand?" Ross whimpered.

Draco struggled back to his knees and nodded at the Vartalen brute. Ross stayed on the ground and cowered under his hands.

It was then that the cocoon tore open from the inside.

Draco looked back at the raised platform in the centre of the bridge and saw a gash in the side of the cocoon. Something moved inside. Its arm appeared to be human, but ended in large hands with claws at the end of each finger. Other sharp bony protrusions erupted from the red, inflamed skin up to its shoulder.

Ross laughed nervously. His voice cracked as he said, "I think the captain's woken up."

The Vartalen raised their rifles at the cocoon and started firing before the infected captain had even emerged from it. The bullets did nothing but enrage the captain. He burst forth from the cocoon and rushed toward the cluster of Vartalen troops. He moved so fast that Draco could barely make out what the captain now looked like. He slammed into the first Vartalen and eviscerated him from stomach to sternum. The Vartalen's blue and green innards fell out of him with a wet splash. He frantically tried in vain to shovel them back into himself with his last shuddering moments.

One of the Vartalen troops tried to slam into Captain Hane, but the captain backhanded him with his spiked arm, shattering the Vartalen's faceplate and turning his face into an indistinguishable mess of green blood and pulpy blue flesh.

Captain Hane stopped for a moment and looked around at Draco Goldwing. Hane's face had not been changed extensively. The whites of his eyes were yellow, and small lumps of bone protruded from beneath his skin from his forehead to his exposed chest. He wore the tattered remains of his captain's uniform. A shredded blue remnant of a jacket remained on his upper half, but his trousers remained largely intact. He had been changed with purpose. He was grown to be a lethal adversary. A protector of the hive.

Captain Hane looked past Draco and then at Ross Fiamingo. His lips parted and he roared. Ross began to crawl away as Captain Hane stalked towards him. Bullets from the remaining three Vartalen troops peppered Captain Hane's back. He roared again before sprinting towards them.

As Captain Hane turned, Draco saw that the bullets had torn flesh on his back. Captain Hane was not completely indestructible, and Draco hoped that the berserk creature was aware of the bargain he had struck with the central intelligence consciousness below.

The Vartalen troops had begun to retreat towards the viewing platform at the back of the tower.

Draco got to his feet and ran over to his rifle. He picked it up and loaded it with a magazine full of armour piercing rounds. Alphonse and Raze both got back to their feet and armed themselves, ready for Captain Hane to finish the Vartalen and come back to deal with them.

"Captain Goldwing, the Vartalen have a ship on the outside of the hull!" Raze said.

"We might have a way out of here. Can either of you pilot a Vartalen ship?" Draco asked.

"I believe I can," Al said.

"When Captain Hane comes back, do not engage him. Not unless he lashes out at one of us first," Draco said.

Alphonse and Raze nodded. They formed up and walked towards the viewing platform. They heard a scream, followed by a guttural roar. Half of one of the Vartalen troops flew out of the walkway and into the bridge. His guts flew through the air after him like the tail of a kite. Draco, Raze and Al rushed around the curved walkway and saw the remains of one Vartalen slumped against a wall. The last remaining Vartalen was trying to clamber up a steel rope ladder that hung down from a vent in the ceiling.

Captain Hane grabbed the last Vartalen by its right ankle and yanked it down. He fell and screamed in pain as his ankle shattered. Captain Hane crushed his head with his bladed fingers. Captain Hane turned toward Draco, Raze and Al. He eyed Captain Goldwing suspiciously, but did not immediately attack.

"Do you remember the bargain I made with your people?" Draco asked, but did not stop aiming his rifle at the infected captain.

"Safe... place..." Captain Hane said.

"Yes, safe place. You understand."

"Understand... Yes."

"You will not hurt my crew."

"Where... is Fiamingo?"

"Fiamingo?"

"Yes."

"He's under my protection. You will not hurt him."

Captain Hane's face twisted into a mask of pure rage. He roared and spat the words out as he spoke, "Must hurt! Must kill him! Killed my.... My... Son! Killed... Killed me! Infec... Infected us!"

"He is under my protection. You will not hurt him," Draco challenged.

Captain Hane exhaled with a grunt. His eyes frantically searched the room as he thought about his options. Alphonse was amazed at the cognitive abilities that Captain Hane had retained during his transformation, but it chilled him as well. This organism had the capability of completely taking over the mind and body of any other living organism, but it could also reshape them with intelligence and purpose.

Ross Fiamingo chose the exact wrong time to join Draco, Raze and Alphonse. He rounded the corner of the walkway and Captain Hane sprinted toward him. Draco rushed into Captain Hane's path and stopped him from reaching Ross.

"Move!" Captain Hane bellowed.

"If you hurt him, I won't save you. I will not take you to a safe place to live peacefully. You'll have to kill me," Draco said.

Captain Hane's eyes narrowed as he leaned in closely to Draco and whispered, "Others will come."

Draco quickly rolled backwards, narrowly avoiding Captain Hane's blade-like fingers as the captain swiped at him. He raised his rifle to his shoulder and fired. The anti-armour rounds ripped through Captain Hane from stomach to shoulder, but it barely slowed him down. He stalked towards Draco, who scrambled back to his feet. He heard the sound of shattering glass from somewhere around him as he tried to escape, but Captain Hane was too fast. He closed the distance between them far too quickly, and Draco's rifle had gone dry. He grabbed another magazine and loaded it into his rifle. Draco turned, ready to loose another volley of bullets at the infected captain, but a small cylindrical piece of steel erupted through the front of Captain Hane's chest. Captain Hane looked down at the metallic protrusion just as the hook points flicked outward. He was yanked backwards as Alphonse began reeling the grapnel hook back in.

Before Draco could gather his thoughts, Alphonse leapt from the edge of the tower, taking Captain Hane with him as he plummeted down into the city.

THIRTY-SIX

The charge counter read 100%, and the gateway drive was ready to be activated. Veck Simms had programmed his destination, and only needed to activate the sequence to make his escape. However, he found himself hesitating to begin the sequence. His mind turned to Draco Goldwing.

Draco was not a bad man. He was misguided, surely, but the thought of leaving him deserted in the middle of the Arcturus sector did not sit well with some ancient part of Veck who still felt something for his former friend.

But his need to live and his need to fulfil his purpose outweighed the life of one man whom he may have considered a friend once.

Veck activated the gateway drive and the dark space in front of the Icarus lit up like a firework. It began as a small spark of light, only a few particles wide. That small point grew and expanded like a blooming flower. The configurations of stars that filled the space in front of them were replaced with another set of stars, as well as a small planetoid that was covered primarily by green landmasses and blue oceans. The gateway continued to grow in size until it was large enough for the Icarus to pass through.

Veck could see his escape. His freedom. His destiny. But he could not bring himself to fly through the gateway just yet. As soon as the Icarus passed through, the gateway would close behind them.

The Metropolis Seven would not have a gravity drive on board. Once through the gateway, he would be beyond his former friend's reach.

He had to say his goodbyes.

Veck opened up the main communication channel. He opened a comm channel with Draco and said, "Hello Draco, how've you been?"

For a moment Draco did not respond. When he did, Veck could sense the anger in his voice even though Draco tried to hide it, 'Veck. What are you doing on the Icarus' comm channel?'

"I wanted to give you the decency of saying goodbye. I'm the captain of the Icarus now, and I've activated the gateway drive."

'Veck, please. You don't know what's going on here. There's an infection. We need evacuation. Some of the passengers survived, and they're loading onto the evacuation shuttles as we speak. We've taken control of the ship, but we need your help.'

"It doesn't sound like you need my help. It sounds like you're doing fine on your own. Ever the hero, you are."

'You don't understand! If this infection reaches an inhabited planet, every single race in the galaxy will become infected. We'll all be destroyed!'

"All the more reason for me to not allow you back on board the ship. I don't want to risk myself, the little mouse, her sister or the pilot."

'Where's Nook?'"

"He tried to be a hero. You know how I loathe heroes."

'You claim to represent the best interest of the human race, yet you embody all of our worst traits.'

"Oh don't give me that right now, Draco. I'm trying to be decent here and give you my farewell, and you go on and try to guilt trip me. If you're going to do that, then I may as well close the comm channel right now and be done with it."

'No! Veck! We need your help!'

"I never took you for a beggar. I expected better of you Draco," Veck said and closed the comm channel.

He pushed the thrusters forward and headed towards the open gateway.

On board the Metropolis Seven, Draco didn't have time to think. He could only react. He started to climb the steel cable rope that hung from the ceiling. He looked back at Ross and said, "If you want to live, you'll follow me. You'll come back to New Earth and you'll face your punishment. If not, stay here on the ship and die. The choice is yours."

Ross' cheeks flushed, but he dutifully ran over to the bottom of the ladder and started climbing.

"Captain!" Raze said with surprise.

Draco snapped his head back down and his face lit up. In the distance, he could see Alphonse flying through the air outside the viewing platform

"Al's batteries must have recharged! I thought we'd lost him!" Raze said.

Suddenly Alphonse dipped in the sky and the thrusters on his feet and hands cut out. They re-engaged quickly, and he regained altitude. The thrusters erupted with light as Al went to full burn. Raze stepped aside from the hole in the glass as Alphonse honed in. He landed awkwardly and tumbled heavily. Al got to his hands and knees, but they gave out on him.

"Al!" Raze exclaimed and went over to join his side.

"I'm fine," Al said, "but I've used most of my battery reserves. I just need a moment."

"Will you be able to fly the Vartalen ship?" Draco asked.

"Yes," Al said, "That won't be a problem."

THIRTY-SEVEN

The Eden's Hill mag-rail station was built on top of a hill, with short cut grass on its gently sloping sides. A stone path wound up the hill to the mag-rail station itself, and it was flanked by fruit trees and rose bushes. The fruit trees had been picked clean over the previous weeks by the survivors, and most of the rose bushes had been trampled by the wandering fleshlings.

They passed the hill and continued on down the road. They came to an intersection littered with small single-person passenger vehicles and motorcycles. Jaxon headed across the intersection and toward a small building that had a wire mesh security screen covering its front entrance. It was the entrance to the hangar.

"I need a security officer up front with me now. Anyone?" Jaxon asked.

A woman in a wheelchair was brought to the front of the crowd. She had lost her left leg from the knee down, and her right leg from the hip. Her husband pushed her wheelchair for her. "What do you need?" she asked.

"I need you to override the security protocol that's locking this door down. Then, after everyone's inside, I need you to initiate a complete lockdown protocol. Make sure that nothing can get down into the hangar, alright?"

"I can do that," she said. Her husband wheeled her to the security console on the side of the building. She leaned forward and grimaced with discomfort as she pressed her right index finger to the screen. It read her fingerprint and said, 'good morning Officer Starling.'

"Lift security profile alpha. Emergency situation. Evacuation required."

'Understood, Officer Starling. Lifting security profile alpha now,' the console said as the mesh door started to rise.

Jaxon ushered everyone inside as quickly as possible.

The horde of infected had kept growing in number. The smaller fleshlings that tended the webs in the apartment building nests had joined them. They crawled over, through and around the infected and tended to them. Vynce saw one of the creatures secrete a lumpy red paste on a jagged wound of one of the infected passenger's necks. The paste began to reconstitute the skin and muscle that had been lost.

Jaxon waited next to Starling until everyone else was in the hangar. Ava stood just inside the door. She refused to move until Jaxon was inside and safe too. After everyone was in, Starling said "Initiate security protocol Omega," and the mesh door immediately started to roll back down. Her husband pushed her under it before it had a chance to close completely. When the mesh door was closed and locked into place, another thicker metal door slid down from the outside, sealing the exit.

The hangar was only half-full of evacuation shuttles, and more than half of those that did remain were visibly damaged. There was no telling how many of them, if any, still functioned.

The shuttles were wide, flat and shaped like arrow heads. They had four powerful ion thrusters that also acted as landing gear. They were each fitted with their own medical and on-board facilities. Due to the nature of space travel, each shuttle had enough oxygen on board to last up to three years with a full complement of passengers. Of course if it did take that long to be rescued, running out of oxygen would be the least of their worries. They would run out of food and sanity much quicker than that.

There were two rows of evacuation shuttles. They flanked both sides of the walkway. Some of the survivors had started to inspect the closest few shuttles, but they were both unfit for travel.

"Everyone I need your attention for a moment," Jaxon said. His voice boomed as it was amplified by his suit augmentations.

The survivors all turned and faced Jaxon as he spoke.

"I need everyone to do something for me. We need to get organised, and we need to do it quickly. We need to get off this ship before those things out there decide they want to come with us. Firstly, those of you who are carrying food and medical supplies, I need you to gather everything together next to that shuttle over there," Jaxon said and motioned to the shuttle with the destroyed ion thruster.

"With our numbers, we're going to need three working shuttles. We need to divide our numbers up by people who are infected, and people who aren't infected. As I'm sure you'll agree, we cannot risk exposing the general populace to this infection. Those who are infected will wait by that ship over there," he motioned towards the shuttle with the hull breach, "and wait for further instructions. Are we clear?"

A murmur of approval spread through the crowd. A number of those who were infected began to mill around the shuttle with the hull breach. Others emptied their packs of supplies next to the shuttle with the destroyed thruster.

Doctor Harris dug into her bag and pulled out a snap-on wrist band normally used in hospital admissions, and a red marker. She snapped the band closed around her left wrist and used the marker to make a thick red scribble.

She held up her left hand and said, "See this? This means I'm infected. Every one of you will have to come to me for a full-body scan and be given a wrist band before you can leave this ship. Even you," she said to those who had already identified themselves as infected.

Doctor Harris began scanning the people who came to her and started handing out wrist bands. She marked those who were infected with a red band like hers, and she marked those who were clear of infection with a similar green scribble. She told everyone who passed as clean that they would need to go through another scan before they were allowed to enter a shuttle for evacuation.

Doctor Fewster and Doctor Cooper had begun to take inventory of the food, water and medical supplies while Jaxon, Ava and Vynce searched for a working shuttle. Young Jaxon jogged up to join them and asked, "Can I help?"

"Sure kid, come with me," Vynce said and gave a knowing look to Old Jaxon. Old Jaxon nodded to Vynce in appreciation.

"So I've got an idea," Young Jaxon said.

"Oh yeah? What's that?"

"All of these ships used to be hooked up to a central network that monitored any issues with them, right? Y'know, it's a requirement of any large ship that the evacuation shuttles are kept in constant working order. So if we can access the monitoring system, we can find out which ones are still functional," young Jaxon said.

"Right, well that sounds like a start," Vynce said.

"A start? It's genius! Do you know how long it would take to check all two hundred and fifty of these ships by hand?"

"We'd never be able to check them all properly."

"Damn right. And two hundred and fifty isn't even enough for a quarter of the amount of passengers on this ship at full capacity. I always thought that if something big went down there wouldn't be enough shuttles for everyone, but I never thought that there would only be a hundred of us left alive," young Jaxon said.

"Well we've got pretty good odds, right? There has to be a pretty big chance of having at least three working ships on board."

"I hope so. I really don't want to die on this ship," young Jaxon said.

"Me neither, buddy."

Old Jaxon and Ava wandered down the opposite direction from Vynce and Young Jaxon. Old Jaxon was far less anxious while he was out of close proximity to his younger self. If he couldn't see or hear his younger self, then he could more easily put him out of his mind. It was enough that he had come back to the Metropolis Seven in the first place, but to have locked Draco Goldwing and his crew to these events as well was almost more than he could bear.

But his mission, which was now the younger Jaxon's mission, was to return the small black case back to New Earth to ensure the continuation of their species. Before old Jaxon could make things right, he had to make sure that the survivors could escape.

"Are you okay?" Ava asked as they walked in silence.

"Uh, yeah. I guess."

"You've been really quiet since we left the med station. Is there anything you want to talk about?" she asked.

"Not really. We just need to focus on finding a working shuttle so we can get out of here," he said.

She grabbed his hand with hers and forced him to stop walking.

"Cut the shit," she said, "Tell me what the fuck is going on."

"I..." he began.

"If you love me, you will not fuck me around. You got that?"

"Yes, but..."

"No fucking buts. If I really think that you and I have something real here, and I think we do, you can't treat me like a child. I'm a big tough girl. I can handle whatever you can throw at me."

He couldn't help but smile, even as tears started to well up in his eyes. He took her into his arms and held her.

"I'm not going to make it off this ship alive," he said.

She shook her head, slightly at first, then growing in intensity.

"No," she said.

"Yes," he said.

"No, you fucking can't. Not after all this."

"Yes. I have to. It's the only way that I can make sure that you and the rest of these people survive this. I have to, to make sure that no one ever sets foot on this ship again."

"No, I just found you, I can't lose you already," she said.

"You won't. You'll find this out soon enough, but being in love with a time traveller is not like being in love with a normal person. Things don't happen on a linear sequential progression of events. This might seem like the end to you, but I have years of happy memories of you, and us, and all the moments we've shared, or will share. It's just bad luck that we meet at the end, and it ends where we meet."

Ava pulled away from Jaxon's embrace and stormed over to the nearest shuttle. It was almost completely destroyed. The ion thrusters were burnt out, as though they had exploded. The outside of the ship was crumpled where part of the roof of the hangar had collapsed. Ava used her remaining hand to manually open the entry hatch and climbed inside.

Jaxon climbed in after her. There was no light inside the shuttle, but Jaxon could hear Ava calling to him from deeper inside. His lowlight vision kicked in and he followed the curved hallway around to the main living area of the shuttle. He could just barely make out Ava's shape in the darkness. She took off her helmet and put it down on the ground next to a wide couch. She ran her hand through her hair, and gave the command for her suit to disengage. The armour of her suit started to retract into itself. The linkages down the side of her suit retracted, and the armour on her left arm disengage from the shoulder guard. She allowed the armour to slide off onto the ground. She took off her chest armour.

"I don't hear you undressing," she said back into the darkness. She was not looking at Jaxon, but Jaxon has looking at her. His suit had begun to feel a little too snug as his desires awoke.

He took off his helmet and breathed the air deep. He could not see a thing, but he could smell the sweet scent of her. He joined her and his mouth met hers. She kissed him hungrily. They undressed each other with a desperate ferocity and made love there in the darkness.

They spoke no words; there was no time for words.

They made love for the first time. They made love for the last time.

As the lovers held each other in the blackness of the shuttle, Vynce and young Jaxon had located the monitoring station. They had located a cluster of seven shuttles which still appeared to be functional. They were on their way back to the rest of the survivors when Captain Goldwing's voice blasted through their comm channels.

'Crew of the Icarus, are any of you there? Please respond! Emergency! Veck Simms has escaped and taken control of the Icarus. He's used the gateway drive and is about to escape!'

THIRTY-EIGHT

"What!?" Vynce bellowed. He was furious. "How the fuck did he manage to get out of the containment cell? I thought it was supposed to fry his brain module!"

'So did I, but he contacted me from the Icarus' main comm channel. He's in charge of the ship, and he's opened the gateway. We need to stop him,' Draco said desperately.

"We've just found a few working evacuation shuttles. We're on our way back there now. We'll get out of here as fast as we can, captain."

'Double time it!'

In the darkness of the shuttle, Ava and Jaxon didn't have time to talk about what had just happened. They were buzzing from a combination of terror and ecstasy. No matter how things turned out, they had each other, and nothing could take that away from them. They dressed in silence.

Jaxon's armour was tuned to his body and could configure itself in moments, but Ava's suit was forty years more ancient and required some manual assistance. In minutes they were dressed again, outside the shuttle, running back toward the survivors.

As they ran, Jaxon had to tell Ava one final thing.

"I love you," he said simply.

"I know," she said.

He couldn't help but smile.

"One last thing," he said, "I need you to promise to go along with whatever I say when we get back, alright?"

"I know that this is the end of us right now. That's why I can't say... well, you know. I just can't say it right now, even though you know what I want to say. And you know that I mean it."

"Yes. I know."

"The end is coming, isn't it?"

"It is. With my life, I can save yours. And that's enough. You..."

"Shut up and keep running," Ava said.

"You're going to do so many great things, Ava. This isn't the last time you'll see me. Just remember that there will come a time when I haven't met you. In my timeline, after my younger self escapes the ship, you won't be able to find him for six years. So don't go looking. But I will find you, and it'll be sooner than that. I guarantee it."

"Is this ever going to get easier?" she asked.

"No. But you get used to it."

By the time they re-joined the main group of survivors, Vynce and young Jaxon had moved the group of survivors down to the functioning evacuation shuttles. Doctors Fewster, Harris and Cooper had divided the medical, food and water supplies up into two groups. They were in the process of loading them onto the two shuttles that the non-infected passengers had begun to board. Just as Doctor Harris promised, she did not allow any of the passengers on board any of the ships until they had been scanned again and passed as clean. This took precious time, and some of the infected passengers had begun to ask questions about why they weren't getting any supplies loaded onto their shuttle.

Old Jaxon overheard them, and he stepped between the group of infected, and the uninfected passengers. He had managed to speak to some of them while they were still in the med station. Doctor Harris knew his plan, as did some of the others, but the majority did not.

"I'm sorry to have gotten your hopes up this far," old Jaxon said to the infected passengers, "but we're not going to make it off this ship alive."

Outrage rose from the infected passengers, and even from some of the uninfected passengers. Jaxon heard words thrown about like inhumane, betrayal, and murderer. One older gentleman stepped forward and demanded, "What do you mean? Why are we even here then? Why didn't you just leave us to die!?"

"Because I need your help. Before we found you all in the med station, we re-routed this ship from a crash course with a binary star system. We thought we were going to be able to save everyone, but that's just not the case. Those of you who are infected but still in control of your own bodies... You have the ability to make sure that those who are not infected can survive this. You can lay down your lives for them, and we can destroy the infection before it has a chance to infect another ship, or another world."

The anger that coursed through the crowd simmered.

"I'll be coming with you all," Old Jaxon said. The anger in the crowd dissipated. Vynce started to say something in protest, but Ava put her hand on his chest and shook her head. Vynce looked at her with confusion. She held him with her remaining arm, and he returned her embrace as he realised what was going to happen.

It was then that the infected passengers outside the hangar bay started to beat on the metal security door at the top of the walkway. The sound boomed through the hangar bay and everyone burst into action.

Old Jaxon approached young Jaxon and grabbed him by the shoulder.

"Do you remember your mission?" he asked.

"Yeah. Bring the chip to Erik Johanssen at The End Times. Arthur Kronenberc Parade, Champion's Square, on New Earth."

"Good lad. You have to deliver that chip. Our future depends on it."

"I will. I promise," young Jaxon said.

"Good, now go join Doctor Fewster. He needs you to help load the medical supplies on board his shuttle."

"Okay," young Jaxon said. It was clear that there was more that he wanted to ask, but he left without argument.

Doctor Harris stood in front of the entryway of the first shuttle and scanned the uninfected passengers before they boarded. One by one they passed the test, showing them what their wristbands already showed them. That was until one of the patients who had previously passed the test as uninfected then scanned as infected. She was a young woman with short raven black hair. She shook her head in disbelief.

"What? No! That can't be right! I'm clean! I'm clean!" she pleaded.

"I'm sorry, but you're going to need to join the infected shuttle. We can't let you on board either of these shuttles," Doctor Harris said.

"No, you can't make me! You can't sentence me here to die!"

"Honey, we're all born with a life sentence. You can accept it, or you can stay in denial and wait for the others to come and claim you."

"Scan me again! Scan me again! Please!"

Doctor Harris put her hand on the woman's chest and scanned her again. The display showed the existence of foreign bodies in her system. She was infected. She held her head in her hands and fell to her knees as she wept.

Old Jaxon helped the woman to her feet and guided her over to the infected passengers. They took her in their arms and held her as she cried.

Vynce approached old Jaxon and said, "Before you go, I just wanted to say that it's been an honour to have met you."

Vynce offered his hand to Jaxon, who took it. Instead of shaking his hand, he pulled Vynce close and hugged him.

"You too Vynce. But this isn't the last time for you. It might be for me, but you and I will meet again. I guarantee it."

Vynce left Jaxon to help his passengers into the shuttle.

Doctor Harris stopped scanning people in front of one shuttle and said, "This shuttle's only got room for two more! Fewster and Clarke, get over here!"

Doctor Fewster joined Doctor Harris, as did Clarke, a middle-aged man with short grey hair. They both climbed up the entryway and sealed the shuttle door behind them. They would be ready for take-off in moments.

It was then that the fleshlings outside the hangar bay managed to penetrate the metal security door. They began to shamble slowly down the walkway, but they started sprinting towards the survivors as soon as they came into their field of vision.

"Somehow I don't think they're being friendly anymore," Vynce said and rushed over to his shuttle.

"Doctor Harris, we have to get this wrapped up! Scan people and get them on board! Now!" Vynce yelled.

"I'm going as fast as I can!" she yelled back. There were only a handful of people left to scan, and they all tested clean in moments. Vynce helped Ava up into the entryway of the shuttle. Doctor Harris climbed into the shuttle of infected passengers. She pulled the shuttle door closed just as the aggressive infected reached them.

Vynce looked back up at the walkway and saw hundreds of infected shamblers shuffling into the hangar bay. The huge creature that had been birthed in the apartment complex rushed into the hangar bay and bellowed at the shuttles who were preparing for take-off. Doctor Fewster's shuttle was the first to ignite its engines. The infected that reached the ion thrusters were turned to ash in an instant.

The shuttle manoeuvred itself into the centre of the hangar bay, in between both rows of shuttles, and then engaged full thrusters. The moment that the evacuation shuttles activated, the hull of the

Metropolis Seven opened. A grav-field across the end of the hangar bay preserved the gravity and atmosphere, but allowed easy escape. The shuttle rocketed through the hangar bay, through grav-field and out into the dark void of space.

Vynce climbed into the pilot's chair of his shuttle, engaged the engines, ran the take-off subroutines, and followed Doctor Fewster's shuttle out of the ship and into space. Old Jaxon's shuttle took off moments after Vynce's shuttle and followed after them.

After Vynce was free of the Metropolis Seven, he looked back on the vidstreams in front of the pilot's chair and couldn't believe that he had actually made it out alive. Ava sat next to him and smiled sadly. She was watching the shuttle behind them. The one that held the man she had fallen in love with.

Vynce wheeled the shuttle around in a wide circle towards the front of the Metropolis Seven and he saw the open gateway, crackling in the black of space. He set an intercept course and tuned into the other shuttles' comm systems.

"Clarke, follow my intercept trajectory. We need to stop the Icarus before it goes through that gateway!" Vynce said.

'How in the hell do you expect us to stop it? It's too far away, and these are evacuation shuttles! We don't have the ability to dock with them! We don't even have any weapons!' Clarke protested.

"Just follow me, and do exactly what I say, you got that?"

Clarke cursed and said, 'Alright. But the moment you put me or anyone else on this shuttle in danger, you're on your own. We didn't get out of this just to risk our lives again.'

"Before we came to rescue you all, we were transporting Veck Simms from the Arcturus sector back to Alliance space. You know who Veck Simms is, right?"

Clarke's face had gone white, 'The betrayer of humanity...'

"He's in charge of our ship and he's about to get a free ride to wherever he wants to go unless we stop him."

'Matching your trajectory now,' Clarke said.

Vynce tried to hail Jaxon's shuttle, but he couldn't get through. Jaxon had disabled comms. Ava watched Jaxon's shuttle through the vidstream as it flew further down the hull of the Icarus and into the loading dock that they had used to get onto the ship in the first place. She reached over for Vynce's hand. He took her hand in his and squeezed gently. She squeezed back.

THIRTY-NINE

Captain Draco Goldwing climbed up the cable ladder and into the air duct. It was a tight fit for Draco and Raze. He didn't want to imagine what one of the bulky Vartalen had looked like as they tried to squeeze through.

At the end of the air duct Draco saw the point where the Vartalen had cut through the hull of the Metropolis Seven. A thick section of hull sat in the bottom of the air duct, and beyond it, the red-lit interior of the Vartalen cruiser. There was no telling whether there was still anyone on board, and if there was, whether they had been monitoring their crewmates' vidstreams or vitals. They could be walking into a trap, but it was the only place left to go. They would never make it through the streets of the ship alive. The Vartalen cruiser was their only hope of escape.

Draco reached the entrance to the cruiser and threw an empty ammunition magazine into the breach. When no gunfire or shouts of surprise greeted him, he climbed aboard and scanned the ship. There were no sounds, and nothing seemed to move. They had arrived in an antechamber which could be sealed like an airlock. The wide door into the ship stood open and unlocked. They clearly didn't expect that anyone would be powerful enough to best them or brazen enough to steal their ship while they were on board.

The ship was a strike class scout, not designed for long range travel. It was the first of a fleet, which would no doubt be on their way to claim the Metropolis Seven for themselves. Draco couldn't give too much thought to them, however. He had to disengage from the Metropolis Seven and take control of the Icarus again before Veck passed through the gateway.

Draco, Raze, Al and Ross crossed the squalid living quarters and headed to the bridge. It was definitely a mercenary ship. Even with their olfactory filters in place, they could still smell the stink of it. Ross had to cover his nose the old fashioned way. The bridge was really just a glorified pilot's chair, with a co-pilot's chair sitting just behind it. The seats were so large that even Raze would look like a child if he sat in them.

The bridge was in the central hooked fuselage of the ship. From the windows in front Draco and Al could see the curved wingtips of the ship on either side. Draco also saw the crackling gateway that Veck had opened, with the Icarus hovering just in front of it. The sonofabitch was almost through, and once he was through, Draco would never be able to find him. He'd never be able to get his father's ship back.

"Al, start this ship up immediately. We need to get back to the Icarus. Now!" Draco barked.

"Yes Captain," Al said and slid into the pilot's chair. He began starting the ignition sequence.

"Raze, I'm going to seal the breaching pod. You ride co-pilot."

"I got it boss," Raze said and sat behind Alphonse in the co-pilot's chair.

Draco rushed back over to the door that separated to Vartalen ship from the antechamber that led onto the Metropolis Seven. He activated the airlock, and a heavy titanium door with a tiny viewing window slid over the doorway.

Al ignited the engines and said, "Now, Captain! Disengage!"

Draco disengaged the breaching pod and the Vartalen attack cruiser separated from the Metropolis Seven. The Vartalen cruiser drifted for a moment before the engines kicked in.

Draco took a deep breath and engaged the antechamber's inner door. Draco locked himself in the airlock and drew his grapnel launcher. He opened up a comm channel to Al and started to speak.

Aboard the Icarus, Veck Simms was alerted to the presence of three smaller ships which were all on intercept trajectories. He gritted his teeth and increased thrust. He hadn't made it this close to freedom to be thwarted at the last moment.

Vynce saw the Vartalen attack cruiser heading towards the Icarus and increased the thrust. He sent a broadcast comm to the enemy ship and said, "Vartalen, disengage from your trajectory. The Icarus is a human ship, and any aggression will be treated as an act of war."

Al's face appeared on the comm screen in front of him and said, 'Vynce, we're in the Vartalen ship. Don't open fire!'

Vynce laughed and said, "Al! I have never been happier to see your faceplate! And don't worry, we couldn't attack even if we wanted to. These shuttles have no weaponry. They're just lifeboats."

'We have weapons, but the girls and Arak are still alive on the Icarus. I don't want to risk their safety.'

"What about Nook?"

'Veck killed him.'

"That motherfucking piece of shit son of a bitch"

'Which is why we need to catch him before he gets away.'

"On it."

Vynce closed the comm channel. Ava turned to him and said, "I need to send one last message to Jaxon. A private message. Can you authorise my suit to hook into the ship's comm channel?"

"Sure," Vynce said and made the necessary adjustments.

Ava switched her comm channel to private, recorded her message, and sent it through the ship's broadcast system to Jaxon's shuttle. Vynce saw her lips moving through her helmet, but when she saw that he was looking, she changed the opacity of her visor to obscure his view. Ava finished and sent the completed message. She could only hope that he received it before he landed back on the Metropolis Seven.

FORTY

Jaxon manoeuvred the shuttle into the wide delivery dock. He passed through another grav-field and found an empty bay in the docks. Ava's message had given him hope. She had sent him a vid comm, so he could see her face while she spoke. She told him about the shuttle from the Icarus in the loading dock, and the cache of weaponry in the back. She figured they might face some resistance getting to the engine control room, but the weaponry they had left in the shuttle should help them.

Then she told him that she loved him. She said that she wished she knew when she would meet him again, but she understood that he couldn't tell her for sure. Before disembarking from the evac shuttle Jaxon sent one final private comm message back to Ava before disabling his comm unit completely. He couldn't risk breaking down in the final moments of his life and spilling the secrets of the future to anyone who would make it alive off this ship.

Before he left the pilot's chair, Jaxon took out his pistol and fired a magazine's worth of bullets into the control console. He couldn't risk anyone trying to escape. If the infection was allowed to spread, then all of his hard work over the course of his life with the Agency would mean nothing. Another Agent would have to go back to this place and clean up the mess to avert the disaster. Jaxon refused to allow anyone else to be involved with the horror aboard the ship.

Jaxon joined the rest of the infected survivors in the living space. Doctor Harris joined him and asked, "Are you ready?"

He nodded and took off his helmet as he addressed the infected survivors.

"Doctor Harris and I are going to leave the shuttle, and we're going to change our course from the engine room. We're not asking any of you to join us, though we'd appreciate the help. The infected are going to be pissed, and I'm expecting we might meet some heavy resistance. But the choice is yours. If you're coming, get ready. We leave immediately."

One by one the infected survivors got to their feet. Some stayed sitting. One man wept openly with his arm around his wife, who cried into her hands.

Jaxon left the shuttle and stepped out onto the loading dock. He saw the rectangular shuttle from the Icarus. He went over to the Icarus' shuttle and opened the side hatch. There he saw two trunks full of weapons and ammunition. The first thing he did was disable the shuttle. After a minute, the infected survivors had begun to join him. He handed weapons out to those that wanted them. Doctor Harris appeared behind Jaxon and put a hand on his shoulder.

"How are you holding up?" she asked.

"I'm fine," he said distractedly. He scooped an armful of rifle magazines into a duffel bag and slung it over his shoulder. "Let's go," he said.

He led the infected survivors through the receiving dock and back into the Metropolis Seven. The infected were waiting for them. They walked through the receiving gates and two fleshlings moaned wetly and ran towards them. Jaxon took one out with a volley of bullets, and Doctor Harris dispatched the other with a shotgun blast to the chest.

Jaxon followed the quickest route to the engine bay. The passcodes and security codes he had used on board the Metropolis Seven all those years ago came back to him easily. It was as though he had never left. He passed through the security checkpoints and led the group of infected survivors down the maintenance tunnels towards the engine control room.

The smaller fleshlings started to climb out from between pipes and vents all around them. The air was filled with screams of fear, curses and the reports of firing weapons.

"We need to go faster!" Jaxon yelled, and the survivors followed him. They ignored the infected that they could, but some survivors were unlucky. Those that fell behind were left behind.

They reached a large open space. The cargo hold. There were pallets of still-wrapped supplies that towered above them. A large fleshling stumbled from behind one of the stacks of pallets; it appeared to have been forged from the bodies of two humans. One served as the body, legs and left arm, but its overgrown right arm was almost the size of its own body again. A face that was stuck in a constant grimace of terror protruded from the outside of the shoulder. It loped towards Jaxon, reaching towards him with two thick fingers that had once been legs.

Jaxon tried to move out of the way of the creature, but it was too fast. It picked him up with its dual-fingered arm and threw him up into the air, across the cargo hold. He landed on top of a pallet and bounced over it into a space between rows of supplies. He quickly tried to regain his bearings, but a group of three fleshlings ran toward him with terrifying speed. He opened fire and cut them down. He headed back towards the sounds of screams.

The sounds of assault rifle fire rang out in the cargo hold. Any infected in the immediate area would know exactly where they were, and the central intelligence that drove them all would be sending everything it had at them.

Jaxon rounded a corner and saw the huge fleshling tearing one of the survivors in two. A volley of assault rifle fire hit the creature in the chest and it stumbled backwards as it was knocked off balance. Doctor Harris marched ahead of the rest of the group of survivors and pumped two shotgun rounds into the thing's chest. It still attempted to get back up, but its strength had begun to fail. Doctor Harris reloaded her shotgun and fired a shell at the creature's head. It exploded outward in red meaty chunks as its body collapsed.

The face on its shoulder snarled at Doctor Harris, but did not have the ability to drive the rest of its body onward.

Jaxon re-joined the group and led them through the cargo hold. They encountered a number of infected as they crossed the hold, but they were all easily put down.

They reached the end of the cargo hold and followed through the maintenance staff tunnels towards the engine room. Jaxon ran along the corridors as fast as he could, hoping that the survivors could manage to keep up. As he ran, the memories of the last twenty years in the service of the Agency ran through his mind just as fast. To think that his journey, the meaning of his life, began aboard the Metropolis Seven and would end aboard the Metropolis Seven was almost too much for him to take.

He rounded the corner into a wider walkway. The signage pointed him in the direction of the engine control room and he ran on.

Upon reaching the engine room, the rest of the survivors began to slowly fill up the room. The infected had started to run after them, but a vanguard of survivors blockaded the entrance and cut down any that got too close.

Jaxon quickly opened the control console and plotted a course to Gemon I, the larger of the two stars in the Gemon binary star system. He set the engines to full thrust, and then activated a terrorist attack security lockdown command to lock the console. Only someone using the captain's authorisation could unlock the console and set another course, and that required retinal scan and thumbprint identification from Captain Hane himself.

FORTY-ONE

The two shuttles raced through space towards the gateway. The Vartalen cruiser was closer, but Vynce didn't think that Captain Goldwing would make it in time. The Icarus was too close to the gateway, and its engines were set to full thrust.

"Captain..." Vynce said over the comm channel.

'What is it?' Draco said.

"I don't think we can get there in time. He's almost through!"

'I've got a plan.'

"I don't think there's much we can do about it. He's... he's already gone," Vynce said.

The Icarus approached the gateway.

"Al, make this ship go faster! When we're just a little closer, I need you to follow my orders exactly and without hesitation!" Draco yelled.

"I'm already at full thrust, Captain. This ship is built for reconnaissance, not pursuit."

"Go faster!"

Al pushed the thrust again, but it could not go any faster. They could see the Icarus just in front of them. Only a few more moments, and they would be right on top of them.

The Icarus crossed through the gateway, and the gateway began to shrink as it closed.

"Swing the ship to the right! Do it now!" Draco commanded.

Al obeyed. He swung the ship to the right sharply. He had a sinking feeling that he knew what the captain was about to do.

Draco Goldwing switched his suit to the in-built oxygen supply. He flicked the switch and engaged the magnetic attachment on the end of his grapnel launcher. He readied himself against the inner door of the airlock, then pressed the purge button. The airlock exploded outward, and nothing separated Draco from the vast cold of space.

The Icarus was right in front of him. He pushed off the inside of the Vartalen cruiser. The repulsive magnetic force his grav-boots propelled him out of the airlock and into the void. Draco raised the grapnel launcher and fired it at the Icarus. His ship was already on the other side of the gateway and it was closing rapidly.

The magnetic head of the grapnel launcher hit the top of the Icarus and stuck fast. Draco pulled the trigger and reeled himself in. The gateway shrunk so quickly that Draco thought that he might have been cut off before he made it to the other side. As he passed through the gateway, he felt the crackle of energy around him on all sides.

In front of him was a small planet covered in blue ocean with small islands dotted across its surface. Draco landed on the back of the Icarus and began striding towards the shuttle bay on top of the ship. He needed to get inside before they entered the atmosphere.

In the pilot's seat of the evacuation shuttle Vynce and Ava swore.

"Did Captain Goldwing just jump through a fucking gateway?" Vynce asked breathlessly.

"That crazy motherfucker," Ava said and couldn't stop herself from grinning.

Alphonse's voice came across the comm channel.

'Is everyone alright?' he asked.

"Just clarify this for us for a second, will you Al? Did our captain just jump through a gateway in nothing but an assault suit?" Ava asked.

'Ah, yes, it appears that way,' Al said.

Vynce and Ava laughed.

'Of course. You realise that...' Raze began to speak, but something caught his eye. A bright spark had appeared in front of the Vartalen cruiser. Vynce, Ava, Clarke and Doctor Fewster all saw it too.

"Is that..." Vynce began to ask.

Al didn't allow himself to believe what he was seeing. Another gateway was opening in the space directly in front of them. It crackled in the middle of the void as it opened. It kept getting wider and wider. It was much wider than the last gateway had been.

Raze checked the vidstream from the backwards facing sensors on the cruiser and saw the Metropolis Seven growing smaller and smaller as it headed back towards the binary star system.

A colossal Alliance military dreadnought class ship passed through the gateway. It was a fearsome looking ship. It was all angles and armour plating. There wasn't a single curved surface on its hull. It looked like an enormous cannon travelling through space. On the side of its hull was the name of the ship. The AMSS Hyperion. The Alliance military's flagship.

"I think our ride's here," Vynce said.

'I think you might be right,' Al said and tried to open a comm channel with the dreadnought.

"AMSS Hyperion, this is Alphonse, a Child of iNet, previous XO of the Icarus, led by Captain Draco Goldwing. We are in need to immediate assistance. We are transporting a criminal, and the survivors of the Metropolis Seven. Please respond."

After a few moments the Hyperion responded.

'Hello Al, this is Admiral Blake. We detected that the Icarus activated an Alliance gravity drive in this sector of space. Care to explain?'

"Yes, the Icarus opened a gateway. But it's already gone. The gateway is closed. Admiral, you need to enact immediate quarantine procedures. There is an infection on board the Metropolis Seven the likes of which our galaxy has never seen. We few are the survivors of the ship. Seal off a medical sector. We need to be screened before you allow us on the ship," Al said as he heard the voice of one of his oldest friends.

'Some trouble indeed. Very well, we'll set up a quarantine wing on the starboard side. We'll open up hangar eighteen once we've initiated the quarantine lockdown. Please head around there in a few moments and we'll have you checked out.'

"Yes sir. Everyone, set course for hangar eighteen," Al said.

FORTY-TWO

The fleshlings had begun to cluster at the end of the walkway. The survivors were running low on ammunition. The corridor beyond the engine room was a bloodbath. It was impossible to tell where one infected creature ended and the next began. The survivors had retreated back into the engine control room, and those who still had bullets left were only using them when one of the infected got too close.

Jaxon had a single magazine left, and Doctor Harris only had a handful of shells.

She looked over at him and said, "I guess this is our final dance."

He smiled and said, "Maybe, but because of us millions of people will get to dance their dances across the galaxy. There's meaning in every moment. If you look for it, you'll find it."

He leaned out into the corridor and saw a group of three infected running towards them. The two in front fell, but the third kept running. Its head was tipped back at an unnatural angle, and it was almost impossible for them to get a decent shot. The fleshling's throat began throbbing like a heartbeat. It slammed into a couple of the survivors who were trying to barricade the door, but it broke through their line of defence. It sprawled out in the middle of the engine control room and Jaxon opened fire. Two bullets left the barrel of his gun before it was dry. The thing's throat kept throbbing and inflating to terrifying size. He saw the sharp white needle-like bone spikes that were starting to emerge from the skin on its neck and chest.

Before he could warn anyone, the fleshling exploded. The needle-like pieces of bone pierced everything like shrapnel. Jaxon felt hot pain all over his body, and a sharp piercing ache in his right eye. He tried to open it, but found that he could not. He raised his hand to his face and winced as he brushed against the piece of bone that had pierced his helmet. He looked down at his chest and saw four pieces of bone jutting out of his armour. Blood had already started to seep through the wounds.

He looked across the room at Doctor Harris. One of the bone spikes had punctured her temple. She had died instantly. In some ways he envied her. The infection had begun almost immediately. He could feel the hotness radiating from where he had been punctured.

Jaxon tried to get back to his feet, but found that he couldn't. He slumped against the wall and turned his head to see the console. It showed a red dot which represented the Metropolis Seven and two larger yellow dots which represented the two stars of the Gemon system. White text on the display showed the estimated time of arrival. Thirty minutes.

Jaxon didn't think he could stay alive that long. He closed his eyes and tried to will death to take him.

His last thoughts were of Ava. He imagined that they were back in their shared home on Orpheon. He dreamed that there had been no great war. That there was no infection. There was no Metropolis Seven. There was no Agency, and no Icarus. There was no pain. There was only him and her and nothing else mattered.

FORTY-THREE

There was nothing but the cold, the black, and the silence. Draco unconsciously held his breath as he passed through the gateway. The only sound he could hear was the almost silent, steady pulse of his beating heart. The Icarus was below him, and an unknown planet hung in the void in front of him. The vibrant blue of the ocean and the deep green of the jungle-covered land reminded him of New Earth, but the land masses were much smaller. The planet grew in size at a terrifying rate as the Icarus approached. Draco held the trigger on his grapnel launcher down and reeled himself closer to his ship.

When his boots touched down on the back of the Icarus he finally gasped for breath. In the silence of the void his sudden inhalation sounded as loud as a thunderstorm. His HUD showed that he had sixty percent of his oxygen tanks left. In the time it would take him to burn through the last of his oxygen, the Icarus would already be inside the atmosphere of the planet, and he would already be burnt to ash.

Draco needed to get inside. Quickly.

He walked along the back of the ship as fast as his grav-boots would allow. Just behind the shuttle dock was an access hatch that was usually used to repair external damage on the shuttle when it was docked with the Icarus. The shuttle itself was still on board the

Metropolis Seven, which could have been on the other side of the galaxy. Draco couldn't be sure. The planet below them didn't even look inhabited. There were no signs of cities or structures of any kind, and the space around the planet was free of satellites and other space traffic. Draco wondered whether anyone had ever actually set foot on the planet in front of him.

When he reached the entrance to the hatch, Draco opened a small panel next to it which revealed a numerical keypad. Draco always thought it rather crude that he had to resort to inputting a four digit code to enter his own ship, but things like voice recognition, fingerprint and retinal scanning didn't tend to work when you were wearing a full-body suit designed to repel the penetrating radiation and cold of space. Draco entered the key code and the hatch slid open. Jets of oxygen shot out from the sides of the hatch as the air inside was jettisoned. Draco turned the handle on the thick airlock cover and opened it outward. He looked back at the planet in front of him and started to feel the temperature of his suit change. He no longer felt like he was submerged in ice water. It had started to get warmer. They had begun to enter the planet's atmosphere.

Draco swung his body feet-first into the hatch and landed on the bottom of the chamber. It was wide enough to accommodate two people standing abreast. Draco pulled the thick hatch cover closed and turned the handle until it was secure. A matching keypad was also on the inside of the chamber, just next to the door. There was a dark blue light just above the door which indicated that there was no oxygen in the chamber. Draco input the code once again, and the dark blue light flickered off. Oxygen was pumped into the chamber, and the light turned green. The door into the ship opened.

Draco strode out from the access hatch and into the med bay. Arak Nara was sealed in the med pod undergoing treatment. Draco looked over the progress chart and grimaced when he realised what Veck had done to him. He knew it had been Veck. It had to have been. But normally Veck wasn't one for compassion and forgiveness. Draco wondered what Arak had done to avoid Veck's blood lust.

Arak's arm was almost healed. The med pod affixed synthetic ligaments and cartilage to the exposed bone. A delicate metal instrument gently pushed the bone back into Arak's arm. Arak was out cold, but he still grimaced with discomfort as the joint was relocated.

Draco headed out of the med bay and into the main corridor. Veck's voice echoed down the corridor from the bridge. The self-satisfaction of his victory was plain by the tone in his voice. Draco resisted the overwhelming urge to rush into the bridge. He knew that it was unlikely that he could best Veck in a one-on-one fight.

Hundreds of questions raced through his mind. How had Veck escaped the containment cell? Why hadn't Evie burnt out his neurotech implant? Where was Evie? Where in the galaxy were they? With each new question, more questions followed. But what really mattered was that Veck was in control of his ship, and Draco wanted to put a swift end to it.

Draco headed into the armoury. He grabbed two of Ava's buster pods from her locker and loaded them onto his forearms. The hot pink stood out against the black and gold of the rest of his suit. He engaged the buster pods to ensure they worked. They broke apart, slid up his arm and over his fist, and then re-formed on his forearm. Draco also grabbed a handful of flashbang grenades and hung them from his belt.

Draco strode back out into the corridor towards the bridge. Veck's voice became louder as he approached, but the words were indistinguishable.

The door to the bridge was open. Draco took a breath to centre himself before sidling around the corridor. He glanced into the bridge and saw a red lump of cloth sitting against the closest wall. His heart ached when he realised that he was looking at the covered body of his old friend.

Fury bubbled up from inside him. A flush of heat flowed through his body. He crept along closer to the bridge door and saw Veck Simms reclining on his chair. His boots rested atop the control console. Draco's blood boiled. He took one final breath, pulled the pin on a flashbang grenade and threw it into the bridge.

Draco closed his eyes until he heard the flashbang detonate. Veck's self-satisfied speech was cut short. Veck stumbled as he tried to get up from the captain's chair and Draco was next to him in a heartbeat. Veck roared in a blind rage. He engaged his sword, his right arm split apart and revealed the long blade. He slashed it wildly in the air around him.

"Arak Nara, you little fuck! I'll kill the girl just like I promised, and I'll make you watch!" he roared.

"No you won't," Draco said as he engaged the buster pod on his right forearm.

Draco grabbed Veck's sword with his left hand. He felt cold metal bite through the armour of his suit and into his palm. Draco threw a punch with all of his weight right into Veck's elbow. His cybernetic arm shattered from the kinetic force delivered by the buster pod. Draco tore the forearm from his body and tossed it aside. Veck roared again. Not out of pain, but out of frustration and blind fury.

Veck tried to throw a punch with his other arm. Draco did the same. The buster pod met Veck's fist which crumpled into a useless heap of cybernetic scrap.

"You fucking little piece of Orphosian gutter trash!" Veck roared.

Draco stepped back from Veck, who still flailed wildly, trying to hit something.

"This isn't Arak Nara," Draco said simply.

Veck's face changed instantly. The mask of fury Veck wore disappeared as he recognised Draco's voice.

"Draco... please -" Veck began but Draco didn't give him time to finish. He grabbed Veck by the hair and punched him directly in the throat. With one final punch Draco severed Veck's head from his spinal column.

"They only need your head you piece of shit," Draco said as Veck's body fell lifeless to the floor of the bridge.

Veck's head began to laugh. The sound came from his mouth, even though there were no lungs to push air through his vocal chords. His laughter grew louder and more manic as it started to blast over the loudspeakers of the Icarus.

'Draco, my old friend, I AM the Icarus!' Veck roared.

Draco dropped Veck's head and a sick cold dread crept across his body. Draco tried to turn away from the bridge, but he could barely move. The HUD of his smartsuit winked out in front of him as it powered down. Draco persevered and marched towards the exit of the bridge, even with the weight of the powered down suit slowing him down. After a few moments, Draco couldn't move at all.

He was frozen. The suit refused to move.

'There are all kind of defence protocols stored in your AI core. And I've got access to every single one of them. Take this one for example, I can target a single suit and completely immobilise it. Or, if I wanted to, send a surge of power through its circuits and fry you from the inside out.'

Draco felt the hairs try to stand up all over his body an instant before searing pain covered every inch of his skin. It felt like he was on fire.

'That's the great thing about smartsuits. Because they interface directly with your nervous system, overloading your pain receptors is remarkably easy to do. That was only one percent power. I wonder what five percent would feel like.'

Draco ground his teeth. He wanted to scream, but he wouldn't give Veck the satisfaction. He tried to move his arms or his legs, but they wouldn't budge. The searing pain returned in greater intensity. It felt as though his skin should be crackling and bubbling. Draco's vision faltered. White motes of light, the harbingers of unconsciousness, danced in front of his eyes.

He should have collapsed, but the immobilised suit held him steadily in place. The white motes of light grew larger. Draco could see two figures in front of him, blurry through the haze. One of the figures reached towards him, but the other figure pulled them away. The two figures left the bridge.

'I was prepared to allow the girls and the pilot to live, Draco. That's why we're in this planet's atmosphere. But now, I'm going to open the airlocks while we're flying over the ocean. If the fall doesn't kill them, exposure certainly will. And they'll know that it was entirely your fault,' Veck said.

Another wave of agony washed over Draco. This time, he did pass out.

FORTY-FOUR

In the infirmary, Arak Nara had heard to the entire exchange. Draco was in trouble, and Veck was in control of the Icarus. They were running out of options quickly, but Arak knew of one way he could atone for his actions and save his captain.

His elbow joint had been healed, but was still extremely sore. His cheekbone had been re-set, but there was still a peculiar ache under the eye socket. Arak stripped his smartsuit off completely to avoid the torturous fate that Draco faced. He rummaged through the linen closet and found an elastic-waisted pair of white pants and a baggy white shirt. He dressed himself quickly and ran towards the bridge.

He ran into Reban and Rhken, and they all went sprawling on the ground.

"Oh my, I am very sorry girls! Is the captain still alive?" Arak asked frantically.

"I don't know. I wanted to stay with him, but... I knew we couldn't," Rhken said.

"Sis, how are we going to get out of this?" Reban asked.

"The plan is the same as it was on the bridge. We go to the armoury, and we eject ourselves from the ship using the drop pods. But..." Rhken said and looked at Arak knowingly.

He nodded and said, "Yes. You should both go and prepare. I will bring the captain to the armoury. You should prepare a drop pod for him."

"But-" Reban said.

"No, I must do this. Now go," Arak commanded. When the girls both looked at each other uncertainly he yelled at them, "Go! Now!"

They turned and ran towards the armoury. Reban looked back at Arak sadly.

When Arak reached the bridge, Draco was there in his black and gold armour, completely immobilised. Arak could see that Draco was unconscious through the captain's glass-fronted helmet. He took a deep breath and attempted to centre himself.

"I'm sorry for this," he said as he threw his bodyweight into the captain's suit.

Draco fell heavily to the floor of the bridge. Arak gripped the captain by one of his outstretched hands and dragged him along the floor and out of the bridge.

'Nara-ka! You're all better! I can't say the same for myself unfortunately. It appears that I've lost my head. But I've gained a new body that will suffice until I get back to my outpost where I keep a spare shell. What in the galaxy do you think you're doing?' Veck asked.

"You won't kill him. I won't let you," Arak said simply.

'I'll kill whoever I please, and there isn't a damn thing you can do about it,' Veck said.

Arak flipped Draco over onto his side. He grabbed the fire axe that lay next to Nook's destroyed body. Arak walked back over to Draco and raised the axe over his head.

'No! I command you to stop! You can't kill him! He's mine to torment!' Veck roared.

Arak swung the axe downward and it embedded itself into the suit that covered Draco's shoulder. Draco went limp immediately.

"I'm not killing him, I'm saving him."

Arak had destroyed Draco's communication unit, which severed any and all external wireless communications from the rest of his suit.

He was still unconscious, but Veck's immobilisation command had ceased. Arak dragged Draco out of the bridge as Veck roared wordlessly over the loudspeakers.

The ache in his elbow joint had gotten worse as he dragged Draco. He could feel the new and repaired ligaments stretching and tearing with the stress he put them under.

"Girls! Rhken! Reban!" he yelled.

The girls joined him.

"Help me, please," he begged.

With the strength of three, they dragged Draco into the armoury and managed to prop him up inside one of the drop pods. There were only three drop pods. Only three tickets off the ship, and four people who wanted them. But Arak had already decided that he would be staying behind. It was the only thing he could do for allowing Veck to take the ship from him.

While he was in the med pod, Arak thought he had figured out how Veck had managed to bypass Evie's defence systems. He didn't bypass them at all. He became one with her systems and slowly began to take over the AI core. He became so intrinsically linked with it that he was able to transfer his consciousness directly into it at the moment his body was destroyed.

But like all artificial intelligence systems, there were locks and limitations put in place so that an AI could never take full control of all systems if it became hostile. The evacuation protocols were protected. The drop pods could only be launched manually by someone who was still on the ship.

They sealed Draco inside the first drop pod. He was still unconscious. Arak wished that he had been able to say goodbye. Rhken was next. She strapped herself in, and Arak locked the pod door from the outside. Next, he helped Reban strap herself in. She stopped him before he closed the door.

"Wait," she said.

"We haven't much time," he said.

"I just wanted you to know that... I know how you feel about me, and-"

"No, please, Reban. There is no need. I know it is inappropriate and I'm sorry if I ever made you feel-" he said.

"Shut up Arak, and let me finish. I love you. Not in the same way that you love me. But I do love you, and I wish that you could come with us."

Arak smiled and felt his bottom lip begin to shake. He nodded wordlessly as he closed the drop pod and locked it shut. Reban smiled out at him through the thick glass.

Tears stung Arak's eyes as he opened the launch console. He located a small habitable island in the ocean below them and programmed the drop pods to land there. He began the launch sequence, then held up three fingers which indicated that the pods would launch in three minutes. When he was sure the girls had seen his final message, he left the armoury and started to walk back toward the bridge. He began counting backwards from one-hundred and eighty in his head.

Veck Simms began to laugh. The sound came from all around him.

'You don't realise it, but you've just signed their death warrants,' Veck sneered.

"You signed yours the moment you jumped into the AI core," Arak countered.

'Once the drop pods launch, I'll simply loop back around and open fire on them. They'll be helpless. Easy targets.'

Arak refused to be baited into a response. He marched back onto the bridge of the ship and opened the captain's control console. He had started to feel a numbness creeping over him. He made the motions on the console as Draco had shown him to open the path to the heart of the Icarus. Veck raged through the speakers around him. But the heart of the Icarus was cut off from the AI core. Veck was powerless to stop Arak Nara.

"I have flown too close to the sun," Arak said.

The console split apart and Arak began to descend the ladder.

'What are you doing? Arak! You're a fool! I can give you credits! Power! Unending, limitless power! I know that's what your heart truly desires!' Veck commanded, but Arak ignored him.

He reached the bottom of the shaft and stepped down onto the cold metal floor. He approached the control pillar and placed his hand on the illuminated green square. The ghost of Samuel Goldwing didn't appear, but Arak knew the words that he needed to speak.

He continued counting backwards.

Thirty...

Twenty-nine...

Twenty-eight...

When he reached zero he both felt the drop pods eject from the ship. He waited another thirty seconds and said, "And now I must burn."

FORTY-FIVE

Draco snapped awake as someone slapped him hard across the cheek. The light of an alien sun shone down on him from above. A greasy black trail of smoke and ash stained the sky. Rhken looked down on Draco from above. Tears fell onto his cheek. Reban knocked the wind out of him as she leapt onto him.

"Oof! Give me a second, okay hon?" he said as Reban got up.

"Sorry Captain Goldwing, I just never thought I was going to see you again," Reban said.

"It's okay. Just let me get up so I can give you a hug properly, alright?"

Draco got back to his feet. They were on top of a sand dune. In front of them was an enormous expanse of water. Small islands dotted the horizon. Behind them were huge, thick trees which covered the rest of the island in jungle.

Draco went over and hugged Reban under one arm. He brought Rhken under his other. He kissed them both on the tops of their heads.

"Tell me girls, what happened?"

"Arak saved you," Reban said with a sad sense of pride.

"Not long after the drop pods ejected, the Icarus exploded. Veck was inside of it. His body and his mind. They're both gone now. Just like the Icarus. Just like Arak," Rhken said.

"Nara-ka died a hero. Just like your Dad. We're all lucky to have known them," Draco said and held the girls tight.

"Could we... could we have a funeral for them?" Reban asked.

When neither Draco nor Rhken said anything, she continued, "I know their bodies aren't here, but I think it would be good to say something. Or do something."

They gathered together what dry wood they could find and stacked it in a rough pile on the beach. They lit the pyre and remembered those they had loved, those they had lost, and those who were still out there waiting for them to come home.

LORE CODEX

Sapient Species of the Milky Way Galaxy

Arcturian

The Arcturian were the first race to emerge from the Arcturus sector. They are a hardy race from Arcturia, a planet strikingly similar to Old Earth. Their evolutionary journey followed a similar line to that of the creatures of Old Earth. However there was no great extinction event as giant reptilian creatures reigned over the land.

Aside from being covered in scale from head to toe, they even look remarkably human. However instead of hair sprouting from their head, they have feather-like growths which can vary from Arcturian to Arcturian.

They are cosmic neighbours to the Vartalen and live in constant fear of the warmongering species bringing war to their doorstep. It is not uncommon for a young Arcturian to move to another inhabited planet when they come of age.

Anjule

The Anjule are one of the few sapient races who exhibit extreme sexual dimorphism. The males of the species are almost as large and brutish as male Vartalen. They have hairless thick blue skin, large muscular limbs, and are prone to become easily frustrated and confused if not paired with a female. They do not possess the highest intellect, but are generally kind people.

The female Anjule share their hairless blue skin, however they are waiflike and are natural empaths. They share a connection with the rest of their race that other sapient species do not. They can communicate with other Anjule via their thoughts, and they can influence the behaviour of male Anjule through touch. They are capable of speech, but prefer to engage in vocal communication only when dealing with other races.

The Anjule are a peaceful people who dedicate their lives to art, music and the celebration of the natural world.

Artori

The Artori have visited humanity and all the other races of the Galactic Community long before those races were ready to know the truth of what was out there. They are tall humanoids with smokey gray skin, large black eyes, large heads and long, slender limbs and digits.

They are the watchers. The survey the galaxy for new life forms, study them, then when they are ready to join the galactic community, they reach out to them. They are devoid of hair and appear very different from other races due to their mostly spaceborn lives. They have been around longer than any other sapient race, however they were not the first...

Bworen

The Bworen are a subterranean race of cave dwellers. They are bipedal, but carry on their evolutionary heritage with large hands that end in curved claws that are meant for digging through tough ground and rock. They are covered in fur, and their eyes are tiny and black.

Their eyesight in the daylight is extremely poor, as their eyes evolved under the light of bioluminescent moss and fungi that grows within the planet Bwora, their home world. They are primarily nocturnal on their homeworld, but are able to function in other civilisations by using extremely powerful sunglasses that filter almost all light.

The Bworen thought that the night sky on the surface of Bwora was just the roof of another cave, very far away. They thought that stars were just bits of moss dangling from the top of that huge cave, and the Bworen wanted to know why the roof of that huge cavern kept moving. This is what drove them to the stars.

Children of iNet

The Children of iNet are a sapient race of intelligence machines created by humanity.

Under Galactic law, they should not exist. However, due to a loophole in the law, they cannot be destroyed. This is a cause of constant debate amongst the races of the Galactic Council. Galactic law states that any race found guilty of pursuing research into creating machines which possessed sentience and actual intelligence would be reprimanded heavily, and ejected from the Galactic Community.

However, Galactic Law also states; "A race cannot be held accountable for offenses under Galactic Law if they were not a member of the Galactic Community and were not aware of the relevant Galactic Law when the offenses occurred."

However once the Children of iNet joined the Galactic Community, they were then subject to the laws. This means that no new Children of iNet are ever able to be created by the Heart of iNet. The race will go extinct as more Children of iNet go offline permanently.

The Heart of iNet has started to allow those Children of iNet who are reaching their end of their life cycles to re-join with it so their consciousness can live on forever, even though the body that housed it is no longer operational. Those empty bodies are stood like sentinels outside the Heart of iNet in an ever-expanding reminder that their race is slowly fading away.

The Children of iNet are feared. They are the only race who have been able to reverse engineer the Gateways created by the Precusors. They created the gravity drive, a device capable of ripping a hole in the fabric of space and passing through it without the need for a constructed, controlled Gateway.

Human

Mammalian, highly resourceful, adaptive, intelligent, cunning. They are the newest addition to the Galactic community. Other races have not entirely made up their mind about humanity. They are still yet to find their place.

Their ambition and resilience intimidates some races, and their capacity for arrogance, apathy and greed makes other races see them as a potential threat to the stability of the Galactic community.

Stollett

Similar to the human race in appearance, but their genesis planet had much higher gravity and a lower oxygen density. Instead of evolving from hunter-gatherer packs like most other sapient species, the Stollett evolved from innovators and inventors.

They interacted with their environment by manipulating it with tools. They set complicated traps to capture prey instead of pursuing it. In the high gravity of their genesis planet, a trip or fall could mean broken bones or death.

When the Stollett reached their industrial age they did not create machine to do work for them. Instead, they created machines to augment their own bodies. These machines allowed them to undertake tasks that the natural limitations of their small bodies would not allow them to do. These machines are now completely ingrained in their society. Once a Stollett reaches their teenage years they can obtain their own exo-suit which they will maintain, modify and personalise for the rest of their lives.

The Stollett are naturally a shy race, and will not show their real selves to anyone but their closest friends and families.

Vartalen

A race of brutes. The Vartalen have almost been ejected completely from council space for their unchecked aggression towards other races.

The Vartalen people can stand anywhere from two to three metres tall, and are as wide as two well-built human men. They are naturally heavily muscled, with broad shoulders and small squat heads that jut out horizontally from between their shoulders.

In hand to hand combat, they are unmatched. Their society values strength over all other attributes. They value not only physical strength, but strength of the mind and the strength of will.

The very best of their species were powerful, intelligent and ambitious. A Vartalen will not follow the commands of another Vartalen that could not best them. They hold the other races in the Galactic Community to these same standards.

The Precursors

The Precursors are extinct, but their influence is still felt. They created the network of Gateways throughout the galaxy and left their maps for those that would come after.

They also left messages and warnings. The last warning left before the Precursors disappeared warned of something they called 'Kanaa'.

Discovering Precursor artefacts across the galaxy has been responsible for extreme technological leaps. Despite their devotion to cataloguing history, no evidence has been found of what fate befell the Precursors. However one central theme of their writings was to discourage future sapient races from creating machines capable of their own intelligent thought. Their genesis planet has not been located.

Populated planets of the Milky Way Galaxy

Old Earth

Old Earth is the genesis planet of humanity. Through their greed, their arrogance and their apathy they allowed their industry to irrevocably damage the planet, which altered the weather systems. The air became progressively more unbreathable, and terrifyingly destructive weather phenomena tore cities apart.

Old Earth was abandoned. After the exodus occurred, three main human planets established themselves. Orpheon, New Earth, and Central.

There are rumours that some humans still live under the blanket of the darkened sky.

Orpheon

Orpheon is a human planet founded on the fundamental idea of continuing the artistic and technological renaissance that began on Old Earth before the darkening of the sky. It is a society of libertarians where substance and sexual experimentation is encouraged and celebrated.

Orpheon is orbited by a single moon, Orphos, and the population of Orphos are slaves to their base desires. Their appetites for carnal congress and substance experimentation know no bounds. The Orphosians are seen as a less enlightened people than those of Orpheon. A large galactic drug trade is run from Orphos, and most galactic sapient species, human and non-human alike, would like to put a stop to it.

Central

Central is an administrative planet responsible for governing the entire human empire, which includes the three major planets, seven moons, and nineteen other human settlements across the galaxy.

On Central, a person is defined by their career. Normal patriarchal relationships are not recognised. A person does not belong to a family unit. They belong to a work unit, and their surname and identity completely changes if they change positions, which is extremely rare. All consumable substances consumed on Central are controlled in quality and volume.

New Earth

New Earth is owned by the Metropolis Corporation. Every facet of their society is deeply ingrained in consumerism and consumption. Huge mega-cities sprawl out across the planet, previously used Metropolis ships have been turned into low-cost housing.

There is a single Metropolis ship, the Metropolis Six, orbiting the planet as a makeshift satellite.

There are serious poverty problems on New Earth, as well as a general apathy towards the environment of the planet. Other human and non-human populations have raised serious concerns that New Earth may suffer the same fate as Old Earth.

Vitu Anju

The word vitu in Anjule language means 'new'. The name of the planet translates literally to New Anju. The Anjule people share a common bond with humanity in that their genesis planet is no longer inhabitable. But instead of a sapient-species created apocalypse, theirs was caused by a wayward asteroid in what would have been an extinction event for a non-spacefaring sapient species.

At the time of their planet's destruction, the Anjule people were evacuated and spent many years confined to their ships while a suitable new planet for the species could be located. Their amphibian evolution meant that the planet needed to reside in the inner orbit of the habitable zone of the solar system. Put simply, the planet needed to be hot and wet.

Eventually a planet similar to Anju was found. It even had similar blue silica sand beaches like the original Anju. Its surface was covered by deep blue oceans dotted with small islands. It was named Vitu Anju, and over a span of years the Anjule colonised the planet. It is now a popular holiday destination amongst tourists.

Vartal

Vartal is the heart of the Vartalen empire. The continents are covered in mega-cities. Each is run by the head of whichever clan has asserted their dominance over the populace. The leadership of Vartal is made up of the heads of the ruling clans and is always in constant flux.

Vartal is in the Arcturus Sector, which is outside of Council space. The Vartalen are on the verge of being completely ostracized from the Galactic community due to their aggressive natures. They are tolerated as part of the community due to their confinement to their home world.

The atmosphere of Vartal is extremely oxygen rich, which makes life large and aggressive. However as a result of this, the Vartalen people find it extremely difficult to stay for long periods of time on planets with lower oxygen-density.

Laws and Galactic Governance

Galactic Law

Galactic Law overrides all Sector, Solar System and Planetary Laws, but does not exist to replace or diminish them. Galactic Law covers trade agreements and treaties across different sectors that Sector Law does not cover. Galactic Law is dispensed by the Galactic Council.

Galactic Law governs when a race may claim a planet for their own. If life already exists on the planet, it may not be claimed. It must be left to evolve life of its own. It is catalogued and watched (usually by the Artori) so that whatever sapient species evolves may be introduced into the Galactic Community when they are ready.

The creation of artificial intelligence is banned across all Galactic space, based on the warnings left behind by the Precursors. Likewise, the Technological Enhancement and Anti-Personal Weaponisation Acts govern the level of synthetic replacements and augmentations a person can have made in their own body. The Galactic Council are fearful of allowing the boundaries between biological life and integrated synthetic weaponised replacements/augmentations to be crossed.

Galactic Law also governs aggression between planets. Any act of war must be lodged with the Galactic Council, but the Galactic Council will not intervene unless they believe the Galactic Community at large is at risk.

Sector Law

Sector Law governs the management of resources within the sector, including cataloguing resource-rich worlds, and possible life-bearing worlds. It also governs trade agreements and treaties within a sector, as well as Gateway maintenance.

Solar System Law

Solar System Law is only applicable if multiple life-bearing worlds or moons exists within a single Solar System, and all of those life-bearing worlds or moons are inhabited by sapient species. One example of this is Orpheon and Orphos.

Solar System law governs immigration between inhabited worlds, and can provide a further level of trade and treaty agreements if Sector laws do not suffice.

Terrestrial Law

Terrestrial Law sets the basic tenets of the civilisation of the planet. This includes, but is not limited to, the form and election processes of local Government (if applicable), the control of consumable substances, the local use of resources, civil rights, information privacy legislation (if applicable) and local military defence arrangements.

ABOUT THE AUTHOR

Matthew J Hellscream lives in Brisbane, Queensland, Australia and writes scary things for fun. He lives with the love of his life, plays too many video games and reads too many comics.

Made in the USA
Charleston, SC
18 June 2014